The Ultimate Attack . . .
A Mysterious Alien Predator . . .
The Omnivorous Chtorr!

Shorty was already turning toward it, sudden realization appearing on his face—and then it was on him. He didn't even have time to yell.

I burned them both. I held the torch on them and *burned.* Bright gouts of flame. Searing tongues of flame . . . I held that trigger firm and squeezed, *squeezed* and screamed. The flamethrower screamed too. I played it back and forth long after the thing had ceased to writhe . . . I didn't stop until the torch was out of fuel.

They had to pry it out of my hands . . .

"SMARTLY PACED AND ARTFULLY WRITTEN.
THIS READER WANTS MHORR ON THE CHTORR!"
—Anne McCaffrey

DAVID GERROLD

A MATTER FOR MEN

The War Against The Chtorr
Book I

PUBLISHED BY POCKET BOOKS NEW YORK

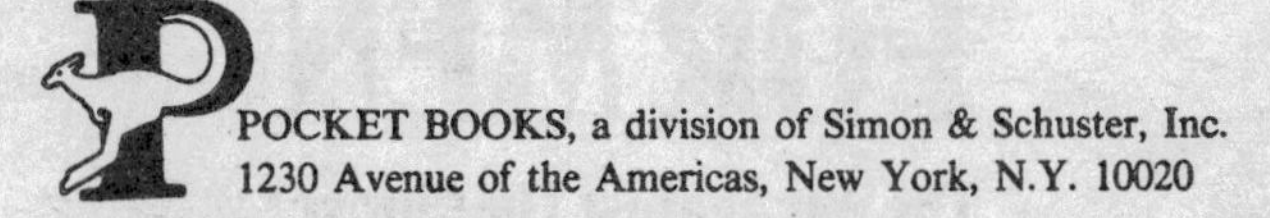

POCKET BOOKS, a division of Simon & Schuster, Inc.
1230 Avenue of the Americas, New York, N.Y. 10020

Library of Congress Catalog Card Number: 82-19571

ISBN: 0-671-45120-0

First Pocket Books Science Fiction printing July, 1984

10 9 8 7 6 5 4 3 2 1

Printed in the U.S.A.

Acknowledgments

The following people have provided valuable support and made significant contributions to this book:

Dennis Ahrens
Jack Cohen
Diane Duane
Richard Fontana
Harvey and Johanna Glass
Robert and Ginny Heinlein
Don Hetsko
Rich Sternbach
Tom Swale
Linda Wright

For Robert and Ginny Heinlein,
with love

Chtorr (ktôr) *n.* 1. The planet Chtorr, presumed to exist within 30 light-years of Earth. 2. The star system in which the planet occurs; a red giant star, presently unidentified. 3. The ruling species of the planet Chtorr; generic. 4. In formal usage, either one or many members of same; a Chtorr, the Chtorr. (See **Chtor-ran**) 5. The glottal chirruping cry of a Chtorr.

Chtor-ran (ktôr-en) *adj.* 1. Of or relating to either the planet or the star system, Chtorr. 2. Native to Chtorr. *n.* 1. Any creature native to Chtorr. 2. In common usage, a member of the primary species, the (presumed) intelligent life form of Chtorr. (*pl.* **Chtor-rans**)

—*The Random House Dictionary of the English Language,*

Century 21 Edition, unabridged

A MATTER FOR MEN

One

"McCARTHY, keep down!"

"Yes, sir."

"—and shut up."

I shut. There were five of us climbing up the slope of a sparsely wooded ridge. We angled diagonally through high yellow grass so dry it crunched. July had not been kind to Colorado. A spark would turn these mountains into an inferno.

Just before each man reached the top he sprawled flat against the slope, then inched slowly forward. Duke was in the lead, wriggling through the tall weeds like a snake. We'd topped five hills this way today and the heat was getting to me. I thought about ice water and the Jeep we'd left back on the road.

Duke edged up to the crest and peered down into the valley beyond. One at a time, Larry, Louis and Shorty moved up beside him. I was the last—as usual. The others had thoroughly read the land by the time I crawled into place. Their faces were grim.

Duke grunted. "Larry, pass me the binoculars."

Larry rolled onto his left side to unstrap the case from his right hip. Wordlessly, he passed them over.

Duke inspected the land below as carefully as a wolf sniffing a trap. He grunted again, softly, then passed the binoculars back.

Now Larry surveyed the scene. He took one glance, then passed the binoculars on to Louis.

What were they looking at? This valley looked the same to me as all the others. Trees and rocks and grass. I didn't see anything more. What had *they* spotted?

"You agree?" asked Duke.

"It's worms," said Larry.

"No question," Louis added.

Worms! *At last!* I took the glasses from Shorty and scanned the opposite slope.

A stream curled through ragged woods that looked as if they had been forested recently. And badly. Stumps and broken branches, ragged sections of trunk, huge woody slabs of bark, and the inevitable carpet of dead leaves and twigs were scattered unevenly across the hill. The forest looked as if it had been chewed up and spit out again by some rampaging, but finicky, prehistoric herbivore of gargantuan proportions and appetite.

"No, down there," rumbled Shorty. He pointed.

I put my eyes to the glasses again. I still didn't see; the bottom of the valley was unusually barren and empty, but—no, wait a minute, there it was—I had almost missed it—directly below us, near a large stand of trees; a pasty-looking igloo and a larger circular enclosure. The walls of it sloped inward. It looked like an unfinished dome. Was that all?

Shorty tapped me on the shoulder then and took the binoculars away. He passed them back to Duke, who had switched on the recorder. Duke cleared his throat as he put the glasses to his eyes, and then began a detailed description of the scene. He spoke in soft, machine-gun bursts—a rapid monotone report. He read off landmarks as if he were knocking items off a checklist. "Only one shelter—and it looks fairly recent. No sign of any other starts—I'd guess only one family, so far—but they must expect to expand. They've cleared a pretty wide area. Standard construction on the dome and corral. Corral walls are about . . . two and a half—no, make that three—meters high. I don't think there's anything in it yet. I—" He stopped, then breathed softly. "Damn."

"What is it?" asked Larry.

Duke passed him the binoculars.

Larry looked. It took a moment for him to find the point of Duke's concern, then he stiffened. "Aw, Christ, no—"

He passed the binoculars to Louis. I sweated impatiently. *What had he seen?* Louis studied the view without comment, but his expression tightened.

Shorty handed the glasses directly to me. "Don't you want to look—" I started, but he had closed his eyes as if to shut out me and the rest of the world as well.

Curious, I swept the landscape again. What had I missed the first time?

I focused first on the shelter—nothing there. It was a badly crafted dome of wood chips and wood-paste cement. I'd seen pictures of them. Close up, its surface would be rough, looking as if it had been sculpted with a shovel. This one was bordered by some kind of dark vegetation, patches of black stuff that clumped against the dome. I shifted my attention to the enclosure—

"Huh?"

—she couldn't have been more than five or six years old. She was wearing a torn, faded brown dress and had a dirt smudge across her left cheek and scabs on both knees, and she was hop-skipping along the wall, trailing one hand along its uneven surface. Her mouth was moving—she was singing as she skipped. As if she had nothing to fear at all. She circled with the wall, disappeared from view for a moment, then reappeared along the opposite curve. I sucked in my breath. I had a niece that age.

"Jim—the glasses." That was Larry; I passed them back. Duke was unslinging his pack, divesting himself of all but a grapple and a rope.

"Is he going after her?" I whispered to Shorty.

Shorty didn't answer. He still had his eyes closed.

Larry was sweeping the valley again. "It looks clear," he said, but his tone indicated his doubt.

Duke was tying the grapple to his belt. He looked up. "If you see anything, use the rifle."

Larry lowered the binoculars and looked at him—then nodded.

"Okay," said Duke. "Here goes nothing." He started to scramble over the top—

"Hold it—" That was Louis; Duke paused. "I thought I saw something move—that stand of trees."

Larry focused the binoculars. "Yeah," he said, and handed them up to Duke, who scrambled around to get a better view. He studied the blurring shadows for a long moment; so did I, but I couldn't tell what they were looking at. Duke slid back down the slope to rest again next to Larry.

"Draw straws?" Larry asked.

Duke ignored him; he was somewhere else. Someplace unpleasant.

"Boss?"

Duke came back. He had a strange expression—hard—and his mouth was tight. "Pass me the piece" was all he said.

Shorty unshouldered the 7 mm Weatherby he had been carrying all morning and afternoon, but instead of passing it over, he laid it down carefully in the grass, then backed off down the slope. Louis followed him.

I stared after them. "Where're they going?"

"Shorty had to take a leak," snapped Larry; he was pushing the rifle over to Duke.

"But Louis went too—"

"Louis went to hold his hand." Larry picked up the binoculars again, ignoring me. He said, "Two of 'em, boss, maybe three."

Duke grunted. "Can you see what they're doing?"

"Uh uh—but they look awfully active."

Duke didn't answer.

Larry laid down the binoculars. "Gotta take a leak too." And moved off in the direction of Shorty and Louis, dragging Duke's pack with him.

I stared, first at Larry, then at Duke. "Hey, what's—"

"Don't talk," said Duke. His attention was focused through the long black barrel of the Sony Magna-Sight. He was dialing windage and range corrections; there was a ballistics processor in the stock, linked to the Magna-Sight, and the rifle was anchored on a precision uni-pod.

I stretched over and grabbed the binoculars. Below, the little girl had stopped skipping; she was squatting now and making lines in the dirt. I shifted my attention to the distant trees. Something purple and red was moving through them. The binoculars were electronic, with automatic zoom, synchronized focusing, depth correction, and anti-vibration; but I wished we had a pair with all-weather, low-light image-amplification instead. They might have shown what was behind those trees.

Beside me, I could hear Duke fitting a new magazine into the rifle.

"Jim," he said.

I looked over at him.

He still hadn't taken his attention from the sight. His fingers worked smoothly on the controls as he locked in the numbers. The switches made satisfyingly solid clicks. "Doesn't your bladder need emptying too?"

"Huh? No. I went before we left—"

"Suit yourself." He shut up and squinted into his eyepiece.

I looked through the binoculars again at the purple things in the shadows. Were those *worms?* I was disappointed that they were hidden by the woods. I'd never seen any Chtorrans in the flesh.

I covered the area, hoping to find one out in the open—no such luck. But I did see where they had started to dam the stream. Could they be amphibious too? I sucked in my breath and tried to focus on the forest again. Just one clear glimpse, that's all I wanted—

The CRA-A-ACK! of the rifle startled me. I fumbled to refocus the binoculars—the creatures still moved undisturbed. Then what had Duke been firing at—? I slid my gaze across to the enclosure—where a small form lay bleeding in the dirt. Her arms twitched.

A second CRA-A-ACK! and her head blossomed in a flower of sudden red—

I jerked my eyes away, horrified. I stared at Duke. "What the hell are you doing?"

Duke was staring intently through the telescopic sight, waiting to see if she would move again. When she didn't, he raised his head from the sight and stared across the valley. At the hidden Chtorrans. A long time. His expression was . . . distant. For a moment I thought he was in a trance. Then he seemed to come alive again and slid off down the hill, down to where Shorty and Louis and Larry waited. Their expressions were strange too, and they wouldn't look at each other's eyes.

"Come on," said Duke, shoving the rifle at Shorty. "Let's get out of here."

I followed after them. I must have been mumbling. "He shot her—" I kept saying. "He shot her—"

Finally, Larry dropped back and took the binoculars out of my trembling hands. "Be glad you're not the man," he said. "Or you'd have had to do it."

Two

I ENDED up in Dr. Obama's office.

"Sit down, McCarthy."

"Yes, ma'am."

Her eyes were gentle, and I couldn't escape them. She reminded me of my grandmother; she had had that same trick of looking at you so sadly that you felt sorrier for her than for yourself. When she spoke, her voice was detached, almost deliberately flat. My grandmother had spoken like that too, when there was something on her mind and she had to work her way around to it. "I hear you had a little trouble yesterday afternoon."

"Uh—yes, ma'am." I swallowed hard. "We—that is, Duke shot a little girl."

Dr. Obama said softly, "Yes, I read the report." She paused. "You didn't sign it with the others. Is there something you want to add?"

"Ma'am—" I said. "Didn't you hear me? *We shot a little girl.*"

Her eyes narrowed thoughtfully. "I see. You're troubled by that."

"Troubled—? Yes, ma'am, *I am.*"

Dr. Obama looked at her hands. They were folded politely on

the desk in front of her, carefully manicured, and dark and wrinkled with age. "Nobody ever said it would be easy."

"You didn't say anything about *shooting children* either."

"I'd hoped we wouldn't have to."

"Dr. Obama, I don't know what the explanation is, but I can't condone—"

"It's not for you to condone!" Her face was suddenly hard. "Duke passed you the binoculars, didn't he?"

"Yes, ma'am. Several times."

"And what did you see?"

"The first time, I saw only the shelter and the enclosure. The second time I saw the little girl."

"And what did Duke do then?"

"Well, it looked like he was going to rescue her, but then he changed his mind and asked for the rifle instead."

"Do you know why he asked for the rifle?"

"Louis said he saw something."

"Mmm. Did you look through the binoculars again to check him?"

"Yes, ma'am—but I looked because I was curious. I'd never seen worms—"

She cut me off. "But when you looked, you saw them, didn't you?"

"I saw something . . ." I hesitated. "I couldn't be sure what it was."

"What did it look like?"

"It was big, and it was purple or red, it was hard to tell."

"The Chtorr have purple skin and varicolored fur. Depending on the light, it can look red, pink, magenta or orange. Was that what you saw?"

"I saw something purple. It was in the shadows, and it kept moving back and forth."

"Was it moving fast?"

I tried to remember. What was fast for a worm? "Kind of," I hedged.

"Then what you saw was a fully grown Chtorr in the active —*and most dangerous*—phase. Duke recognized it, so did Larry, Louis and Shorty. They signed the report."

"I wouldn't know—I've never seen a Chtorr before. That's why I'm here."

"If they said it was a Chtorr, you can be sure it was—but that's why they passed the binoculars, just to be sure; if Duke had been wrong, one of the others would have been sure to spot it."

"I'm not arguing about the identification—"

"Well, you should be," Dr. Obama said. "That's the *only* reason you could possibly have for not signing this report." She tapped the paper on her desk.

I eyed it warily. Dad had warned me about signing things I wasn't sure of—that's how he had married Mother. Or so he'd always claimed. I said, "It's that little girl we shot—I keep seeing her skipping around that pen. She wasn't in danger; there was no reason to shoot her—"

"Wrong," said Dr. Obama. "Wrong, twice over. You should know that."

"I shouldn't know *anything!*" I said, suddenly angry. "I've never been *told* anything. I was transferred up here from a reclamation unit because somebody found out I had two years of college-level biology. Somebody else gave me a uniform and a rule book—and that's the extent of my training."

Dr. Obama looked startled, resigned and frustrated, all at once. Almost to herself—but loud enough so I could hear it too—she said, "What the hell are they doing anyway? Sending me kids. . . ."

I was still burning. "Duke should have shot at the Chtorr!" I insisted.

"With *what?*" Dr. Obama snapped back. "Were you packing artillery?"

"We had a high-powered rifle—"

"And the range to the Chtorr was more than seven hundred meters on a windy day!"

I mumbled something about hydrostatic shock.

"What was that?"

"Hydrostatic shock. It's what happens when a bullet hits flesh. It makes a shock wave. The cells are like little water balloons. They rupture. That's what kills you, not the hole."

Dr. Obama stopped, took a breath. I could see she was forcing herself to be patient. "I know about hydrostatic shock. It doesn't apply here. You're making the assumption that Chtorran flesh is like human flesh. It isn't. Even if Duke had been firing point blank, it wouldn't have done any good unless he was lucky enough to hit one of their eyes—or unless he had an exploding cartridge, which he didn't. So he had no choice; he had to shoot what he could." Dr. Obama stopped. She lowered her voice. "Look, son, I'm sorry that you had to come up against the harsh realities of this war so quickly, but—" She raised her hands in an apologetic half-shrug, half-sigh, then dropped them again. "—Well, I'm sorry, that's all."

She continued softly, "We don't know what the Chtorr are like inside—that's why we want you here. You're supposed to be a scientist. We're hoping you'll tell us. The Chtorr seem to be pretty well armored or segmented or *something.* Bullets don't have much effect on them—and a lot of good men died finding that out. Either they don't penetrate the same way, or the Chtorrans don't have vital organs that a bullet can disrupt—and don't ask me to explain how that one's possible, because I don't know either. I'm just quoting from the reports.

"We do know, though—from unfortunate experience—that to shoot at a Chtorran is to commit suicide. Whether they're intelligent or not—as some people think—makes no difference. They're very deadly. Even without weapons. They move fast and they kill furiously. The smartest thing to do is not to shoot at them at all.

"Duke *wanted* to rescue that child—probably more than you realize—because he *knew* what the alternative to rescue was. But when Louis saw Chtorr in the woods, Duke had no choice—he didn't dare go after her then. They'd have read him halfway down the hill. He'd have been dead before he moved ten meters. Probably the rest of you too. I don't like it either, but *what he did was a mercy.*

"That's why he passed the binoculars; he wanted to be *sure* he wasn't making a mistake—he wanted you and Shorty and Larry to double-check him. If there was the slightest bit of doubt in any of your minds, he wouldn't have done what he did; he wouldn't have had to—and if I thought Duke had killed that child unnecessarily, I'd have him in front of a firing squad so fast he wouldn't have time to change his underwear."

I thought about that. For a long moment.

Dr. Obama waited expectantly. Her eyes were patient.

I said, suddenly, "But Shorty never looked at all."

She was surprised. "He didn't?"

"Only the first time," I replied. "He didn't look when we saw the child and he didn't look to confirm it was Chtorr."

Dr. Obama grunted. She was writing something on a note pad. I was relieved to have her eyes off me even for a moment. "Well, that's Shorty's prerogative. He's seen too many of these—" She finished the note and looked at me again. "It was enough that he saw the enclosure. But it's you we're concerned with at the moment. You have no doubt, do you, that what you saw was Chtorr?"

"I've never seen a Chtorran, ma'am. But I don't think this could have been anything else."

"Good. Then let's have no more of this nonsense." She pushed the report across the desk. "I'll take your signature on the bottom line."

"Dr. Obama, *if you please*—I'd like to know why it was necessary to kill that little girl."

Dr. Obama looked startled again, the second time since the interview began. "I thought you knew."

I shook my head. "That's what this whole thing is about. I *don't.*"

She stopped. "I'm sorry . . . I really am sorry. I didn't realize—No wonder I couldn't sandbag you. . . ." She got up from her desk and crossed to a filing cabinet. She unlocked it and pulled out a thin folder—it was lettered SECRET in bright red—then returned to her seat. She held the folder thoughtfully in her hands. "Sometimes I forget that most of what we know about the Chtorr is restricted information." She eyed me carefully. "But you're a scientist—"

She was flattering me, and we both knew it. Nobody was anything anymore. To be accurate, I was a student on leave, temporarily contracted to the United States Armed Services, Special Forces Operation, as a full-time exobiologist.

"—so you should be entitled to see these things." But she still didn't pass them over. "Where are you from?" she asked abruptly.

"Santa Cruz, California."

Dr. Obama nodded. "Nice town. I used to have some friends just north of there—but that was a long time ago. Any of your family still alive?"

"Mom is. Dad was in San Francisco when it—when it—"

"I'm sorry. A lot of good people were lost when San Francisco went under. Your mother still in Santa Cruz?"

"I think so. Last I heard, she was helping with the refugees."

"Any other relatives?"

"I have a sister near L.A."

"Married?"

"Yes. She's got a daughter, five." I grinned at the thought of my niece. The last time I had seen her, she had been barely beyond the lap-wetting stage. I went sad then, remembering. "She used to have three. The other two were boys. They would have been six and seven."

Dr. Obama nodded. "Even so, she's very lucky. So are you. Not many people had that many members of their family survive the plagues." I had to agree with her.

Her face went grim now. "Have you ever heard of a town called Show Low?"

"I don't think so."

"It's in Arizona—it *was* in Arizona. There's not much left of it now. It was a nice place; it was named after a poker game—" Dr. Obama cut herself short; she laid the folder on the desk in front of her and opened it. "These pictures—these are just a few of the frames. There's a lot more—half a disk of high-grain video—but these are the best. These pictures were taken in Show Low last year by a Mr. Kato Nokuri. Mr. Nokuri apparently was a video hobbyist. One afternoon he looked out his window—he probably heard the noise from the street—and he saw *this.*" Dr. Obama passed the photographs across.

I took them gingerly. They were color eight-by-tens. They showed a small-town street—a shopping center—as seen from a third-story window. I flipped through the pictures slowly; the first showed a wormlike Chtorran reared up and peering into an automobile; it was large and red with orange markings on its sides. The next had the dark shape of another climbing through a drugstore window; the glass was just shattering around it. In the third, the largest Chtorran of all was doing something to a—it looked like a body—

"It's the last picture in the bunch I want you to see," said Dr. Obama. I flipped to it. "The boy there is only thirteen."

I looked. I almost dropped the picture in horror. I looked at

Dr. Obama, aghast, then at the photograph again. I couldn't help myself; my stomach churned with sudden nausea.

"The quality of the photography is pretty good," she remarked. "Especially when you consider the subject matter. How that man retained the presence of mind to take these pictures I'll never know, but that telephoto shot is the best one we have of a Chtorran feeding."

Feeding! It was rending the child limb from limb! Its gaping mouth was frozen in the act of slashing and tearing at his struggling body. The Chtorran's arms were long and double-jointed. Bristly black and insectlike, they held the boy in a metal grip and pushed him toward that hideous gnashing hole. The camera caught the spurt of blood from his chest frozen in midair like a crimson splash.

I barely managed to gasp, "They eat their—their prey *alive?*"

Dr. Obama nodded. "Now, I want you to imagine that's your mother. Or your sister. Or your niece."

Oh, you monster—I tried not to, but the images flashed across my mind. Mom. Maggie. Annie—and Tim and Mark too, even though they were seven months dead. I could still see the boy's paralyzed expression, the mouth a silent shriek of *why me?* startlement. I could see that expression superimposed on my sister's face and I shuddered.

I looked up at Dr. Obama. It hurt my throat to swallow. "I—I didn't know."

"Few people do," she said.

I was shaking and upset—I must have been white as a scream. I pushed the pictures away. Dr. Obama slid them back into the folder without looking at them; her eyes were studying me. She leaned forward across her desk and said, "Now, about that little girl—do you have to ask why Duke did what he did?"

I shook my head.

"Pray that you never find yourself in the same situation—but if you do, will you hesitate to do the same thing? If you think you will, take another look at the pictures. Don't be afraid to ask; any time you need to remember, come to my office and look."

"Yes, ma'am." I hoped I wouldn't need to. I rubbed my nose. "Uh, ma'am—what happened to Mr. Nokuri, the photographer?"

"The same thing that happened to the boy in the picture—we think. All we found was the camera—"

"You were there—?"

"—the rest of the place was a mess." Dr. Obama focused on something else for a moment, something very far away. ". . . There was a lot of blood. All over everything. A lot of blood. . . ." She shook her head sadly. "These pictures—" She straightened the folder on her desk meaningfully. "—an incredible legacy. This was our first real proof. The man was a hero." Dr. Obama looked at me again and suddenly snapped back to the present. "Now you'd better get out of here. I have work to do—oh, the report. Take it with you and read it again. Bring it back when you've signed it."

I left. Gratefully.

Three

I WAS lying on my bunk when Ted, the other fellow up from the university, came gangling in. He was a lanky smart-aleck with a New England twang. "Hey, Jim boy, chow's on."

"Uh, no thanks, Ted. I'm not hungry."

"So? You want me to call the doc?"

"I'm okay—I'm just not in the mood to eat."

Ted's eyes narrowed. "You still brooding about what happened yesterday?"

I shrugged where I lay. "I dunno."

"You talk to Obie about this yet?"

"Yeah."

"Ah, that explains it—she gave you the shock treatment."

"Well, it worked." I turned on my side and faced the wall.

Ted sat down on the bunk facing mine; I could hear the springs creak. "She showed you the Arizona pictures, didn't she?"

I didn't answer.

"You'll get over it. Everybody does."

I decided I didn't like Ted. He always had *almost* the right thing to say—as if he took his lines from a movie. He was always being just a little *too* wonderful. Nobody could be that cheerful all the time. I pulled the blanket over my head.

He must have gotten tired of waiting for a response, because he stood up again. "Anyway, Duke wants to see you." He added, "*Now.*"

I turned around, but Ted was already out the door.

So I sat up and ran a hand through my hair. After a moment, I slipped on my shoes and went looking for Duke.

I found him in the recreation room talking to Shorty; they were sitting on one of the couches going over some maps together. There was a pot of coffee on the table before them. They looked up as I approached. "Be with you in a minute," said Duke.

I hung back politely, keeping my attention focused on the opposite wall. There was an old photograph on it, a faded magazine shot of President Randolph Hudson McGee; I studied it with no interest at all, the square jaw, the shiny gray hair, and the campaign-convincing blue eyes. Finally, Duke mumbled something to Shorty and dismissed him. To me he said, "Sit down."

I did so, nervously.

"Want some coffee?"

"No, thanks."

"Have some anyway—be polite." Duke poured out a cup and set it before me. "You've been here a week, right?"

I nodded.

"You've talked to Obie?"

"Yes."

"Seen the pictures?"

"Yes."

"Well, what do you think?"

I said, "I don't know. What am I supposed to think?"

"Never answer a question with a question, for one thing."

"My father used to tell me that's the only way to answer a rhetorical question."

Duke slurped his coffee and grimaced. "Ugh. It gets worse every day. But don't tell Sergeant Kelly I said so." He looked at me speculatively. "Can you operate a flamethrower?"

"Huh?"

"I'll assume that's a 'no.' How fast can you learn? By the end of the week?"

"I don't know. I guess so. Why?"

"I need a backup man. I thought you might want the job." I started to protest—Duke ignored it. "This time it's not just a scouting foray; it's a search and destroy. We're going back to do what we should have done yesterday. Burn some worms." He waited for my answer.

"I don't know," I said at last.

His eyes were steady. "What's the problem?"

"I don't think I'm much of a military type; that's all."

"No, that isn't all." He fixed me with his steely gray eyes and waited.

I felt transparent before him. I tried to glance away, but I felt drawn back to his face. Duke was grim, but not angry—just patient.

I said slowly, "I came out here to *study* the worms. This . . . doesn't exactly fit my expectations. Nobody told me I'd have to be a soldier."

Duke said, "You're getting military credit for it, aren't you?"

"Service credit," I corrected. I'd been lucky. My biology background had qualified as a "needed skill"—but just barely.

Duke made a face. "So? Out here we don't draw lines that thin. There's no difference."

"I beg your pardon, Duke, but there's a lot of difference."

"Eh? How so?"

"It's in my contract. I'm attached as a scientist. Nowhere does it say I have to be a soldier."

Duke leaned back in his chair. "Better take another look at that contract, boy—the 'special duties' clause."

I quoted from memory—we had studied it in school; Duke raised his eyebrows, but let me continue. " 'In addition, the employee may be required by the employer, as represented by his/her immediate, or otherwise superiors, to perform any special or unique duties for which he is properly and duly equipped, whether by training, nature or other; and which relate or pertain to the basic obligation as herein detailed—' " Duke smiled. I continued, " '—*except* where those duties are in direct conflict with the intent of this contract.' "

Duke was still smiling. "That's right, McCarthy—and the duties I'm asking of you are not in direct conflict. You're not under a 'peaceful intention' clause, are you?"

"Uh, I don't know."

"You're not. If you were, you'd have never been sent up. Every man here has two jobs—his own and killing worms. Do I have to say which one takes priority?"

I said slowly, "What does that mean?"

"That means," said Duke, "that if the mission is military, *everyone* is a soldier. We can't afford to watch out for deadheads. I need a backup man. You want to study worms, learn how to operate a flamethrower."

"That's what you mean by 'special duties,' huh?"

He said calmly, "That's right. You know I can't order you, McCarthy. Any operation requiring a risk to life has to be entirely voluntary. And not the old-fashioned 'I'll take you, you, and you' kind of volunteering either." Duke put down his coffee cup. "But I'll make it easy on you. You have till tomorrow to choose. When you do, go see Shorty. Otherwise, you're shipping out on Thursday's chopper. Got that?"

I didn't answer.

"Did you get it?"

"I got it!" I snapped.

"Good." Duke stood up. "You already know what you're going to choose, Jim—there's no question about that. So quit obsessing over it and get on with the job. We don't have the time."

He was right, and I knew it, but it wasn't fair, his pressuring me.

He caught the meaning of my silence and shook his head. "Get off it, Jim. You're never going to be any readier than you are now."

"But I'm *not* ready at all!"

"That's what I meant. If you were, we wouldn't need to have this conversation. So . . . what is it?"

I looked up at him.

"Yes . . . ?"

"Uh—I'm scared," I admitted. "What if I screw up?"

Duke grinned. "There's a very simple test to know if you've

screwed up. If you have, you've been eaten. Everything else is success. Remember that."

He picked up his coffee cup to carry it back to the kitchen. "I'll tell Shorty to expect you. Wear clean underwear." Then he turned and left, leaving me staring after him.

Four

LEGALLY, I was already in the army.

Had been for three years. Sort of.

You were automatically enlisted when you showed up for your first session of Global Ethics, the only mandatory course in high school. You couldn't graduate without completing the course. And—you found this out only afterward—you hadn't completed the course until you'd earned your honorable discharge. It was all part of the Universal Service Obligation. Rah.

The instructor was somebody named Whitlaw. Nobody knew much about him. It was his first semester here. We'd heard some rumors though—that he'd once punched a kid for mouthing off and broken his jaw. That he couldn't be fired. That he'd seen active duty in Pakistan—and still had the ears of the men and women he'd killed. That he was still involved in some super-secret operation and this teaching job was just a cover. And so on.

The first time I saw him, I believed it all.

He stumped into the room and slammed his clipboard down onto the desk and confronted us. "All right! I don't want to be here any more than you do! But this is a required course—for *all* of us—so let's make the best of a bad situation!"

He was a squat bear of a man, gruff-looking and impatient. He had startling white hair and gun-metal gray eyes that could drill you like a laser. His nose was thick; it looked like it had been broken a few times. He looked like a tank, and when he moved, he moved with a peculiar rolling gait. He rocked from step to step, but he was surprisingly graceful.

He stood there at the front of the classroom like an undetonated bomb and looked us over with obvious distaste. He glowered at us—an expression we were soon to recognize as an all-purpose glower of intimidation, directed not at any of us individually, but at the class as a unit.

"My name is Whitlaw!" he barked. "And I am not a nice man!"

Huh—?

"—So if you think you're going to pass this class by making friends with me, *forget it!*" He glared at us, as if daring us to glare back. "I don't want to be your friend. So don't waste your time. It's this simple: I have a job to do! It's going to get done. You have a job to do too. You can make it easy on yourself and own the responsibility—or you can fight it and, I promise you, this class will be worse than Hell! Understand?"

He strode to the back of the room then, plucked a comic book out of Joe Bangs's hands and ripped it up. He tossed the pieces in the trash can. "Those of you who think I'm kidding—let me disabuse you of that now. We can save ourselves two weeks of dancing around, testing each other, if you will just assume the worst. I am a dragon. I am a shark. I am a monster. I will chew you up and spit out your bones."

He was in motion constantly, gliding from one side of the room to the other, pointing, gesturing, stabbing the air with his hand as he talked. "For the next two semesters, you belong to me. This is *not* a pass-or-fail course. *Everybody* passes when I teach. Because I don't give you any choice in the matter. Most of you, when you're given a choice, you don't choose to win. That guarantees your failure. Well, guess what. In here, you don't have a choice. And the sooner you get that, the sooner you can get out." He stopped. He looked around the room at all of us. His eyes were hard and small. He said, "I am a very ugly man. I know it. I have no investment in proving otherwise. So don't expect me to be anything else. If there's any adapting to be done in this classroom, I expect *you* to do it! Any questions?"

"Uh, yeah—" One of the clowns in the back of the room. "How do I get out?"

"You don't. Any other questions?"

There were none. Most of us were too stunned.

"Good." Whitlaw returned to the front of the room. "I expect a hundred percent attendance, one hundred percent of the time. There are no excuses. This class is about results. Most of you use your circumstances as reasons to not have results." He looked into our eyes as if he were looking into our souls. "That's over, starting now! From now on, your circumstances are merely the things you have to handle so you can have results."

One of the girls raised her hand. "What if we get sick?"

"Are you planning to?"

"No."

"Then you don't have to worry about it."

Another girl. "What if we—"

"Stop!" Whitlaw held up a hand. "Do you see? You're already trying to negotiate a loophole for yourselves. It's called, 'What if—?' 'What if I get sick?' The answer is, make sure you *don't.* 'What if my car breaks down?' Make sure it doesn't—or make sure you have alternate transportation. Forget the loopholes. There aren't any! The universe doesn't give second chances. Neither do I. Just be here. You don't have a choice. That's how this class works. Assume that I'm holding a gun to your head. Because I am—you don't know what kind of a gun it is yet, but the fact is, I *am* holding a gun to your head. Either you're here and on time, or I pull the trigger and splatter your worthless brains on the back wall." He pointed. Somebody shuddered. I actually turned to look. I could imagine a red and gray splash of gore across the paneling.

"Do you get that?" He took our silence as assent. "Good. We might just get along."

Whitlaw leaned back casually against the front edge of his desk. He folded his arms across his chest and looked out over the room.

He smiled. The effect was terrifying.

"So now," he said calmly, "I'm going to tell you about the

one choice you do have. The *only* choice. All the rest are illusions—or, at best, reflections of this one. You ready? All right—here's the options: you can be free, or you can be cattle. That's it."

He waited for our reactions. There were a lot of puzzled expressions in the room.

"You're waiting for the rest of it, aren't you? You think there has to be more. Well, there isn't any rest of it. That's all there is. What you think of as the rest is just definitions—or applications. That's what we're going to spend the rest of this course talking about. Sounds easy, right? But it won't be—because you'll insist on making it hard; because this course is not just about the definitions of that choice—it's about the *experience* of it. Most of you aren't going to like it. Too bad. But this isn't about what you like. What you like or don't like is not a valid basis for choice in the world. You're going to learn that in here."

That's how he started out.

It went downhill from there—or uphill, depending on your perspective.

Whitlaw never entered the room until everybody was seated and settled. He said it was our responsibility to run the class—after all, he already knew the material; this class was for us.

He always began the same way. When he judged we were ready, he entered—and he always entered speaking: "All right, who wants to start? Who wants to define freedom?" And we were off—

One of the girls offered, "It's the right to do what you want, isn't it?"

"Too simple," he countered. "I want to rip off all your clothes and have mad passionate intercourse with you, right here on the floor." He said it deadpan, staring her right in the face. The girl gasped; the class laughed embarrassedly; she blushed. "What keeps me from doing it?" Whitlaw asked. "Anyone?"

"The law," someone called. "You'd be arrested." More laughter.

"Then I'm not completely free, am I?"

"Uh, well . . . freedom is the right to do whatever you want as long as you don't infringe on the rights of others."

"Sounds good to me—but how do I determine what those

rights are? I want to practice building atomic bombs in my back yard. Why can't I?"

"You'd be endangering others."

"Who says?"

"Well, if I were your neighbor, I wouldn't like it."

"Why are you so touchy? I haven't had one go off yet."

"But there's always the chance. We have to protect ourselves."

"Aha!" said Whitlaw, pushing back his white hair and advancing on the unfortunate student. "But now *you're* infringing on *my* rights when you say I can't build my own A-bombs."

"Sir, you're being ridiculous now. Everybody knows you can't build an A-bomb in your back yard."

"Oh? I don't know that. In fact, I *could* build one if I had access to the materials and enough time and money. The principles are well known. You're just betting that I don't have the determination to carry it through."

"Uh—all right. But even if you did, the rights of the individual still have to be weighed against the safety of the general public."

"How's that again? Are you telling me that one person's rights are more important than another's?"

"No, I—"

"Sure sounded like it to me. You said my rights have to be weighed against everyone else's. I want to know how you're going to determine them. Remember, all of us are supposed to be equal before the law. And what are you going to do if I don't think your method is fair? How are you going to enforce your decision?" Whitlaw eyed the boy carefully. "Try this one—it's more likely: I'm a plague victim. I want to get to a hospital for treatment, but if I even approach your city, you're going to start shooting at me. I claim that my right to medical care guarantees me entrance to that hospital, but you claim that your right to be free of contamination gives you license to kill. Whose rights are being infringed upon the most?"

"That's not a fair example!"

"Huh? Why not? It's happening in South Africa right now—and I don't care what the South African government says about it, we're talking about rights. Why isn't this a fair example? It's your definition. Sounds to me like there's something wrong with your definition of freedom." Whitlaw eyed the uncomfortable boy. "Hm?"

The boy shook his head. He gave up.

"So, let me give you a hint." Whitlaw turned to the rest of us again. "Freedom is *not* about what you *want.* That doesn't mean you can't have what you want—you probably can. But I want you to recognize that going for the goodies is just going for the goodies, nothing else. It has very little to do with freedom." He sat down on the edge of the desk again and looked around. "Anyone have another?"

Silence. Embarrassed silence.

Then a voice: "Responsibility."

"Eh? Who said that?"

"I did." A Chinese boy in the back of the room.

"Who's that? Stand up there. Let the rest of the class see what a genius looks like. What's your name, son?"

"Chen. Louis Chen."

"All right, Louis. Repeat your definition of freedom for the rest of these louts."

"Freedom means being responsible for your own actions."

"Right. You have your A for the day. You can relax—no, you can't; tell me what it means."

"It means you can build your A-bombs, sir, but if you aren't taking proper precautions, then the government, acting on behalf of the people, has the right to take action to guarantee that you do, or shut you down if you don't."

"Yes—and no. Now we have something else to define. *Rights.* Sit down, Louis. Give someone else a turn. Let's see some hands."

Another boy in the back. " 'Rights: that which is due a party by just claim, legal guarantee, or moral principle.' "

"Hm," said Whitlaw. "You surprise me—that's correct. Now close the book and tell me what it *means.* In your own words."

"Uh . . ." The fellow faltered. "That which is rightfully yours. The right of . . . the right to . . . I mean, it's what you're entitled to . . ." He became flustered and trailed off.

Whitlaw looked at him with a jaundiced expression. "First of all, you can't use a concept to define itself. And secondly, nothing is *rightfully* anyone's. We've already covered that one, remember? There's no such thing as ownership; there's only *con-*

trol. Ownership is just a temporary illusion, so how can there be any such thing as rights? You might as well insist that the universe owes you a living." Whitlaw grinned abruptly. "As a matter of fact, it does—but it's a lifetime job to collect."

He resumed his machine-gun attack. "Look, I'm going to make this easy for you. All that stuff that we call rights—that's just a lot of stuff that politicians say because it sounds good, so people will vote for them. They're actually ripping you off because they're confusing the issue, putting a lot of stuff in the way between you and the source of it all. So I want you to forget for a moment all of that stuff that you believe about rights. Because the truth is, it doesn't work. In fact, you can even forget about rights in the plural sense. There's only one right—and it isn't even a right in the traditional meaning of the word at all."

He was in the center of the room. He turned slowly around, meeting the eyes of all of us as he spoke. "The *defining* condition of adulthood is responsibility. So what's the one thing you need to experience that responsibility? It's so simple you won't get it—it's the *opportunity.*" He paused a moment to let it sink in, then repeated, "The opportunity to be responsible for your*self.* That's it. If you're denied that one, then you're not free, and all of the other so-called rights are redundant. Rights are opportunities—that's the definition. And opportunity demands responsibility."

A hand went up. "What about people who can't take care of themselves?"

"You're talking about the insane and the immature. That's why we have keepers and parents—to watch out for them, to clean up their messes and paddle their behinds and teach them not to make any more messes—and not turn them loose upon the world *until* they learn. Part of the responsibility of adulthood is seeing that others *also* have the opportunity to reach adulthood and be responsible for themselves too. Mentally as well as physically."

"But that's the government's job—"

"*What?* Somebody call the asylum—one of the lunatics is loose. Surely you don't mean that, son."

The boy looked stubborn. "Yes, I do."

"Mm, okay," said Whitlaw. "Justify yourself."

"It's the government's responsibility," he said. "By your definition."

"Eh? No, I said it's the people's responsibility."

"The government *is* the people."

"It is? Not the last time I looked—according to the book, the government is the *representative* of the people."

"That's not fair, sir—you wrote the book."

"I did?" Whitlaw looked at the text in his hand. "Hm, so I did. All right, point for your side. You caught me begging the question."

The boy looked smug.

"—But you're still wrong. No, you're only half wrong. The purpose of a government—the *only* justifiable reason for its existence—is to act on behalf of the member population in a delegated area of specific responsibility. Now, what's a 'delegated area of specific responsibility'?" Whitlaw didn't wait for someone to guess at it—he bulldozed on. "It works out to be anything that enough people are committed to—*whether it's right or wrong.* Get this! A government, acting on behalf of the member population—*and in their name*—will do *whatever* it is delegated to do, regardless of any defined morality in the matter. If you want proof, read a good history book." He plucked one off his desk. "A good history book is one that tells you what happened. Period. Forget the ones that explain history to you—they're ripping you off of the opportunity to see the *whole* picture."

He sat down on the edge of his desk again. "Listen, the government does what *you* want it to. If you say that you don't make a difference, you're guaranteeing that you won't. The fact of the matter is that anyone who is committed enough to enroll other people into the same commitment *will* make a difference. I want you to know that it does *not* take a majority. Some of the games that specific segments of this nation's population have enrolled the rest of us into include an extensive military organization, a space exploration agency, an interstate highway system, a postal service, a pollution control agency, an economic management bureau, a national education standard, a medical insurance service, a national pension plan, a labor management bureau and even a vast and complicated system of taxation so that each of us can pay for his or her fair share of those services—whether we wanted them or not in the first place." Whitlaw stabbed at us with one long bony finger, making his points in the air like a shrike impaling its prey on the thornbush. "So the conclusion is inescapable. *You* are responsible for the actions of your government. It acts in your name. It is your *employee.* If you don't properly supervise the actions of your employee, you're not *owning* your responsibility. You'll deserve what you get. Do you know why the government is in the shape it is today? Because you aren't doing your job. After all, who *else's* responsibility *could* it be? I mean, can you imagine anyone in his right mind *deliberately* designing such a system? No—no one in his right mind would! The system is continually falling into the hands of those who are willing to manipulate it for short-term gain—because *we* let them."

Someone raised his hand. Whitlaw waved it down. "No, not now." He grinned. "I'm not through 'brainwashing' you. I know that's what some of you think this is—I've seen the editorials in the newspapers too, the ones calling for the end of 'political indoctrination classes.' Let me just say this about that: you'll notice I'm not telling you what you *should* be doing. Because I don't know what that is. It's *your* responsibility to determine it for yourselves—you get to create your own form of participation. Because that's the only real choice you ever get in your whole life—whether or not you're going to participate. You might want to notice that *not* participating is also a decision—it's a decision to be a victim of the consequences. Refuse to handle your own responsibilities and you will get the consequences. *Every time!* You can count on it.

"So here's the punch line—pay attention. 'Let George do it' is not just the slogan of a lazy man—it's the credo of the slave. If you want to be taken care of and not have to worry, that's fine; you can join the rest of the cattle. Cattle are *comfortable*—that's how you recognize them. Just don't complain when they ship you off to the packing plant. They've bought and paid for the privilege. You sold it to them. Now if you want to be free, then get this: freedom is *not* about being comfortable. It's about seizing and using opportunities—and using them *responsibly.* Freedom is not comfort. It's *commitment.* Commitment is the willingness to be *un*comfortable. The two are incompatible, but there are damn few free men on welfare.

"The free man, class, doesn't just *survive*—he *challenges!*"

Whitlaw was right, of course. He usually was. If he'd ever been wrong, none of us had ever caught him at it. And after a while, we'd gotten pretty good.

I knew what he would say. The choice was mine. Even if I could have asked him for advice, he would have only said, "I can't answer that question for you, son. You already know the answer. You're just looking for agreement."

Right.

I couldn't depend on the good will of the universe any more. Five big plagues and a score of little ones had seen to that.

My coffee had gone cold.

So I went looking for Shorty.

Five

SHORTY TOWERED over me like a wall.

"Here," he said and thrust a flamethrower into my arms. "Don't flinch," he grinned. "There's nothing to be afraid of. It's not charged."

"Oh," I said, not at all reassured. I tried to figure out how to hold it.

"Watch it," he warned. "That'd be a good way to burn off your—here, hold it like this. One hand on the flame control there, the other on the stock—see that handle? That's right. Now, hold still while I fix your straps. We'll work without the tanks until you get the feel of it. You know, you're lucky—"

"Oh?"

"That torch is a Remington. Almost new. Designed for the war in Pakistan, but never used. Didn't need to—but it's perfect for us now because it'll take anything that burns and flows. See, the trick is this: you can shoot a stream of pure fuel alone—jellied gasoline is best—or you can shoot a barrage of exploding pellets, soaked in the fuel. Or you can shoot both at once. The pellets are pressure-loaded in this chamber here. Because they're pellets, you have a greater range, and because they explode on impact, you get a larger splash. The effect is terrific—don't point that at the ground, or you'll take off."

"Uh, Shorty . . ."

"Something wrong?"

"Napalm was outlawed almost ten years before the Pakistan conflict. What was the government doing with flamethrowers?"

He let go of the straps he was adjusting. "You're gonna need shoulder pads." He turned away. I thought he wasn't going to answer the question, but as he came back from the Jeep, carrying the pads, he said, "Same thing they were doing with A-bombs, nerve bombs, bacteriological weapons, hallucinogenic gases, nerve gases and poison vectors. Stockpiling them." He stopped my next question before I could ask it. "I know, they're illegal. That's why we had to have them—because the other side had them too. Letting them know was the guarantee. That's why the treaty worked."

"But—I thought the purpose of the whole thing was to outlaw inhumane weapons."

"Nope. Just to keep 'em from bein' used. There's always a difference between what you say and what you really want. If you're sharp enough to know what you really want, then it's easy to figure out what to say to get it. That's what that whole conference was about." He paused sourly. "I oughta know. I was there."

"Huh?"

Shorty looked like he wanted to say something, but he stopped himself. "Never mind. Some other time. Let me ask you this: what is it that makes a weapon inhumane?"

"Uh . . ." I thought about it.

"Let me make it easier for you. Tell me a *humane* weapon."

"Um—I see your point."

"Right. There's no such thing. It's like Christmas—it's not the gift, it's the thought that counts." He came around behind me and started fitting the pads under the straps. "A weapon, Jim—never forget this, lift your arms—is a tool for stopping the other fellow. That's the purpose—*stopping* him. The so-called humane weapons merely stop a man without permanently injuring him. The best weapons—you can put your arms down now—are the ones that work by implication, by threat, and never have to be used at all. The enemy stops himself.

"It's when they don't stop"—he turned me around to adjust the fittings in front—"that the weapons become inhumane, because that's when you have to use them. And so far, the most effective ones are the ones that kill—because they stop the guy permanently." He had to drop to his knees to cinch the waist strap. "Although . . . there's a lot to be said for maiming—"

"Huh?" I couldn't see his eyes, so I didn't know if he was joking or not.

"—but that's asking too much of both the weapon and its user." He straightened again and rapped the buckle in the center of my chest. "Okay, that's the quick-release latch. Flip that up and the whole thing falls apart. That's in case you have a sudden need to run like hell. And if you do, you'd better. Five seconds after you drop that, it blows itself to bits. All right, I'm gonna hang the tanks on you now."

"You were going to say something about the Moscow Treaties before, weren't you?" I prompted.

"Nope." He headed for the Jeep.

I flexed my arms. The harness was stiff, but it wasn't uncomfortable. I guess Shorty knew what he was doing.

He came back with the tanks. They sloshed lightly. "They're only half full. I don't want you starting any forest fires. Turn around."

As he hung the tanks on my shoulders, he said, "You want to know about the treaties? They were dishonorable. To make false rules about 'I won't use this if you won't use that' may seem civilized because it lessens the brutality—but it isn't. It just makes the brutality tolerable for a longer time. And that's not civilized at all. If we're in a situation where we have to stop the other fellow, then let's just *stop* him. It's more efficient. There, how does that feel?"

I tested my balance. "Uh, fine—"

He scowled. "No, it isn't. You're off balance. They're too low. Hold still." He lifted the tanks off my back and began readjusting the straps of the harness. "This torch—" he said, "—this torch is a truly beautiful weapon. It has a maximum range of sixty meters. Eighty with a supercharger. It makes you a totally independent fighting unit. You carry your own fuel, you choose your own targets, point and squeeze. *Vrr-o-oomm!* It'll stop a man instantly—or a worm. It'll stop a tank. It'll burn out a pillbox. There isn't anything that can resist a torch—except very thick armor or a lot of distance. It is not"—he gave a hard yank—"humane. You pull that trigger and that's not a man in front of you anymore; it's a private piece of hell. You can watch him turn black and shrivel as his blood boils out of his skin. You can feel his flesh roasting. Sometimes you can even hear the scream of the air exploding out of his lungs." He gave another sharp pull at the straps. "And that's good, Jim, that's very good. You *should* be right down there next to what you're doing. If you're going to be a killer, you should do it personally, so you *experience* what you're doing. That's the civilized way." He poked me. "That torch is *not* humane, but it is civilized."

My mouth was very dry. I managed to say, "Civilized—?"

"It stops them, doesn't it? Hold still, here come the tanks again. A weapon should let you sleep well at night. If it doesn't, there's something wrong with the war."

He caught me unprepared. I almost staggered. I stiffened against the weight. But he was right. The balance was better this way.

He must have seen the look on my face. "Jim—war isn't polite. Especially not this one. We don't have the time to be fair. That torch will burn a Chtorran like fluff, and that's all that matters—you don't get a second chance with worms. They come at you at a good sixty-five kilometers an hour—two hundred and twenty-five kilograms of angry worm. And they're all teeth at the business end. If it's purple, burn it. That's a standing order. You don't have to wait for permission."

"I won't."

He locked eyes with me and nodded sharply; his expression was hard. "There's one more thing. Don't ever balk because you might hit a man. Don't hesitate because you think you might be able to save him—you can't. Once a Chtorran starts eating, there's no way to stop it. It *can't* stop. Not even if it wanted to. Burn them both, Jim. And burn them fast. He'd thank you for it if he could." He studied my face. "Can you remember that?"

"I'll try."

"It's like that little girl. It's the kindest thing you can do."
I nodded and shouldered the flamethrower. I didn't like it—I probably never would. Too bad. "Okay," my mouth was saying. "Show me how to work it."

Six

RECONNAISSANCE CONFIRMED that there were only three worms in the valley, as Duke had guessed, but also that they were very busy with something. When Larry reported that, Duke frowned. He didn't like worms being so active—that made them hungry.

Dr. Obama ordered satellite pictures and the USAF ROCKY MOUNTAIN EYEBALL sent us a full-spectrum series, a twelve-hour surveillance of the valley and surrounding regions. The frames started arriving within an hour of Dr. Obama's request.

We all studied them, particularly the infra-red ones, but they told us little we didn't already know.

"Look here," said Larry, "the igloo." It was a bright red blotch; the frame was pseudo-color enhanced to show heat sources. "Something very hot in there. They must be large."

"And very active," grunted Duke. "That's almost too much heat." He poked Shorty. "What do you think? How much mass are we looking at?"

Shorty shrugged. "Hard to say. Three tons at least. Probably more. The resolution on the infra-red is lousy. The wavelength's too long."

"Yeah," said Duke. "I guess that settles it. We'll take three teams."

We left just before dawn. Chtorrans don't like direct sunlight, so we figured to drive all morning and catch them in the hottest part of the day, when they were most likely to be torpid. We hoped.

There were twelve of us. Four men with torches, three with grenades and two with rocket launchers. And the three Jeep drivers would be carrying laser-sighted AM-280s. The 280 was recoilless and could fire twenty-three hundred rounds per minute. A mere touch on the trigger would put fifty rounds inside a seven-centimeter circle—whatever the target beam touched. You could shoot from the hip and aim it like a flashlight. The 280 could chew holes in a brick wall—it was the high volume of fire that did it. If any gun could stop a Chtorran, it would have to be the 280.

I'd heard only a single complaint about the guns—from Shorty, of course. Denver had sent up some specially loaded magazines for them. Every hundredth round was a needle dart packed with a variety of particularly nasty germs. The reasoning was that if we failed to kill the Chtorrans right away, the bugs might get them later. Shorty had snorted contemptuously. "It's in case we don't come back. That's how much faith they have in us." He looked at me. "Listen, boy—that's not the way we do it here. We plan on coming back. Got that?"

"Uh . . . yes, sir."

The Remington hadn't been that hard to master. I'd spent the first couple of days starting forest fires—clearing brush and widening the scorched area around the camp; then had switched to target practice—trying to burn an asbestoid-and-wire framework dragged behind a Jeep.

"Now, be careful," Shorty had warned. "If you fire too soon, the Chtorran will veer off—but you won't be able to see that until the smoke clears. By then it's too late. Wait as long as you can before firing."

"Until I see the whites of his eyes, huh?"

Shorty grinned as he got back into the Jeep. "Sonny, if you

get close enough to a worm to see the whites of his eyes—you're lunch." He drove off and began his run.

I missed, of course. I waited too long and nearly got knocked down by the cage.

Shorty braked to a stop, stood up in the Jeep and rang a big triangular dinner bell. "Come and get it, Chtorrans! Dinner is served! Nice fresh human—not dangerous at all! Come and get it!"

I waited till he was through. "I assume that means I was too slow."

"Too slow—? Of course not. You just move too long in the same place."

We tried again. This time he drove straight at me. The Jeep bounced across the field, the asbestoid worm in hot pursuit but never quite catching up. I planted my feet solidly and counted slowly. Not too soon, now—

I missed again.

This time Shorty got out of the Jeep and strode back to the target. He pulled a fifty-casey note out of his pocket and stapled it to the cage. "There," he said. "I'm betting fifty C's that you can't hit it." He started back to the Jeep. "You know, you really ought to learn how to run faster. Make the worms earn their lunch. We don't want any fat Chtorrans on this planet, do we?"

"We don't want any at all," I said.

"That's the idea," he grinned. "I thought you forgot. Want to try it again?"

"Yeah. This time I'll get it."

He hooked a thumb at the target. "I've got fifty caseys says you won't—prove me wrong." He gunned the engine and jolted off.

While he circled, I tried to figure out what I was doing wrong. Obviously I was waiting too long to fire—but Shorty had said not to fire too soon or the Chtorran would have time to veer off.

On the other hand, if I held off too long I might not get the chance to fire at all.

Hmm. The best time to shoot had to be at just that moment when it was too late for the Chtorran to change course. But when was that? How close did a Chtorran get before the bloodlust took over? Fifty meters? Twenty-five? Hmm, think of a stampeding elephant. Call it fifteen meters. . . .

Hey, wait a minute—! This torch had a range of almost seventy. What was Shorty trying to pull? I could burn worms long before they got close enough to chomp me!

I waved at him and tried to attract his attention, but he only grinned and waved back. He started heading toward me. Fast. He was beginning another run.

Well, I'd show him. I reset the range of the flamer to maximum. This time I'd fire as soon as the target got close enough. I wouldn't wait one second longer than necessary.

I focused on the wire-mesh worm, estimated its range, waited till it bounced across an invisible line and squeezed the release. The flame whooshed out with a roar, startling me with its intensity. The asbestoid worm disappeared in a ball of orange fire. Oily black smoke rose from it.

Shorty leapt from the jeep, howling. I cut off the torch hastily. But he wasn't mad at all about his fifty caseys—not even angry about his singed eyebrows. He just ran over and pulled the plug on my battery pack.

"Now you're thinking like a worm-burner," he said. "Fire as soon as they get within range."

I glowered at him. "Why didn't you tell me that in the first place?"

"What—? And let you miss the excitement of learning how to outthink a Chtorran? That's what the lesson was all about."

"Oh," I said. Then, "Can we try it again?"

"Uh, I think not." He was feeling the damage to his eyebrows. "At least not until I get a longer towline for that target."

We never did get the longer towline, what with preparations for the big burn and all, but it worked out all right anyway. A couple more days of shooting at the target—Shorty wore his asbestoid pajamas—and I was ready for the real thing. At least Shorty and Duke were willing to take the chance. I wasn't as sure. I'd heard that worms could be as long as four meters and weigh as much as nine hundred kilos. Or more. Maybe those were exaggerations—I'd find out for myself soon enough—but I'd been brought up to worry.

It's a family tradition. Good worrying is never wasted.

Well, I'd certainly done enough this time—and just in case I hadn't, I was doing a little extra in the Jeep. Just to be on the safe side.

Duke noticed it, of course. We were both in the second car. "Relax, Jim. It's not white-knuckle time yet."

"Sorry," I said, trying to grin.

"We won't be there for hours." He leaned back against the seat and stretched his arms. "Enjoy the morning. Look at the scenery."

"Uh, shouldn't we be on the lookout for worms?"

"We are."

"Huh?"

"Shorty's in the first Jeep. Louis and Larry are in the last one. You don't know what to look for—that's why you're in the second. And I have more important things to think about." He folded his arms behind his head and appeared to go to sleep.

"Oh," I said.

I was beginning to get it. In this man's army, you don't worry unless you're ordered to—and if I want you to have an opinion, I'll give you one.

In other words, this was not the army I had thought I was joining—the Teamwork Army. That was dead and gone. I don't know why I hadn't realized. This was something else altogether.

Seven

WHITLAW TALKED about the army once.

One of the girls—one of the older ones; her name was Patricia—had been complaining about how her draft board had rejected her choice of "needed skill." (Well, Creative Anarchist had been pretty far out. I couldn't blame them.) "I might as well join the army and be a whore," she said.

"Mmm," said Whitlaw. "With an attitude like that, you probably wouldn't be a very good one."

The class laughed, but she looked miffed. Insulted, even. "What do you mean by that?"

"I mean, you might not be acceptable to them. Morale is very important in the army these days."

"Morale—?" The girl seemed astonished. "They're only a bunch of sweat-pushers—! What about *my* morale? I'm a political scientist!"

"Not in here, you're not." Whitlaw sat down on the edge of his desk, folded his arms and grinned. "And, obviously, not to your draft board either. Maybe a little honest sweat is exactly what you need to appreciate its value."

She sniffed proudly. "But my work with my brain is much more valuable than their work with their bodies."

"Wrong," said Whitlaw. "Your work is valuable only when it's needed. And *you're* only valuable when your particular skill is scarce. It takes time to train a biological engineer or a quantum mechanic or even a competent AI hacker—but if we had a hundred thousand of them, how much do you think a single one would be worth?"

She didn't answer.

"The only reason we haven't trained that many is that we don't need them. If we did, our society could produce them in two to four years. We've proven that time and again. Your grandfathers proved it when they needed computer programmers and engineers and aerospace technicians and a thousand other specialties to put the first man on the moon—and most of those specialties had to be invented as the needs arose. By the end of the decade, it seemed as if they were as plentiful as sweat-pushers; in fact, some of them actually *had* to start pushing sweat to survive when the space program was cut back."

"But that was . . . just economics," she insisted. "It's the education that makes a person valuable, isn't it?"

"Is it?" Whitlaw looked at her blandly. "How do you define value? Can you fell a tree? Or milk a cow? Do you know how to operate a bulldozer? Can you lay bricks?"

"Of course not—"

"Then by some standards, you're not valuable at all. You're not a survivor type."

"But—that's manual labor! Anybody can do that."

Whitlaw blinked. "But *you* can't?"

She looked surprised. "Why should I have to?"

Whitlaw stopped. He eyed her curiously. "Haven't you read any of the assignments?"

"Of course I have, but I'm talking about the *real* world now."

Whitlaw stopped in mid-turn toward his podium. He looked back at her, a startled expression on his face. "I beg your pardon."

The class groaned—*uh oh*—we knew what was coming.

He waited until her mouth ran out of momentum. "Let me explain something to you. In the whole history of the human race, in all the time since we first climbed down out of the trees and stopped being monkeys and started learning how to be people, in all those years, we have managed to maintain what passes for modern civilization for only a very short period. I mark the beginning of modern times with the first industrialization of electricity. That makes the—ah, you should pardon the expression—*current* era less than two centuries long. That's not a long enough test. So it still isn't proven that civilization isn't a fad. I'm betting on history—it's got the track record. Do you understand what I'm trying to tell you? What you think of as the *real* world is actually a very *unreal* world, an artificial environment that has come into existence only by the determination of a lot of sweat-pushers looking for a way to make their lives easier, and by the good will of the universe—and the latter condition is subject to change without notice. That alone guarantees that this"—he lifted his hands wide to take in the room, the building, the city, the world—"is just a temporary condition. Certainly on a cosmic scale it is." He brushed his white hair back with one hand. There was fire in his voice as he added, "Listen, you're capable—that's not the question. You just refuse to acknowledge your own capability—and that's your problem. Did you know that in the Soviet Union today there are more women bricklayers than men? And it's been that way for at least fifty years. No, your only excuse is that you're not *trained* for it. And that's also the reason why you wouldn't be a good whore—you don't know how to be. But you could be, if you had the training. The fact is, you can be anything you choose if you have the training—and you would if it meant the difference between eating or starving."

"I'm sure I could," she said. "I could learn to milk a cow, if I had to—"

"I'm sure you could too. It'd only take a few minutes." He eyed her. "Or longer."

"—but then what?"

"Then you'd milk cows, of course!"

"But I don't want to milk cows!"

"Neither do I—but if the cow has to be milked, someone has to do it! That's what makes it a *needed* skill. Listen—" He turned to the rest of us now. "Too many of you sitting in this classroom have been separated from those very necessary skills for too many generations. It's given you some very peculiar ideas of your own importance. Let me relieve you of that foolishness right now—most of you have to depend on too many others for your survival, and that makes you vulnerable. It wouldn't be a bad idea to learn a few of those basic skills, because as far as the society you live in is concerned, it's the training that's valuable, not the individual.

"Right now, most of our laborers in the army take a lot of pride in what they're doing—believe it or not. So what does it matter that some of them were sixth-generation welfare recipients? They're not anymore! Now they're taxpayers, just like the rest of us. And the skills they learn in the army may be enough so that they'll never have to go back on welfare again. And at least *they* can see the physical fact of what they're accomplishing—most of *us* never do. I don't. I doubt you'll remember a tenth of what I tell you a year from now—and you don't know how frustrating that is for me to realize—but *they* can point to a new park or a reclaimed building and say, 'I did *that.*' And that's quite a feeling. I know! This country benefits from their labor, you and I benefit—and most of all *they* benefit, because their lives are enriched. They gain skills, they gain pride and they regain their self-respect, because they're doing a job that makes a difference!"

Whitlaw stopped and took a breath. I found myself wondering again about his limp, where he had gotten it. He covered it well. I hadn't noticed it until someone else pointed it out to me. He looked at the girl whose comment had sparked this discussion as if to say, "Do you get it?"

She made a mistake. A little one, but it was enough. She sniffed.

Whitlaw's expression froze. I'd never seen him looking so angry. He said quietly, "You know something? If you were a whore, you'd probably starve to death."

Nobody laughed. Nobody dared to.

Whitlaw leaned in close to her, his face only inches away from hers. In a stage whisper, he said, "You've been ripped off. You've been allowed to turn yourself into an egocentric, selfish, spoiled brat—a self-centered, empty-headed, painted little cock-tease. You think the sanctity of your genitals is important? You're *already* a whore and you don't even know it!"

"You can't talk to me that way—" She started to rise—

—but Whitlaw didn't back away. He leaned in even closer.

There was no room for her to rise, and she fell back in her seat. "Listen, I've seen you. You shake your tits and simper and expect the football team to fight for the privilege of sitting next to you in the cafeteria. You pout at Daddy and he hands you his credit cards. Someday you'll make a deal to screw twice a week and some poor sucker will give you a house and a car and a gold ring to wear. If that isn't whoring, I don't know what is. The only difference between you and a licensed courtesan is that he or she gives honest service."

"Hold on there—!" One of the fellows in the back of the room stood up suddenly. He was red in the face. He looked ready to punch Whitlaw. I didn't know whether to be scared for him or Whitlaw.

"Sit down, son!"

"No! You can't badger her like that!"

"How would you like me to badger her? *Sit down!*" Whitlaw turned to the rest of us, not bothering to look and see if the fellow had followed instructions or not. "How many of you think I'm out of line here?"

Most of the class raised their hands. Some didn't. Not me. I didn't know what to think.

"So get this! I don't care what you think! I've got a job to do! And if that means hitting some of you broadside with a shovel, I'll do it—because it seems to be the only way to get your attention! Listen, dammit! I am not a babysitter! Maybe in some of your other classes they can pour the stuff over you like syrup and hope some of it will stick; but in this class, we do it *my* way—because my way produces *results!* This class comes under the authority of the Universal Service Act—and it's about growing up!" He poked the girl harshly. "You can go home and complain to your daddy if you want—I know who you are—and he can go and complain to the draft board. Mean old Mr. Whitlaw is picking on Daddy's little girl! They'll just laugh in his face. They hear three or four of those a week. And they love them—it proves I'm doing my job." He learned in close to her again. "When things get uncomfortable, do you always run to Daddy? Are you going to spend the rest of your life looking for daddies to defend you against the mean old Mr. Whitlaws of the world? Listen, here's the bad news—you're going to be a grownup soon! You don't get to do that anymore!" He reached out and took her chin in his hand and pointed her face back toward him. "Look at me, Patricia—don't hide from it! There are tigers outside—and you are fat and plump and tender. My job is to toughen you up, so you have a chance against them. If I let you get away with this bullshit that you run on everybody else, I'd be ripping you off of the opportunity to learn that you don't need it. That you're bigger than all of that 'sweet little Daddy's girl' garbage. So leave it at the door from now on. You got that?"

She started to cry. Whitlaw pulled a tissue from his pocket and dropped it on the desk in front of her. "That racket won't work in here either." She glared at him, then took it and wiped at her eyes quickly. For the rest of the session she was very quiet and very thoughtful.

Whitlaw straightened and said to the rest of us, "That applies to the rest of you too. Listen, this is about *service.* Most of you are operating in the context that the obligation is some kind of *chore,* something to be avoided. Do you know you're cheating yourself? The opportunity here is for you to use the resources of the United States government to make a profound difference for yourselves and the people you share this planet with. And we'll be talking about specifics later in the course. You just need to get one thing—this isn't about you serving others as much as it's about you serving yourselves." He stumped to the back of the room and faced the entire class. We had to turn in our seats to see him. His face was flushed, his eyes were piercing.

"Listen," he said. "You know about the Millennium Treaties—the final act of the Apocalypse. I know what you've been taught so far. In order to guarantee world peace, the United States gave up its right to have an international military force. We lost a war—and this time, we had to take the responsibility for it. Never again would an American president have the tools of reckless adventurism at such casual disposal—it's too dangerous a risk. The Apocalypse proved that.

"So what we have instead is the Teamwork Army—and what that means to you is that your service obligation is no longer a commitment to war, but a commitment to peace. It's an opportunity to work not just here, but anywhere in the world, if you so choose, attacking the causes of war, not the symptoms."

Abruptly, Whitlaw stopped there. He shoved both his hands into his jacket pockets and returned to the front of the room.

He stood there with his back to us, peering at his notes on the podium. He stood like that long enough for the classroom to become uncomfortable. Some of us traded nervous glances. Without looking up from his clipboard, Whitlaw said quietly, "Paul, you have a question?"

It was Paul Jastrow, in the back of the room. How had Whitlaw known that? "Yeah," said Paul, standing up. "I've been reading here"—he held up one of the texts—"our situation is like that of Germany at the end of World War One, right?"

Whitlaw turned around. "In what way?"

"Well, we're being punished for starting a war. So we're not allowed to have the kind of military that could be used for starting another war, right?"

Whitlaw nodded. "One thing—in our case, it isn't a punishment. It's a commitment."

"Yeah," said Paul. "I hear you—but the terms of it are the same, no matter what you call it. We don't have a real army—not one that carries guns." He looked angry.

"Only the domestic service, of course," Whitlaw noted. "But essentially, you're right. So what's the question?"

"I'm getting to it. It's this 'Teamwork Army'—" He said it with disdain. "It sounds an awful lot like what the Germans had after World War One. They had all these work camps and youth groups and they drilled with shovels instead of rifles and they did public works and all that kind of thing. And all that was really just a fake, because when the time came, these guys put down their shovels and picked up rifles and turned into a real army again. And we know how that turned out."

"Yeah," said Whitlaw. "So?"

"So—what about our so-called Teamwork Army? I mean, couldn't they be turned back into a military force?"

Whitlaw smiled. For some reason, it made him look dangerous. "Yep," he said, looking straight at Paul.

"Well—?" asked Paul.

"Well what?"

"Was that intentional?"

"I don't know." Whitlaw's tone was casual. Perhaps he really didn't know.

"Well, doesn't that mean the Teamwork Army's a fake?"

"Is it?" Whitlaw asked. "You tell me."

Paul looked uncertain. "I don't know," he said.

Whitlaw stood there for a moment, waiting. He looked at Paul, he glanced around the room at the rest of us, then looked back to Paul. "Is that an observation, Paul, or is there a question in there somewhere?"

"Uh, yeah. There's a question in there, but I don't know what it is. It's just—I don't get it."

"I see that. And thanks for being honest about it—that's good. So let me work with that for a second. Let's start with the facts about the Teamwork Army. These are men who are building things. People who build things tend to be very defensive about the things they build. It's called territoriality. It turns out they make very good soldiers. Yes, the possibility is there. The Teamwork Army could be converted to a regular military force in . . . oh, let me see, now—what did that report say?" He made a show of returning to his clipboard and calling up a specific page of notes. "Ah—twelve to sixteen weeks."

He paused. He let it sink in. He looked around the classroom, meeting the gaze of everyone who dared to look at him. I think we were horror-struck; I know I was. It wasn't the answer I wanted to hear. After a long, uncomfortable silence, Whitlaw said quietly, "So *what?*" He stepped out into the middle of the room again. "The question is not *why* is that possibility there—because there is *always* that possibility of military adventurism—the question is *what,* if anything, do we do about it?"

Nobody answered.

Whitlaw grinned at us. "That's what this course is about. *That responsibility.* Eventually it's going to be yours. So your assignment is to look at how you'd like to handle it. What would *you* do with the army? It's *your* tool. How do you want to use it? We'll talk about that tomorrow. Thank you, that'll be it for today." He returned to the podium, picked up his clipboard and left the room.

Huh—? We sat and looked at each other. Was that it?

Patricia looked unhappy. "I don't like it," she said. "And I still don't know what to do about my draft board."

Somebody poked her. "Don't worry about it," he said. "You'll think of something. You've got time."

But he was wrong.

She didn't have time—and neither did any of the rest of us. She was dead within six months. And so were most of the rest of my classmates.

Eight

WHEN THE plagues first appeared, the medical community assumed they were of natural origin, simple mutations of already familiar diseases. Hence the names: Black Peritonitis, African Measles, Botuloid Virus, Comatosis and Enzyme Reaction 42—that last one was particularly vicious. They were so virulent and they spread so fast that it wasn't until afterward that all of them were identified.

I remember Dad frowning as he read the newspaper each night. "Idiots," he muttered. "I'm only surprised it didn't happen sooner. Of course you're going to get plague if you put that many people into a place like Calcutta."

Within a couple of weeks, the frown gave way to puzzlement. "Rome?" he said. "I thought the Italians were more careful than that."

When it hit New York, Dad said, " 'Nita, I think we should move up to the cabin for a few weeks. Jim, you'll come with us, of course."

"But, I've got school—"

"You can afford to miss it. I think I'll call your sister too."

At first, the doctors thought they were dealing with only one disease—but one with a dozen contradictory symptoms. They thought that it took different forms, like bubonic and pneumonic plague. Then they thought that it was so unstable it kept mutating. Everyone had a theory: the super-jumbos were the vectors; we should ground all air travel at once and isolate the disease. Or the bacterio-ecology had finally developed a widespread tolerance for our antibiotics; we shouldn't have used them so freely in the past. Or it was all those experiments with fourth-dimensional physics; they were changing the atmosphere and causing weird new mutations. Things like giant centipedes and purple caterpillars.

The first wave swept across the country in a week. A lot of it was carried by the refugees themselves as they fled the East Coast, but just as much was spread by seemingly impossible leap-frog jumps. Airplanes? Or something else? There was no direct air service at all to Klamath, California, yet that city died before Sacramento.

I remember one broadcast; this scientist—I don't remember his name—was claiming that it was biological warfare. He said there were two kinds of agents: the Y-agents for which there were vaccines and antitoxins, and the X-agents for which there were no defenses at all. Apparently, he said, some of these X-agents must have been released, either accidentally or perhaps by terrorists. There was no other way to explain this sudden outbreak of worldwide uncontrollable death.

That idea caught on real fast. It made sense. Within days the country was in an uproar. Screaming for revenge. If you couldn't kill the germ, at least you could strike back at the enemy responsible for releasing it.

Except—who was that? There was no way of knowing. Besides—and this was the horrible thought—what if the bugs were *ours?* There were just as many people willing to believe that too.

After that, things fell apart real fast. We heard some of it on the short wave radio. It wasn't pretty.

We were fairly well isolated where we were, even more so after somebody went down to the junction one night and set the bridge on fire. It was an old wooden one and it burned for hours, until it finally collapsed into the stream below. Most of us who lived on the hill knew about the shallow place two miles upstream. If necessary you could drive a vehicle across there, but Dad had figured that the burned-out bridge would stop most refugees from trying to come up the mountain. He was almost right. One of our neighbors down the hill radioed us once to warn of a caravan of three land-rovers heading our way, but not to worry. A while later we heard some shooting, then nothing. We never heard anything more about it.

After that, however, Dad kept a loaded rifle near the door, and he taught all of us how to use it—even the kids. He was very specific in his instructions. If we did shoot someone, we were to burn the bodies, *all* their belongings, their cars, their animals and everything they had touched. *No exceptions.*

We stayed on the mountain all summer. Dad phoned in his programs until the phones stopped working; then he just kept working without sending them in. I started to ask him once why he kept on, but Mother stopped me. Later, she said to me, "Jim, it doesn't matter if there's ever going to be anyone again who'll want to play one of his games—he's doing them for himself. He has to believe—we all do—that there *will* be a future."

That stopped me. I hadn't thought about the future—because I hadn't comprehended the awesome scale of the pestilence. I had stopped listening to the radio early on. I didn't want to know how bad it was. I didn't want to hear about the dead dying faster than the living could bury them—whole households going to bed healthy and all of them dying before they awoke. I didn't want to hear about the bodies in the streets, the panic, the looting, the burnings—there had been a firestorm in Los Angeles. Was anybody left alive?

We stayed on the mountain all winter too. It was rough, but we managed. We had a windmill, so we had electricity—not a lot, but enough. We had a solar roof and a Trombe wall, we wore sweaters and we stayed warm. We'd used the summer to build a greenhouse, so we had vegetables, and when Dad brought down the deer, I understood why he had spent so much time practicing with the crossbow. We survived.

I asked him, "Did you know that something like this would happen?"

He looked up at me across the body of the deer. "Something like what?"

"The plagues. The breakdown."

"Nope," he said, wiping his forehead. The insides of that animal were *hot.* He bent back to his task. "Why do you ask?"

"Um, the crossbow, the cabin—and everything. Why this particular mountain? I always thought you were a little bit . . . well, wobbly for making such a thing about being self-sufficient. Now it seems like awfully good planning."

He stopped and laid down his knife. He wiped the blood off his gloves. "It is impossible to work in weather like this." His breath was frosty in the air. "And I can't get a grip through these gloves. No, I didn't know—and yes, it was good planning. But it wasn't my idea. It was your grandfather's. I wish you could have known him better. He used to tell me that a man should be prepared to move suddenly at least three times in his life. That is, if you're planning to live a long life. You know why, of course. Pick any period of history, any place. It's hard to find seventy years of unbroken peace and quiet. Somebody's tree is always too crowded." He sighed. "When the screeching starts, it's time to go someplace quieter." He picked up the knife and went back to his evisceration of the buck. "Our family has a history of narrow escapes—wait a minute. Hold that—ah, there! One of your great-grandfathers left Nazi Germany in 1935. He kept heading west until he got to Dublin—that's why your name is McCarthy today. He forgot to marry your great-grandmother in a church."

"Oh," I said.

"Your grandfather bought this land in 1986. When land was still cheap. He put a prefab on it. Came up here every summer after that and built a little more. Never saw the sense of it myself until—let's see, it was before you were born—it would have had to have been the summer of '97. Right, we thought that was going to be the year of the Apocalypse."

"I know," I said. "We studied it in school."

He shook his head. "It's not the same, Jim. It was a terrifying time. The world was paralyzed, waiting to see if they would drop any more bombs. We were all sure that this was it—the big one. The panics were pretty bad, but we came through it all right, up here. We spent the whole year on this mountain—didn't come down till Christmas. The world was lucky that time. Anyway, that's what convinced me."

We began pulling the buck around and onto the sled. I said, "How long do you think we'll have to stay up here this time?"

"Dunno. Could be a while—maybe even a couple years. In the fourteenth century, the Black Death took its time about dying out. I don't expect these plagues to be any different."

I thought about that. "What do you think we'll find when we do go back?"

"Depends."

"On?"

"On how many people have . . . survived. And who." He looked at me speculatively. "I think you'd better start listening to the radio with me again."

"Yes, sir."

About a month after that, we caught a broadcast out of Denver, the provisional capital of the United States. Martial law was still in effect. The thirty-six surviving members of Congress had reconvened and postponed the presidential election for at least six months. And the second-generation vaccines were proving nearly sixty percent effective. Supplies were still limited though.

Dad and I looked at each other and we were both thinking the same thing. *The worst is over.*

Within a month, Denver was on the air twenty-four hours a day. Gradually, the government was putting its pieces back together. And a lot of information was finally coming to light.

The first of the plagues—they knew now there had been several—had appeared as isolated disturbances in the heart of Africa. Within a few weeks, it had spread to Asia and India and was beginning its westward sweep across the world. The second plague came so hard on its heels that it seemed like part of the same wave, but it had started somewhere in Brazil, I think, and swept north through Central America—so fast, in fact, that many cities succumbed before they even had a chance to identify it. By the time of the third plague, governments were toppling and almost every major city was in a state of martial law. Almost all travel worldwide was at a standstill. You could be shot for trying to get to a hospital. The fourth and fifth plagues hit us like tidal waves, decimating the survivors of the first three. There was a sixth plague too—but by then the population density was so low, it *couldn't* spread.

Some areas had been lucky and had remained completely unaffected, mostly isolated out-of-the-way places. A lot of ships just stayed at sea, particularly Navy vessels, once the admiralty recognized the need to preserve at least one military arm relatively intact. Then there were remote islands and mountaintop settlements, religious retreats, survival communities, our entire Nuclear Deterrent Brigade (wherever they were), the two lunar colonies, the L5 construction project (but they lost the ground base), the submarine communities of Atlantis and Nemo and quite a few places where someone had the foresight to go down and blow up the bridge.

But even after the vaccines were in mass production and the plagues had abated (somewhat), there were still problems. In fact, that was when the *real* problems began. In many parts of the world, there was no food, the distribution systems having broken down completely. And typhus and cholera attacked the weakened survivors. There was little hospital care available anywhere in the world; the hospitals had been the first institutions to go under. (Any doctor who had survived was automatically suspect of dereliction of duty.) Many large cities had become uninhabitable because of fires and mass breakdown of services. Moscow, for instance, was lost to a nuclear meltdown.

It was the end of the world—and it just kept on happening. So many people were dying of exposure, starvation, anomie, suicide, shock and a thousand other things that people didn't usually die of but which had suddenly become fatal, that it seemed we were caught up in a larger plague with no name at all—except its name was despair. The waves of it rolled around the world and kept on rolling and rolling and rolling. . . .

Before the plagues had broken out, there had been almost six billion human beings on the Earth. By the end of it, nobody knew how many were left. The United States government didn't even try to take the next national census. If anybody in authority had any idea how many people had survived, they weren't saying. It was almost as if they were afraid to make it real. But we heard on the short wave one night that there had to be at least a hundred million dead in this country alone. Whole cities had simply ceased to exist.

We couldn't comprehend that, but there were all those reports on the radio and pictures on the TV. Large areas of the countryside were returning to wilderness. There were ruins everywhere. Burned-out houses were commonplace—frightened neighbors had tried to halt the spread of the disease by burning the homes of the dying, sometimes not even waiting until the dying were dead. Everywhere there were abandoned cars, broken windows, faded billboards, uncut lawns and more than a few mummified corpses. "If you come upon one," said the voice from Denver, "exhale quickly, don't inhale, hold your breath, don't touch anything and back away—practice it till it becomes a reflex. Then place yourself in quarantine—there may be a chance for you, *maybe*—and call a decontamination squad. If you're in a place where there are no decontamination units, set a fire. And pray you've been fast enough."

We stayed up in the mountains through spring. And listened to the radio.

Denver reported that it looked like the plagues were beginning to die out. There were less than a thousand outbreaks a week worldwide, but people were still dying. There were famines now—there were crops that hadn't been planted—and mass suicides too. If the plague without a name had been despair before, then now it was madness. People slipped into and out of it so easily it was recognized as a fact of life—a complaint so common that no one was untouched, so universal it became transparent. Like air, we couldn't see it anymore, but nonetheless we were enveloped in it every moment of existence.

The news reported only the most shocking or disturbing cases, the ones too big to ignore. We listened, wondered and sometimes cried. But there was just too much hurt to handle. Most of it we buried. And some of it we didn't—we just avoided it the best we could. Somehow we managed not to care too much. Somehow we managed to survive.

I was afraid that we would never be able to come down from the mountain—but we did, eventually. In April, Dad and I took the station wagon and ventured slowly down the hill and across the stream. If anyone was watching us, we didn't see them. We paused once to wave a white flag, but there was no answering "Halloooh."

It was as if we'd been traveling to another star for a hundred years and had only just returned. We felt like alien explorers—we felt as if we didn't belong here anymore. Everything was both familiar and different. The world looked deserted and empty. And it was uncannily quiet. But there were burned-out buildings everywhere—scorched monuments to the dead. Each one was testimony—a body had been found here.

We had to wend our way carefully around abandoned vehicles and fallen trees. I began to get uneasy. We saw nothing for miles until we came to a pack of dogs trotting down the highway. They started barking when they saw us. They chased the car for almost a kilometer. My unease gave way to fear.

Later we saw cattle wandering free; they looked thin and sickly. We saw a dazed young woman walking up the road. We tried to stop her, warn her about the dogs, but she just kept on walking past us as if we weren't there. After that we saw a naked boy hiding in the trees, but he turned and ran when we called to him.

"Too soon?" I asked.

Dad shook his head. "Not soon enough. There's work to be done, Jim." And his face tightened in pain.

We stopped to fill our gas tank—there was an official-looking sign on the station, proclaiming that it had been nationalized for the duration of the emergency and whatever fuel and supplies still remained were freely available to all registered survivors.

"But aren't they afraid someone will steal it?"

"Why bother?" Dad said. "There's more than enough for everyone now."

I thought about that. The plagues had been fast. A thousand frightened people had scrambled aboard a super-jumbo in New York, and by the time the plane was over St. Louis, half of them were dead and the other half were dying. Only the flight crew, in their locked cabin, survived—but they were dead too, because there was no airport in the country that would let them land. And even if they could have landed, there was no way to get that flight crew out of the plane except through the passenger cabin. That happened three times. The one plane that did land was burned immediately as it rolled to a stop. The other two flight crews took the faster way out. After that *all* the airports were shut down.

Dad was saying, "It's all still here, Jim—almost everything. There wasn't time for a panic. That's how fast it happened." He shook his head sadly. "It's as if the human race has gone away and isn't coming back. There isn't any reason to steal anymore, no need to hoard—only to *preserve.*" He smiled sourly. "For the first time in the history of the human race, there's more than enough of everything for everybody. We've all been made suddenly wealthy." He sounded very sad.

Eventually, we came to a town. Two men with rifles met us at a roadblock. They were very polite about it, but we would not be allowed to pass until we had been cleared through decontamination. Their guns were very convincing.

It was an uncomfortable fifteen minutes. We stood by the car, our hands held away from our sides, until the decontamination team arrived. They pulled up in a white van with a large red cross on each side. We stripped naked and two helmeted figures in white safety-suits sprayed us with foam—our station wagon too. inside and out. I was glad it was a warm day. They took blood samples from each of us and disappeared back into their truck; they were gone for a long time. I began to shiver, even in the afternoon sun.

Finally the door opened and they came out again, still masked. Dad and I looked at each other worriedly. They came up to us, each one carrying a pressure injector. The shorter one grabbed my arm and held the nozzle against the skin. Something went *pssst* and my arm felt suddenly cold and wet. I flexed my fingers experimentally. "Relax, you'll be all right," she said, pulling off her hood—they were women! And they were grinning.

"They're clean!" shouted the gray-haired one; she turned to Dad. "Congratulations." Dad handled it with remarkable aplomb. He bowed.

I was already reaching for my jeans. The guards laid their guns aside and ran up to shake our hands. "Welcome to Redfield. Is either one of you a teacher? Or a sewage engineer? Do you know anything about fusion systems? We're trying to get the northwest power-net up again. Can you handle a stereo cam?"

I rubbed my arm; it was starting to sting. "Hey—what's this mark?"

"Coded tattoo," said the one who had vaccinated me. She was very pretty. "Proves you're clean—and immune. Stay away from anyone who doesn't have one. You might pick up spores and not know it."

"But we've got family!"

"How many? I'll give you extra vac-pacs to take with you—and coveralls. And foam! Oh, damn! I don't have enough! You'll have to stop at the med-station. Listen to me—you can't come in direct contact with your own people again until they've been vaccinated too. Even though *you're* immune, you can still carry spores—you could be very dangerous to anyone who isn't inoculated. Do you understand?"

I nodded. Dad looked worried, but he nodded too.

"Good."

We went first to the med-station, formerly a drugstore across the street from the two-story city hall. The teenager in charge gave us complete decontamination and vaccination kits, and very thorough instructions on how to use them. She gave us extra vac-pacs for our neighbors on the mountain too.

Then she sent us to the Reclamation Office to register. "First floor, city hall," she pointed. "It's not exactly mandatory," she said, "but it'll be better for you if you do."

I asked Dad about that as we crossed the street. He shook his head. "Later, Jim—right now, we play by the rules."

The "office" was a desk with a terminal on it. It asked you questions, you answered. When you were through, it spat out a registration card at you. Dad thought for a moment, then registered only himself and me. No mention of Mom or Maggie or the boys. "There'll be time enough later, if it's necessary," he said. "Let's see if we can pick up some supplies. I really miscalculated on the toilet paper."

That was the strangest shopping trip I'd ever been on. Money wasn't any good anymore. Neither was barter. There was a wizened little old man at the checkout counter of the mall, a few other people moving in and out of the shops. He was shaking his head in slow rhythmic beats, and he couldn't focus his eyes on anything for long. He told us that the mall was under the authority of the local Reclamation Office—Dad and I exchanged a look—and we were free to claim what we needed. "When you leave, stop by here and show me your card. I punch it in. That's all."

"But how do we pay for it?"

"If you're lucky, you won't have to." He giggled.

Dad pulled me away. "Come on, Jim. Get a cart. I think I understand."

"Well, I don't! It sounds like legalized looting!"

"Shh, keep your voice down. Now, think about it. What good is money if you can walk into any empty house or store and walk out with handfuls of it—or whatever else you find? A year ago, there were enough goods in this country for three hundred and fifty million Americans—not to mention goods produced for export. Look around, Jim—how many people are left? Do you want to take a guess at the percentage that survived? I don't—I don't want to scare myself. But it's fairly obvious, isn't it, that in circumstances like this even barter is unnecessary. These people here have worked out an answer to the immediate problem of survival. The goods are here. The people need them. We can worry about the bookkeeping later. If there is a later. For many of them there may not be—at least not without this kind of help. It all makes sense—sort of."

"But if they're giving things away, then why the registration cards?"

"To give a semblance of control, maybe. To give us the feeling there's still some authority in the world. You notice how industrious some of these people seem? Maybe it's to keep themselves going—because if they stop for even a moment and realize—" He caught himself. "Come on, get that cart."

We picked up toilet paper, a couple of radiophones, some cartons of canned goods and freeze-dried foods, a new first-aid kit, some vitamins, some candy for the kids, *a newspaper,* rifle shells and so on. The only things we couldn't afford were the fresh meats and vegetables. Those had to be paid for—in United Nations Federal Kilo-Calorie notes, caseys for short.

"Aha—yes. The nickel drops."

"What?"

"What's the only thing in short supply today, Jim?"

"People."

"Trained skills. That's what they're trading here. Ability. Labor. That's the new money-standard. Or it will be." He looked almost happy. "Jim"—he grabbed my shoulders abruptly—"it's over. These people are organizing for survival, for a future. There's work to do and they're doing it. They have hope." His grip was tight. "We can come down from the mountain now. We're *needed.* All of us. Your mom's a nurse. Maggie can teach. . . ." His eyes were suddenly wet. "We made it, Jimmy. We made it through to the other side!"

But he was wrong. We hadn't even seen the worst of it yet.

Nine

THE PLAGUES weren't over.

But this time we were better prepared. We had vaccines, and the lower population density and all the precautions still in effect from the first calamitous waves slowed the spread of the new plagues to a containable crawl.

The one that hit us was supposed to be one that you could recover from, although it might leave you blind or sterile—or permanently deranged. It had been around since the beginning—it just hadn't been noticed until the others were contained. Not controlled, just contained.

We lost the boys to it—Tim and Mark—and we almost lost Dad too. Afterward, he was a different man. He never fully recovered. Haggard and gray, he was almost a zombie. He didn't smile anymore. He'd lost a lot of weight and most of his hair, and suddenly he looked old. It was as if the mere act of surviving had taken all of his strength; he didn't have any left for living. A lot of people were like that.

And I don't think Maggie ever forgave him for the death of her sons. It had been his decision to bring us down from the mountain by July, but he couldn't have known. No one did. We all thought it was over.

The last time I saw him was when he left for San Francisco. They'd "drafted" him—well, not quite drafted, but the effect was the same. Someone was needed to manage the reorganization of the Western Region Data Banks, and Dad was one of the few free programmers left. Most of those who'd survived had already nested themselves into security positions; programmers were *valuable*—without them, the machines would stop. But Dad was still a free agent, and therefore subject to the control of the Labor Requisition Board. He'd been right to be cautious about registering. When we came down from the mountain, his orders were waiting for him. He appealed, but it was rejected. The national welfare came first.

I drove Dad down to the train station that last day. Mom couldn't get away from the clinic—she'd made her goodbyes the night before. Maggie wouldn't come. Dad looked very thin. He carried only a single small suitcase. He didn't say much while we waited for the train to arrive. We were the only ones on the platform.

"Dad? Are you all right? You know, if you're ill—"

He didn't look at me. "I'm all right," he snapped. And then he said it again in a quieter tone. "I'm all right." He still wasn't looking at me, he was still staring down the track, but he reached over and put his hand on my shoulder.

"Do you need to sit down?"

He shook his head. "I'm afraid I might not be able to get back up." He said, "I'm tired of this, Jim. I'm so tired. . . ."

"Dad, you don't have to go. You have rights. You can claim the shock of—"

"Yes, I do," he said. And the way he said it left no room for argument. He dropped his hand from my shoulder. "You know about the guilt, Jim—survivor's guilt? I can't help it. There were people who *deserved* to live. Why didn't I die instead?"

"You did what you had to!"

"Just the same," he spoke haltingly, "I feel . . . a responsibility now . . . to do something, to make amends. If not to the rest of the world, then to . . . the babies. Tim and Mark."

"Dad"—this time I put my hand on his shoulder—"listen to me."

He turned to me. "And I can't stand the look in her eyes anymore!"

"Maggie?"

"Your mother."

"She doesn't blame you!"

"No, I don't think she does. And she has every good reason to. But it's not the blame, Jim—it's the pity. I can't stand that." He faltered, then said, "Maybe it'll be better this way." He stooped to lower his suitcase to the ground. Very slowly, he put his hands on my shoulders and pulled me close for a last hug. He felt even thinner in my arms than he looked.

"Take care of them," he said. "And yourself."

He pulled back and looked at me, searching my face for one last sign of hope—and that was when I saw how old he had become. Thin and gray and old. I couldn't help it. I felt sorry for him too. He saw it. He had been looking for my love, and instead he saw my pity. I knew he could tell, because he smiled with a false heartiness that felt like a wall slamming into place. He clapped me on the shoulder and then turned quickly away.

The train took him south to San Francisco and we never saw him again.

It took the Bureau of Labor Management a lot longer to catch up to me, almost a year.

I had gone back to school. They had reorganized the State University system and you could get study credits for working on a campus reclamation team, saving and preserving the state of human knowledge as it existed before the plagues. It seemed in those first hectic months that everyone was an official of some kind or other. *I* even held a title or two. For a while, I was Western Regional Director of the Fantasy Programmers' Association—I only did it because the president of the organization insisted. She said I owed it to my father's memory as an author. I said, "That's hitting below the belt, Mom," but I took the job. My sole responsibility was to sit down with a lawyer and witness a stack of documents. We were claiming the copyrights of those authors who had not survived and for whom no surviving kin could be located. The organization was becoming the collective executor of a lost art form, because no one had the time for large-scale fantasy games anymore.

Halfway through the spring semester, I was drafted—really drafted, not labor-requisitioned.

The army was one of the few institutions that was structured to cope with massive losses of manpower without loss of structure; its skills were basic, widespread and nonspecialized. Therefore, it was the army that managed the process of survival. The army reestablished communications and maintained them. The army took charge of resources and utilities, protecting and allocating them until local governments were again able to assume the responsibilities of control. The army distributed food and clothing and medical aid. The army contained the plague districts until decontamination teams could be sent in—and as ugly as that latter task was, they handled it with as much compassion as was possible under the circumstances. It was the army that carried the country through the worst of it.

But that wasn't the army that I was drafted into.

Let me say this: I hadn't believed in Chtorrans any more than anybody else.

Nobody I knew had ever seen a Chtorran. No reputable authority had ever come forward with any proof more solid than a blurred photo, and the whole thing sounded like another Loch Ness monster or Bigfoot or Yeti. If anyone in the government knew anything, they weren't saying—only that the reports were "under investigation."

"Actually, the truth should be obvious," one of the coordinators—they didn't call them instructors if they didn't have a degree—at the university had said. "It's the technique of the 'big lie' all over again. By creating the threat of an enemy from outer space, we get to be territorial. We'll be so busy defending our turf, we won't have time to feel despair. That kind of thing is the perfect distraction with which to rebuild the morale of the country."

That was *his* theory. Everybody had an opinion—everybody always does.

And then my draft notice arrived. Almost two years late, but still just as binding. Congress had amended the draft act just for us survivors.

I appealed, of course. So they gave me a special classification. "Civilian Personnel, Attached." They were doing that a lot.

I was still in the army—

—and then Duke shot a little girl.

And I knew the Chtorrans were real.

The human race, what there was left of us, was at war with invaders from space. And I was one of the few people who knew it. The rest of them didn't believe it—and they wouldn't believe it until the day the Chtorrans moved into their towns and started eating.

Like Show Low, Arizona.

Ten

WE LEFT the Jeeps at an abandoned Texaco station and hiked across the hills—and that flamethrower was *heavy.* According to the specifications in the manual, fully loaded and charged, tanks and all, it should have weighed no more than 19.64 kilos—but somewhere along the way we lost the decimal point, and Duke wouldn't let me go back and look for it.

So I shut up and climbed.

Eventually—even with Tillie the Ten-Ton Torch on my back—we reached the valley where we had spotted the worms less than a week before. Duke's timing was just right; we arrived at the hottest part of the day, about two in the afternoon. The sweat had turned the inside of my clothing clammy, and the harness for the torch was already chafing.

The sun was a yellow glare in a glassy sky, but the valley seemed dark and still. The grass was brown and dessicated and there was a light piney haze hanging over the woods; it looked like smog, but there hadn't been any smog since the plagues. This grayish-blue haze was only natural hydrocarbons, a byproduct of the trees' own breathing. Just looking at it I could feel the pressure in my lungs.

The plan was simple: Shorty and his team would go down on the right flank, Larry and his would take the left, Duke would take the center. I was with Duke's squad.

We waited on the crest of the ridge while Shorty and Larry moved to their positions with their men. Meanwhile, Duke studied the Chtorran igloo. There was no sign of life; but then we hadn't expected any, didn't *want* any. If we had guessed correctly, all three of the worms would be lying torpid within.

When the binoculars were passed to me, I studied the corral in particular. There weren't any humans in it, but there was *something*—no, there were a lot of somethings. They were black and shiny, and covered the ground like a lumpy carpet. They were heaving and shifting restlessly, but what they were I couldn't make out at this distance.

Shorty signaled then that he was ready, and a moment later so did Larry.

"Okay," said Duke. "Let's go."

My stomach lurched in response. *This was it.* I switched on my helmet camera, hefted the torch and moved. From this moment on, everything I saw and everything I heard would be recorded for the log. "Remember," Duke had said, "don't look down if you have to take a leak—or you'll never hear the end of it."

We topped the ridge without any attempt to conceal ourselves and started moving down the slope. I suddenly felt very naked and alone. My heart was thudding in my chest. "Oh boy . . ." I said. It came out a croak.

And then *remembered the recorder!* I caught myself, took three deep breaths and followed Duke. Was anybody else this scared? They didn't show it. They looked grim.

This side of the valley was rocky and treeless; it was the other side that was dangerous. Duke signaled and I stopped. We waited for the others to take the lead. Count to ten. Another signal and we advanced. We were going leapfrog fashion; two men would move while the other two kept lookout, then the first two would watch while the second two advanced. All three groups moved forward this way. I kept my torch charged and ready; so did Duke, but the climb down the hill was slow and uneventful. And painful.

Nothing moved in the woods opposite. Nothing moved in the

valley. And certainly nothing moved near the igloo—we watched that the hardest. Everything was still. We approached cautiously, three groups of four men each, spaced about a hundred meters apart.

Where the ground leveled off, we paused. Duke sniffed the air and studied the forest beyond the chunky dome. Nothing. Still, he looked worried.

He motioned Larry's team forward. They had the Mobe IV with them—they called it "Shlep." The dry grass crunched under its treads. We waited till they were about a hundred meters forward, then followed. After a bit, Shorty and his men took up their position to the rear.

It seemed to me that the three groups were spread too far apart. Maybe Duke thought he was being careful by having us stretched across more territory; it'd be harder for the worms to overpower or surprise us. On the other hand, though, maybe he was being a little reckless too. Our combined torch ranges overlapped, but not by very much; we couldn't come to each other's aid as fast.

I was about to point this out to him when Larry's team stopped ahead of us. We approached to about thirty meters and then waited till Shorty's group was an equal distance behind. Then we all started moving again. Duke looked a little less grim and I started to breathe easier myself—but not much; this was still worm country.

We were close enough now to see the construction of the igloo in detail. I estimated it was four meters at its highest point and fifteen in diameter. It was made of layered rows of light-colored wood paste and chips; it looked fairly strong. All around the base was a jumble of dark vegetation so purple it was almost black. The scent was faint, but cloying nonetheless—like honeysuckle, but tasting of something fruitier.

I would have expected the dome to be more cone-shaped, like a beehive because of the way it must have been built, one layer at a time; but no, it was more of a mound—a spherical section with a flattened top. The door was a large arched opening, wider than it was high, and shielded by an interior baffle—like the "spirit wall" the Chinese used to put behind their front gates to keep ghosts out. We couldn't see into the hut. There was no telling if there were worms inside or not.

Larry paused at a safe distance and unlocked the Mobe. The rest of us stopped too, all keeping our same relative positions. Larry stood up again and sent two of his men to circle the igloo; he and the remaining man, Hank, moved around the opposite way. Shlep waited alone, its radar turning back and forth in patient unquestioning rhythm. The rest of us watched the front door.

In front of the dome was something I hadn't noticed before—had it been there last time? It was a kind of . . . totem pole. Only it looked like—I don't know, a piece of blast art perhaps. Like something half-melted, a liquid shape frozen in the act of puddling. What the hell was it? A signpost? A mailbox? It was made out of the same stuff as the dome and the corral. There was one large hole in the base of it, then three more of decreasing sizes placed almost casually above, oddly off center, and a score of ragged tiny holes all around. The thing stood more than two meters high, half the height of the dome, and directly in front of it.

After a bit, Larry and his men reappeared, each having circled the dome completely. Larry signaled that it was all clear. There was no back door; we couldn't be taken by surprise that way.

"All right," Duke signaled back. "Send in the Mobe."

Larry waved and turned to Hank. He unfolded the remote panel on the man's back and armed Shlep. The Mobe's bright red warning lights began to blink; it was now unsafe to approach. If its sensory apparatus detected a large heat-radiating body close by, the EMP-charge on its back would flash, instantly roasting everything in the dome and probably a good way beyond—like a microwave oven, but faster.

EMP stands for Electro-Magnetic Pulse; it's a burst of wide-spectrum high-energy radio noise.* *Very wide* spectrum. From radio to gamma. *Very high* energy. Linearly amplified.

It probably would have been simpler to just toss a grenade into the hut and duck, but Duke wanted to capture this shelter intact. We needed to learn everything we could about the Chtorrans.

---

*An EMP-grenade will cook or curdle any living matter within a radius of *(CLASSIFIED)*. A single charge will yield as many as *(CLASSIFIED)* usable pulses. There is also the tendency of the flash to destroy all unshielded electronic gear within the larger radius of *(CLASSIFIED)*.

The EMP-flash would kill them without destroying them or the dome.

Larry waved again and Duke snapped, "All right, everybody down." This was probably the most dangerous part of the mission—we had to lie down in the grass to minimize the effects of stray radiation from the flash, but the position left us vulnerable because we couldn't use the flamethrowers if we were surprised.

Hank lay down with the remote panel and sent the Mobe rolling forward. He had his eyes pressed into the stereo sight and was looking solely through the eyes of the Mobe now. Beside him, Larry kept uneasy watch. The other two men had stretched a protective flash-foil in front of all four of them—the remote antenna stuck up beyond it—but the Mylar struts were refusing to stay anchored and the men were having to hold them up by hand. The rest of us were far enough back not to need foil, but we stayed down anyway.

The Mobe was in the dome now. Again we waited. The minutes ticked off with deliberate hesitation. The only motion was Hank's hands on the Mobe controls. He was murmuring as he worked and Duke was listening to his comments on a disposable (it would have to be) earphone. I couldn't hear what he was saying.

Hank stopped disgustedly and said something to Larry. Larry stood up, swearing softly. Hank turned back to his panel and did something, then sat up. The others let the flash-foil collapse. The Mobe was coming out of the hut now, operating on its own guidance. Had it flashed? No, the red warning blinker was still going. Hank hit the remote and disarmed it; the light went out. The rest of us stood then, brushing ourselves off and checking our weapons.

The Mobe said there were no worms in the hut—but Duke never took a machine's word for anything. Mobes had been fooled before. Maybe the worms were cold-blooded, or perhaps they didn't give off much heat while they were torpid. Larry was going in to see.

The supposition was that at this time of day the worms should be slow and Larry should be able to burn them before they came fully awake and active. We wanted that shelter, and any piece of worm we could get. So he was going to try to scorch them lightly—enough to kill, not enough to destroy. It was tricky and dangerous and not recommended for those who wanted to die in bed. But if they were in there, Larry would get them. If not . . .

Well, that was why the rest of us were waiting outside with torches.

Larry put on his O-mask then, stooped and entered, the man with the grenades right behind him. Insurance. The grenades had suicide fuses. I didn't envy either of them. They bent low inside the "foyer" and disappeared to the right of the spirit wall.

Silence. And again we waited. A bee—or something—buzzed around my right ear and I brushed at it in annoyance. A drop of sweat trickled from my armpit down my side. The insect buzzed again.

I studied the plants around the base of the dome through the binoculars. They were scraggly clumps of something that looked like midnight ivy, mixed with something else that looked like sweet basil—or black marijuana. Both were a deep, intense shade of purple, almost black and almost impossible to see clearly. The coloring of the ivy must have shaded off into the ultraviolet because it seemed oddly out of focus in the bright sunlight—as if each curling leaf were outlined with hazy red neon. The ivy was streaked with fine veins of white, the basil stuff was spattered with red. We were close enough for the cloying scent to be annoyingly pungent. I assumed it was a product of the basil stuff. At closer range it would be overpowering.

At last Larry and the other man reappeared, angrily pulling off their masks. Larry's face was white. "It's empty!" he shouted. "There's nothing here!"

Duke said, "Damn," and kicked at a rock. "Shorty, keep an eye out. McCarthy, come with me." Then, abandoning his carefully staked-out position, he stalked toward the dome. I followed, struggling to keep up.

"How long has it been empty?" Duke asked.

Larry shrugged. "Beats the hell out of me. You know as much about their nesting habits as I do. But it smells *warm*. . . ."

Duke shoved past him and ducked into the doorway. I started to follow, despite myself, then stopped—my mouth was dry. I stared at that dark hole of an entrance as if it were death. I couldn't take another step. And yet—I wanted to, more than anything. I peered cautiously, but couldn't see beyond the foyer. The interior was unlit. I took a step forward, tried to convince myself to make it two—

Abruptly, Duke exited, straightening and almost bumping into me. He shot me an absentminded look of annoyance, then turned to Larry. "Check the enclosure. See what's in it. Post lookouts on the other side—but keep in sight of each other." He turned back to me. "You. You're supposed to be a scientist. I'll give you ten minutes to inspect the inside of that nest. Then I'm going to burn it."

"Huh? But we're supposed to—"

"Never mind what we're supposed to. *That thing is full of eggs!* You think I'm going to leave them here to hatch?"

I didn't bother to answer. The question was rhetorical. I bent and entered the worm hut.

The spirit wall was more than just a baffle behind the door. It joined the roof low enough to force me into a crouch, forming a circular cross section and becoming two inward-curving passageways, one to either side, that followed the wall of the dome—how far around, I couldn't see; the ends were lost beyond the curve. The passages were ramped upward; the floors were made of the same material as the walls and the roof, only the floors seemed spongier.

I crouch-crawled into the branch on the right; that was the way Duke had gone. The passage led up and around through ninety degrees of arc and opened onto a circular room eight or nine meters in diameter and just tall enough to stand in. The left-ward passage opened up in the wall opposite.

I had a flashbeam, but it wasn't necessary here. There was an opening two meters across in the center of the roof. Light streamed in through this, as well as fresh air, but the temperature wasn't as cool as I had thought it would be inside. In fact, it was almost stuffy. There was a strong, stifling smell about the nest, somehow familiar; a sickly sweetish odor, but I couldn't place it easily. . . .

The room seemed smaller than I'd expected and the ceiling was lower than it had appeared from outside—of course, those upward-sloping ramps—this was the *top* part of the dome.

Was there a bottom section? There had to be. Or was it all foundation? There were several openings in the floor, all of them ominously dark. I stood there, hesitating. I was a scientist—*supposed* to be a scientist; at least that's what it said on my pay vouchers—but that didn't keep me from being afraid. I stood there indecisively and sniffed—that odd-flavored smell. . . .

As my eyes adjusted to the dim light, I noticed something about the walls; they had a peculiar way of reflecting the light. I forgot the holes in the floor for the moment and turned off my flashbeam; the walls seemed almost—no, they *were*—translucent. The glare from outside was forcing its way through the material of the dome.

I inspected closer—and found that it wasn't a hardened wood paste at all, but some kind of dried wood-foam—a much lighter substance, but no less sturdy. Wood chips were suspended in it like raisins. I poked it with my knife and it was like carving hard paperboard. The walls of this dome were actually tiny bubbles of cellulose-based glue. That explained their peculiar light-transmitting properties, and they were probably excellent insulators as well. I sliced off as large a chunk of the wall as I could and dropped it into my sample pouch.

The rest of the room was featureless, except for those holes. There was an absolute lack of artifacts, excepting some chunks of chewed-up *something,* globs of grayish material like masticated asbestos. Some of the globs were almost a meter in diameter. They were stuck casually to the walls like pieces of chewing gum. I shrugged and cut off a sample and bagged it. If these Chtorrans were truly intelligent creatures, you couldn't prove it by this dwelling.

I wondered—where were the eggs that Duke had seen? Probably down one of the openings. There were three of them spaced equidistantly around the sides of the dome. The largest was against the inner side of the spirit wall. The other two holes were against the outer walls of the dome.

I inspected the largest hole first. I shone the flashbeam down it, but it was only another room like this one, and apparently just as empty. The overripe stench was particularly strong here; I decided not to climb down. Besides, there didn't look to be an easy way to climb back up.

The next hole was some kind of a well. It just went straight down and disappeared in blackness. A toilet, perhaps? Could have been; it smelled like it. I didn't know—what kind of droppings did Chtorrans leave? I was beginning to realize all the things I should have known, but didn't.

The last hole was the one with the eggs.

The hole was against the back wall and it was full of them. They were shiny things, each about the size of a tennis ball, deep red but bathed in a milky white ooze that made them look pearlescent. There must have been hundreds of them—*how deep was the hole?* It was almost perfectly circular and about two meters wide; it seemed to be as deep as the others, but the level of eggs was almost close enough to touch.

So I did something stupid.

I laid down the torch. I unbuckled the tanks and took them off. Then I sat down on the floor and lowered my feet into the hole and started to climb down.

I miscalculated though, and slipped. I dropped—*squish!*—into the eggs; it was like tumbling into oyster-flavored Jell-O. For an instant, I thought I was going to lose my footing and topple face first into them, but I caught myself against one wall. Then I thought I was going to be sick. My throat went tight, and I had to swallow quickly—and painfully—to keep from retching.

I was standing in a red and slimy-white mess up to my knees.

Thankfully, these eggs were fairly recent. I don't think I could have stood it if I had found myself in embryonic Chtorrans. Carefully—I couldn't move too fast because of my unsure footing—I gathered up as many of the still intact eggs as I could reach, bagged them and stuffed them into my pouch. I tried to lean against the wall as much as possible. The feel of those eggs was . . . uneasy.

I was shuddering when I finally braced my hands against each side and levered myself out of that hole. Those eggs were sticky, and they smelled like raw fish left out in the sun too long. If I never saw another one, it would still be too soon.

I was trembling violently as I shrugged back into the tank harness and picked up my torch again. Even if it had been only for a minute, that was still sixty seconds too long to be unarmed in a worm nest.

I looked around then for something else to take samples of. There was nothing. Just the walls and the globs of Chtorran chewing gum, and I already had samples of those. I inspected the other two holes again. The pungent smell from the center one seemed stronger, which surprised me—I should have been used to it by now—but otherwise there was nothing I hadn't seen.

I went out through the left-side passage. It was identical to the right.

Duke was standing there, waiting for me. He glanced at the mess on my legs, but didn't say anything. Instead, he gestured over his shoulder. "Go take a look in the corral. Larry's found something interesting."

I wasn't sure I wanted to. I remembered what had been in that enclosure a week ago. I nodded and kept moving.

The enclosure resembled a large frontier-type stockade about ten meters across, only circular. Its walls were nearly three meters high and slanted inward as if the whole were an incomplete dome. The material was the same as the nest, but thicker and darker. There were the same dark plants around the base—the ivy and the basil stuff. I bagged a couple of smaller ones as specimens; the basil was the one with the cloyingly sweet smell. The leaves of the ivy were waxy and had a sticky feeling to them.

There was no opening in the corral wall. Instead, a steep ramp leaned against the side and up beyond by an equal length; it was rough-hinged to seesaw down into the center. Larry was perched at the top. He waved when he saw me. "Come on up."

The ramp was steep, but ribbed horizontally. It was not quite a ladder and not quite stairs, but something of both. Even though I had to use my hands, the climb was easier than I expected.

"What do you make of that?" said Larry, pointing down inside.

I straightened carefully, making sure I had my balance before I looked. Even so, I was startled, and Larry had to grab my arm to steady me.

The interior of that stockade was a swarming mass of—*insects.* Or, if not insects, then something very much like them. They were large, most of them almost a half-meter long—although some were longer—and black and shiny. Their bodies were slender and jointed like metal-covered wire. Each was fringed with hundreds of flashing legs. They moved across the shadowed floor, twisting and whirling like an explosion of metal pieces.

"Centipedes," said Larry. "Giant centipedes."

"Millipedes," I corrected. "*Thousand*-leggers."

He shrugged; it was all the same to him. "You ever seen anything like that before?"

I shook my head. The floor of the corral was seething. The creatures were oblivious to each other. They raced back and forth across the dirt or curled into balls. They climbed over each other's bodies or just stood and twitched nervously. Or they explored the periphery—several of them were chewing methodically at the walls.

"Look, they're escaping," I said.

Larry shook his head. "Watch."

I did so. One of the largest of the millipedes, nearly a meter long, seemed just on the verge of breaking through. He was almost directly under me and chewing with a vengeance; the sound was a sticky, vicious kind of crunching, like sizzling fat or grinding light bulbs. Abruptly he stopped and backed away. He waved his feelers about in confusion, then began to wander aimlessly—until he came to another section of wall. He tested it cautiously. After a moment, he began chewing again, though not as industriously as before.

"What happened?" I asked.

Larry pointed. "He broke through."

I looked closer. Where the millipede had been chewing was a tiny black hole. A dark, pitchy substance was oozing out of it. "This is a double wall," said Larry. "The inside is filled with something they don't like."

I nodded silently. Elsewhere around the edges, other millipedes were repeating the performance of the first one, and there were numerous other holes with hardened plugs of the same dried, pitchy substance to testify to the millipedes' persistence.

"I didn't know centipedes grew so big," said Larry.

"They don't," I answered, suddenly remembering something from my plague-aborted course in entomology. "And they don't have four antennae either. Their mouths aren't shaped like miniature garbage disposals, their eyes aren't so large and they aren't herbivorous—they shouldn't be eating those walls at all. These aren't millipedes."

Larry shrugged. "Well, if they're not, they'll do until the real thing comes along."

"I don't know *what* these are," I said. "I've never seen anything that even resembles them before. Real millipedes don't have as many legs or body sections. Look how they're segmented—and what are those humps behind the eyes? And what are they doing *here?*" I indicated the enclosure.

"Isn't it obvious? This is the Chtorran larder. They like their food fresh. They keep it in this corral until they're hungry. Look." He pointed again. "See that? Somebody was having a snack earlier."

I saw a pile of discarded shells and disjointed body sections. I repressed a shudder—these millipedes were nothing more than food for Chtorrans. They were live lunch from the planet Chtorr! "Hey! These things are extraterrestrial too! The Chtorrans brought them! I've got to catch one!"

He stared at me. "Are you crazy—? Those things might be man-eaters."

"I doubt it," I said. "If they were, they wouldn't be chewing on wood." It sounded good to me.

"They might be poisonous—"

I shook my head again. "Herbivorous creatures never are; they don't need it."

"How do you know they're *only* herbivorous? They might have a taste for meat as well."

That made me pause—but not for long. "There's only one way to find out. Help me down."

He set his jaw stubbornly. "No."

"Larry," I said, "this is every bit as important as burning worms. Anything we can find out about them will help us destroy them."

"I'm not going to help you get killed."

"Then I'll do it myself—" I took a step upward on the ramp; another one and I was beyond the wall; a third and it began to teeter precariously. Larry took a step back down to stop it.

"Look," I said to him, "somebody's got to do it."

He didn't answer, just took another step downward to counterbalance my weight. I stared at him until he looked away. I took another step up. One more and the ramp began to lower slowly on my side. I took another step and the rate of swing increased.

Larry started to move—too slowly. He said a word and gave up. He adjusted his position to keep the ramp from moving too fast. "Okay," he growled, "but if you get your legs chewed off, don't come running to me."

I grinned. "Thanks,"—then had to grab suddenly to keep from toppling off. The ramp kept swinging—Larry rose above me unhappily—till my end touched ground near the center of the corral with a *thump.* I found myself balanced in an awkward position and had to scramble around in order to climb down more easily—or *up,* if I had to. I looked down warily. A couple of the millipedes had already begun inspecting the foot of the ladder, and one of them had even begun to chew on it. But so far, none of them had made any attempt to climb out. If anything, most were moving *away* from it. Had they learned already to associate the lowering of the ramp with predatory Chtorrans? It seemed likely.

I swallowed and began climbing down. About a foot above the ground, I paused. I held my leg out carefully to see if they would jump or snap at it. One of them rose halfway up as if to sniff, but almost immediately lost interest. I waved my foot above another. He rose up too, and even grabbed hold; I flinched, but held still and waited as he flicked his antennae back and forth across the toe of my boot. After a second, he lost interest too and dropped away. I managed a weak grin and lowered my foot to the ground. "Well, that's one more giant step for mankind." I was breathing a little easier.

The millipedes showed no alarm at my presence. If one did come in contact with my shoes, he either turned away or climbed over them as if I were just one more bump in the landscape. Mostly, they ignored me.

I wondered if it would be safe to pick one of them up with my bare hands, or even with my gloves on. I poked one of the creatures with the tip of the torch and immediately it curled into a ball, showing only its shiny black shell. Okay, so maybe that established they were cowards, but they still had mouths like miniature scrap-metal processors—you know, the kind that can reduce a new Cadillac cruiser into assorted pellets of steel and plastic, none larger than an inch across. I decided to play it safe.

That was when I found out how ill-equipped my sample pouch really was. I didn't have anything to carry them in. A plastic bag? Uh uh, they could go through that in seconds; a creature that can chew its way through wood foam and wood chips isn't going to be stopped by anything less. I wished I'd had the foresight to bring some wire-based netting. Should I risk my canvas pouch? It didn't seem a good idea. I had no guarantee that a captured millipede would stay politely curled up all the way back to base or until I could find a proper cage for it.

I wondered—I was wearing a polymer-asbestoid liner between myself and the torch harness, also a shock vest. The vest alone should be enough—at least I hoped it would—so I began shrugging out of the tanks again.

"Hey!" called Larry. "What the hell are you doing?"

"Taking a shower," I called back. Then, "Relax. I know what I'm doing."

He scowled doubtfully, but shut up and looked unhappy. I took off the liner and dropped it to the ground, then I pulled the tanks back on. Two of the millipedes explored the plastic-looking shirt without much curiosity, then wandered away. Good. I hoped that meant they'd found it inedible.

Quickly, I poked the three nearest specimens with the nozzle of the torch. They curled up obediently. I rolled them onto the asbestoid cloth, made a sack out of it and tied it at the top by looping the sleeves around and tying them in a hasty knot. My pouch was beginning to bulge like the belly of a pregnant hippo—and I must have looked every bit as proud. As a sample-collecting trip, this was turning into quite a bonanza. First the eggs; now the millipedes. For good measure, I added a piece of the enclosure wall and some of the pitchy substance that filled it, also a few of the discarded shells and body sections from the recent Chtorran snack.

Larry was visibly relieved when I began climbing out. I think the idea of a man going willingly into a Chtorran larder—even if only to look around—was too much for him. He waited until I was almost to the top and then shifted his weight to seesaw the ramp up from the center and down on the outside.

We climbed down together; it was wide enough for that. At the bottom, Larry looked at me with grudging respect. "I gotta admit," he said, "that took guts. I wouldn'ta done it. I don't like bugs of any kind."

I shrugged. "I was only doing my job."

"Well, I wouldn't trade with you," he said. This from the man who had gone into the dome first to see if there were worms inside. "Come on, let's go see if Duke has figured out where the worms are hiding—"

And then all hell broke loose.

There was a purple *chirruping* sound and a sudden cry. Larry went white and grabbed for his grenade belt. We heard the roar of a torch and from the other side of the nest puffed a gout of black smoke. I dropped my sample pouch and went charging after Larry.

I saw Shorty first. He had his legs braced firmly apart and was stabbing a finger of flame at something large and black and writhing. It was totally enveloped by the fire and smoke—the burning carcass of a worm!

I kept running—now I could see beyond the curve of the nest. There was another Chtorran there. I skidded and stopped in sheer horror—I had seen the pictures, yes, but they hadn't prepared me for the incredible size of the creature! It was huge! Nearly twice the length of a man, bright red and more than a meter thick at the head! Its eyes were black and lidless. It reared up into the air and waved its arms and made that chirruping sound again; its mouth was a flashing maw. *"Chtorr!"* it cried. *"Chtorrrr! Chtorrrrrr!"*

I was fumbling with the safety on my torch; the damn thing seemed frozen. I jerked at it unmercifully.

I glanced up, half expecting to see that crimson fright charging down on me—but no, it was still reared up in the air, half its length. Its fur was standing stiffly out from its body, revealing its skin of deep purple. Abruptly, it came back to ground and lowered its head; its eyes were like black searchlights fixed directly on me. I braced my legs as Shorty had shown me and steadied my flamer—damn! Larry was blocking my shot! He was just pulling the pin on a grenade—

The worm moved then. So did I, sliding sideways to catch it before it could bear down on Larry; he was closest. It turned toward him and streaked across the ground like hot lava, a flowing red silkiness. Stiff-armed he flung the grenade. It arced high—simultaneously, Shorty's flame flicked across that purple and red horror. It exploded in a tongue of orange—and then exploded again as the grenade shattered its writhing form.

There was another explosion in the distance, and then it was all over. Shorty cut off his flamer and its roar became a sigh, then faded out altogether, leaving only the sizzle of burning worm, the insistent crackle of its blackening flesh, and a smell like burning rubber.

Duke came stumbling through the smoke. "Anybody hurt over here?" He gave a wide berth to the still burning carcasses.

Shorty called back. "We're okay. I got 'em both easy." He grinned. "And Larry wasted a grenade."

Larry mock-scowled. "Well, I couldn't wait all day for you." To Duke: "Everybody all right on the other side?"

Duke nodded. "No problem. That worm never had a chance, but I was worried when I saw the other two headed this way."

"Hell, boss, you oughta know better than that," Shorty boomed jovially. "Fact is, Jim here saw how well me and Larry were doing; he decided to take a nap."

Duke's eyes flickered over me. "He better not have," he muttered.

Shorty ignored it. "How big was the one you got?"

Duke shrugged. "About the same as these. Maybe a little bigger."

"How about that," Shorty said, directing it toward me. "We just burned two and a half tons of worm."

Duke said sourly, "We were almost caught by surprise." He turned to Larry. "I thought you said that dome was empty."

"Huh? It was—!" His face looked confused. "You saw that yourself!"

"I didn't inspect it all, Larry—I took your word for it. I only checked for eggs. It was your responsibility to check the other holes."

"I did!" Larry repeated. "They were empty! The Mobe tapes will confirm it!"

Duke narrowed his eyes. "Larry, those worms came charging out of that dome. I saw it myself."

"And I tell you that dome was empty—if it wasn't, you think I'd be standing here now?"

"I can confirm that," I said. They both looked at me. "Remember? I went into the dome too, and I poked my nose into everything. I didn't see any worms."

Duke closed his mouth. He studied his boots for a moment. "All right," he said. "Let's drop it for now." He turned and walked off.

Larry looked at me. "Thanks, kid."

"For what?" I said. "That dome *was* empty. Duke's gotta be wrong. The worms must have come from the woods."

"Uh uh," said Larry. "If Duke says he saw them come from the dome, then that's where they came from. There was something we missed, Jim—both of us. We haven't heard the end of this."

I shrugged and followed him. We passed between the two crackling worm carcasses toward where Duke and the others were gathering. Larry looked unhappy, so much so that I wanted to say something more to him, but Shorty caught my arm. "Leave him be, Jim. Let him work it out for himself. Larry's that way."

"But it's not his fault—and nobody got hurt."

"But somebody *could* have been," said Shorty. "It was his responsibility to check out that nest and he thinks he failed. In Larry's eyes, a reprimand from Duke is pretty serious." He added, "If it were me, I'd be feeling that way too."

"Oh," I said. I thought about it. "Okay." Then I remembered. "Oh, I forgot my sample pouch. I dropped it when the excitement started. Wait a minute—" I broke away and started back toward the enclosure.

Shorty nodded. "I'll wait here."

It took only a moment. I dashed around the smoking worms and up to the foot of the ramp. The pack was where I had left it. I scooped it up and hung it on one shoulder, checking the contents as I walked back.

I came around the nest in time to see the biggest worm of all attacking Shorty.

Shorty was just turning toward me, grinning—then there was that chirruping sound, *"Chtorrrr! Chtorr!"* and a section of the nest wall next to him fell away. A thick, purple-red body streamed out, all mouth and grabbing arms. *I couldn't reach my torch!* The goddamn pack was in the way! *"SHORTY!"* Shorty was already turning toward the worm, sudden realization appearing on his face—and then it was on him. He didn't even have time to yell.

I found my hands and I burned them both. I held the torch on them and *burned.* Bright gouts of flame. Searing tongues of flame. Red and black and orange! Roaring, cleansing fire! I held that trigger firm and squeezed, *squeezed* and screamed. The flamethrower screamed too. I played it back and forth across the worm long after the thing had ceased to writhe. Then I turned it on the nest and burned that too. I didn't stop until it was completely aflame and the roof had collapsed.

But by then the torch was out of fuel anyway and they had to pry it out of my hands.

Eleven

WE RODE back in silence. I sat and stared at the sample pouch in my lap and tried not to think of the price Shorty had paid for my stupidity. It was my stupidity, wasn't it? I mean, to carry the pouch like that.

Duke was in the front seat, conferring softly with Hank. I tried not to listen, but the wind kept whipping their words back to me. They were battering at the facts, replaying them over and over again. "That fourth Chtorran—" Duke insisted, "—it shouldn't have been there."

Hank was making noises in response, quacking duck-billed platitudes. "Aww, Duke—we don't know enough about them yet—"

Duke ignored him. "—I thought that shelter looked a little too big—damn Reconnaisance! They're going to hear about this. I should have flashed that damned Mobe, and to hell with the cost."

"Hey, how about the kid—?"

"Huh?"

"He's taking it pretty hard."

"We all are."

"But he's the one who pulled the trigger."

"It's a risk we all have to take," Duke said. "You know that."

Hank glanced back at me. "Still . . ." he said quietly, "it wouldn't hurt to have a word with him . . . or something."

Duke didn't answer for a moment. When he did, his voice was strained. "Damn you, Hank. Just once I want to lick my own wounds first—Shorty was my friend too." He fell silent, then turned away in his seat and stared at the passing hills; they were shadowed in dusk. The clouds were shiny pink against a pale gray horizon.

I pulled my jacket tighter around me. The wind kept slapping at my hair and eyes; it was cold and dusty, and I was miserable, both inside and out. Occasionally, the millipedes would start to move; the bag would squirm uneasily, but a gentle rap with my hand was enough to make them curl up again; three hard little knots the size of cantaloupes.

It was past nine when we got back to base. It had been a boys' camp once, but now it was a makeshift Special Forces base. As the Jeeps pulled up in front of the mess hall, men began pouring from its doors. "How was it? How many worms did you get?" Their voices were loud and excited.

Almost immediately, though, they caught our mood, and when Duke said, "Shorty's dead," an uncomfortable silence fell over the group. They followed us into the mess hall where Sergeant Kelly was pouring out coffee in her usual don't-bother-me manner and distributing platters of hot biscuits with businesslike dispatch. I snagged a couple of biscuits—I could live without Sergeant Kelly's coffee—and faded into a corner. Nobody paid me any attention, for which I was more than grateful.

Duke also stood alone. Holding his mug by the bowl, not the handle, he sipped his coffee steadily, grimacing at its taste and ignoring the occasional question. The other men from the mission were tumbling out their stories as fast as they could talk. When they came to the part about Shorty some of the men glanced toward me and lowered their voices, but an excited murmur rose from the rest of the group. "A *fourth* worm—? Impossible!" But incredulity was met with insistence and the discussions splintered into speculations.

Dr. Obama came in then and took Duke off to one side where they conferred for a few moments; once they looked over in my direction, but when they saw me looking back at them they turned away; then Duke put down his coffee cup and the two of them left.

Abruptly, Ted was standing in front of me. He was hunched over, with his hands thrust deep into the pockets of his jeans. He had a peculiar expression on his face, like someone looking at an auto accident.

"Are you all right?"

"I'm fine."

He sat down opposite me, folded his arms and leaned across the table on his elbows. "Quit trying to be brave. You look like hell."

"You don't look so hot yourself," I muttered. His sandy hair was rumpled, his face was puffy. He looked like he'd just gotten out of bed. Was it that late?

He ignored it. "I hear you had a pretty rough time."

I didn't answer.

He eyed my sample pouch. "Did you find anything interesting?—Hey, it's moving!"

I rapped the bag quickly and it stopped.

Ted gaped. "What've you got in there?"

"Some of the bugs from the corral. That's what you can do. Go find a cage."

"A cage—? How big? Would a chicken coop do?"

"As long as there isn't any wood in it."

"Uh uh. Aluminum and wire." He scooted out the door.

Some of the men were trickling out now, headed for the rec room, probably. Others refilled their mugs, slurped noisily, and followed them—that was probably the loudest sound in the room. I thought Sergeant Kelly was in the kitchen flashing more biscuits, but she wasn't. "Here," she said, putting a chicken sandwich and a glass of milk in front of me. "Eat." Her expression was difficult to read, as if her face had been detached from her emotions.

I looked back down into my lap. "I'm not hungry."

"So?" she snapped. "When did that ever stop you from eating?"

"Sergeant," I said, lowering my voice, "I had to kill Shor—"

"I know," she said, cutting me off. "I heard." She placed her hand gently on my shoulder. When I didn't look up, she reached over and cradled my head into her hands—they were *huge*—and pulled me to her. I couldn't help myself. I started crying, bawling like a baby into her lap. Sergeant Kelly is the only person in the world who has a lap standing up. I buried my face in it and sobbed. It was the first time I had cried all day. "That's my boy," she said. "That's my good boy. Let it out. Let it all out. Mamma's here now. Mamma's here."

After a while, I stopped. "Sergeant," I said, wiping my nose on her apron, "thank you." I looked blearily up at her; her eyes were bright. "I love you!"

"Uh . . ." For a moment, her composure seemed uncertain. She looked startled. She said, "I left something in the kitchen," and bustled quickly off. I thought I saw her wiping her eyes as she ducked through the door.

When I turned back to the table, Ted was standing there with the chicken coop. How long he had been there, I didn't know—and didn't want to ask. He didn't say anything about my red eyes; he just set the coop down on the table and waited.

I covered my embarrassment by fumbling with the pouch. Ted opened the top of the coop and I put the asbestoid shirt with the millipedes into it. I loosened the knot and tumbled them out, three hard, black nuggets. Then I latched the cage securely.

"That's it?" asked Ted. He sounded disappointed. "Those are actual Chtorran animals?"

I nodded. The millipedes were still rolled up in balls; their shells seemed almost metallic. If they were still alive, they hadn't shown it yet.

"They're not much to look at, are they?"

"Wait'll they open up," I said. "They're cute as baby spiders."

Ted made a face.

Meanwhile, Sam, the camp mascot—a large gray and white tabby cat who had adopted us—hopped up onto the table to inspect. "*Mrowrrt?*" he asked.

"No, Sam, that's not to eat." That was Ted.

Sam sniffed in annoyance. He turned his attention instead to my chicken sandwich and milk, an unexpected bonanza. Neither Ted nor I pushed him away. He ate noisily. Dainty bites, but noisy ones. He was purring appreciatively while he ate.

Louis sauntered over next. He'd stripped down to his T-shirt. He was beginning to show a layer of fat on his middle-age spread.

I guess the army couldn't afford to be too choosy any more. "Is that the bugs from the worm camp?" He peered close. "How come they're all rolled up?"

I shrugged.

"Have you tried feeding them yet? Maybe that's the trouble. Maybe they're hungry."

"Or scared," I suggested.

He ignored it. "What do they eat?"

I shrugged again.

"Don't you know?"

"How could I? Could be anything. When I caught them, they were chewing on the walls of their enclosure."

"Well, you gotta feed them something," he insisted. Two or three other men had wandered over. A small crowd was forming. One or two of them muttered agreement.

"I'll have to make some tests," I mumbled. "To see what they like."

"Aah, you don't know anything about animals. I grew up on a farm—" He put his finger up to the mesh and clucked. "I'll bet they're just like chickens. Chtorran chickens. Come on, little bugs, come on—see what Daddy's got for you—" He shoved a little piece of biscuit through the wire. "Come on—"

I was hoping the millipedes would ignore him, but one of them chose that moment to uncurl. No longer restrained, and finding no reason to keep hiding, it began exploring its surroundings; its antennae waved tentatively, first forward, then back, then randomly in all directions. After a moment, it slithered across the floor and even part way up the walls of the cage, giving me a good look at its soft underside. Soft? It was a deep disturbing purple with dark bands separating the—what?—they looked like segments. I could see how all the shells were jointed; the creature's body was a train of tiny armored cars on legs.

The millipede tested the aluminum frame with its feelers and tried to poke its head through the wire mesh. For a moment, it seemed to be staring right at me; its eyes were black discs the size of quarters. They made me think of Chtorran eyes. They weren't faceted like normal insect eyes.

It pulled back then and continued exploring, coming at last to the sliver of biscuit. The millipede touched it lightly with its probing antennae, then ate it. It simply moved forward, chewing as it went, until there was no more left. "Hey," said Louis, grinning. "He likes it. Here, have some more." He shoved the rest of the biscuit into the cage.

The millipede made short work of this piece too. One of the others uncurled then and also began exploring the coop.

"Hey, Louis," said one of the men. "Now you gotta feed the other one."

Louis glanced around. His eye fell on the chicken sandwich that Sam was still working on. "'Scuse me, kitty, but I need this."

"*Maoww—*" Sam protested loudly, but to no avail. Louis tore the bread into pieces and pushed it through the mesh. Sam licked his chops deliberately, hoping the chicken wouldn't follow.

He was wrong. "Let's see what else they like," said Louis, and the chicken was pushed through the wire as well. Also the lettuce and tomato.

"Looks like we have to apologize for hurt felines," remarked Ted. "Here, Sam, drown your sorrows in some milk."

"*Mrowwt,*" said Sam. But he drank the milk.

Meanwhile, the third millipede had uncurled and joined its fellows in consuming the feast before them. "Look, they like chicken too."

"And lettuce. *And* tomato." Ted looked at me. "I wonder if there's anything they *don't* like."

"The stuff inside the enclosure wall," I said. "They don't like that. I brought back a sample for you to analyze." I pulled the plastic bag from my pouch.

Ted opened it and sniffed. "I hate to tell you what it smells like." He wrinkled his nose and closed it up again.

Louis was still at the cage. He poked his finger through the mesh and clucked. "Pretty baby, come to Poppa. . . ." I could understand his fascination with them. They seemed somehow more *intelligent* than mere insects. It was their eyes; they were large and round and dark, they were almost soft—like puppy eyes; they were all pupil. And it was the way they looked at you through those eyes—peering and turning toward every sound, studying each object with dispassionate curiosity. They seemed *knowing.* These creatures were to ordinary bugs as an owl is to other birds—clearly the same type of creature, but definitely something *more.* One of the millipedes rose up into the air to sniff Louis's finger—

—and suddenly bit it.

"Aaii—*Hey!!*" He jerked his finger back, but the millipede had a firm grip. For a moment, Louis was caught there while the creature thrashed about within the cage—then he broke free, blood streaming from the missing joint. "Aaah! Son of a bitch!" he gasped.

Someone wrapped a paper napkin around his hand; it quickly stained red. "Get him to the doctor!" said someone else. Two men hustled Louis out the door. He was making little gasping sounds.

In the cage, the millipedes were unperturbed. Their black eyes were suddenly baleful.

"I should have warned him," I said.

Ted looked at me. "Did you know they would do that?"

I shook my head.

"Then shut up. It was his own fault for putting his finger in the cage. Sometimes Louis can be a real fool. Tonight he outdid himself. The bugs must have thought it was still feeding time." He put on a thoughtful expression. "These things do have an appetite, don't they?"

"So do Chtorrans," I said, remembering. "Here. These were in the enclosure too." I passed him the empty shells and body sections.

Ted raised an eyebrow.

"Lunch," I explained. I pointed at the cage. "The Chtorrans eat them."

"Sounds risky," he quipped. "But it makes sense. And better them than us." Then he thought of something. "Say, how did you catch them without getting attacked yourself?"

"I don't know—they just didn't seem interested in me. I thought I was safe and I was."

"Hm." Ted frowned. "There must have been a reason."

"Maybe I'm just inedible."

"So? Stick your finger in the cage and prove it."

"On the other hand," I said quickly, "maybe there's some other reason."

Ted looked disappointed. "Spoilsport—it would have been a valid test."

"If you're so eager, you stick *your* finger in."

"Ah, but it's not my inedibility we're testing. No, you're right;

there must be some other reason. You're probably edible, just not very tasty. How did you go into the enclosure? Just hold your nose and jump?"

"No, I tested with my foot first. I waved it above their heads to see if they'd attack."

"Well, so you're smarter than I thought. I would have guessed you crossed your fingers and hollered 'King's X!' Maybe they just don't like shoe leather—let's find out." He pulled off a boot and pressed one side of it against the mesh. All three of the millipedes attacked it. "Well, that settles that."

Then he tried to pull his boot away. But their combined grip was too strong. "Aww, come on, now—" Not wanting to hurt them by pulling harder, he let go of the boot. It hung there while the insectoids chewed at it and the men around us snickered. The millipedes ate until they could chew no further and the boot clunked to the floor.

Ted picked it up sadly and fingered the holes in it. "My best pair of boots," he mourned. He sighed and pulled it back on, all the while shaking his head. He looked at me. "Okay, let's have one of yours—"

"Huh? Are you crazy? You just got through proving that they *like* shoe leather—why do you want to ruin my boots too?"

"Dummy," he said patiently, "this is a scientific experiment to determine why you're still walking around. Now, let me have one of your boots before I break off your leg and beat you to death with it."

He was right. I'd seen the way the millipedes had attacked his footgear. It was identical to mine and the millipedes had ignored me. I pulled off my boot and handed it across.

He held it up to the mesh. The millipedes tested it with their antennae, then lost interest in it and wandered away. Ted tried it again on the other side. The millipedes did the same thing.

Ted frowned and held the boot close to his face. He sniffed. Once, twice, a third time, curiously. "Smells fishy. What'd you step in?"

"Nothing," I said. Then remembered. "Uh—eggs."

"Eggs—? You mean like in chicken, cluck-cluck-cluck?"

"No. I mean like in Chtorran."

His expression was incredulous. "You stepped on Chtorran eggs—?"

"It was inside the nest—"

"Inside the nest—? Yipe! I take it all back, Jimmy boy. You're not smart at all. There's a safer way to kill Chtorrans than by walking into their nests and stomping on their eggs. What do you think flamethrowers are for?"

"I didn't *mean* to step on the eggs. It was an accident."

"I hope you told that to Mamma Chtorran."

"Besides, Duke was going to burn them anyway, so I climbed down and saved a few."

For a moment there was silence.

Then Ted said, "Do you have them with you?"

I upended the pouch and tumbled them out onto the table. There must have been a dozen, at least.

Ted stared; so did the two other men who still remained. I didn't know their names. The eggs were blood-red and smooth, still moist-looking and slightly translucent. There was something dark inside. Gingerly, Ted picked one up and sniffed it. "Raw fish, all right." He held it against the side of the millipede cage. They tested it incuriously, then lost interest. "Well, that's what saved your life, Jimbo—the fact that you're such a clumsy retard. You must have had egg all over you."

I thought back. "You're right. I know I had it up to my knees and all over my arms." I shuddered at the thought of what might have happened if I hadn't. And that was probably why my three specimens hadn't tried to chew their way out of the sample pouch—the smell of the eggs around them.

"Uh huh—" Ted was holding the egg up to the light.

"See anything?" I asked.

"It says, 'Disregard previous egg.' " He replaced it on the table. "I can't tell."

"You know what these remind me of?" I said. "Ant eggs."

"Ant eggs?"

"Uh huh. They have that same kind of almost-translucency. And their shells are soft too. Look, see how they bounce? What does that suggest?"

"Handball?"

I ignored it. "It means we can begin to learn something about how they evolved. Birds and reptiles have hard-shelled eggs—it's for extra strength and water retention. This might indicate a lower level of development. Insects or amphibians."

"Worms are a little bit of each?"

"Maybe." I picked up the egg again. "On the other hand, maybe the Chtorran atmosphere is humid enough so that moisture retention is not a very important survival factor. And this shell seems to be awfully thick, almost cartilaginous. That might provide the protection the embryo needs, particularly if Chtorr *does* have a higher gravity than Earth. That's what some of the fellows around here think. It would explain the Chtorrans' extreme strength and mobility." I frowned and held the egg up to the light. "I don't know. The shape of an egg and the texture of its shell should tell you things about the conditions it's meant to hatch under—and that should give you clues about the nature of the parent and the offspring. But I don't know how to begin to figure this one out. My brain hurts—there are too many questions. Like, for instance, how come if these millipede things are so incredibly voracious they aren't interested in the eggs?" I pressed the egg to the mesh again. "It doesn't make sense."

"Maybe they can tell it's a Chtorran, and they're afraid of it even before it hatches."

"Sorry, I can't imagine these creatures passing up a free meal. There must be something about these eggs that's distasteful."

Ted blinked. "Wow! An egg with its own defense mechanism." He looked up. "What are you planning to do with them?"

"I was thinking of rigging up an incubator."

Ted whistled softly. "Jimmy, I've got to admire your . . . bravado. Or something. You're either the smartest damn fool around here—or the dumbest. It's not enough you have to rescue Chtorran eggs from the incinerator; now you want to hatch them. When Duke hears about this, he's going to have a fit."

I hadn't thought about Duke. "Why? What's wrong with the idea?"

"Oh, nothing; it's just that the purpose of this Special Forces operation is to kill worms, not breed them."

"Not entirely," I insisted. "You and I were sent up here to study the Chtorrans."

"That doesn't mean we have to make pets of them."

"And how else are we going to get close enough to study them? Do you know a better way to observe one long enough to learn anything? On a hunt, as soon as you see a worm, you burn it. No, the only way we're going to be the scientists we were sent up here to be is to put some worms in a cage and watch to see what makes them tick—and if we can't capture a live one, then we'll have to grow our own."

"Simmer down, I'm on your side. I think. It's just that I don't think the idea is going to be very popular around here; this isn't a P.O.W. camp—and that's another thing; even if you do hatch a few worms, where are you going to keep them?"

"We'll think of something," I mumbled. I was trying to think of something.

"We?" He raised an eyebrow.

"Yes. *We.* Remember, you're an exobiologist too."

"Oh, yeah—I forgot." Ted looked unhappy. "But I think this is one of those times when I'd rather be a botulinus tester." He said, "I mean, raising the worms is going to be the easy part—"

"Huh?"

He clapped me on the shoulder. "Jimbo, put the bugs to bed. I'm going to talk to Duke."

"Want me to come along?"

"Uh, better not. Duke's had a . . . rough day. I think I can be more tactful. You just tuck 'em in for the night and leave the rest to me."

"Well . . . okay."

I left the millipedes in the mess hall for the night, with a canvas draped over the coop and a sign that said DANGER! on it. The eggs were slightly more difficult, but I borrowed Ted's electric blanket and put them in a cardboard box with it draped across the top as a makeshift incubator. To keep the eggs from drying out, I lined the box with a layer of plastic, then a layer of towels, and then sprayed it all with warm water—enough to keep the towels damp, but not soggy. It was just a guess. I'd have to work out something more permanent in the morning.

I had trouble falling asleep. I couldn't help it. Someone was screaming in my head, *Shorty's dead!*

I kept telling myself that I had barely known him; I shouldn't be feeling it this hard. But I hurt all over, and—oh hell, I couldn't help it; I started crying again.

I was still awake, just lying there, aching, when Ted came in. He didn't turn on the light, just undressed in the dark and slipped into his bed as quietly as he could.

"What did Duke say?" I asked.

"Huh? Oh, I didn't know you were awake."

"I'm not. Not really. What did Duke say?"

"Nothing. I didn't talk to him."

"You were gone an awfully long time."

"Yeah," he said. "I'll tell you in the morning. Maybe." He rolled over and faced the wall.

"Ted," I said, "Shorty died because I wasn't fast enough, didn't he?"

"I don't know," he mumbled. "I wasn't there."

"It's *my* fault, isn't it?"

"Shut up, will you?"

"But—"

"It'll all be settled tomorrow. There's going to be a hearing."

"A what?"

"An inquest, stupid! An inquest. Now, go to sleep, damn you!"

Twelve

THE INQUEST was held in the mess hall. Duke, Hank, Larry, two of the other men from the mission (whose names I still didn't know) and myself. Dr. Obama, doubling as medical officer, sat at the head of the table. She had a yellow, legal-sized pad of paper in front of her, covered with precise little notes. Ted sat just to her left with a transcriber terminal; his job was to answer the machine's questions about sound-alike or mumbled words. I was at the opposite end—with sweaty palms. Dr. Obama was looking very quiet and when she finally did speak, I had to strain to hear her. "All right, Duke," she said. "What happened?"

Duke told her, quickly and efficiently. He left out nothing, but neither did he waste time on elaborate descriptions. Dr. Obama showed no reaction throughout, other than an occasional nod, as if she were ticking off each of Duke's facts on a mental check-list.

"We followed procedure all the way," concluded Duke. "That's the annoying thing. If there were only something I could identify as a mistake—some error in judgment, even my own, that I could find—at least we might learn something; but I've been over this thing a hundred times, and I just don't know. We did everything by the book. . . ." He hesitated. "Maybe the book is wrong." He fell silent, spreading his battered hands out on the table before him; they had been scrubbed unnaturally clean for this hearing. "I have no explanation how we missed those worms."

Dr. Obama was thoughtful. She didn't look at Duke at all. At last, she cleared her throat slightly and murmured, "It seems we have several areas of investigation here." She shifted the pad of paper in front of her and read from it: "First, where were the Chtorrans hiding that they were undetectable to the Mobe sensors, as well as to Duke, Larry—"

Ted murmured something, his fingers suddenly moving on the terminal keyboard.

"Eh? What's that?" Dr. Obama looked annoyed.

"Last names," whispered Ted. "The record requires it."

"Oh." Dr. Obama went blank for a moment, trying to backtrack her train of thought. "Uh—" She looked at her yellow pad again. "Where were the Chtorrans hiding that they were undetectable to Captain Archibald 'Duke' Anderson, Lieutenant Lawrence Milburn, Corporal Carlos Ruez and Observer James McCarthy—who else was inside the hut?"

"No one," said Duke. "Just the four you listed."

Dr. Obama seemed not to hear him; she continued on to her second point, "Next. *Why*—and this is a very important point to consider—why did *all* of them miss detecting the Chtorrans? That the Mobe also missed the Chtorrans is very important. . . ." She glanced at Ted. "This part is off the record, Jackson." Ted stopped, hit a button and rested his hands by the sides of the terminal. To the rest of us, Dr. Obama continued, "While I may know each of you personally and am willing to vouch for your integrity, there are those who prefer to look for scapegoats when something like this happens. In most cases, they would sooner take the word of a machine and suspect the human beings of carelessness. Machines rarely have ulterior motives. Count it as a blessing that the machine agrees with you here." She nodded at Ted, then continued with a touch more formality. "That the Mobe was unable to detect the Chtorrans confirms your story that the dome was to all appearances empty. The Mobe is supposed to be able to detect things beyond the range of normal human senses—and, vice versa, a human observer also has capabilities that the machine lacks, not the least of which is a sense of *judgment.* Wherever the Chtorrans were, both kinds of observation failed to detect them, indicating—as do certain other facts which we will consider—that the standard procedures do not allow for every contingency."

She referred again to her notes. "Third, the assumption was made that the Chtorrans would be torpid within their shelter. This has been the pattern in the past, but now we must ask, were they in fact within the shelter the whole time? And were they in fact in their most inactive state? It has been a general experience, not just in this area, but in other locations as well, that when worms—excuse me, Chtorrans—go inactive they do so as a group, and generally they go to the coolest part of their shelter; that is, the second level, the underground half. If they were there, the Mobe should have detected them, as should have any of the aforementioned individuals. Which brings up two more questions: What range were the Mobe's sensors set for? How were these parameters determined? On what basis? Perhaps we will have to reexamine that particular aspect of our procedure. Yes, Hank?" To Ted, "Henry Lannikin."

Hank cleared his throat uncomfortably. "Well, Dr. Obama, there *is* a window in the sensing matrices—but it shouldn't have been big enough to let a Chtorran slip through, let alone three—I mean, four—of them. A hot Chtorran within ten meters will trigger the flash, but with a cold one—that is, one that's inactive—the Mobe has to be within four meters. Sorry, but they work so far in the infrared, they can't help but be nearsighted. The point is, if those worms were in the hut, whether hot or cold, the Mobe should have flashed. The only way it could have missed cold ones, they'd have had to have been too far away—like *out* of the hut. And we know that wasn't the case, because we didn't see them."

"Maybe those domes are getting bigger on the inside," Larry offered.

Dr. Obama looked at him coldly. "Do you think that's possible?"

"Hell, I don't know," said Larry. "Every other one I've been into has only had two levels, top and bottom. If the worms started digging deeper than that, I didn't see 'em."

Dr. Obama considered the thought. "It isn't impossible that

the wor—*Chtorrans* have changed their life style, but we have several other discrepancies to consider as well." She looked annoyed. "This has been a very atypical affair all around." She resumed her professional manner. "Sixth question, *why* was there a *fourth* Chtorran in the nest? Where did it come from? And why did it delay its attack? What was there different about this one that caused it to hang back for several moments? Also notice that it was the largest of the four Chtorrans encountered—*significantly* larger. What is the importance of that? Finally, is such an event likely to be encountered again in the future? Obviously we will have to modify our existing procedures to allow for that possibility.

"Seventh and eighth questions. What, if any, is the significance of the plant life surrounding the Chtorran shelter? We have not found such plants around the shelters in the past. Why here? Why now? Are these, in fact, specimens of native Chtorran vegetation?"

I'd transplanted all of my samples, each into its own pot. I had no idea how to handle them. Were they dangerous—or what? I wasn't even sure how to test them. Dr. Obama's questions barely scratched the surface.

She continued, "And what about the creatures observed in the Chtorran corral—those were burned as well? Ah, good. What is *their* place in the Chtorran ecology?" She stopped, looked around the table. "Are there any other questions that we want to consider? Yes, Duke?"

"What about Shorty?"

Abruptly, my stomach dropped.

"Yes." Dr. Obama looked to her notes, but she'd already turned to a blank page. There was no answer there. "We all feel bad about that."

"That's not what I meant," said Duke, very quietly.

I wondered if I was going to be sick.

"I know what you meant, Duke." Dr. Obama was every bit as quiet. "All right," she said. "Let's get it over with. Could you have saved him?"

"No," said Duke.

"Is there anyone here who could have saved Sergeant Harris?" asked Dr. Obama. She looked around the room. Larry was studying his fists; they were buried in his lap. He almost looked like he was praying. Carlos and Hank didn't say anything either; even Ted's hands were motionless on his keyboard.

"I should have been faster," I said. The words seemed unnaturally loud in the mess hall. Everyone but Dr. Obama looked at me, but having said it, I felt relieved. There, it was out. "I should have been faster, but the specimen pack was in the way. I couldn't get at my torch quick enough. If I'd been faster, maybe I could have saved him; maybe I could have gotten the worm before it—"

Dr. Obama said, "I doubt it. Sergeant Harris himself checked you out on that torch." She was still looking at her notepad. "And I approved his certification of you. Under the circumstances, that makes me equally responsible. As well as Duke."

"Thank you, ma'am. I recognize what you're trying to do—but I know that I was carrying the pack wrong."

Dr. Obama shook her head. "There's no one else who saw that. Despite your good intentions, McCarthy, I can't accept your statement as evidence."

"Excuse me," I said.

"Something else?"

"Yes," I insisted. "There is." I was suddenly aware that everyone in the room was looking at me. "I was wearing the helmet. I made a sound and video record. I—I think that there's some question here about what I did, and whether or not I—uh, acted properly. And I think that the video could clear that up. I'd like to have it shown. Please."

"I'm sorry. That's not possible."

"Huh—?"

"Duke and I tried to look at it last night. Unfortunately . . . um . . . the memory clip was defective."

"*What?*"

"The write-protect tab was out—"

"That was a brand new clip! I loaded it myself."

"—so the camera and microphone signals were not recorded. The clip was *blank.*" She said it firmly and looked at me, as if daring me to argue with her.

"But—" I'd tested that clip myself! I—saw the look on Ted's face and—stopped. "Yes, ma'am."

She gestured to Ted and Ted switched off the transcriber again. She said, "Look, it's irrelevant. No matter what we decide here, it won't bring back Shorty. I promise you, he's going to stay dead. So if you're trying to justify your guilt feelings, please stop wasting our time. It doesn't produce much result."

"I'm sorry, ma'am," I protested. "I understand what you're saying—but I should have done better—I mean, if only—"

"Stop!" She glared down the table at me. "Jackson, is that thing off?" He checked and nodded. "Thank you," she said. "You're not getting it. So let me give it to you another way. Listen, McCarthy, the responsibility for putting that weapon in your hands was *mine*—do you get that?"

I nodded.

"So if there was an error there, it's *my* error too. Do you get *that?*"

I nodded again.

"And I don't make errors. Not of this kind. You were handed that weapon because you were judged to be capable of handling the responsibility. Shorty thought so. Duke thought so. I thought so. Are you telling us now that all three of us were wrong?"

"Uh—no, but—"

"No buts about it. Either we were wrong or we were right. This thought you have that you screwed up is nothing more than an attempt to avoid the responsibility, and pass the error back up the line to the people who authorized the weapon for you. I'm sorry, but we're not accepting delivery. You took the job. You knew what was involved. You accepted the responsibility. So I don't care how *you think* you handled it. You handled it appropriately." She glared at me with eyes like fire. *"Can you get that?"*

"Y-yes, ma'am." I shoved my fists into my lap and stared at them. She didn't want to hear me.

Dr. Obama stopped and cleared her throat, coughing into her clenched fist. She took a drink of water, then looked up again without focusing on anyone in particular. She nodded to Ted. He switched the transcriber back on. "Does anyone else have anything to add?" She waited without expression. "Then I take it that all of you here are convinced that Shorty Harris's death was unavoidable. Is there anyone who disagrees? Is there anyone who disputes the validity of McCarthy's response? No one?" She looked at Duke. Duke did not meet her gaze. He seemed troubled and for a moment I thought he was going to speak; then, instead, he just shook his head.

Dr. Obama waited a moment longer, then exhaled softly. She seemed relieved. "All right, let the record show that this hearing has determined that James McCarthy acted with dispatch and fortitude. Those present at the scene confirm that McCarthy's actions were appropriate and above reproach. Furthermore, it is the opinion of this body that McCarthy's professed clumsiness is an expression only of his feeling of inexperience in combat, not negligence."

She looked around the table. Duke nodded his reluctant approval. Everyone else seemed . . . deliberately nonchalant.

"All right, before we adjourn is there anyone who has any information which would cast any light on any of these questions we've brought up?" She waited only a second. "I thought not. It is hereby determined that this board of inquiry is unable to reach a conclusion about the circumstances of yesterday's operation, and for all the usual reasons: we simply do not have the knowledge of the Chtorran species that we need. It is the sense of this session and the conclusion of this panel that we have only the questions and none of the answers. We therefore make no recommendations of any kind. This meeting is adjourned. File that, Jackson, and put a copy on the wire—no, let me see it before you send it out." She stood up, gathered her notepad, and nodded. "Good day, gentlemen."

Thirteen

DUKE AND I were left alone in the room.

He looked haggard and very old. He was leaning on his elbows and staring into yesterday. His bony hands were clenched, two knotted fists pressed hard together, pressed against his jaw.

"Uh, Duke . . ."

He looked up, startled. When he saw it was me, his face tightened. "What is it?"

"Um—I have some specimens."

Duke blinked. For a moment, he wasn't there; then he remembered. "Right. You'll find a set of handling cases in the storeroom. Do you know where it is? It's bungalow six. We'll send them out on Thursday. Try and keep those eggs and millipedes alive."

"I think the bigger problem would be killing them—" I saw that he had disappeared inside himself again. He had dismissed me. "Uh—Duke?"

He came back impatiently. His eyes were red. "Yeah?"

"Uh, did Ted talk to you yet?"

"No, he hasn't. About what?"

"He said he was going to. We thought that maybe—I mean, I am supposed to be an exobiologist—"

Duke held up one hand. "Spare me the story. What do you want?"

"A lab," I said quickly. "So I can do some of my own observations on the millipedes and eggs and that purple stuff from around the dome."

He looked annoyed. "I don't want you damaging those specimens before they get to Denver! I've got enough problems—"

"I'm not gonna *'damage'* anything!"

Duke snorted.

I said, "Duke, if you're pissed at me, then say so."

"I am not pissed at you—"

"I don't believe you." I walked around and sat down in Dr. Obama's chair and faced him. "What's going on here, Duke? This was the stupidest inquest I've ever been to—" He looked up at that, a question in his eyes. "Three," I answered before he could ask, "—not counting this one. Nothing was established here. Nothing at all. I grant that there aren't a lot of answers yet to most of our questions—but the questions that could have been answered *weren't.* They were whitewashed. So excuse me for being suspicious, but what was all this about?"

Duke shook his head. He stared at his hands. "You don't want to know."

"Yes, I do!"

Duke let that sink in. Then he said quietly, "You were only doing what Shorty told you to do. You were following orders."

I sniffed. I quoted from somewhere, " ' "I was only following orders" is not an excuse—it's an indictment.' "

"Who said that?"

"I just did."

Duke's expression was scornful. "Don't give me slogans, son. I've got a low threshold of bullshit. Especially today."

"I heard it in Global Ethics. And it's no slogan. It's true for me. Look—there's something I want you to know."

"I don't really want to hear it," he said. "In fact, I don't want to talk at all right now."

"Neither do I," I said. I could feel my voice starting to quaver. "But I have to! Until someone just *listens* to me!" My throat was tightening and I was terrified I was going to start crying. It was all bubbling up. I didn't even know what it was. I said, "I'm the guy who pulled the trigger, Duke. I'm the guy responsible. You and Dr. Obama can say whatever you want in an inquest, but I'm still the guy who did the job."

He looked like he was going to say something else, but he stopped himself. "All right, say what you have to then, and get it over with." His voice was very quiet.

"I didn't sleep last night. I couldn't. I needed someone to talk to. I wanted to talk to you. I even got up once and went looking for you. I got as far as your door. I almost knocked. And I didn't—I don't know why. Yes, I do—I was scared. See, I didn't know if I did wrong yesterday or not. I wanted some . . . help. But all I could hear was Shorty's voice saying, 'Figure it out yourself.' Like he did with the manuals. So I didn't knock. And besides, I saw the light was on under your door. And I thought I heard voices. And I didn't want to interrupt anything—"

Duke started to say something, but I cut him off. "No, I want to finish this. Then you can talk. I didn't go right back to my room. You know the hill behind the camp? I went up there and sat by myself for a while. And—I let myself cry. At first I thought I was crying for Shorty, only after a while, I found out I wasn't. I was crying for myself, because of what I was realizing. And it has nothing at all to do with Shorty being dead."

I realized I was trembling. My hands were trembling on the table. I thrust them between my legs and held them there with my knees pressed together. I felt very small and very cold. I looked at Duke and said, "What I realized was that—even if Shorty hadn't told me to do what I did—I still would have done it, done the same thing."

Duke was genuinely surprised. "You would?"

I swallowed hard. It wasn't easy to speak. "Duke, it was the only thing to do. That's why I've been so . . . crazy. I'd been trying real hard to convince myself that I did it because Shorty told me to—only *I knew I hadn't.* There wasn't time to think about it—it just happened. I didn't remember what to do or what I'd been told. I just did it—*without thinking.*" I was looking down into my lap now. "Duke, I've never killed anyone before. I never thought I'd ever have to. All I knew was that it was something I never wanted to do—and then, yesterday afternoon, I found out that I *could* do it—and do it *easily.* And I've been going crazy ever since trying to explain it to myself. I keep looking for a way to make it *all right.* I keep saying that it was the circumstances, except that I know it *wasn't* the circumstances at all. It was me! And now—after this inquest—I can't even have it be a mistake! It was me. I did it. Nobody else. And I have to live with that now—that I can kill people." I added, "It's not really something that I want to know."

Duke was silent a moment, just studying me. I studied back. His face was craggy and weathered, his skin was sun-darkened and crinkled with use. His eyes were sharp and alive again and boring straight into mine. I stared right back.

Abruptly, he said, "All right, you've got your lab."

"Uh—*thank you!*"

"Yeah, I'll see how you feel in a week. Where did you want to set up this zoo?"

"The new bath house."

Duke looked at me sharply. "Why?"

"It's obvious. It's the only building in camp that's suitable. It's got concrete walls and very high small windows. Nothing could escape. At least, not easily. Nobody's using it because the plumbing was never completed; we could bring in portable heaters and fix up the interior any way we need."

Duke nodded. "That's exactly where I would have chosen. But I would have chosen it for you because it's a good safe distance from the rest of the camp. You'll have to clear out the stuff that's already in there. Tell Larry what you'll need in the way of special equipment or if you need anything built. He'll find some men to help you."

"Yes, sir—and thank you."

He lifted his hand the barest distance from the table, a wait-a-minute gesture. "Jim?"

"Sir?"

"This is no party. Make your results count. Those specimens were awfully expensive." When he looked at me, his eyes were shinier than I'd ever seen. He looked haunted.

"I know," I said. It was suddenly very hard to speak. "I—I'll try."

I left quickly.

Fourteen

AN HOUR after I started cleaning out the bathhouse, Ted showed up with a sour look on his face. I told him what I wanted to do and he pitched in, but without his usual repartee of puns, wisecracks and pontifical observations. Usually, Ted radiated a sense of self-importance, as if he were coming straight from some very important meeting. He always seemed to know what everyone else was involved in. But this morning he seemed chastened, as if he'd been caught with his ear to the keyhole.

After a while, Larry and Carl and Hank joined us and the work moved a lot faster. They didn't speak much either. There was a Shorty-shaped hole in all our lives now and it hurt too much to talk about it.

There was a lot of work to be done. It took us half the afternoon just to clear out the lumber and other supplies that had been stored in the concrete-brick bunker, and the rest of the day to make the place millipede-proof. There were vents to be covered with mesh and windows to be sealed, and we had to install doors too; the latter had to be wrapped with wire mesh, and we had to mount metal plates on the bottoms too, just in case.

The final touch was provided by Ted, a brightly painted sign which stated in no uncertain terms:

THE BENEDICT ARNOLD HOME FOR WAYWARD WORMS

TRESPASSERS WILL BE EATEN!!

No bugs, lice, snakes, snails, toads, spiders, rats, roaches, lizards, trolls, orcs, ghouls, politicians, lifers, lawyers, New Christians, Revelationists or other unsavory forms of life allowed. Yes, this means you!

Visitors allowed only at feeding time.
Please count your fingers when leaving.

—Ted Jackson,
Jim McCarthy,
Proprietors.

The interior of the bath house was divided into two rooms. One had been intended as a shower room; the other would have been for changing clothes and drying off, a locker room without lockers. We decided to use the locker room for the millipedes and the shower room for the eggs—if we had to choose one or the other to put in a tile-lined room behind two solid doors, it had to be the eggs because of the *potential* danger they represented. An escaped millipede would be far less serious than an escaped Chtorran.

We installed two large work tables in each room, connected the electric lighting and heaters, built a special incubator for the eggs and a large metal and glass cage for the millipedes. Sergeant Kelly was happy—she had her mess hall back—and so were we; we had a lab.

By suppertime, we were seeing our first results. We determined that the millipedes were omnivorous to a degree that made all other omnivores look like fussy eaters. Primarily, they preferred roots, tubers, shoots, stems, flowers, grasses, leaves, bark, branches, blossoms, fruit, grain, nuts, berries, lichens, moss, ferns, fungi and assorted algae; they also liked insects, frogs, mice, bugs, lice, snakes, snails, toads, spiders, rats, roaches, lizards, squirrels, birds, rabbits, chickens and any other form of meat we put before them. If none of the above were available, they'd eat whatever was handy. That included raw sugar, peanut butter, old newsprint, leather shoes, rubber soles, wooden pencils, canned sardines, cardboard cartons, old socks, cellulose-based film and anything else even remotely organic in origin. They even ate the waste products of other organisms. They did not eat their *own* droppings, a viscous, oil-looking goo; that was one of the few exceptions.

After three days of this, Ted was beginning to look a little dazed. "I'm beginning to wonder if there's anything they *won't* eat." He was holding one end of a typewriter ribbon and watching the other end disappear down a millipede maw.

I said, "Their stomachs must be the chemical equivalent of a blast furnace; there doesn't seem to be anything they can't break down."

"All those teeth in the front end must have something to do with it," Ted pointed out.

"Sure," I agreed. "They cut the food into usable pieces, particles small enough to be dissolved—but in order to make use of that food, the stomach has to produce enzymes to break the complex molecules down into smaller, digestible ones. I'd like to know what kind of enzymes can handle such things as fingernail clippings, toothbrush bristles, canvas knapsacks and old video-disks. And I'd like to know what kind of stomach can produce such acids regularly without destroying itself in the process."

Ted looked at me, one eyebrow raised. "Are you going to dissect one and find out?"

I shook my head. "I tried it. They're almost impossible to kill. Chloroform hardly slows them down. All I wanted to do was put one to sleep for a while so I could examine it more closely and take some skin samples and scrapings—no such luck. He ate the cotton pad with the chloroform on it."

Ted leaned forward; he put his elbows on the table and his face into his hands. He peered into the millipede cage with a bored, almost weary expression. He was even too tired to joke. The best he could manage was sarcasm. He said, "I dunno. Maybe they're all hypoglycemic. . . ."

I turned to look at him. "That's not bad. . . ."

"What is?"

"What you just said."

"Huh?"

"About the blood sugar. Maybe something keeps their blood sugar permanently low, so they're constantly hungry. We may make a scientist out of you yet."

He didn't look up; he just grunted, "Don't be insulting."

I didn't bother to respond. I was still considering his offhand suggestion. "Two questions. How? And why? What's the purpose? What's the survival advantage?"

"Um," he said, guessing. "It's fuel. For growth?"

"Yeah . . . and then that raises another question. How old are these things? And how big are they going to get? And does their appetite keep pace? And what *is* their full size? Or is this it?" I sat down on the edge of one of the tables, facing the glass wall of the millipede cage. I began chewing on the end of my pencil. "Too *many* questions—" Hanging around the millipedes was affecting *my* eating habits. I folded my arms across my chest. "And what if we're not asking the right questions in the first place? I mean, what if it's something so simple and obvious that we're overlooking it?"

"Hm," said Ted; then, "Maybe they're not getting the right kind of food—and that's why they stay so hungry. . . ."

"Hey!"

Ted looked up. "What?"

I pounced on the thought. "Try this: maybe they're *dextro-* and we're *levo*—they're made out of right-handed DNA! And they need right-handed proteins to survive! And this is a left-handed world!"

"Um," said Ted. He scratched his nose and thought about it. "Yes and no. Maybe. I have trouble with the right- and left-handed idea. I don't think it's possible. It's certainly improbable."

"The worms themselves are improbable," I pointed out.

He scratched his nose again. "I think the fact that they can safely eat any Earth-based organic matter without immediately falling down, frothing at the mouth in deadly convulsions, is a pretty good sign that our respective biologies are uncomfortably close. If I didn't know better, I'd say almost related."

Another idea bobbed to the surface. "Well, then—try it this way. Earth isn't their native planet, so maybe they have to eat a lot of different things to get all of their daily requirements. I mean, their metabolisms *must* be different because they've evolved for a different set of conditions, so they have to be unable to make the best use of Earth-type foods—it follows, doesn't it?—so they'd have to increase their intake just to survive."

"Um, but look, if that were true of the millipedes, then it would have to be true for the worms. They'd have to be even more ravenous than they already are. They'd be eating everything in sight."

"Well, they do, don't they?"

He shrugged. "Who knows what's normal for a worm?"

"Another worm?" I suggested.

"Mm," he said. And then added, "—Except, there are no normal worms on this planet."

"Huh?" I looked at him suddenly.

"It was a joke!" he said.

"No—say it again!"

"There are no normal worms on this planet."

"What did you mean by that?"

He shrugged. "I don't know; it just seemed . . . obvious. You know? I mean, we don't know what the worms are like in their own ecology; we only know them in ours—and we don't even know how they got here. So if there's something—*anything*—that's making them or their behavior atypical, we wouldn't know, would we? And neither would any other worm on this planet, because they'd all be experiencing the same effects."

"That's great!" I said, "It really is—I wonder if anyone else has realized that yet."

"Oh, I'm sure they have—"

"But I'll bet that's part of the answer. We're dealing with crazy Chtorrans! And I like your other idea too—about something keeping their blood sugar permanently low. I just wish I had a good biological justification for it." I scribbled it into my notebook. "But it fits in with something else. Here, look at these—" I went rummaging through the mess on the desk behind me and came up with a folder marked UGH. I pulled out a sheaf of color eight-by-tens and passed them across. He stood up to take them. He leaned against the table and began to leaf through them.

"When did you take these?"

"This morning, while you were on the terminal. I finally found my close-up lenses. There's some real high-power stuff there. Look at the structure of their mouths."

He grimaced. "They look like worm mouths."

I shrugged. "Similar evolutionary lines, I guess. What else do you see?"

"The teeth are like little knives."

"You notice anything else? The teeth are slanted inward. Here, look—compare these two pictures where he's eating the cigar. When the mouth is at its widest, the teeth are pointing straight up and down and just a little bit outward; but as the mouth closes, they curve inward. Here, see how they mesh? Once a millipede bites something, the teeth not only cut it, they push it down the throat. A millipede *can't* stop eating—not until the object is finished—*because he can't let go.* Every time he opens his mouth, he automatically takes another bite; every time he closes, he pushes it down his throat. That's why his teeth have to grind and cut and slash—otherwise, he'd choke to death."

"Um, I doubt that last," he said. "I don't think they're capable of choking. With a mouth arrangement like that, they wouldn't have a swallowing mechanism that could so easily kill them. It would be self-defeating. I'd guess that the arrangement of the teeth is so they can get a good hold on their prey and, if nothing else, get one good bite out of it—like Louis."

"Have it your own way, Perfessor—but I watched him eat the cigar, and that's the way he used those teeth."

"But, Jimbo—that doesn't make sense. What happens to the little bastard who gets stuck to a tree?"

"He eats or dies," I offered. "Remember what you learned in school: 'Mother Nature doesn't give a shit.' "

"Um," Ted said, shaking his head. He continued paging through the photographs. "How did you shoot this one?" He was staring down the wide-open mouth of one of the millipedes.

"Which one? Oh, that. I shot that through a pane of glass. There's a spot of grease smeared on it; he's trying to bite it off. The focus isn't so good because of the grease, but it was the only way I could look down his mouth. They learned real quick that they couldn't get through the glass, so they stopped lunging at it when I held up a finger. That's why the grease. Here, this one's sharper—this was before he scratched the glass."

Ted peered close. "Hand me that magnifying glass, will you? Here, look—what do you make of this?"

"Hey! I didn't notice that before—a second row of teeth!"

"Mm," said Ted. "I wonder if he ever bites his tongue."

"Those are molars!" I said. "See? They're not as sharp. The first row is for cutting; these are for grinding. And look—do you see anything farther back?"

"Uh, I'm not sure. It's awfully dark down there."

"We can digitize this and bring up the resolution, but doesn't that look like a third row?"

"I can't tell. It could be."

I looked at him. "Ted, maybe these things have teeth all the way down their throats. That's why they can eat so much, and so many different things. By the time the food reaches the stomach, it's been ground to pulp. They'll still need strong stomach acids, but now the food has a lot more surface area exposed to the action of the enzymes."

"Well, this makes them a little more . . . believable." Ted grinned. "I find it very hard to trust any kind of creature that eats tennis shoes, wallpaper and baseballs, not to mention bicycle seats, clotheslines and Sergeant Kelly's coffee."

"Ted, give me a break. Please."

"All right—they wouldn't drink the coffee. That's probably what the Chtorrans use in that corral fence to keep them from getting out—Sergeant Kelly's coffee grounds."

"Oh, no," I said. "Didn't I tell you?"

He looked up. "What?"

"You should have guessed. What's the one thing the millipedes won't eat—the one *organic* thing?"

He opened his mouth. He closed it.

"That's right," I said. "Used food. No creature can live in its own excrement—those are the things its metabolism *can't* use. And that's what the worms put between the double walls of their corral. As soon as the millipedes sense it, they back away."

"Wait a minute, boy—are you telling me the worms are going around gathering up millipede droppings for fence insulation?"

"Not at all. I didn't say anything about millipede waste. I just said it was waste"—he opened his mouth to interrupt; I didn't let him—"and it's not terrestrial waste either. Remember we were wondering why we never found any worm droppings? This is why. Evidently, the worms have been using it to keep their 'chickens' from escaping. The worms and the millipedes must be similar enough so that it doesn't make any difference. What a worm can't use, neither can a millipede. The tests on the droppings from the enclosure and the specimens we've got here show a lot of similarities. Mostly the differences are dietary, although a lot of the special enzymes don't match up. If I had more sophisticated equipment, I'd be able to spot the subtler differences."

Abruptly, Ted's expression was thoughtful. "Have you written any of this down?"

"I've made some notes. Why?"

"Because I heard Duke talking to Dr. Obama about you—about us. He wants Obie to send us to Denver."

"Huh?"

Ted repeated it. "Duke wants Obie to send us to Denver. With the specimens. On Thursday."

I shook my head. "That doesn't make sense. Why should Duke do any favors for us?"

Ted perched himself on the edge of the table. The three millipedes looked at him with patient black eyes. I wondered if the mesh of their cage was strong enough. Ted said, "Duke's not doing us any favors. He's doing it for himself. We don't belong up here and he doesn't want to be a babysitter. And after what happened with Shorty—well, you know."

I sat down again. I felt betrayed. "I thought . . . I mean . . ." I shut up and tried to remember.

"What?" asked Ted.

I held up a hand. "Wait a minute. I'm trying to remember what Duke said." I shook my head. "Uh uh—he didn't say anything. Not about this. I guess I just thought I heard—" I stopped.

"Heard what?"

"I don't know." I felt frustrated. "I just thought that we were going to be part of the Special Forces Team."

Ted dropped off the table, pulled the other chair around and sat down opposite me. "Jim boy, sometimes you can be awfully dumb. Listen to your Uncle Ted now. Do you know where these Special Forces Teams came from? I thought not. These are—or *were*—top-secret crack-trained units. So secret even our own intelligence agencies didn't know they existed. They were created after the Moscow Treaties. Yes, illegally—I know—and you used a flamethrower last week, remember? It saved your life. Guess what the Special Forces were for—and a lot of other innocuous-looking institutions. Too bad you slept through history, Jim, or you'd understand. Anyway, the point is, these men have lived together and trained together for years. And they're all weapons experts. Have you ever seen Sergeant Kelly on the practice range?"

"Huh? No—"

"Well, you should—or maybe you shouldn't. You'd be too terrified to complain about her coffee. These people think and act as a family. Do you know what that makes us? Just a couple of local yokels. We're outsiders—and there's nothing we can do that will change that. Why do you think Duke gave us this lab—practically shoved it on us? Because he wants an excuse to send us packing. And this is it. He'll be able to say we're too valuable as scientists to be risked out here in the field."

"Oh," I said. "And I was just beginning to like it here."

"Better than Denver?" Ted asked.

"I've never been to Denver."

"Trust me. You'll love it. It'll be just like civilization. Jim, do you really want to stay here, where the odds are seven to one that you'll end up in a Chtorran stewpot? Or didn't you know that?"

I didn't answer right away. At least now I knew why Ted had been so cooperative these past few days. But I still felt as if a rug had been yanked out from under me. I looked across at Ted. He was peering into my face, still waiting for my reaction.

"Damn," I said. "I wish you weren't always so . . . ubiquitous."

He shrugged. "So what? You'll thank me for it in Denver."

"I know. *That's* the annoying part!"

Fifteen

THE THURSDAY chopper was pushed back till Saturday, so we had four days left—if we were going. They still hadn't told us. Ted said that was the army way. If they told us, we'd only worry about it. This way, we didn't have anything to worry about.

I worried anyway—and made the best use I could of the time.

I borrowed the helmet camera and set it up in front of the millipede cage. I digitized the image, fed it into one of the computers—and I had an activity monitor. The program counted the number of pixel changes per second, noted the scale of change, the time and the temperature. As it built up information, it correlated trends, fit them into curves and made them available for display on continually updating graphs.

The bugs did not like heat. Temperatures above twenty-five degrees Centigrade made them lethargic, and higher than thirty-five degrees they refused to move at all. Generally they seemed to prefer a ten-degree environment, although the remained active at temperatures as low as freezing. Lower than that, they would curl up.

I repeated the tests under different lighting conditions. The bath house had been rigged with two bare twelve-hundred-lumen plates; when I replaced them with outdoor lamps, some of the vari-temp, night-into-day lights for hydro- and aeroponics, the millipedes curled up as if to shield themselves, regardless of the temperature. Clearly, they did not like bright light.

But I wanted to measure their activity levels through a full range of lighting conditions, charting the curve all the way from pitch dark to bright sunlight—and through a complete range of temperatures too.

We borrowed the air conditioner from Dr. Obama's office—we didn't dare try to take the one from the mess hall—and Larry found a spare heater for us somewhere. Between the two I was able to achieve most of the test temperatures I wanted. I rewrote the program, put the lights on a rheostat with a photodiode to measure the lumens and connected everything to the computer.

The result was a two-dimensional data-base demonstrating the millipedes' reactions to a variety of environments.

But it was inconclusive. The bugs liked low temperatures and dim lights. They tolerated high temperatures. They didn't like bright lights at any temperature. That didn't make sense. It was too simple. Did they come from a dark planet? There wasn't enough data.

So I repeated the whole series of tests another dozen times, but now with the lights tweaked to a different color each time.

This left me with a *three*-dimensional graph—now I was nine times as certain that I didn't trust the results. There was a funny anomaly at the low end of the spectrum. I knew it meant something, but I was more confused than ever.

I was still sitting in front of the terminal, leaning back in my chair, arms folded across my chest, staring at the screen and waiting for inspiration to strike me, when Ted bounced in. "Okay, Jimmy boy! Pack your comic books! It's time to go."

I didn't even look up. "Later. Not now—"

He grabbed my chair from behind and pulled me back away from the terminal. "Come on—Obie wants to see us."

"About what?"

"Huh? Have you forgotten? Denver, remember? It's a large city in Colorado . . . next to a mountain?"

"Oh, yeah." I said, "I can't go."

"Huh?"

"I'm not done." I leaned over to the terminal and touched a button. The screen started cycling through the pages of my report and over a hundred different three-dimensional graphs. There were cross sections too. I pointed. "Look at that activity curve, Ted! It doesn't make sense. These things look like they should be nocturnal—but their behavior pattern with light and temperature variations says they're not. And look at the way it spikes on the spectrum tests—what does that mean?"

Ted pulled me to my feet. "What it means is congratulations!" He pumped my hand heartily. "You've just won a free trip to Denver!"

"—But the job is incomplete!"

"It's good enough! You don't have to interpret it! They have *real* brains in Denver. They'll take one look at what you've done and have the answer for you in no time. You'll probably get a nice footnote in somebody's report." He placed one hand in the middle of my back and *shoved.* "Now, move! The chopper's already on its way—yes, it's a day early; Larry's bringing packing crates—is your data disked? Here, take it. Let's go!" We were out the door and on our way before I even had a chance to punch him.

We tumbled into Dr. Obama's office like a small stampede. We were both out of breath and flushed. Dr. Obama barely glanced up as Ted snapped a precision salute. I realized what he had done and hastily followed suit, only not as precise.

Dr. Obama almost smiled. She said, "I see you've heard." She handed across two envelopes. "Well, we might as well make it official—here are your orders."

We read them together. I finished first and looked up. "Thank you, ma'am." And then I added, "I think—?"

She nodded. "You're right. I'm *not* doing you a favor. Denver isn't going to be any more pleasant, but you'll find that out for yourselves. You'll both want to be real careful."

"Ma'am?" I asked.

"I mean, don't screw it up—you're going to be playing in a much bigger game. There are worse things than being eaten." She looked unhappy. She said, "I suppose I should wish you luck and tell you I'm proud of you. But I won't. I'm not proud of you, and you're going to need a lot more than luck. Let's have no illusions. I didn't want you up here, either of you, and I'm going to be glad to have you out. This is no place for untrained replacements. But I'll give you this much. You did your jobs—and you were appreciated. You're both intelligent. Wherever you end up, you should do fine"—she looked at Ted, she looked at me—"each in your own inimitable style." She glanced at her watch. "The chopper's already on its way. You have less than an hour. Pack your specimens and be in front of the mess hall at twelve-thirty. Duke is driving you to the helipad. There are metal cages for the bugs and an insulated box for the eggs right outside. Try not to get sent back."

"Yes, ma'am. Thank you." I started to rise.

"Don't be so quick—there's one more thing. Jackson, would you excuse us a moment? Wait outside. And, ah—this time, would you please *not* eavesdrop?"

"Huh? Who, me?" Ted looked puzzled as he stood. "I don't know what you're talking about, ma'am."

"Yes, I'm sure you don't," Dr. Obama said quietly as the door closed after him. She opened her desk drawer and pulled out a small flat lockbox the size of a paperback book. "I have a . . . personal favor." She lowered her voice, "There's a Lieutenant Colonel Ira Wallachstein attached to Project Jefferson. Would you please deliver this to him?"

"Certainly, ma'am—"

"I want you to *personally* place it in his hands."

"Yes, ma'am."

"If for any reason that's not possible, take this out to an open field and punch the date into the lock. Then walk away quickly. Thirty seconds later, it'll self-destruct. Any questions?"

"No, ma'am."

"Repeat it back to me."

I did so and she nodded in satisfaction. "Good," she said. "Thank you. That'll be all."

The helipad was a kilometer down the mountain. It took five minutes to drive there. Duke was tight-lipped all the way. What was it about the Special Forces anyway that they didn't let you in unless you were terminally nasty?

Ted was stretched across the back. I was sitting in the front, half-turned toward Duke. "Uh—Duke?"

"Don't talk." He said it very flatly.

I shut up. And wondered what was eating him now—

Abruptly, Duke said, "Listen, both of you—you've both taken the oath and you're both entitled to wear the Special Forces insignia. I would prefer that you didn't."

"Sir?"

Did Duke look annoyed? The expression flashed so quickly, I wasn't sure. He said, "What you need to know is this: if you wear your insignia, you will attract the attention of people who will ask you questions that you are not prepared to answer. That could be very embarrassing for you. Or worse. Got that?"

I started to say, "I don't understand—" but Ted poked me in the ribs. *Hard.* "We got it," he said.

I looked at him. He looked back at me. I remembered what we had talked about the day before. "Oh," I said.

We pulled up at the helipad then—actually just a large clear space next to the road, bulldozed flat and surrounded by automatic lights and plastic markers. The chopper was nowhere in sight yet. Duke glanced at his watch. "Looks like we're a little early."

"Or they're a little late." That was Ted. He hopped out of the Jeep and walked off a way to admire the view.

"Duke," I said. "I want to thank you."

He looked at me skeptically. "For what?"

"For lying to me."

"Eh?"

"I went and reread my contract. I'm 'scientific personnel attached to the military, specifically exempt from military duties and functions.' I'm not in the army at all."

"I never said you were. I didn't lie to you, McCarthy. You told me your contract requires you to obey your immediate superiors and I agreed with you." He grinned. "I just didn't tell you that neither Dr. Obama nor myself are in that chain of command. Except by courtesy. Legally, you're an independent agent."

"Um," I said. "Well, thank you for fooling me."

"I didn't fool you. You fooled yourself. What I said was this: 'If the mission is military, *every* man is a soldier.' That has nothing at all to do with your contract. You could have stood your ground as a 'scientist,' and there wouldn't have been a thing I could have done about it—except, you would have never seen a worm. That's all. Either way, you still get sent to Denver—but this way, I'll shake your hand and mean it." He held out his hand.

His grip was firm. I looked at him and his eyes were bright. Almost smiling? No, it must have been a trick of the sun. I looked away, embarrassed.

The chopper appeared in the distance then and Duke sat up in his seat to see it better. "By the way," I asked, "if neither you nor Dr. Obama has the authority to give me orders, who does?"

Still peering into the distance, he said, "That's in your contract too."

"No, it isn't," I said. "There's not a word about where I fit into the chain of command."

He looked at me then and grinned. "That's what I meant. You're your own man—all civilian attached personnel are. But we try to keep you from finding out, else you're hard to put up with. I can't give you orders, only recommendations. Same for Dr. Obama and every other officer. Take a look at your papers on the way up. You're carrying pinks, not yellows; you're a free agent, responsible only to the team or task you're assigned. But, ah—don't get cocky. You still have to earn the right to talk to a Special Forces man."

We could hear the chopper now, a distant blurring in the air. Duke was already getting out of the Jeep. "Come on, I'll help you with your gear."

By the time we had unloaded the last of it, the chopper was already overhead, engines screaming and stirring up clouds of choking dust with their downdraft. It was one of the new Huey Valkyrie 111s; with jet-assisted flight, its range was more than two thousand miles—at least, that's all the army would admit. Privately, it was said to be a lot more. The landing gear flexed and gave as the copter settled its weight to the ground, but its rotors continued to strop the air. The thunderous roar of the jets muted temporarily to an impatient whine. We picked up our bags and ran for it.

Ted was up the ladder first. I bumped into him as he did a sudden stop in the door. The pilot was an impeccable-looking redhead in jumpsuit and major's insignia, Army Air Corps. I wondered if she was friendly. She looked through us as we climbed aboard with the specimen cases. "Secure those boxes in the back, then get out. I'm in a hurry." No, she wasn't.

"Uh—" I said, "—we're coming with."

"Forget it—I don't carry passengers." She booted my duffel casually out the door.

"Hey!" I yelped, but she was already turning to Ted.

He was unbuttoning his pocket. He handed her our orders. She didn't even bother to look, just snapped, "I said, 'Forget it.' "

Ted and I exchanged a glance—

Duke called up, "What's the matter? What's going on?"

—and I shouted back, "No problem. We're just going to have to find some other transportation, that's all. Come on, Ted—I'll get the eggs, you unstrap the cages."

"Hold it, Charlie!" she barked.

"Just hold it yourself!" I barked right back. "We have a job to do too!" It worked. She stopped—but only for a moment. "You'd better read our orders," I said, very calmly.

She took them from Ted and scanned them quickly. "Pinks!" she snorted, handing them to me. "Doesn't mean a thing. Those are just advisories."

"Right," I said. I kept my voice innocent as I carefully refolded and pocketed our papers. "We're advised to deliver these specimens. And you're advised to take us."

"Uh uh." She shook her head. "Nobody told me about it. I'm only taking those." She pointed at the cages.

"No way." I cleared my throat and prayed that my voice wouldn't crack. "If we don't go, they don't go. Duke, hand me that duffel?"

She looked at me, then really looked. I glared right back. She had very bright blue eyes—and a very dark expression. She flicked her glance briefly over Ted, then back to me again. I was already stowing my bag. She said a word, a not-very-ladylike word, then, "The hell with it—I don't care! Fight it out with Denver. How much do you turkeys weigh?"

"Seventy-three kilos," grunted Ted. He didn't look happy.

"Sixty-four," I said.

"Right." She jerked her thumb at me. "You sit on the left." To Ted: "Secure that box on the other side. Both of them. Then belt up." She didn't even wait to see; she pulled the door shut behind us with a slam, secured it and climbed forward again. She checked to see that Duke was clear—I just had time to wave; he nodded back—and punched us up into the air.

The mountain dropped quickly, then angled off and slid sideways as we described a sharp sweeping turn. The acceleration pressed me against the wall of the cabin. We had hardly leveled off—I had to trust my eyes for that; my stomach was no longer speaking to me—when the jets cut in and a second press of acceleration forced me deep into my seat. The cabin tilted steeply and my ears popped as we climbed for height.

There was nothing to see out the window except clouds; the stubby wing of the copter blocked my view of the ground and the bulge of the jet engine was not enough to hold my interest. The scenery in the distance, what little of it I could see, was too far away to be impressive.

I realized the pilot was speaking to us: "—be in the air a couple hours. If you're hungry, there's a ration box plugged into the wall. Don't eat all the chocolate ice cream."

Ted was already rooting around in it. He came up with a couple of sandwiches and a container of milk. Grinning hungrily, he went forward and plopped into the copilot's seat.

The redhead eyed him. "You got a certificate?"

"Well, no—but I am licensed." He gave her what he probably hoped was a friendly smile; it came out as a leer.

"*Jeezus!* What is it with you guys? Go sit in the back with the rest of the passengers."

"Hey, I'm only trying to be friendly."

"That's what stewardesses are for. Next time, take a commercial flight."

"And, uh—I wanted to see how this thing flew," he added lamely.

She did something to the control panel, set a switch and locked it in place. "Okay," she shrugged. "Look all you want. Just don't touch." Then she unstrapped herself and came aft. The tag on her jumpsuit said L. TIRELLI.

"What's in the boxes?" she asked. She nudged the insulated one with her foot.

"Eggs," I grunted.

"And in here?"

"Bugs," I said. "Big ones."

She looked disgusted. "Right. Bugs and eggs. For that they cancel my leave. Oh, yeah. I always get the good ones." Still muttering, she turned her attention to the ration box. "Damn! Clot-head took all the chicken." She pawed through the remaining sandwiches sourly.

"Uh—I'm sorry," I offered.

"Forget it. Everybody's an asshole. Here, have a sandwich." She picked one at random and tossed it at me before I could say no. She took another one for herself and dropped into the seat opposite. "What's so special about *your* bugs and eggs?"

"Uh—I don't know if I'm allowed to—" I looked to Ted. "Are we top secret?"

"What've you got—more Chtorrans?" To my startled look she said, "Don't worry about it. It's no secret. I carried a live one into Denver a month ago."

"A live *Chtorran?*"

"Uh huh. Just a small one. They found it in Nevada, dehydrated and weak. I don't know how they caught it. I guess it was too sick to fight back. Poor little thing, I felt sorry for it. They didn't expect it to live, but I haven't heard if it died."

Ted and I looked at each other. "Some scientists we are," I said. "They don't tell us anything."

"Well, there goes our big claim to fame," he added. "We thought we had the only live specimens around."

"That's a pity," she said, around a mouthful of sandwich. "But don't worry about it. They wouldn't have let you take the credit anyway."

"Thanks for the encouragement."

She wiped at her mouth with a napkin. "Don't thank me. It was free. Worth exactly what you paid for it. I'd have done the same for anyone."

She started to go forward again, but I stopped her. "What's the *L* for?"

"Huh?"

I pointed at her name tag.

"Oh—it's Liz. Short for Lizard."

"Lizard?" I raised an eyebrow.

"I come by it honestly. You'll find out."

"I think I already have."

"Just eat your sandwich," she said. "You're getting skinny."

And then she climbed forward and back into her pilot's seat. Ted smiled hopefully, but she just jerked her thumb rearward and paid him no further attention.

He sighed and came back, and strapped himself into the chair where she had been sitting. "Whew!" he whispered. "I remember her. She bumped into the *Titanic* once and sank it."

"Oh, I don't know. I think she's terrific!" I didn't think she had heard me, but the tips of her ears turned pink. At least, I think they did.

Ted merely grunted, curled up sideways in his seat and went to sleep.

I finished my sandwich and spent the rest of the trip thinking about a tall spiky anomaly at fifty-nine hundred angstroms. I wished I had a terminal so I could study the data first hand instead of in my memory. Something about the millipedes' behavior—something so obvious I couldn't see it—was staring me right in the face. It was frustrating as hell—because I couldn't *not* think about it! It was a bright red vision, a blood-colored room with a table in the middle, and sitting on the table, a cage full of skittering active millipedes. Why? I leaned my head against the window and studied the clouds and thought about rose-colored glasses.

The chopper banked then and the sun flashed in my eyes, leaving a brilliant afterimage. I put my hand over my eyes, closed them and watched the pulsating blob of chemical activity on my retinas. It was white and yellow for a while, then it was crimson and it looked like a star—I decided it was Chtorr, and wanted to blow it up. After a while, it started turning blue and faded away, leaving me with only its memory and another dozen questions about the possible origin of the Chtorran invasion. I also had a niggling suspicion about something. More than ever, I wanted to get back to a terminal.

The chopper banked again and I realized we were coming in toward Denver. And Major Tirelli was about to demonstrate a "stop and drop."

She'd brought us straight over the Rockies without bothering with a descending glide path—and now that we were over the city there wasn't room for one, at least not without a long swing over eastern Colorado to shake off ten kilometers of altitude. So instead, she cut in the rotors, baffled the jets down and let us fall. The technique had been developed eight years earlier, but never used; the army had wanted a way to boost men and supplies quickly over enemy territory, never coming low enough to be in range of their portable ground-to-air missiles. It was one more thing to be grateful to the Pakistan war for. Even if your nerves forgave you for such a landing, your stomach never would.

"Wow," gasped Ted when he realized what she was doing; we'd been dropping for several decades, even though my watch insisted it was only two and a half minutes. "Either she's a real hot shot, or somebody wants to see us in an awful hurry."

"Both," she called from up front. She was downchecking the auto-monitor.

Ted looked embarrassed; he hadn't realized she could hear us.

She got on the radio then to warn them we were dropping in. "Stapleton, this is Tirelli. Clear the dime—I've got that high-pri cargo and I'm putting it right where I said I would."

A male voice answered immediately. "Negative, Tirelli. Your priority's been double-upped. They need the chopper for some brass. Veer off and drop it next door on Lowry. There's a truck waiting for you on north zero-six."

"Oh, hell," she said. But she began cutting in the jets, firing short bursts to bring us around and slow our descent. The deceleration was sideways. And bumpy.

"By the way," added the radio. "Tag your auto-monitor for inspection. We lost some of our remote metering just before you voiced in."

"Naw, that was me. I was downchecking."

"Damn it, Liz! You're not supposed to do that in the air."

"Relax, Jackie. You had me on your scopes. I saw the beeper. You didn't need the telemetry or the inertial probe anymore. And I'm in a hurry."

"Liz, those systems are for your safety—"

"Right. And worth every penny of it." She grinned. "I can't talk anymore, Jackie. I'm gonna drop this thing." She switched off the voice circuit. The auto-monitor continued to flash.

"Uh," I said, "maybe I don't understand—"

"You're right," she cut me off. "You don't." Without taking her eyes off her controls, she explained, "The excuse I gave him was a blind. What I'm really doing is cutting the control monitors. I don't want him knowing I'm not using noise abatement—it takes too much power from the engines."

"Oh," I said. "But what about the people below?"

"I try not to think about them," she said. And then added, "Would you rather be a considerate spot of red jelly on the runway—or rude and in one piece?"

"I see your point." I shut up.

"Besides," she continued, "anyone who lives that close to an airport deserves it—especially now, when half the city is empty." The copter was caught by a crossdraft then and we slid sideways. For a moment I thought she'd miscalculated and we were going to miss the runway, but she did nothing to correct our descent. Then I caught sight of the truck and realized that she'd even outthought the wind. We were being blown *toward* our landing spot.

A moment later we touched ground easily. It was the last easy thing in Denver. Even before the jets whined down to a stop, a ramp was slammed into place and the door was being pulled open.

It popped outward with a whoosh of pressurized air and slid sideways. Almost immediately, a hawk-nosed major with red face and beady eyes was barking into the cabin, "All right, Liz, where are the—"

And then he caught sight of me and Ted. "Who're you?" he demanded. He didn't wait for an answer, but snapped at Major Tirelli, "Dammit, Liz, there wasn't supposed to be any deadheading on this flight!" He was wearing a Sony Hear-Muff with wire mike attached. "Hold a minute," he said into it.

"We're not deadheading," Ted said.

He blinked at us, annoyed.

Ted poked me. "Show him the orders."

"Orders? What orders?" To the mike: "Stand by. I think we got a foul-up."

I pulled the papers out of my jacket pocket and passed them over. He took them impatiently and scanned them with a growing frown. Behind him, two middle-aged privates, obviously tapped for the job of carrying the specimen cases, peered at us with the usual mixture of curiosity and boredom.

"What the hell," he muttered. "This is a bloody nuisance. Which one are you?"

"I'm McCarthy, that's Jackson."

"Right. McCarthy. I'll remember you." He handed our orders back. "Okay, grab your cases and lug them down to that cruiser." He turned and ducked out. "You two are dismissed. They sent their own flunkies." He had all the charm of a drill press.

Ted and I exchanged a glance, shrugged and reached for the boxes. Major Tirelli finished her power-down, locked the console, and squeezed past us toward the door.

As we stumbled down the ramp after her, I noticed that the two privates had parked themselves in the V.I.P. seats of the wagon, leaving the service seats for us. The major—already I disliked him—was standing by the hood, talking to an unseen someone. "Yeah, that must be it. . . . Well, find someplace to bed them down until we can figure out what to do with them—I don't care where. . . . What? . . . I don't know. They look like it. Wait, I'll find out for sure." He glowered over at us. "Are you boys fairies?"

"Oh, honey!" Ted gushed at him. "When are you going to learn? The word is *faggot!* Don't they teach you anything at those fancy eastern schools?" Before I could react or step away, Ted had hooked his arm through mine. "Jimmy, we've got a lot of consciousness-raising to do here."

"Ted!" I jerked away and stared at him angrily.

"Yeah, they are," the major was saying. "Put them somewhere out of the way. Let's not give our Fourth World friends any *more* ammunition. . . . Right. Out." He looked at the two privates. "Move it! Make room there for Major Tirelli!" To us, he just growled, "Stash those in the back! You'll have to crawl in with them; there's not enough room up front." He planted himself beside a weary-looking driver.

I scrambled in behind Ted and tried to make myself comfortable—Hah! That bus hadn't been designed for comfort. There must have been an army regulation against it. We bounced across the field toward a distant building.

"What was *that* all about?" I hissed at Ted.

Ted half-shrugged, half-grinned. "I don't know. Seemed like a good idea at the time."

"Not to me!"

Ted reached over and patted my arm affectionately. I glared at him. He said, "Jimbo, take a look around you. It's a *beautiful* day. And we are back in civilization! Not even the army can spoil that!"

"I'm not a fairy!"

"I know, dear—but the major was looking for a reason to dislike you and I didn't want to disappoint him. Wow! Look at that sky! Welcome to Denver!"

Sixteen

OUR FIRST stop was Specimen Section, ET-3. Ted and I pushed the cart down the long disinfectant-smelling hall of the section, while Major Bright-Eyes and his honor guard followed us—glowering.

At one point we passed a heavy steel door with a very tantalizing sign:

LIVE CHTORRAN OBSERVATION

AUTHORIZED PERSONNEL ONLY

I craned my neck as we passed, hoping to peer in through the windows in the doors, but there was nothing to see. And Major Shithead gave me a dirty look for my trouble.

We went all the way to the end of the hall through a pair of double doors marked SUPERVISION. The person in charge of the section was a surprisingly unmilitary little old lady, who peered at us over the tops of her half-frame spectacles. "Well, hello!" She gave us a twinkly-sweet smile. "What did you bring me today?" She took the clipboard from the major and peered at it, smiling and blinking as she did so. "Uh huh, yes . . . yes, very good. . . ." She had rosy pink cheeks and shiny white hair piled and curled on top of her head. She was wearing a white lab coat, but where it was open at the neck I could see the collar of a green and blue flowered dress. Her nametag said M. PARTRIDGE, Ph.D.

"Millipedes, yes . . . uh huh, eggs . . . uh huh, wall scrapings . . ." She thumbed through the rest of the specimen list, squinting carefully as each page flashed up on the clipboard. "What's this? *Purple Coleus?* Whose classification is that?"

"Mine." I raised my hand.

"Oh, yes." She blinked at me. "And you are—?"

"McCarthy, James. Special Forces."

"Ah, yes," she said. "Well, James, please don't classify specimens anymore. Leave that to those who are better qualified for the task. I know you were only trying to be helpful—"

"Excuse me," I interrupted. "But I am qualified."

"Eh?" She looked up at me. And blinked.

"I'm Special Forces, ma'am. Extraterrestrial Section. I gathered those specimens myself. *At some risk.* And I've had several days in which to observe them. I've also had access to the entire Scientific Catalog of the Library of Congress. 'Purple Coleus' is an accurate description of that plant, regardless of the qualifications of the person pointing to it and saying, 'That's a purple coleus.' " I looked at Ted, but he was busy admiring the ceiling. It was very well plastered.

The major was glaring at me. Dr. Partridge shushed him and turned to me. "James, we receive many, many specimens every week. I have no way of knowing whether this is the first time we've seen samples of this particular species or not. This may not even be a Chtorran species at all—"

"It was growing in a carefully cultivated ring all around the Chtorran igloo—" I started to explain.

"Yes, yes, I know." She held up a hand. "But please let *us* make that confirmation. If we accepted the classifications of every person who brought in specimens, we'd have fifty different descriptions of every single plant and animal." She patted my hand like a forgiving grandmother. "I know you'll remember that with the next batch of specimens you bring us."

"Uh, ma'am—" I fumbled my orders out of my pocket. "We've been reassigned here. We're detached from the Rocky

Mountain Control District to function as independent observers in the National Science Center, Extraterrestrial Division."

She blinked. And blinked again. "Goodness," she said. "Well, it wasn't cleared with me. How do they expect me to run a section if they don't keep me informed?" She took the pink copy of my orders, adjusted her glasses on her nose and looked down at it. She held it almost at arm's length. When she finished scanning, she said, "Hm," very quietly. She passed the paper back almost absentmindedly. "Yes. Well, I'm sure we can find something for you boys to do. Come and see me on, ah . . . Tuesday. No, wait a minute—where did I leave my calendar?—oh, here it is. Let's see, now. No, Thursday will be better—"

"Uh, ma'am?" She stopped and blinked and gave me that wide-eyed look again. "We'd like to get to work *immediately.* If you could assign us a terminal . . . ?"

"My goodness, are you Special Forces boys always in such a hurry?"

"Yes, ma'am, we are. There's a war on." I remembered something Shorty had said and added, "It's the first invasion ever fought on American territory." I held up my disk meaningfully. "A terminal? And can we get our live specimens settled in?"

Major Bombast interrupted then. "Dr. Partridge—it's already Friday afternoon, and you have a reception and a plenary session—"

"Yes, I know." There was an impatient edge to her voice. She caught herself and smiled sweetly at him. "I'll finish up here, and you can pick me up for the briefing in—ah, forty-five minutes." The major hrumphed and disappeared. Dr. Partridge stepped to a desk and hit a buzzer. "Jerry!" she called.

Jerry was a dumpy-looking potato of a human being hiding a rubbery face behind thick glasses and a frazzle of dirty blond hair. He appeared in a smudged lab coat and was carrying a disemboweled modulator. He didn't seem to be aware that he still had it in his hands. His nametag said J. LARSON, and he wore a slightly confused frown, as if he were perpetually preoccupied in some minor befuddlement.

Dr. Partridge gave him a cloying smile. "Oh, there you are. Will you handle James and—what is your name? Ted? Will you help them out? They're here as observers."

"Oh," said Jerry. He stared at us as if we were intruders. He looked to be somewhere in his mid-thirties, but he could have been any age from twenty-five to fifty. "Do you have orders?" he asked.

I passed them over. As he glanced through them, Dr. Partridge chirped, "I know that Jerry will take good care of you. If there's anything you need, just see him. He represents me. Now, if you'll excuse me—" And she disappeared into an office.

Jerry finished reading our orders and passed them back. "Special Forces, I see." He coughed. "My uncle's in the Special Forces. My Uncle Ira."

I nodded politely. "Sorry. I don't know him. Look, can we get on with this? I need a terminal. And I want these millipedes installed under special conditions."

Jerry rubbed his nose, then looked at me with a flat expression. "I'll have to have you cleared before I can assign you a terminal and work space. It'll take two weeks."

"Oh, terrific," I said. "Look—I'm in the middle of a process here. I can't wait two weeks." I pointed to the cases on the cart. "Those eggs and millipedes have to be installed under special conditions—"

"What kind of conditions?" Jerry had stepped over to the cart and was opening the metal handling cases and peering in.

"A cool, dry place for the eggs. The millipedes too—a cool room with dim light. I can give you specific recommendations."

"That won't be necessary."

"Ahh—I strongly suggest it."

Jerry opened another case. "Why?"

"Because that's what they like." I stepped over to the cart next to him. "Use a little common sense. Look at the size of their eyes. They're all pupil. Of course they're not going to like bright light."

Jerry hmphed.

I said, "Hazy sunshine blinds them. Indoor light blinds them. Even dim light blinds them. They can maneuver in twilight or dusk, but they can only see well in the dark."

Jerry looked skeptical. "Even *absolute* dark?"

I nodded. "I think their eyes are heat sensitive. I wasn't able to test it, but it looks as if they can see pretty far into the infra-red."

Ted spoke up then, for the first time. "Tell him what that means, Jim."

"Uh . . ." I wished he hadn't done that. I said, "They're not nocturnal—"

Jerry looked up from the case, frowning. He shoved his hands into the pockets of his lab coat. "I don't get that."

"—on their home planet. On Earth, they have to be."

"Huh?"

"Well," I said, "it's the size of their eyes. That really suggests that they've evolved under much poorer lighting conditions than we have here. It's compensation. Either their home planet is farther from its primary, or the primary doesn't put out as much light in the visible spectrum as Sol. Or both. That makes the planet noticeably cooler than Earth; probably its temperatures range between five and twenty degrees Centigrade. Maybe it's in a long glaciation. The millipedes seem most comfortable between ten and thirteen degrees, but that depends on the amount of light hitting them."

Jerry began to look interested.

"Earth daylight is too bright," I continued. "It slows them down, even makes them curl up. At a light level approximating dusk, they're at their most active across the widest possible temperature range—that's when they really *move.* When we found them, they were torpid—but only by comparison. I take it to be a pretty good indication of the general level of brightness to be found on Chtorr. Hence, the big eyes."

Jerry said, "Hm," and looked back into the millipede case with studied thoughtfulness.

"If I had access to a terminal," I hinted, "I could tell a lot more. It's very interesting how sensitive to light and temperature differences these creatures are. That suggests to me that the climate on Chtorr is incredibly stable. The nights must be fairly warm in relation to the days. I'd guess that the planet has a fairly hazy atmosphere with a lot of carbon dioxide in it; that would create a greenhouse effect and keep the nights from cooling too much. I also think the planet may not have any moons—or maybe only very small ones. Nothing that can exert strong tidal effects. That would make the planet stormy, not hazy."

"Hazy, huh?" Jerry pursed his lips as he thought. His whole rubbery face deformed. "I do know a little bit of theoretical ecology," he said. "You might be right—" Then he added, "—but I doubt it."

"Oh, thanks." I folded my arms across my chest. "Listen, if you know a little bit, then you know a little bit isn't enough."

He nodded his agreement. "I know. I took my degree in T.E."

"B.S.?"

"Ph.D."

"Oh." Suddenly, I felt stupid.

"Listen, I applaud your industriousness—as well as your imagination—but your theory has holes in it big enough to drive a worm through."

"Name six."

"Just one will do." He closed the lid on the case again. "If Chtorr has a hazy atmosphere, then that means they can't see the stars. If the atmosphere is hazy enough, they won't see any moons either, especially not if they're small. That means no celestial objects in the sky to attract their interest—and that means no incentive for an intelligent race to discover space travel. If your theory is correct, these bugs shouldn't be here, and neither should the worms who brought them."

"Their eyes are much more sensitive than ours," I replied. "They should be able to see celestial objects under far worse viewing conditions. Look—" I took a deep breath. "To an exobiologist, the species filling the bottom rungs of the ladder are very efficient little monitors of the physical conditions of the planet—its rotation, its temperature cycles, its light levels, its weather patterns and a thousand and six other variables. You can extrapolate the context of the ecology out of the content, if you know what to look for. Based on this evidence, Chtorr is a perpetually smoke-filled room. Or haze, or smog, or something. The point is, the atmosphere is thick and the primary is dim, but how much of each, I don't know—oh, but I can tell you what color it is."

"Huh?" Jerry's jaw dropped. "How?"

"That's what I've been working on." I tapped my disk. "It's all on here."

He blinked. "What is it?"

"It's a three-dimensional graph—the variables are temperature, light intensity and light frequency, demonstrated by millipede reactivity."

"Oh," said Jerry. He looked impressed.

"Well, hey—!" put in Ted, "What color *is* it?"

"It's red," I grinned. "The star is dark red. What else?"

Jerry considered that. His face was thoughtful. "That's fairly well advanced along the sequence. I can see why the Chtorrans might be looking for a new home; the old one's wearing out." He looked at me. "How do you know?"

"Serendipity," I admitted. "I thought I could approximate darkness with a two-hundred-lumen output in the red band—well, it works in a dark room; why not here? I got tired of stumbling into things. But then the new measurements didn't fit the curve I'd already established. The bugs were way too active. So I started thinking about the wavelengths of their visual spectrum. All last night I had the computer varying the color temperature of the plates at regular intervals. I gave the bugs eighteen different colors. Most of them provoked no response at all. The yellow gave some, the orange a bit more, but it was the red that made them sit up twice. A little more testing this morning showed they like it best no brighter than a terrestrial twilight—and then it correlates almost perfectly with the other set of tests."

"It sounds like a good piece of work," said Jerry. Suddenly, he grinned. On his face, the effect was grotesque. "It reminds me of a project I did once. We were given three disparate life forms and we had to extrapolate the native ecology. It was a two-year project. I used over twenty thousand hours of parallel processing." He grew more serious. "So please don't be upset when I tell you that your conclusions might be premature. I've been through this exercise once. I know some of the pitfalls. You can't judge a planet by a single life form. There's a lot of difference between rattlesnakes and penguins. You don't know if these millipedes are representative or just a special case. We don't know what part of the planet they're from, or what kind of region—are they from the poles or the equator? Are they representative of mountainous fauna on Chtorr, or swampland creatures? Or desert, or grasslands, or *what?* And what would that identification imply about conditions on the rest of the planet? What kind of seasons are these bugs geared to—how long are they? What kind of biological cycles? How long are the days, months, years? If they have no moons, or more than one, do they even have cyclical equivalents of months? The real question about these specimens is, where do these millipedes *fit* in the Chtorran ecology? All you have here are indicators: the worms like to eat bugs, and the bugs like to eat anything—is that a general or arbitrary condition? What can we imply about the shape of their food chain? And what about their breeding—what is their reproductive cycle like? What are their growth patterns? Their psychology—*if* they even have one? Diseases? And I haven't even *begun* to ask questions."

"That's what we're here for," I said. "To help ask questions—and to help find answers."

Jerry accepted that. "Good." He said, "I'll see that your information gets passed along to those who can make the best use of it. You've probably opened up a valuable area of inquiry." He held his hand out for the disk.

"Sorry." I shook my head. "No terminal, no disk."

"Uh—" Jerry looked annoyed. "If you have information about any extraterrestrial or suspected extraterrestrial life forms, you know you're required by law to report it to the federal authorities. This is the agency." He held out his hand again.

"No way," I said. "A man died for this information. I owe it to him to see it delivered. I don't want it disappearing down some rabbit hole."

"It's against regulations to let you on a terminal before you're cleared." He looked unhappy. "What branch of Special Forces did you say you were with?"

"Alpha Bravo."

"And what do you do?"

"We burn worms."

"I wouldn't phrase it like that, if I were you. At least, not around here." He thought for a moment, then made a face. "Phooey on regulations. You've got a green card, haven't you? All right, I know how to do it. Come on." He led us to a nexus of four terminals, powered up two of them, logged himself in on one and slaved the second one to his control. "Go ahead," he said. "Create a password for yourself. You too—Jackson, is it? You'll be operating on a special department account for V.I.P.s—oh, and don't tell anyone I did this. Now, first thing—I want you to *dupe* that disk—"

Seventeen

THE BUS station was next to the PX. There were fifteen or twenty people standing around and waiting, most of them dressed in evening clothes or uniforms.

Hardly anybody looked up as we approached. "What's up?" I whispered.

Ted said, "I'll find out," and disappeared into the crowd. He left me standing there looking after him.

Our intention had been to ride into town and take in a show or a tribe-dance. Now I just stood in front of the bus terminal, staring at the big wall-screen. It was flashing: NEXT BUS—22 MINUTES. There was a blinking dot on the map, showing its present location.

I shoved my hands into my pockets and turned around. Almost immediately, I found myself staring into the face of a thin, pale little girl who couldn't have been more than sixteen at most, probably younger; she was hanging on the arm of a large, bombastic-looking man. He was puffy and florid-faced, and obviously drunk. He was old enough to be her father. He wore a plaid kilt and a rumpled military jacket. I didn't recognize the nationality; he could have been anything from Australian to Scot. I pegged him as a colonel. Or a buffoon. I was just about to give the girl a smile when he noticed me studying them. He glared and I turned away embarrassed.

I looked at the two WACs instead—at least, I assumed they were WACs. They could just as easily have been whores. Dad always said the way to tell the difference was that "whores dress like ladies, and ladies dress like whores." But I never understood what he meant by that. I always thought a whore *was* a lady. By definition. These two were murmuring quietly to each other, obviously about something neither of them cared about. They were swathed in elegance and indifference. They should have been waiting for a limousine, not a bus; but—well, the whole crowd was an odd conglomeration. Maybe they were with the three Japanese businessmen in Sony-suits who were arguing so heatedly over something, while a fourth—obviously a secretary—kept referring to the readouts on a pocket terminal.

There were four black delegates speaking some unidentifiable African language; I would have guessed Swahili, but I had no way of being sure. Three men and a tall, striking woman with her hair in painful-looking corn rows. All were in bright red and gold costumes. The woman caught me looking at her, smiled and turned away. She whispered something to one of the men and he turned and glanced at me; then he turned back to his companion and the two of them laughed softly together. I felt myself getting hot.

I was embarrassed. I turned and stared into the PX window. I stayed that way, staring at faded packages of men's makeup kits until Ted came up grinning and punched my arm. "You're gonna love this!" he said.

I turned away from the dusty window. "What did you find?"

"Oh . . . something." He said it smugly.

"For instance?"

"An orientation reception. You know what's going on here?"

"Chtorran studies, I hope."

"Better than that. The First Worldwide Conference on Extraterrestrial Life, with especial emphasis on the Chtorran species, and particular objectives of contact, negotiation and coexistence."

"What about control?"

"I guess that's implied. There is a subsection on defensive procedures and policies, but it seems to be downplayed. In any case, this is a major effort. There are five hundred of the best scientists—"

"Best *remaining,*" I corrected.

Ted ignored me. "—in the world. Not just biologists, Jim boy, but psychologists, ecologists, anthropologists, space scientists—they've even got the head of the Asenion Foundation coming in."

"Who's he?"

"It's a group of speculative thinkers. Writers, artists, filmists, programmers—like your dad—and so on. People with a high level of ideational fluency. People who can extrapolate—like futurists and science fiction writers."

"Oh," I said. "Crackpots. I'm whelmed."

"You gonna come?"

"Huh? We're not officially invited are we?"

"So? It's about Chtorrans, isn't it? And we're Chtorran experts, aren't we? We have as much right as anybody to be there. Come on, the bus is here." It was a big Chrysler hydro-turbine, one of the regular shuttles between the base and downtown. The driver had all her lights on and the big beast gleamed like a dragon.

I didn't get a chance to object. Ted just grabbed my arm and pulled me aboard after him. The bus was moving even before we found seats; I wanted to head for the back, but Ted pulled me down next to him near a cluster of several young and elegantly dressed couples; we rumbled out the front gate and onto the main highway and I thought of a brilliantly lit cruise ship full of revelers in the middle of a dark and lonely ocean.

Someone up front started passing a flask around and the party unofficially began. Most of the people on the bus seemed to know each other already and were joking back and forth. Somehow, Ted fit himself into the group and within minutes was laughing and joking along with them. When they moved to the lounge at the front of the bus, he waved for me to come up and join them, but I shook my head.

Instead I retreated to the back of the bus—almost bumping into the thin, pale little girl as she came out of the lavatory. "Oops, sorry!"

She flashed a quick angry look at me, then started to step past.

"I said I'm sorry."

"Yeah—they all are."

"Hey!" I caught her arm.

"What?!"

I looked into her face. "Who hurt you?"

She had the darkest eyes. "Nobody!" she said. She pulled her arm free and went forward to rejoin her friend, the fat florid colonel.

The Marriott-Regency was a glimmering fairy castle, floating like a cloud above a pool of silvery light. It was a huge white pyramid of a building, all dressed up in terraces and minarets, and poised in the center of a vast sparkling lake. It towered above Denver like a bright complacent giant—a *glowing* giant. Starbursts and reflections twinkled and blazed across the water—there were lights below as well as above—and all around, shimmering laser beams played back and forth across the sky like swords of dancing color; the tower was enveloped in a dazzling halo.

High above it all, flashing bursts of fireworks threw themselves against the night, sparkling in the sky, popping and exploding in a never-ending shower of light. The stars were dimmed behind the glare.

By comparison, the rest of the city seemed dark and deserted. It was as if there were nothing else in Denver but this colossal spire, blazing with defiant life—a celebration for the sheer joy of celebration.

A gasp of awe went up from some of the revelers. I heard one lady exclaim, "It's beautiful! But what are they celebrating?"

"Nothing," laughed her companion. "Everything. Just being alive!"

"They do it every night?"

"Yep."

The bus rolled down a ramp, through a tunnel and up into the building itself, finally stopping on an interior terrace overlooking a frosty garden.

It was like stepping into a fairy tale. The inside of this gaudy diamond was a courtyard thirty stories tall, bathed in light, divided by improbable fountains and exuberant forests, spotted with unexpected plateaus and overhung with wide terraces and balconies. There were banners hanging everywhere. I got off the bus and just stared—until Ted grabbed my arm and pulled me along.

To one side was a lobby containing the hotel's registration desk and elevators, on the other was a ramp leading down into the heart of the courtyard. A Marine Corps band in shining silver uniforms occupied one of the nearby balconies and strains of Tchaikovsky's *Sleeping Beauty March* filled the air. (It used to be a waltz, until the Marines got ahold of it.) Everywhere I looked, I saw uniforms—from every branch of the service, and quite a few foreign ones as well. Had the military taken over the hotel?

There was a young lieutenant—good grief! When had they started commissioning them that young?—at the head of the ramp. He was seated behind a porta-console, checking off each person against the list in the computer. Although we didn't see him prevent anyone from going down the ramp, his authority to do so was obvious. I wondered how Ted was going to get us past.

It turned out to be no problem at all. Ted had attached himself to the buffoon with the sixteen-year-old girl, showing interest only in the buffoon and none at all in the girl. He looked like a hustler in his gaudy flash-pants; now he was acting like one. We approached the console in a group; Ted hooked one arm through the buffoon's, the other through mine. "Now, come on, Jimmy-boy," he said. "Don't be a party-poop." The looey looked up at all four of us, tried unsuccessfully to conceal his reaction and nodded us past without comment.

Turned out the buffoon was one of the better known buffoons in Denver. As well as his predilections for—well, never mind. The girl was not his daughter. But she *was* hungry.

I shook off Ted's arm and pulled angrily away. I stopped on the ramp and let them keep going without me. Ted just nattered along, barely noticing my departure.

I stood there watching them, Ted gushing on one arm of the buffoon, the girl on the other, and hated all three of them. This wasn't what I'd come to Denver for. I felt hot and embarrassed, a damn fool.

Screw them. I went looking for a phone.

Found one, inserted my card and dialed home.

Got a recorded message. "Not here now, back tomorrow." *Beep.*

Sigh. "Mom, this is Jim—"

Click. "Jim, I'm sorry I missed you. I'm not in Santa Cruz anymore. I've moved down the coast to a place called Family. It's on the New Peninsula. We take care of orphans. I've met a wonderful man here—I want you to meet him. We're thinking of getting married. His name is Alan Plaskow; I know you'll like him. Maggie does. Maggie and Annie send their love—and we all want to know when we'll be seeing you again. Your Uncle Ernie will be in town next month, something to do with the Reclamation Hearings. Please let me know where I can get in touch with you, okay?" *Beep.*

"Hi, Mom. I got your message okay. I don't know when I'll be able to get away, but as soon as I can I'll come home for a few days. I hope you're well. I hope everyone else is okay too. I'm in Denver right now at the National Science Center and—"

A metallic voice interrupted: "It is required by law to inform you that this conversation is being monitored for possible censorship under the National Security Act."

"Terrific. Anyway, Mom, I'll be in touch with you as soon as I can. Don't try to call me here; I don't think you'll have much luck. Give my love to everyone." I hung up. I tried calling Maggie, but the lines to Seattle were out, or busy, or something. I left a delayed message, pocketed my card and walked away.

I found myself in front of a newsstand, studying headlines. It was the same old stuff. The President was calling for unity and cooperation. Again. Congress was in a wrangle over the economy. Again. The value of the casey had jumped another klick. Bad news for the working man. Again.

On an impulse, I picked up a pack of Highmasters, opening them as I headed back.

I stopped to light up at the top of a ramp.

"Who's that?" said someone behind me.

"Who's who?" someone answered.

"The preacher."

"Oh, that's Fromkin. Ego-tripping again. He loves to play teacher. Whenever he comes to these things, he holds court."

"Looks like a full house."

"Oh, he's a good speaker, never dull—but I've heard him before, and it's always the same sermon: 'Let's be unreasonable.' Let's go somewhere else."

"Okay."

They wandered off. I studied the man they were talking about for a moment, then headed down the ramp for a closer listen. He did look like a preacher. The effect was accomplished by a ruffled silk shirt and a black frock coat—he looked like he'd just stepped out of the nineteenth century. He was lean and spare and had a halo of frosty-white hair that floated around his pink skull like a cloud.

His eyes sparkled as he spoke; he was very much enjoying himself. I edged into the crowd and found a place to stand. One of the women at his feet was saying, "But I don't see how it's possible to inflate a labor economy, Professor. . . . I mean, I thought that everything was *fixed.*"

"It's really quite simple," Fromkin said. "Just devalue your counters."

"But that's what I mean. I thought the point of the whole thing was to create an economy that *couldn't* be devalued."

"Sure. But—oh, hell, it requires too much explanation. Wait a minute, let me see if I can boil it down. Look, the theory of money is that it's a tool to allow a social organism to manipulate its energy—that is, money units are the corpuscles of the cultural bloodstream; it has to flow for the system to be able to feed itself. You like that, huh? What we think of as money is really only counters, a way of keeping score which organ in the social body—that means you—is presently using or controlling this piece of energy. It's when we start thinking that the counter is valuable that we confuse ourselves. It's not—it's only the symbol."

"I could use a few of those symbols," one wag remarked.

Fromkin looked at him with withering gentleness. "So create some," he said. Suddenly, I knew who he reminded me of—Whitlaw!

"I'd love to. How?" said the wag.

"Easy. Create value—for others. The truth is that you can only measure your wealth by the amount of difference you make in the world. That is, how much do you contribute to the people around you? And to how many people do you contribute?"

"Huh?" The wag had stopped being funny. Now he was honestly curious.

"All right, stick with me. The physical universe uses heat to keep score. Actually, it's motion, but on the molecular level we experience it as heat. Just know that it's the only way one object ever affects another, so it's the only way to measure how big a difference an object *really* makes. We measure heat in BTUs. British Thermal Units. Calories. We want our money to be an accurate measure, so we use the same system as the physical universe: ergo, we have the KC standard, the kilocalorie."

A chubby woman in a bright-flowered dress giggled nervously. "I used to think we were spending pieces of fat. I thought I'd be rich." Fromkin acknowledged her attempt at humor with a noncommittal smile, and she gushed happily.

The man next to her asked, "How much *is* a pound of flesh these days?"

"Um, let's see—a pound is two-point-two kilograms. . . ."

"It'd be three caseys," I said. "A pound of flesh is three thousand calories." I looked back to Fromkin.

He was ignoring the interruption. He took a final sip from his drink and put it down. Someone immediately moved to refill it, a thin, bony-looking woman with basset-hound eyes.

Fromkin returned his attention to the brunette who had asked the original question. "Still with me? Good. Okay, this is what the casey teaches us about the law of supply and demand. The purchase price of an object is determined by how much of your labor you're willing to trade for it. The difference between the purchase price and its actual value is called *profit.* Stop wrinkling your nose, my dear; profit is not a dirty word. Profit is a resource. It is a necessary part of the economic process; it's what we call the energy that the organism uses for reinvestment if it is to continue to thrive and produce. This apple, for instance, is the apple tree's profit—the meat of it is used to feed the seeds inside, and that's how an apple tree manufactures another apple tree. So you cannot charge less than an item costs in energy, but you can charge more; in fact, you *must.*"

"So why does a kilo of Beluga cost more than a kilo of soya?" someone asked. "The soya has more protein."

Fromkin smiled. "Isn't it obvious? As soon as you have one unit less than the number of willing buyers, you have an auction going. The price will rise until enough people drop out and you have only as many buyers as units to sell; it's called 'whatever the market will bear.' "

He stood up then and stepped to a nearby buffet table and started loading a plate. But he kept talking. The man was incredible. "Under the labor standard, a nation's wealth is determined by its ability to produce—its gross national product. Cut the population and you cut the wealth of a country. Automatically. But the amount of counters still in circulation remains high. And there's no easy way to cut back the coinage; it can't help but inflate—and even if you *could* cut back all the excess cash in circulation, it wouldn't be enough. The system is still pegged to its history. Bonds, for instance—a government sells bonds on the promise of paying interest on them. Interest can only be paid when the system is in a growth situation. If there's no growth, then interest is only a promise by the government to continue inflating the economy and further reduce the value of the counters—the money. That's why I oppose letting the government borrow money—under *any* circumstances. Because it sets a bad precedent. If it can't pay it back, then it has to borrow more, and the inflationary spiral is endless. Let the government go into debt and we're mortgaging our own future incomes. This country—the whole world, in fact—is in an extreme no-growth situation, yet the interest will still be paid on all outstanding bonds. It has to be; it's the law. So . . . the more cash in circulation, the less each bill is worth. Thank God we still have the dollar—that's at least backed by paper, and it can't inflate as fast as the casey can under these circumstances—and it'll continue that way for a long time. It *was* a commodity; someday soon it'll be money again. We're at the beginning of a long recede—"

"Beginning—?" said the brunette. "I thought—"

"Nope." Fromkin was sitting again, eating. He paused to chew and swallow. "You're wrong. That was a population crash. When four and a half billion people die in two years, that's a crash. The U.N. definition of a recede specifies seven percent or more over an eight-month period—but when it's seventy percent, that's a crash. We're just coming out of the crash now; the curve is finally starting to level off. Now we're going into the recede. The *real* recede. It's the aftershock of the crash. But it's a lot more than that too. Believe it or not, the human race may have been knocked below the threshold of viability. There may not be enough of us left to survive."

"Huh?" That was a newcomer to the group. His posture was military even though he was wearing a dress jacket. He was standing with a plate in one hand and a drink in the other. "Are you serious? Fromkin, I think you're ignoring the fact that the human race has survived a long time—and we've only been above one billion individuals for a little more than a century."

Fromkin looked up. He recognized the man and grinned. "You'd better stick to your spaceships, Colonel Ferris. Someone make room for the colonel here, thank you. You're right about your figures, of course—I saw the same report—but the figures alone don't tell the whole story. You need to know the demographic cross section. Right now, we are not functioning from a stable population of family or tribal groups. The human network is mostly disjointed—we're all individual atoms, swirling in chaos. We haven't reformed into molecules—although that process has begun—let alone crystals and lattices. We're still a very long way from the creation and operation of the necessary social organisms that a self-generating society needs to survive—and I'm still only talking about survival; I haven't even touched upon anything beyond that—like celebration."

Ferris looked unhappy. Some of Fromkin's other listeners looked puzzled.

"Okay, let me put that in English for you. We are not a population yet. We are just a mish-mash of people who've been lucky enough—or perhaps I should say *unlucky* enough—to survive." He looked at Ferris as he said it. "Each of us has his own horror story."

Now I knew him. Jarles "Free Fall" Ferris. The Lunar Colony. One of the seventeen who made it back. We never heard how they chose who stayed and who returned. I wondered if we'd ever find out.

Fromkin was saying, "The fact is, we're still getting after-effects of the plagues. We'll be getting them for another year or three—but we're nowhere better equipped to handle them for a small, spread-out, disorganized population than we were able to handle them for a large, dense, organized one. If anything, an individual's chances are worse now for survival. There are still ripples of those plagues circulating. Slowly, but surely, we're going to lose another half-billion people—that's the guess of the Rand-Tanks. Then, of the survivors, we're going to lose ten percent who will have lost the will to live. Anomie. Shock. The walking wounded—and just because you don't see them wandering around in herds anymore doesn't mean they're not there. The we'll lose the very old and the very young who won't be able to take care of themselves. And the very ill too. Anyone on any kind of maintenance is in danger, even if it's something as easily controllable as diabetes. There simply won't be either the medical care or the supplies. We lost nearly eighty percent of the world's supply of doctors, nurses and support technicians. We'll lose a lot of children because there won't be anyone around to parent them. Some will die, some will go feral. The birth rate will be down for a long time. We're going to lose all the babies who won't be born because those who could have been parents are no longer capable or willing. We'll lose even more babies who are born to parents who can't or won't maintain them. Should I go on? No? Okay—but we're real close to the edge. It'll look like positive feedback on the cultural level: psychoses creating more psychoses, distrust and suspicion leading to more distrust and suspicion. And if enough people start to perceive that there isn't enough of anything to go around—food, fuel, whatever—they'll start fighting over what's left. And by then we'll be into serious problems with population density; the survivors—a rag-taggle conglomeration of misfits by any definition—may be too spread out to meet and mate. Those few left who are capable and willing to be responsible parents may not be able to find each other. I expect the recede to take us right down to the level where it will be questionable if we can come back. Which means, by the way, that the casey was a noble experiment, but I'm afraid it's going to be overinflated and worthless for a long time to come. I wish I were wrong, but I've already converted most of my holdings to property or dollars. I'd advise the rest of you to do the same. With a shrinking tax base, the government is going to have to take drastic steps soon, and you're going to have to protect your wealth, or you might find yourself turned into a pauper overnight by a paper revaluation. That's happened a couple times in the past two decades, but this next one ought to be a wowzer."

He paused to take another bite of food and wash it down with a drink.

Maybe it was my high-school reflexes—I had to say something. He was talking about the fact that the dying hadn't ended yet, that we were going to lose one-third, maybe even one-half, of the remaining human beings left on the planet. He wasn't talking about how to save them; he was talking dispassionately about how to avoid economic discomfort. No—he was talking about how to profit from it. I couldn't help myself. "Sir—"

He looked up. His eyes were shaded. "Yes?"

"What about the people?"

"Say again?"

"The people. Aren't we going to try to save them?"

"Save whom? From what?"

"You said at least another half-billion people are going to die. Can't we do something about that?"

"What would you have us do?"

"Well—save them!"

"How?"

"Um, well—"

"Excuse me—I should have asked, 'With *what?*' Most of us are spending most of our energies just staying alive. Most governments are having too much trouble just maintaining internal order to mount a rescue effort even for their own populations, let alone others. And how *do* you rescue people from the criss-crossing wave fronts of five different plagues, each wave front more than a thousand kilometers wide? We may have identified the plagues, but we haven't finished identifying the mutations. By the way, are you vaccinated?"

"Sure, isn't everybody?"

He snorted. "You're vaccinated because you're in the army, or the Civil Service, or something like that—someone considers you valuable enough to justify keeping you alive; but that vaccine costs time, money—and, most valuable of all, human effort. And there isn't enough of the latter to go around. Not *everybody* is vaccinated—only the ones that the government *needs* to survive. We don't have the technicians to program even the automated laboratories. We don't even have the personnel to *teach* new technicians. We don't have the people to maintain the equipment. We don't have—"

"I get the point—but still, isn't there something—?"

"Young man, if there were something, we would be doing it. We *are* doing it. Whatever we can. The point is, that even with our best efforts we are still going to lose that half-billion people. It's as unavoidable as sunrise. We might as well acknowledge it because, like it or not, that's what's so."

"I don't like it," I said.

"You don't have to." Fromkin shrugged. "The universe doesn't care. God doesn't take public opinion polls. The fact is, what you like, what I like, what anyone likes—it's all irrelevant." His expression was deceptively cordial. He seemed almost deliberately hostile. "If you really want to make a difference, then you need to ask yourself this question about *everything* you do: will this contribute to the survival of the species?" He looked around the gathering. "Most of us here are breeders. Would you have us compromise that breeding potential in favor of some altruistic gesture of ultimately questionable value? Or let me put that another way: you can spend the rest of your life raising and teaching the next generation of human beings, or you can spend it nursing a few dozen of the walking wounded, catatonics, autistics and retards who will never be able to contribute, who will only continue to use up resources—not the least of which is your valuable time."

"I hear you, sir. But to sit calmly and eat caviar and strawberries and bagels and lox while talking about global death and benevolent genocide—"

He put down his plate. "Would it be more moral if I starved while I talked about global death and benevolent genocide? Would starving make me care more? Would it increase my ability to do something—other than *hurt?*"

"You shouldn't be talking about it so dispassionately at all," I said. "It's unthinkable."

A flicker of annoyance crossed his face, but his voice remained steady. "It is *not* unthinkable." He said it very deliberately—was he *angry?* "In fact, if we do *not* think about it, we will be risking the consequences of being caught by surprise. One of the basic fallacies of sophomoric intelligence—don't take it personal, son; I insult everybody equally—is moral self-righteousness. Merely being able to perceive the difference between right and wrong does not make you a moral person; it only gives you some guidelines in which to operate." He leaned forward in his chair. "Now, here's the bad news. Most of the time those guidelines are irrelevant—because the pictures we hold in our heads about the way things *should* be usually have very little relation to the way things actually *are.* And holding the position that things should be some way other than what they are will only keep you stuck. You'll spend so much time arguing with the physical universe that you won't produce any result at all. You'll have some great excuses, but you won't have a result. The fact that we can do nothing about the circumstances that are sending us into a long recede is unpleasant, yes—now let's stop arguing about the situation and start handling it. There is still much we can do to minimize the unpleasantness—"

"One half billion human deaths is more than just an unpleasantness—"

"Four and a half billion human deaths is more than just an unpleasantness too." He looked at me calmly. "And please, lower your voice—I'm sitting right here."

"Sorry. My point is, this whole discussion seems inhumane."

He nodded. "Yes, I have to grant that. It does *seem* inhumane." He changed his tone suddenly. "You know any crazy people?"

"Damaged," I corrected. "Crazy is a negative connotation."

"Sorry," he amended. "I grew up in a different time. Old habits are hard to break. I still hadn't gotten used to women having the vote when the next thing even lawyers wanted to ride in the front of the streetcars. Do you know any *mentally dysfunctional* human beings? Any *damaged* people?"

"A few."

"Did you ever stop to consider why they were that way?"

"They were irrational, I suppose."

"Were they? Sometimes irrationality is the only *rational* response to an irrational situation. It's a very human thing—and it's not limited to humans alone." He said softly, "That's what we're doing here—the only rational response to an irrational and very frightening situation. Quite possibly—no, quite *probably*—of the people in this room"—and he gestured to include the whole reception, spread out across several acres of hotel—"less than half of us may be alive next year at this time. Or even next week." He shrugged. "Who knows?"

The sweet young thing, whose knee he was resting his hand on, went pale at that. He patted her gently, but otherwise ignored her. He continued looking at me. "All of a sudden, there are a lot of things out there that can kill human beings. And there isn't a lot left to stop them. You know, we've had our way on this planet far too long. Nature is always willing to take advantage of our weaknesses. Remember, Mom's a bitch. We've spent centuries building a technology to isolate us from the real world. That isolation has left most of us survival-illiterate and vulnerable. But the machine has stopped—is stopping *now*—and most people are going to be at the mercy of the contents of their stomachs. Nature doesn't care; she'll finish the job the plagues started and never miss us. Humans weren't always the hunter at the top of the food chain—we were just a passing fad. Now we're going to be prey again, like in the old days. Ever seen a wolf pack?"

"No. . . ."

"We've got them running loose in the streets of Denver. They're called poodles, terriers, retrievers, Dobermans, shepherds, collies, St. Bernards and mutts—but they're still wolf packs. They're hungry and they can kill. We could lose another thirty million people to animals, formerly domestic and otherwise, right there. Probably more. I'm talking about worldwide, of course. And I'm including people packs in that estimate too—those are animals of another sort. We'll probably lose a hundred million people who would not have died otherwise, but there's no longer the medical care to take care of the injuries and illnesses that they'll incur in the next twelve months. Did you know that appendicitis can be fatal? And so on—" He stopped, looked at me and smiled. I was beginning to understand his charm. He never intended anything personally. "So, my young friend—much as I respect your indignation and the emotions on which it is based—what we are doing here tonight is quite probably the most rational thing we can be doing. I notice you haven't tried to excuse *your* presence here; perhaps you're quite rational too. In fact, there is only one thing more rational for a person to do that I can think of."

"What's that?"

He went soft for a moment, *gentle.* "Make love to someone you care about. You're not immortal, you know. If you don't take the opportunity to tell someone you love them tonight, you may never get another chance."

He was right. I thought about a whole bunch of someones.

Fromkin stood up and offered his arm to the girl. She and another woman both tried to take it. Fromkin smiled and offered his other arm. He smiled at me again, knowingly, and then the three of them moved off and away.

Yes, just like Whitlaw. He got the last word too.

Eighteen

I TURNED to go and almost bumped into a dream. "Oops, excuse me—" I caught her to keep from stumbling, then forgot to let go.

"Hello!" she said, laughing.

"Uh—" I flustered, unable to speak. I was mesmerized—her eyes were soft and shiny gray, and I was lost in them. Her skin was fair, with just the faintest hint of freckling. Her face was framed by auburn curls that fell in silk cascades down to her shoulders. Her mouth was moist and red.

I wanted to kiss her. Who wouldn't?

She laughed again. "Before you ask," she said, "the answer is *yes.*"

"Huh?"

"You *are* going to proposition me, aren't you?" Her voice was dusky velvet, with just the slightest hint of Alabama in it.

"Uhh . . ." I took a step back. My feet stayed where they were, but I took a step back.

"Are you shy?" Yes, Alabama. Definitely. She spoke each word so slowly I could taste it. And she smelled of honeysuckle and lilac—and musk.

I found my voice. "Um, I used to be. . . ."

"I'm glad to see you got over it," she said, laughing. She put her arm through mine and started walking me toward the elevators to the garage levels. "What's your name?"

"Jim. Uh, what's yours?"

"Jillanna. Everyone calls me Jilly."

I felt suddenly embarrassed. I started to speak—"Um . . ." —and then shut up.

She looked at me, her head slightly tilted. "Yes?"

"Nothing."

"No, tell me."

"Well, I . . . uh, I guess I'm just a little startled."

"Why?"

"I've never been picked up like this before."

"Oh. How do you usually get picked up?"

"Um. I don't," I admitted.

"Goodness. You *are* shy!"

"Um. Only around women."

"Oh, I see," she said. "Are you gay?"

"I don't think so. I mean, I never tried."

She patted my arm. Did she mean that as reassurance? I didn't ask.

"Uh, I'm here on research," I offered. "I mean, I'm with the army. That is, I'm doing research for them."

"Everyone is," she said. "Everyone in Denver is working on Chtorrans."

"Yeah," I thought about it. "I guess so."

"Have you ever seen one?" She said it casually.

"I . . . burned one . . . once."

"Burned?"

"With a flamethrower."

She looked at me with new respect. "Were you scared?"

"No, not at the time. It just happened so fast. . . . I don't know—it was kind of sad, in a way. I mean, if the Chtorrans weren't so hostile, they could be beautiful. . . ."

"You're sorry you burned it?"

"It was awfully big. And dangerous."

"Go on," she said. Her hand tightened around mine.

I shrugged. "There isn't much to tell. It came out of the hut and I burned it." I didn't want to tell her about Shorty, I don't know why. I said, "It all happened so fast. I wish I'd seen it better. It was just a big pink blur."

"They have one here, you know." Her grip was very intense.

"I know. I heard from the Lizard."

"You. Know. *Her?*"

"No, not really. She was just the pilot who flew us in. Me and Ted."

"Oh." Her grip relaxed.

"She told us about the Chtorran they have. She flew it in too."

We took the elevator down to the third level of the garage where she had a custom floater waiting in one of the private pads. I was impressed, but I didn't say anything. I climbed in silently beside her.

The drive whined to life, cycled up into the inaudible range, and we eased out onto the road. The light bar on the front spread a yellow-pink swath ahead. The bars of the incoming traffic were dim behind the polarized windshield.

"I didn't know any of these had actually hit the market," I said.

"Oh, none of them did. Not really. But several hundred of them did come off the assembly line before Detroit folded up."

"How did you get this one?"

"I pulled strings. Well, Daddy did."

"Daddy?"

"Well . . . he's like a daddy."

"Oh."

Abruptly she said, "Do you want to see the Chtorran?"

I sputtered. "Huh? Yes!" Then, "—But it's locked up. Isn't it?"

"I have a key." She said it without taking her eyes off the road. As if she were telling me what time it was. "It's in a special lab. One that used to be a sterile room. If we hurry, we can watch them feeding it."

"Feeding? It?"

She didn't notice the way I'd said it. "Oh, yes. Sometimes it's pigs or lambs. Mostly it's heifers. Once they fed it a pony, but I didn't see that."

"Oh."

She went on babbling. "They're trying to duplicate what it eats in the wild. They're hunters, you know."

"I'd . . . heard something like that."

"They don't kill their prey—that's what I find interesting. They just bring it down and start eating. Dr. Mm'bele thinks there's a kill reflex involved. This one won't eat dead meat unless it's very, very hungry, and even then only when it's being moved around so he can attack it."

"That's interesting."

"They say that sometimes they eat human beings. Do you think that's true? I mean, doesn't that seem atypical to you?"

"Well—"

She wasn't waiting to hear. "Dr. Mm'bele doesn't believe it. There aren't any reported cases. At least, none that have been verified. That's what the U.N. Bureau says. Did you know that?"

"No, I didn't." Show Low, Arizona. "Um—"

"There was supposed to be one once," she said, "but—well, it turned out to be just another hoax. They even had pictures, I heard."

"A hoax, huh?"

"Yep. You didn't know that, did you?"

"Uh, how did you hear about it?" I don't think she noticed, but I was riding at least three lanes away from her.

"I work here. I'm permanently stationed. Didn't you know?"

"Oh. What do you do, exactly?"

"Executive Vice-Chairperson, Extraterrestrial Genetic Research Coordination Center."

"Oh," I said. Then, "Oh!" Then I shut up.

We turned off the main highway onto the approach road. There had been very little traffic going either way.

"Is there anything interesting about the Chtorrans? I mean, genetically?"

"Oh, lots. Most of it is beyond the lay person, but there is a lot to know. They have fifty-six chromosomes. Isn't that odd? Why so many? I mean, what is all that genetic information for? Most of the genes we've analyzed seem to be inactive anyway. So far, we've been unable to synthesize a computer model of the way the whole system works, but we're working on it. It's just a matter of time, but it would help if we had some of their eggs."

"I—uh, never mind. I'm just amazed that they have chromosomes and genes."

"Oh, well, that's universal. Dr. Hackley proved it almost

twenty years ago—carbon-based life will always be built on DNA. Something about the basic molecular structure. DNA is the most likely form of organic chain—almost to the point of inevitability. Because it's so efficient. DNA is almost always there first—and if other types of organic chains are possible, DNA will not only outgrow them, it'll use them as food. It's really quite voracious."

"Um," I said. "How appropriate."

She burbled on. "It's really amazing, isn't it? How much we have in common with the Chtorrans?"

"Um, yeah. Amazing."

"I mean sociobiologically. We both represent different answers to the same question—how can life know itself? What forms give rise to intelligence? And what . . . structures do these forms have in common? That would tell us what intelligence is a response to, or a product of. That's what Dr. Mm'bele says."

"I've, uh, heard good things about him."

"Anyway, we're trying to put together a program to extrapolate the physiology of the Chtorran animal from its genes, but we don't have anyone who can write a program for it yet. You're not a programmer, are you? The lack of a good hacker will probably add anywhere from two to three years to our research schedule. And it's a very important problem—and a double-edged one. We don't know what the genes are supposed to do because we don't know the creature, at least not very well. And we can't figure out the creature because we don't understand the genes. Some really peculiar things." She took a breath. "Like, for instance, half the chromosomes seem to be duplicates of each other. Like a premitosis condition. Why is that? We have more questions than answers."

"I'm sure," I said, trying to assimilate what she was telling me. "What about the millipedes? Didn't they give you any clues?"

"You mean the insectoids? They're another whole puzzle. For one thing, they all seem to be the same sex—did you know that? No sex at all."

"Huh?"

"We haven't found any evidence—nobody has—that there's any sexuality in them at all. Not physically, not genetically; no sex organs, no sexual differentiation, no secondary sex characteristics, no markings and not even any way to reproduce."

"Well, they must—"

"Of course they must, but the best we've found are some immature structures that might—just *might,* mind you—be undeveloped ovaries or testes—we're not sure which—and a vestigial reproductive tract, but they've been inoperative in every specimen we've dissected. Maybe they're just growth glands. But even if they were sexual structures, why are they buried so high up in the abdomen with no apparent connection to any outlet?"

She stopped at the main gate just long enough to flash her clearance at the scanner, then zoomed forward, turning sharply right and cutting across a lot toward a distant L-shaped building.

"The Chtorrans have some sexuality, don't they?"

"Oh, yes. Quite a bit. We're just not sure how it works. The one we have—we thought it was a female. Now we're not sure. Now we're guessing it's a male. At least, I think it is, but . . . we don't have anything to compare it with. We've been able to dissect some dead ones in the past couple months—two we think were females, one pretty definite male and two we're still not sure of. The big one was definitely male," she repeated. Her voice went funny then. "I wish I could have seen that one alive. He must have been magnificent. Two and a half meters thick, maybe five meters long. We only got the front half. The back half was . . . lost. But he must have been magnificent. What a warrior he must have been. I'll bet he ate full-sized cattle."

"Um," I said. I didn't know what else to say. I was beginning to wonder—was this part of getting laid? Or what? I wasn't sure I wanted to any more.

The floater slid to a stop before the building. It wasn't L-shaped, but X-shaped. We had parked in one of the corners. Bright lights illuminated the whole area. As I got out, I paused to look up at the poles. Just as I thought, there were snoops on every tower; that's what the lights were for. Security. Nothing was going to get in—or out—without being recorded.

I wondered if anyone was looking at the recordings.

And then I wondered if it mattered.

There were eleven other people already in the room. It was long and narrow and dimly lit. Two rows of chairs ran the length of the room, facing a wall of glass. I could make out five women, six men. The men all seemed to be civilian types, but I couldn't be sure. I didn't know if the women were their colleagues or their companions for the evening. If the latter, I couldn't help but wonder at their choice of entertainment. The men waved to Jillanna and looked curiously at me. I waved back, half-heartedly.

Jillanna's eyes were wide with excitement. "Hi, guys. Have we started yet?"

"Smitty's just getting ready."

"What's on for tonight?"

"Coupla dogs they picked up from the shelter."

One of the women, the redheaded one, said, "Oh, that's awful."

"It's in the interest of science," someone answered. I wasn't convinced.

Jillanna shouldered her way up to the glass. "Okay, make room, make room." She squeezed a place for me.

The glass slanted diagonally out over a deep room below us; we overlooked it as if on a balcony. The light was dim below, hardly much brighter than the viewing room. There was a distinct orange cast to the illumination. I felt pleased at that—so someone else had discovered the same thing!

Deep, slow-paced sounds were coming from two wall speakers. Something breathing.

I stepped forward to look. There was an inclined notebook rack at the bottom of the glass; I had to lean out over it to see.

A layer of straw—it looked orange in this light—was spread across the floor. The room was high and square, a cube, but the bottom half was circular. The corners had been filled in to make a round enclosure four meters high; the top of it came right up to the window. There were cameras and other monitoring devices on the resulting shelves formed in the corners.

The Chtorran was directly below me. It took a second for my eyes to adjust.

It was a meter thick, maybe a bit more; two and a half, maybe three meters, long. Its fur was long and silky and looked to be deep red, the color of blood-engorged skin. As I watched, it humped forward once, twice, a third time, then stopped. It was circling against the wall, as if exploring. It was cooing softly to itself. Why did that unnerve me? As I watched, ripples—like waves moving through sluggish oil—swept back across its body.

"That means he's excited," breathed Jillanna. "He knows it's dinner time."

It slid forward into the middle of the room then, began scratching at the straw on the floor. From this angle, I could see its cranial hump quite clearly—underneath that fur, it was helmeted across the shoulders. A bony carapace to protect the brain? Probably. Its long black arms were folded now and held against its sides like wings, but I could see where they were anchored to the forward sides of the helmet. The brain bulge was directly behind the creature's two thick eyestalks. From this angle, the Chtorran looked more like a slug or a snail than a worm.

"Does he have a name?" one of the women asked. She was tall and blond.

Her date shook his head. "It's just *it.*"

Sput-phwut went the speaker. *Sput-phwut.*

"What was that?"

Jillanna whispered, "Look at his eyes."

"It's facing the wrong way."

"Well, wait. He'll turn."

"Be a good show tonight," the guy at the end said as he lit a cigarette. "Saint Bernard and a Great Dane. I'm betting the Bernard puts up a better fight."

"Aah, you'd bet on your grandmother."

"If she still had her own teeth, I would."

Jillanna leaned over to me. "He needs fifty kilos of fresh meat a day. They have a real problem getting a steady supply. Also, they're not sure that terrestrial animals provide all the nutritional elements he needs, so they keep varying the diet. Sometimes they pump the animals up with vitamins and stuff. Sometimes he rejects the food; I guess it smells bad to him."

Sput-phwut.

The Chtorran humped around and looked at us with eyes like black disks. Like dead searchlights. It humped up, lifting the front third of its body into the air, trembling slightly, but focusing its face—like the front end of a subway, flat and emotionless—toward us. I stepped back involuntarily, but Jillanna pulled me forward again. "Isn't he beautiful?" Her hand was tight on my sleeve.

Sput-phwut.

It had blinked. The sound was made by its sphincter-like eyelids, irising closed and open again. *Sput-phwut.* It was looking right at me. Studying dispassionately.

I didn't answer her. I couldn't speak. It was like looking into the eyes of death.

"Don't worry. He can't see you. I think. I mean, we're pretty sure he can't."

"It seems awfully interested." The Chtorran was still reared up and peering. Its tiny antennae were waving back and forth curiously. They were set just behind the eyes. Its body rocked slightly too. I wished I had a closer view—something about the eyes; they weren't mounted *in* a head, but seemed instead to be on swiveled stalks inside the skin. They were held high above the body and gimbaled independently of each other. Occasionally one eye would angle backward for a moment, then click forward again. The creature was constantly *alert.*

The Chtorran lowered suddenly and slid across the floor, right up to the wall below us and halfway up it, bringing its face within a meter of the glass. I got my wish—a closer look. It angled its eyes upward, bringing them even closer. Its mandibles—sinuous like an underwater plant—waved and clicked around its mouth. Its eyes opened as wide as they could. *Sput-phwut.* "Too interested. You sure it can't see us?"

"Oh, he tries that almost every night," called the guy on the end with the funny-smelling cigarette. Laced with dream dust? Probably. "It's our voices he hears. Through the glass. He's trying to find out where the sound is coming from. Don't worry, he can't reach up here. He has to keep at least half his length on the ground to support himself when he rears up. Of course, if he keeps growing—as we think he will—we'll have to move him to a bigger lab. There might come a day when he won't wait for Smitty. He'll just come right up here and help himself."

The women shuddered. Not Jillanna, just the women. They moved instinctively closer to their dates. "You're kidding," the redheaded one said plaintively. "Aren't you?"

"Nope. It could happen. Not tonight, though—but eventually, if we don't get him into a bigger tank."

The Chtorran unfolded its arms then, like a bird flapping its wings once to settle them, but instead of refolding, the arms began to open slowly. They came away from the hump on the back and now I could see exactly how the shoulders were anchored, and the curve of that bony structure beneath the fur, how the skin slid over it as the muscles stretched, how the arms were mounted in their sockets like two incredible gimbaled cranes. The arms were covered with leathery black skin and bristly black fur. They were long and insect-like. How long and thin they were, and so peculiarly double-jointed. There were *two* elbows at the joint! And now the arms came reaching upward slowly toward us. The hands—they were claws, three-pronged and almost ebony—came tapping on the glass, sliding and skittering up and down it, seeking purchase, leaving faint smudges where they touched. There were soft fingers within those claws. I could see them pressing gently against the glass.

The eyes stared emotionlessly, swiveling this way and that—and then both of them locked on me. *Sput-phwut.* It blinked. And kept on staring.

I was terrified before it. I couldn't move! Its face—*it didn't have a face!*—was searching mine! If I had stretched, I could have touched it. I could see how narrow its neck was—a shaft of corded muscle terminating in those two huge, frightening eyes. I couldn't look away! I was caught like a bird before a snake—its eyes were dark and dispassionate and deadly. What kind of god could make a thing like this?

And then the moment broke. I realized that Jillanna was beside me, breathing heavily.

One more *Sput-phwut* and the Chtorran began sinking back down to the floor. It slid away from the wall and began roving around the room again, sometimes humping like a worm, other times seeming to flow. It left a swept trail through the scattered straw and sawdust. There were several bales of it against one wall. It stopped to pull at one of them, did something with its mandibles and mouth, then left behind a small mound of weak-looking foam.

"Building instinct," Jillanna said.

"It doesn't seem very intelligent," the redhead whispered to her date.

"It isn't. None of them are," the man whispered back. "Whatever kind of invaders these Chtorrans are, they don't seem to be very smart. They don't respond to any kind of language—or any attempts at communication. Then again, maybe these are just the infantry. Infantry doesn't have to be very smart, just strong."

I realized then that we were all whispering. As if it could hear us.

Well, it could, couldn't it?

"Look at the way his arms fold up when he's not using them," Jillanna pointed. "It's like they're retractable. They're not bones, you know, just muscle and some kind of cartilage. Very flexible—and almost impossible to break. You'll see them in action when he's fed—oh, here we go now."

A slit of light appeared at the base of the left wall; it slid upward to become a door, revealing a closet-shaped cubicle. The Chtorran arced around quickly—amazing, how fast the thing could move. Its eyes rotated forward, up and down, in an eerie disjointed way. The sliding door was completely open now. A Great Dane stood uneasily in the lit cubicle before the Chtorran. I thought of horses—Great Danes, with their lumbering huge paws, long legs and heavy bodies, always made me think of horses. I could just barely hear a low rumbling growl coming from the dog.

For a moment, everything was still: the Chtorran, the dog, the watchers at the glass. Below, in the glow of light reflected from the cubicle, I could see a dark window just across from us. It looked as if there were someone behind the glass, watching.

The moment stretched—and broke. The Chtorran's arms came slightly out from its body. I thought of a bird getting ready to fly. It was a gesture of readiness, the way they were poised—the claws open, ready to grab.

The Chtorran slid forward.

The dog jumped sideways—

—and was caught. One of the arms reached out at an impossible angle and snatched the dog in mid-leap, knocked it to the ground on its back. The Chtorran *bent* sideways in mid-flow—as if the dog in its claw was a pivot and it was pulling itself around. The other arm came around. The Chtorran flowed. Its great black jaw was a vertical open hole that split the front of its crimson body. The dog was pinned by both arms now—I could see how the claws dug into its flesh like pincers. It thrashed and kicked and snapped and bit. The red beast raised and stretched and arced—and came down upon the hapless Dane almost too fast to follow. There was a thrash and slash and flurry—and then stillness. The back half of the Dane protruded from the Chtorran maw.

Was that it? The Chtorran was holding the dog like a snake with a mouse, frozen in lidless contemplation before commencing the long process of swallowing. Its mandibles were barely moving, just a slight ready trembling barely visible against the Dane's side. The Chtorran held the dog between its claws; its mouth was stretched impossibly around it. Its eyes stared impassively off, as if thinking—or savoring.

Then something awful happened. One of the dog's hind legs kicked.

It must have been a reflex reaction—the poor animal couldn't have been still alive—

It kicked again.

As if it had been waiting for just that thing, the Chtorran came to life and began to chew its way forward. Its mandibles flashed shiny and red, slashing and cutting and grinding. The kicking leg and tail were the last parts of the dog to disappear.

Blood poured onto the floor from the Chtorran mouth. The mandibles continued to work with a dreadful wet crunching. Something that looked like long sausages drooled out, dripped on the floor. The Chtorran sucked it back in. Casually. A child with a strand of spaghetti.

"Wow!" said someone. It was one of the women, an unafraid one. The blonde. The redhead had hidden her eyes the moment the door slid open to reveal the dog.

"He'll take a moment to digest," said the guy at the end, the one who would bet his grandmother. His name, I found out later, was Vinnie. "He could eat another one without waiting, but it's better to give him a moment or two. Once he ate too fast and threw up everything. Jee-zus, what a mess that was. It would have been hell to clean up, but he ate it again almost immediately."

The cubicle door dropped closed and the dim figure in the window across from us disappeared into the deepness behind it. Two more people came in silently behind us, both men, both smelling of alcohol. They nodded at Jillanna; they obviously knew her. "Hi, Vinnie. Did we start yet?"

"Only a Great Dane, but it wasn't much. The Saint Bernard will be better."

"You hope," said his friend, the man he'd made the bet with.

Vinnie won the bet. The St. Bernard did put up a better fight than the Dane. At least, that's what the sounds coming from the speaker suggested. I was looking at my shoes.

"Well, that's it," said Vinnie. "Let's go pay the man and finish getting drunk."

"Hold it," said the speaker. Smitty? Probably. "I've got one more. Dessert."

"I thought you only got two from the pound."

"I did—but we caught this one digging in the garbage, been turning over cans for weeks. Finally trapped him this evening. We were gonna send him down to the shelter. But why bother? Let them save the gas."

When the door slid open this time, there was a hound-sized mutt standing there, his nose working unhappily. He was shaggy with matted pinkish-looking fur, stringy and dirty—as if he'd been hand-knit by a beginner. He was all the beat-up old mutts in the world rolled into one. I didn't want to look, but I couldn't stop—he was too much the kind of dog I would have cared about, if . . . the kind of dog that goes with summer and skinny-dipping.

The Chtorran was lying flat in the center of the room. Engorged and uninterested. His eyes opened and closed lazily. *Sput . . . phwut.*

The dog edged out of the cubicle—he hadn't seen the Chtorran yet. Sniffing intensely, he took a step forward—

—and then every hair on his back stood up. With a *yowp* of surprise, the dog leaped backward into the nearest wall. Something about the Chtorran lying there in a pool of dark red blood smelled very bad to this poor creature. He cowered along the wall, slunk toward the space behind a bale of hay—but it smelled even worse there; he froze indecisively, then began backing away uncertainly.

The Chtorran half-turned to watch him move. Twitched. One arm scratched lazily.

The dog nearly left his skin behind. He scrambled toward the only escape he knew, the tiny lit cubicle. But Smitty had closed it. The dig sniffed at it and scratched. And scratched. Frantically, with both front legs working like pedals, he clawed at the unyielding door. He whined, he whimpered, he pleaded with terrible urgency for impossible escape.

"Get him out of there!" It wasn't me who said it—I wish it had been—it was the redhead.

"How?" said Vinnie.

"I don't know—but do something. *Please!*"

No one answered her.

The dog was wild. He turned and bared his teeth at the Chtorran, growling, warning it to keep back; then almost immediately he was working at the door again, trying to get one foot under it, trying to lift it up again—

The Chtorran moved. Almost casually. The front half of it curled up into the air, then came down again, making an arch; the back half barely moved forward. It looked like a toppled red question mark, the mouth flush against the floor where the dog had been.

The Chtorran stayed in that position, its face directly against the straw-matted concrete. Blood seeped outward across the dirty stained surface.

There hadn't even been time for a yelp.

"That's it?" asked Vinnie.

"Yep. That's it till tomorrow," replied the loudspeaker. "Don't forget to tell your friends about us. A new show every night." Smitty's voice had a strange quality to it. But then, so did Vinnie's. And Jillanna's.

The Chtorran stretched out again. It looked like it was asleep. No, not yet. It rolled slightly to one side and directed a stream of dark viscous fluid against a stained wall, where it flowed into a trough of running water.

"That's all that's left of last night's heifer," snickered Vinnie. I didn't like him.

Jillanna led me downstairs and introduced me to Smitty. He looked like an ice-cream man. Clean-scrubbed. The kind who was a compulsive masturbator in private. Very fair skin. Wisps of sandy hair. Thick glasses. An eager expression, but haunted. I did not shake hands with him.

"Jillanna, did you tell him?"

"Oh, I'm sorry. Jim?" She turned to me and went all coquettish, twisting two fingers into the material of my shirt. She twinkled up at me—a grotesque imitation of a woman, this creature who was sexually aroused by the death of three dogs to a giant day-glow caterpillar. She lowered her voice. "Uh, Jim . . . will you give Smitty fifty caseys?"

"Huh?"

"It's for . . . you know." She cocked her head toward the other side of the wall where something pink was trilling softly to itself.

I was so startled that I was already reaching for my wallet. "Fifty caseys?"

Smitty seemed apologetic. "It's for . . . well, protection. I mean, you know, we're not supposed to let unauthorized personnel in here—and especially not when we're feeding it. I'm doing you a favor letting you be here."

Jillanna solved it by plucking my wallet out of my hand and peeling a crisp blue note from it. "Here, Smitty—buy yourself a new rubber doll."

"You should talk," he said, but not very strongly. He pocketed the bill.

I took my wallet back from Jillanna and we left. There was a dark pressure at the back of my skull. Jillanna squeezed my hand and the pressure grew darker and heavier. I felt like a man walking toward the gallows.

I stopped her before we reached the floater. I didn't want to say it, but I didn't want to continue with this horror one moment more.

I tried to be polite. "Uh, well—thanks for showing me," I said. "I uh, think I'll call it a night."

It didn't work.

"What about *us?*" she asked. She *demanded.* She started to reach for me.

I held her back. I said, "I guess I'm . . . too tired."

She toyed with the hairs on my arm. "I have some dream dust. . . ." she said. Her fingers tiptoed toward my elbow.

"Uh—I don't think so. That just makes me sleepy. Listen, I can walk back to my barracks from here—"

"Jimmy? Please stay with me—?" For just a moment, she looked like a lost puppy, and I hesitated. "Please . . .? I *need* someone."

It was the word *need* that got me. It felt like a knife in my gut. "I—I can't, Jillanna. Really. I can't. It's not you. It's me. I'm sorry."

She looked at me curiously, one beautiful eyebrow curling upward like a question mark.

"It's, uh—that Chtorran," I said. "I wouldn't be able to concentrate."

"You mean you didn't find him *sexy?*"

"Sexy—? My God, it was horrible! That poor dog was frantic!"

"It was just an old mutt, Jim—the Chtorrans are something magnificent. They really are. You have to look at them with new eyes. I used to think it was awful too, but then I stopped anthropomorphizing—stopped identifying with the dogs and started looking at the Chtorrans objectively. The strength, the independence—I wish humans had that kind of power. I want to do it like that. Please, Jim, stay with me tonight. Do it to me!" She was plucking at my jacket, at my shirt, at my neck.

"Thanks—" I said, remembering something my father used to say. Something about knowing what you're getting into. I disengaged myself from her hands. "—But, no thanks." I wanted to say something else, but a vestigial sense of tact prevented me from telling Jillanna what I really thought of her. Perhaps the Chtorran had no choice in being what it was. She did. I began to pull away—

"You *are* some kind of queer, aren't you?"

To hell with tact. "Are *you* the alternative?" And then I turned and walked away from her.

She didn't say a thing until I was halfway across the lot. Then she hollered, "Faggot!" I turned around to look, but she was already roaring off in the floater.

Shit.

By the time I found my way back to my barracks, I was chilled. But I wasn't trembling anymore, and I wasn't angry anymore. I was only . . . sick. And tired. I wanted to be young again, so I could cry into my father's lap. I was feeling very, very much alone.

My bed was like an empty grave and I lay in it shivering, trying to feel compassionate, trying to understand—trying to be *mature.* But I couldn't be mature—not when I was surrounded by idiots and assholes, blind and selfish and wallowing in their own sick games and fetishes and power ploys. What I really wanted to do was hit and kick and burn and smash and destroy. I wanted to pound and pound and pound. I wanted to grab these people and shake them up and down so hard their eyes would rattle in their heads.

I wanted to feel safe. I wanted to feel that someone, somewhere—*anywhere*—knew what he was doing. But right now, I didn't think that anyone in the world knew what he was doing, not even me.

Were they *all* that blind or sick—or stupid?

Why couldn't they see the truth in front of them?

Sput-phwut.

Why couldn't they see it?

Show Low, Arizona, was no hoax!

Nineteen

TED STAGGERED in at six in the morning, slamming into the room, switching on the lights and banging and clattering his way from wall to wall to bathroom. "*Hooboy!*" he shouted. "I am going to be limp for a week—and walk funny for two." The rest of it was lost under the sound of running water.

An axe would be too messy, I decided. It would have to be a gun.

"Hey, Jim! You awake?"

"I am now," I grunted. No, the gun would be too quick. I wanted it to be painful. I'd use my bare hands.

He lurched into the room, grinning. "Hey—you getting up?" What was left of his makeup was smeared.

"Yeah. I've got something I want to do."

"Well, let it wait. This is more important. You're lucky I had to come back for clean clothes. You can ride back with me—but hurry up!"

I sat up on the edge of the bed. "Ride back where?"

"Back to the hotel. The first session isn't until ten, but I've got a breakfast meeting—"

"Breakfast meeting?"

"Yeah—you got any sober-ups?"

"I dunno. I'll have to look—"

"Never mind, I can get some at the hotel. Come on, get dressed—"

"Just a minute—" I sat there, rubbing my eyes. My head hurt. I granted him a temporary stay of execution while I reviewed the evidence. "What's this all about? Where were you all night?"

"Painting the town black and blue. Come on—" He pulled me to my feet. "—Into the shower with you. I did a party-walk—"

"Party-walk?"

"Is there an echo in here? Yeah, a party-walk." He was punching up a cycle on the shower panel. "Come on, get out of those—unless you're going to shower in your underwear."

"Wait a minute—I" I started to sit down on the commode.

"We haven't got a minute." And suddenly, he was lifting me up bodily, stepping into the shower and holding me under the running water. "Goddammit!" Not even a phone call from the governor would save him now. All I needed was a jar of honey, an anthill and four stakes.

My paper underwear was already shedding off. He handed me the soap, then shredded off his own sopping shirt. He peeled off his kilt—it was real—and tossed it out of the shower onto the bathroom floor.

I had to ask. "Did you leave them somewhere?"

"Leave what?"

"Your underwear?"

"Never wear any. It's traditional. Nothing's worn under a kilt." He grinned foolishly. "Well, it's a little worn this morning, but give me a couple days—I'll be all right."

I turned away from him, stuck my head under one of the shower heads and just stood there. *Aahhh.*

"Anyway—" he continued, "—I went for a party-walk." Maybe if I let the water run into my ears, I wouldn't be able to hear him. "Only this time, I did it with a purpose. I started out on the main floor of the reception with Colonel Bustworth—remember him? The one with the girl? He's a very important man to know—he's in charge of requisitions, supplies and transportation for the whole Denver area. He's the perfect bureaucrat—he makes the paper run on time. Anyway—Jim, stand a little closer to the soap! We're in a hurry! Anyway, I stuck with him long enough to get into a private party in the penthouse. The Conference Committee. Sat in the corner near three of the armpieces and listened to them gossip. In fifteen minutes I knew who was important in that room and who wasn't. Another fifteen minutes and they knew who I was—Senator Jackson's nephew from Mormon University!"

"Huh—?"

"Shut up and scrub—I haven't finished my story."

"Ted, you can't tell lies like that—"

"How should I tell them?"

"You know what I mean. Not to congressmen and generals and God knows who else!"

"Jim, it didn't matter. No two of them were paying any attention to anything except what was coming out of their own mouths—or going in. And when they were ready to drift on to the next party, I drifted with them. And met another roomful of people and did it again. I listened to the gossip and picked out the most important—it's easy to tell, the gossip gets particularly nasty—and got as close to them as I could. I went through seven parties that way, each one better than the last. There was a United Nations reception, just for the diplomatic corps—did you know half the world is here? Your Uncle Sam rented a ballroom—I met a senator over the guacamole dip—but it was the Communists who had the most lavish spread. They were in the Imperial Suite. And I even got into the Society for Wholesale Aggression; now, there's a weird bunch. But useful. Do you know how important mercenaries are to the balance of world power?"

"No, and I don't care." On second thought: "Do they do assassinations? And how much do they charge?"

"Only character—and if you have to ask, you can't afford it."

I started getting out of the shower, but Ted grabbed me. "Wait a minute—you haven't heard the best part."

"Yes, I have!"

He pulled me back into an affectionate hug. "You're beautiful when you're angry—"

"Knock it off, Ted!"

"—and I love it when you play hard to get." But he let me go. I stepped away hotly. The only thing keeping Theodore Andrew Nathaniel Jackson alive now was my inability to think of a convenient way to dispose of the body.

I stood under the shower again—he'd gotten soap all over my back. The spray was alternating between warm rain and hot needle-jets. "I want you to cut that out, Ted."

"You don't have to worry—everybody knows it's all over between us now, anyway. I met this girl last night, and let her 'cure' me. Oh, I didn't want to, Jim. I tried to be faithful—I told her I had made a solemn commitment—but she convinced me to try it once the *other* way—and she was right. That was all I needed."

"Terrific. I'm very happy for you. You've not only convinced everybody I'm a fag—now I'm a jilted fag. And I don't even know how the whole thing started." I turned around under the shower, lifting my arms to rinse underneath them. At the exact same moment, the water spray went icy—a sudden pummeling jackhammer of very cold water, the run-off from the local glacier. "*Aahhh!*" said Ted. "Doesn't that feel great? Doesn't that just wake you up?"

I couldn't answer. I was too busy swearing—I was out of the shower and shivering into a towel before the walls stopped echoing. I was now completely awake, and it didn't matter anymore whether I had a way to dispose of the body or not.

"Answer the door, Jim!"

"Huh?"

"The door—can't you hear the knocking?"

I grouched out of the bathroom and puddled over to the door. "Yeah—?" I snarled.

It was a bony-looking woman with bassett-hound eyes. Why did she look familiar? Oh, yeah—the one who'd refilled Fromkin's drink. She'd been waiting on him all evening, now that I thought about it. "Hi, Jim," she said. "We haven't been formally introduced—" She grabbed my hand and pumped it. "—I'm Dinnie. Are you guys ready yet?" She had bad teeth.

"Uh—no."

"Okay, I'll wait." She swept past me and parked herself in the room's one chair.

"Uh—right. You do that." I grabbed some clothes and retreated to the bathroom.

"God," said Ted, stepping out of the shower bay. "Isn't morning wonderful?" He poked me in the ribs as he passed.

"Yeah." I was thinking that no jury in the country would convict me. I pulled my clothes on quickly.

When I came out of the bathroom, Dinnie was just handing Ted a light brown T-shirt that said: NOT JUST ANOTHER LOVE STORY . . . "Here," she was saying, "This will drive the women crazy. It shows off your muscles."

"Especially the one between his ears," I muttered. They ignored me.

Ted grinned and pulled on the shirt and a maroon windbreaker. He picked up his carryall and started for the door. "Come on, everybody ready? Let's go."

I grabbed my jacket and followed them. I squinted back sudden tears as we came out into the morning sun. I hadn't realized how bright Colorado could be in the daytime. Ted was already falling into the driver's seat of a long silver—

"Ted! Where did you get *this?*"

"I told you. Colonel Bustworth is an important man to know. You like it?"

"Isn't it a little . . . ah . . . extravagant?"

"There is no such thing as a *little* extravagance," Ted replied. "Are you getting in?" He turned the key and the engine roared to life with a guttural rumble that rattled windows for a kilometer around.

I climbed into the back. Ted didn't even wait for me to close the door, just hit the acceleration and climbed into the air at an angle steep enough to scare the nickels out of my jeans.

"*Wheee-oww!*" hollered Dinnie, with elaborate enthusiasm. She applauded the takeoff, and bowed in her seat to the pilot. Maybe it should be a double murder.

Ted leveled off into an easier climb. Dinnie turned around to look at me. "So wasn't Uncle Daniel terrific, Jim?"

"Who?"

"Dr. Fromkin."

"He's your uncle?"

"Well, not legally." She pointed her nose upward. "He's my *spiritual* uncle. Ideationists are all one big family, you know."

"Oh," I said.

"You met Fromkin?" That was Ted. "You didn't tell me."

"You didn't ask. He's um—interesting." I said to Dinnie, "Do you work for him?"

"Oh, no—but we're very good friends. I probably know him better than anybody. The man's a genius."

"If you say so." I didn't know. He had seemed like just another pompous ass to me.

She said, "Plowboys should never pull on number-one guns. You're lucky he was in a good mood." She explained to Ted. "Jim challenged him."

"Jim?" Ted was quietly incredulous. *"Our Jimmy?"*

"I just asked him about—oh, never mind." My face was burning.

Dinnie turned to me. "So how was Jillanna?"

"Huh?" said Ted. "Who's Jillanna?"

"Jim went off with her last night. Everybody noticed."

"I hadn't realized I was so . . . popular," I mumbled.

"Oh, it wasn't you. It's Jillanna. She's got quite a reputation. There was this Air Force colonel who died in the saddle—a 'massive coronary event'—but Jillanna didn't stop; not until she finished her own ride. You've got to respect a woman with that kind of control. And let's face it—how many can fuck you till your ears bleed?" Dinnie looked at me with wide-eyed frankness. "So, punkin? Was she good enough to stop your heart?"

"Mmfle," I mmfled. "I didn't do anything with her." Maybe I should just throw myself from the car.

"That's our Jimmy," said Ted. I could see the grin even on the back of his head.

"What a waste," said Dinnie, turning forward again. "Jillanna is so beautiful. She even put the make on me once, but I had to turn her down. Now I wish I hadn't, but I had taken a vow of celibacy for a year. Just to prove I could. There were just too many people trying to climb into my panties. Mother! I was wearing myself out."

Something in the back of my head went *twang.* Ted had gone social climbing last night—*deliberately*—and come up with this?

She continued on, candidly. "It was a good thing I did, though. It made me appreciate things all the more. I mean, I must have come at least *eleven* times last night. I know *you* did," she said to Ted. "Then I lost count."

Good lord! I folded my arms across my chest and turned to the window. Did I really need to hear all this? Below, I could see huge burned-out areas—swaths of blackened rubble that marred the even march of avenues to the horizon.

Hardly anything moved. No cars, no buses, no pedestrians, no bicyclists—there was nothing. I saw three dogs trotting down the middle of a street and that was all. The stillness of that silent landscape was unnerving.

Someone had inscribed a giant graffito along a block-long wall. The letters must have been three meters high; it was readable even from the air. It said: WHERE HAVE ALL THE PEOPLE GONE?"

There was dust, sweeping down in yellow gusts, piling up against a wall or curb or house. Would there be desert here—or what? Or would the prairie just reclaim the land, preserving almost perfectly a record of the last days of our civilization for some distant unseen archaeologists?

What would they make of us, those prying future eyes? I found myself resenting them. How dare they dig into our tragedy!

Dinnie broke the mood.

She was patting her hair into place with one hand; it was a peculiar orange color. "So many people just don't understand how sensitive he is; I do. The man is too talented. If he ever learns to control his tools, he'll be dangerous."

I looked at Ted, wondering—what had he been thinking of?—but he was expressionless now. Occasionally he would nod or grunt, but his reactions were only noncommittal acknowledgments. Dinnie didn't seem to notice, or if she did, she didn't seem to mind. Good lord! Didn't her tongue ever get sunburned?!

"What's your meeting about?" I asked Ted.

He opened his mouth to answer—and Dinnie said, "It's the Spiralist Free World Association."

"Spiralism? You're going in for Spiralism now? I—" Stopped myself. "Never mind—" I held up both my hands. "—It's not my business. Everybody gets to go to hell in their own handbasket."

"It's only a breakfast, Jim—" he started to say.

Dinnie plowed right over him. "They're *really* charming people. And it's at Ragamuffin's, which is one of the *few* places that knows how to serve a *decent* continental breakfast—although I have to say, I *don't* think their wine list is very good, so I wouldn't recommend them for anything past brunch. Did I tell you how I once sent back the *sommelier?*"

Suddenly, I was no longer angry at Ted. He'd found a far more appropriate fate than anything I could plan for him. "Well, it certainly sounds . . . uh, interesting. Um—will they be drinking the blood of any gentile babies this morning?"

I saw Ted's quick glance to the rearview mirror—he caught the expression on my face, how far my tongue was in my cheek. At least it was in my *own* cheek.

"Listen, Jim," he said, seriously. "I'm going to leave you off outside the hotel. But it's not really a hotel anymore. Uncle Sam's taken it over, using it as a temporary conference center. For the duration. So that makes it permanent. Anyway, I've gotten us both C-clearances—don't ask—so you'll have access to just about every formal session and most of the informal ones. I don't know if that includes the red-lined ones. You'll have to scout that out yourself—but carefully. Listen, you don't want your credentials examined too closely; you're valid, but just barely, so try to be inconspicuous, okay?"

"Sure—sounds good to me. But how *did* you do it?"

"I come from a long line of dog-robbers. Now, listen—you'll have to check in, first thing. Dial CORDCOM-REG; any of the terminals can rewrite your card. Oh, and by the way, your clearance also entitles you to use the vehicle pool. Unlimited access. It's very convenient. You don't have to bother with Rec-Rec's paperwork. You can have almost anything except the President's limousine or a Patton charger."

"Now, why would I want a laser-equipped tank?"

Ted shrugged. "For the fun of it?" The car bumped as it hit the road, bounced once and settled heavily. Ted touched the brakes lightly to bring the cruising speed down.

"You *could* get it, you know, if you really wanted it. Because you're—um, military. *Special,* you know? That's where the clearances came from too. All you have to do is take a couple hours training. And prove you have a real need for it."

"I'll pass, thanks."

"Well, keep it in mind. Could you imagine the look on Duke's face—*or Obie's*—if you drove up in one of those?"

I thought about it. No, I couldn't imagine it.

Ted turned onto a ramp and pulled up at a convenient side entrance. "I'll see you later, okay?"

"Sure. Uh, nice meeting you, Dinnie." I stepped back as they rolled away. *Spiralism?*

I shoved my hands into my jacket pockets and headed into the hotel—huh? What was *this?* Oh, Dr. Obama's lockbox. I'd almost forgotten I was carrying it.

I found a row of terminals and slid into a booth. It took only a moment to REGister with CORDCOM. My card disappeared into the slot, then rolled out again, overprinted with a yellow stripe. A large C in a red box had also been printed in the upper right corner. Was that it?

I cleared and punched for DIRectory, Lieutenant Colonel Ira Wallachstein.

The screen flashed: SORRY, NOT FOUND.

Huh?

Maybe I had miskeyed. I typed it again.

SORRY, NOT FOUND.

Well, that was . . . weird. I called up PROJECT JEFFERSON next, tried to list its personnel.

SORRY, NOT AVAILABLE.

Tried the Denver Area Military Directory. He wasn't listed there either.

I sat puzzled for a moment, wondering what to do next. I scratched my head. Why would Dr. Obama give me a package for somebody who wasn't here? Or maybe this Colonel Wallachstein had moved on and hadn't let Obama know? Maybe I should call Dr. Obama and ask. No, something told me not to.

I took the box out of my pocket and looked at it. There was nothing extraordinary about it, just a one-piece lightweight unit. Rounded corners. No markings, other than the printed keyboard and the lock. Not much rattle to it either. I had to think about this. I didn't want to destroy it. Not yet. That would feel like failure.

I slid it back into my pocket. Maybe tonight, back at the barracks. Maybe I'd missed something obvious.

I cleared the board and called up the day's conference schedule. The general session on Chtorran biology and behavior began at ten o'clock. Apparently it was a weekly session. I scanned the rest of the calendar, hard-copied it, logged off and went in search of breakfast.

I had bagels and lox and strawberries and cream. I ate alone, and I was still in better company than Ted.

Twenty

THE MAN at the podium looked unhappy.

There were too many empty seats. The auditorium was only a third full.

I hesitated at the back of the room. The audience had already begun to segregate themselves into sections.

The military attendees were seated up close, but on the sides. I hadn't realized it was possible to sit at attention. The funny-looking types were all in the first five rows. Of course, I'd never been to a convention where it hadn't been so. The serious types scattered themselves in the center of the room. The turbans and the burnooses—and there were an awful lot of them—were milling in the aisles, chattering away at each other as fast as they could, ignoring the frowning man on the dais.

The room roared with the noise of a thousand separate conversations—a babbling torrent of words. Didn't they realize how loud they all were? Each one was shouting to be heard above all the rest, and as each one raised his or her voice, all the rest became correspondingly louder too. It wasn't hard to see why the man at the podium was so unhappy.

I found an empty row halfway to the front and took a seat

near the center. I put a fresh clip into my recorder and slipped it back into my pocket.

The unhappy man stepped to the edge of the stage and whispered something to an aide, the aide shrugged, the man looked unhappier. He checked his watch, I checked mine—the session was already fifteen minutes late. He stepped back to the podium and tapped the microphone. "Gentlemen? Ladies?" He cleared his throat. "If you would please find seats, we can begin—?"

It didn't work. The noise of the conversations only increased as each speaker shouted to make himself heard over the public address system. I could see that this was going to take a while.

"Delegates? *If you please—?*" He tried again. "I'd like to call this session to order."

No one paid attention. Each and every one of them had something so important to say that it superseded every other event in the auditorium.

The unhappy man tried one more time, then picked up a tiny mallet and started striking an old-style ship's bell that was perched on top of the podium. He hit it four quick times, then four times more, then again and again. He kept on striking it, over and over, a steady rhythmic dinging that could not be ignored. I saw him looking at his watch while he did it. Apparently he'd been through this before.

The groups began to break up. The various conversations splintered and broke off—they couldn't compete any longer—and the participants began drifting into their separate seats. The only conversation still going full bore was one between three deaf women—or maybe they were interpreters—in Ameslan.

"Thank you!" the unhappy man said at last. He touched some buttons on the podium in front of him and the screen behind him lit up with an official-looking announcement. It repeated itself every fifteen seconds, each time shifting to a different language: French, Russian, Italian, Chinese, Japanese, Swahili, Arabic—I couldn't identify the rest. The English version said: "English interpretations of foreign language speakers may be heard on channel fifteen. Thank you."

He waited while the various delegates inserted earpieces or put on headphones. They rustled and gobbled among themselves, each one taking an impossibly long time.

Something on the right caught my eye—Lizard! Major Tirelli!

She was on the arm of a tall black colonel; they were laughing and chatting together as they found seats three rows forward. I wondered if I should call hello, then decided against it. It would probably only annoy her, and besides the auditorium was filling up now and it would be conspicuous, and probably embarrassing. I wondered if I should save a couple of seats for Ted and Dinnie—except I didn't want to—until finally the question was answered for me when a dark, handsome woman sat down on my right, and a second later, a pair of lieutenants took two of the three seats on my left. The handsome woman was in a lab coat and was carrying a clipboard. She switched it on while she waited and began reading through some notes.

I took my recorder out of my pocket to turn it on, and she touched my arm. "Not a good idea," she said. "Some of this may be classified."

"Oh," I said. "Thanks." And dropped it back into my pocket, thumbing it on anyway as I did so. I don't think she saw.

The unhappy man began banging his bell again. "I think we can begin now. For those of you who don't know, I'm Dr. Olmstead, Dr. Edward K. Olmstead, and I am the acting director of the Extraterrestrial Studies Group of the National Science Center here in Denver. I'd like to take this opportunity to welcome all of you to this special session of the Continuing International Conference on Extraterrestrial Affairs.

"I am required by the rules of this conference to remind you that much of the material that we will be presenting here is generally classified on a need-to-know basis. While that includes all of our registered attendees and their respective staffs, we still want to stress that the material is for your use only and should be treated as confidential. We are not yet prepared to release some of this information to the general public. The reasons for this will be discussed in tomorrow's session on culture shock. Your cooperation is greatly appreciated. Thank you.

"This special Saturday session is being held for the convenience of those delegates who will not be here for the full conference schedule. As always, this session is going out live on channel two. If you need more information on any specific subject, that access is available through the project network, of course. Please feel free to tap in. If you don't already have a clearance number, check with the desk.

"As you can see by your schedules, we're going to try to present all of the scientific material in the first two and a half hours, and follow up with the more important questions of contact and containment procedures this afternoon—after a reasonable break for lunch, of course. As I'm sure most of you have already discovered, the hotel here has an excellent buffet. Tomorrow we will spend the morning session on the cultural and psychological questions, and the afternoon meeting will deal with the economic sphere. We do apologize for presuming on so much of your time, and we thank you in advance for your cooperation. This is, of course, a working weekend, so at this time I'd like to turn the microphone over to our conference chairperson, Dr. Moyra Zymph."

There was a spattering of polite applause as Dr. Zymph came up to the dais. She was a stout woman, slightly disheveled, and she moved like a truck driver. When she spoke, it was with a gravelly, I-mean-business voice. "All right, let's get to it." She slapped her clipboard down onto the podium. "I know that most of you are more interested in finding out the answers than in listening to the questions. Unfortunately, all we have right now are questions. We have *lots* of questions . . ." She paused for effect. ". . . and a few educated guesses, which I will share with you.

"I want you to think of a jigsaw puzzle—with most of the pieces missing and no picture on the cover of the box to guide you. Now think of a warehouse full of similar incomplete jigsaw puzzles. Now mix them all up. Now find someone who's never seen a jigsaw puzzle before in his life, and put him in the middle of this pile of mixed-up pieces and ask him to figure out what's going on here. At the point he realizes what a jigsaw puzzle is, he's won the game. He's solved the hardest part of the problem.

"I want you to hold that picture in mind, because that's what we're up to here. We've got a warehouse full of pieces. We know what individual pieces look like, but we don't know what the pictures look like—we do know for sure that this is a warehouse full of incomplete puzzles. We've solved the *hard* part. And we'll tell you about that.

"Now, some of you are not going to like what you hear. You are especially not going to like the implications. Some of you may be so disturbed by the material presented that you'll want to question its validity. You'll want to dismiss our conclusions because you can't accept the facts. Please do not make that mistake.

"I want you to know that it's *all right* to be uncomfortable with the material. We certainly are . . . and we've been living with it for a while. Just don't use that discomfort as an excuse to hide from the urgency of the situation." She paused long enough to let that sink in, looking around the auditorium as if daring anyone to object.

No one did. Not yet. Dr. Zymph nodded and continued. "Good. So what we're going to do here today is show you some of the pieces that we are certain about and then go from there to the larger pattern. I will not be showing you all of our puzzle pieces—we don't have the time—but I will be showing you those items which you most need to know about."

She switched her clipboard on and began referring to it. "First off, we can tell you this. The Earth, this planet that we live on, is experiencing an ecological infestation. The source of the infestation is presumed to be extraterrestrial." She touched a hidden control on the podium and the screen behind her came back to life, showing two views of the Earth, front and back. There were red splotches blinking across the larger land areas. It looked like a case of measles. She continued: "The infestation has appeared on all five major continents: Asia, Africa, both of the Americas and to a lesser extent—although we don't know why yet—Europe. We have not yet confirmed any signs of infestation in Australia or Antarctica. So far, the evidence suggests that it is generally limited to the temperate zones of the planet, the same areas in which the bulk of our human population is established. That is, the *remaining* human population." She stopped and looked out at the room. "The—uh, population crisis will be discussed at tomorrow's session. I urge all of you to be there. We do have some specific recommendations, but they have to be implemented immediately. And I want to point out that our primary concern is not *just* saving our human resources, but putting them to work in ways that contribute to the larger effort." She looked uncomfortable. She bent back to the security of the notes on her clipboard.

"The infestation has manifested itself in several distinct forms that we are aware of—and probably quite a few more that we have not yet discovered." She stopped, touched a control, looked behind her to see that the screen was showing the appropriate slide—some kind of red sludge floating on a lake—and continued. "While most of the attention has been focused on the more, ah, dramatic aspects of this infestation, I want to make you aware that that there is considerable ecological impact in other areas as well. We are experiencing events in the microbial and botanical spheres, for instance, that are every bit as serious, though perhaps not as noticeable.

"I'm going to give you only a few examples to demonstrate the scope of the problem. Please be assured that it is far worse than these examples suggest. This first one is a kind of algae. It breeds fast, it floats on the surface of the ocean and it's moderately toxic. It tends to occur primarily in the offshore regions, but it can also be found on still lakes and backwaters. Once it establishes itself, it tends to choke out most other plant life. It does not use chlorophyll for photosynthesis, which explains its red to red-purple color." Behind her, the screen showed muddy crimson breakers crashing on a long stretch of shore. The pink sand was stained with dirty streaks that looked like clotted blood.

"As I said, it is moderately toxic, and I want to take a moment to expand on this. The sludge exudes a particularly nasty set of byproducts, including some interesting long-chain molecules that seem intended for use by the next creature in line in the ecology; but whatever that creature is, it hasn't manifested itself yet. And I don't know whether to be thankful or not.

"Sludge-infested water usually feels oily—and the oil is particularly difficult to clean off. But if you do get the oil on you, it's essential to get it off as quickly as you can, because it very effectively clogs human pores and reduces the skin's ability to breathe. For the record, it also smells bad—so at least you have that much warning.

"If you are unlucky enough to *swallow* sludge-infested water, you will definitely regret it. You'll experience nausea, diarrhea, vomiting and fever. If you're strong, you'll survive. If not, you won't.

"Now, I want you to think about the fish and the plants in that same water—unlike you, they can't get out to go lie down for a while. Prolonged exposure to the sludge is *always* fatal to them. The smaller the creature, the quicker it dies.

"Wherever the red sludge appears, the plankton disappears—followed by the fish that feed on the plankton and the predators that feed on them, all the way up the food chain. The red sludge turns ocean into desert. This is going to have a disastrous effect on the global food chain if it is not controlled. If the seas die, *we* die. And already the red sludge has infected three-tenths of a percent of the world's farmable waters, and that figure is climbing at an alarming rate. Now, I know that three-tenths of a percent doesn't sound like a lot, but when you consider that two-thirds of the Earth is covered by water, then you have to realize that we are already talking about several hundred thousand square miles—and it may be in the millions already; we don't know for sure. But you can extrapolate from that." The screen showed the map of the world again. There were red streaks off the coast of China, California, Brazil and parts of Africa. "These are the areas of primary infestation," she said. "At the present rate of spread, within two to five years most of the world's richest sea farms will be lost.

"I *do* wish to alarm you about this—because this may be the single most threatening aspect of the infestation. So far, the sludge has resisted most of our attempts to control it. It does not seem to be temperature sensitive, and it can survive a wide range of water conditions. We've had some success at inhibiting the growth of the sludge with tailored bacteria, but it is a limited success. To date, our best results have been obtained by pouring crude oil on the water and setting it on fire. I'm sure I don't have to say much about the unacceptability of *that* solution."

She stopped to take a drink of water, checked her notes, then brought up another series of pictures on the screen—some kind of insect-looking bug; but it stood on two legs. Its front four legs were very short, they looked atrophied, except that each terminated in a very strong-looking claw. The grasshopper in its mandibles established a sense of scale. The bug was the size of a sparrow. "This is not an insect," Dr. Zymph said. "Do not fall into the trap of thinking that it *is* an insect, because to do that is to wear blinders to the possibilities that the creature has some very un-insectlike capabilities."

The next picture showed the creature standing—almost *lurking*—in a dark corner. It stood erect, and its long black shell-casing enveloped it like a cape. The shape of its head as well as its posture made me think of Jack the Ripper. "We call this fellow the nightwalker," Dr. Zymph said. "He's a comparatively recent discovery, so we can't tell you too much about him. He eats most kinds of terrestrial insects, and is not averse to the occasional mouse, bird or frog. This is a small one. We've found them as big as twenty centimeters. We hope that's as big as they get. We're not sure. They are not poisonous, but the bite is painful. An interesting thing about that bite—most predatory insects liquify their food to eat it; this fellow is large enough, he doesn't have to bother. He uses his mandibles like teeth. We believe that his digestion is something like a bird's in that he may have to swallow small pebbles to help grind the food in his stomach. This is a good place to note that he is a serious competitor for the birds' place in the ecology. He has a voracious appetite and will undoubtedly provide some very powerful competition to all of our smaller predators."

Another set of pictures—this time, it was a pink puffball thing. "We're still not sure if this one is plant or animal. We call it the cotton candy bug. It's as light as a dandelion, and it's as easily spread. It is nontoxic, it is edible and, as far as we have been able to determine, it does not appear to endanger its surroundings. What that means is that we still haven't determined what kind of a danger it is—and I'll touch on that point in a minute too.

"First, I want to show you this cute little fellow—" There was polite laughter as the slide came up on the screen. "We call him the pipe cleaner bug, because he looks like he's made out of pipe cleaners. Again, do not be misled by the fact that he looks like an insect. That's just the ecological niche he lives in. He does not have a segmented body, and his exoskeleton is covered with a thick skin and that soft white fur that you see. That fur is actually a very sensitive olfactory organ. The creature smells the air with his whole body. Now note the bunny feet: those pads are also sensory organs, even more sensitive. He's not just standing on that leaf, he's tasting it as well. The creature's eyes are on the tip of those two antennae, and they *are* regenerative. This fellow eats the cotton candy bugs; he is eaten by the nightwalker. I can't tell you much more than that. We know nothing about his breeding habits. We can tell you that he moves very fast and can eat twice his own weight in leaves every day. We expect to be seeing a lot more of him next summer. Or even sooner."

The next picture was of a scarlet-leafed field of ivy. "We call this one red kudzu for obvious reasons. The leaves are bright red and veined with white. It likes marshes and shallow water, and it breeds like madness, advancing at the rate of two meters per week. So far, we've only found it in the Louisiana bayous, but we expect to see it spread throughout the entire Gulf Coast if it isn't controlled."

The audience was beginning to get uneasy. There were too many of these creatures.

"Now this one—looks like an Earth millipede, except for the hump across its, ah, shoulders—we're not even sure it belongs here in this catalog. There's some evidence to suggest that it may be a terrestrial creature; we know that there were several of them under study at the African Ecology Center in Nairobi more than twenty years ago, but they were lost in the firestorm that destroyed the city. These creatures are omnivorous, and they're capable of short bursts of speed across open territory. We think they serve primarily as scavengers in the Chtorran ecology. We've not seen a lot of them. Now, this next one—"

Huh? Was that it? She hadn't said *anything* about the millipedes! And why did the Chtorrans have a corral full of them?

"—looks like the *anopheles* mosquito, but again, please do not be fooled by the resemblance. It's only superficial. There are significant internal differences. We call this a stingfly. It feeds on blood—human blood is fine, but it's just as happy with cats, dogs, cattle, horses—anything else it can find. It's not choosey, and for that reason we suspect it to be a primary vector for disease. . . ." She had to pause here; there was an excited hubbub in the audience. After a moment, she raised her voice and continued over it. "We *suspect* it; we are not yet certain. There are too many questions still unanswered. But"—and she leaned forward on the podium now, steepling her hands in front of her—"we *are* looking at it as the most likely mechanism for introducing the plagues into the human population." She was well aware of the ramifications of that statement. And so was her audience.

She said loudly, "I want you to get this—it's still only a theory! We do know that two of the plagues appeared in more than one form—like the bubonic and pneumonic forms of the Black

Death. And most of them can be spread by a sneeze, or by touching a contaminated cup or blanket. So what we're looking at here—this stingfly—is not a primary vector, merely a method of introduction. If that. But this does lead right into the next point . . . the plagues themselves.

"We are now operating on the theory that the seven major infections and nine minor ones that have decimated the human species must also be considered as part of the overall pattern of ecological infestation. I want you to know that we came to this realization slowly. When you look at the overlapping patterns of disease and infestation, the relationship is obvious; but even as recently as several months ago, when most of us were still reeling from the initial impact of the disaster, we simply did not have enough reliable information to establish the correlation.

"Um, I'm not going to go into the political and psychological arenas here, but I do want to point out the reasons why conclusive identification of the diseases as extraterrestrial was delayed until the early part of this year. Convincing our respective governments—and I do not mean this as criticism—that there was a very real *presence* on this planet was, under the circumstances, the hardest part of the job. We had very little hard evidence, and it was difficult to have our voices heard during the, ah, worst of the hysteria. We *cannot* afford to let confusion like that happen again!" She stopped herself. Apparently, she realized she was getting angry. She took a sip of water and looked at her notes. She seemed to do that a lot when she was dealing with an uncomfortable subject. Was that for herself or her audience? I wasn't sure. When she was ready, she looked out over the room again.

"I want to say something here. I want to deal with certain avenues of speculation. During the early days of the plagues, there were a number of accusations—on all sides—that they were a weapon of war. At that time, it was assumed that there was a human agency responsible. We know that not to be the case now. The devastation has touched all of us equally, and no nation on this planet has profited by the plagues. And, of course, now the biological evidence is also falling into place—so we must put our distrust and our suspicion behind us. *Now!* The situation is too urgent for us to have our energies divided."

She placed her hands on both sides of the podium. She looked around the room, as if she were looking into the eyes of each and every one of us in the auditorium. She said, "The accusation that the plagues are a weapon of war is not entirely accurate—because *it's too shortsighted!* They are actually a tool of ecological engineering. We as humans may be somewhat biased about the application of such a devastating tool, but as scientists we cannot help but admire the skill with which this particular tool was applied. Almost eighty percent of the members of the dominant species of this planet have been excised as neatly as a surgeon cutting out a cancer with a laser. If that is how they see us, then they should have no problem with the subsequent applications of—continuing with the same metaphor—chemotherapy. We shall see. But if that was their goal, then they have accomplished most of their objective in a very short time. Less than two years." She stopped and wiped her forehead with her handkerchief. She took another drink of water.

When she spoke again, her voice was lower, slower and steadier. The gravelly quality was muted somehow, and she seemed suddenly very serious. "We have been speaking of this as an ecological infestation, because we can't prove that it's anything more. We have specifically *not* called this an invasion, because *we have not been able to find an invading force.* We have no evidence of extraterrestrial landings, no sightings of ships, no evidence of advanced technology of any kind. If we are being invaded, then *where* are the invaders?

"For a while, we suspected that the large purple and red creatures that we have been calling Chtorrans were our alien visitors, but this theory is rapidly falling into disrepute, because we have not been able to prove that these creatures even have the *potential* for intelligence—let alone the *capabilities* necessary to mount such an invasion across the vast distances of space. We are assuming, of course, that this ecological infestation has as its source a planet in another star system—it could not possibly have originated on any of the planets in our own solar system. I refer you to Dr. Swale's analysis for the reasons why we have come to that position. So the question remains: *where* are the invaders?

"I'm actually going to answer that—in a way. But it's a circuitous route. You'll have to bear with me a bit, because in order to find out who the culprit is, we have to take a good long look at the evidence.

"When we look at the overall pattern—the stingflies, the nightwalkers, the red kudzu, the sea sludge, the bacteria that caused the plagues, even the, ah, Chtorrans themselves—we find that there is a pronounced tendency toward voraciousness, as if all of these life forms have evolved in a much more competitive ecology, not only surviving, but succeeding in that environment. Here on Earth, without their natural predators—all the checks and balances of a stable ecology—these life forms cannot help but run wild. We're seeing it happen all over the planet.

"We expect to find that *none* of these creatures are harmless to the Terran ecology—*especially* not the ones that *look* harmless. They're the ones that represent the biggest danger, because they're the ones we're *most* likely to underestimate. We have one hundred and fifty-four new species identified, and there are probably a lot more that we haven't yet discovered. And that's because we don't have the people. For all practical purposes, most of the world's ecological maintenance agencies have ceased to exist. And that leaves us particularly vulnerable to this kind of ecological infestation—twice over. Once because we don't know all of what's happening out there, and twice because even where we do have monitors in the field, we do not have the resources to respond. We need to rebuild those agencies—without delay! If we mobilize now, there is still the chance that we can create a strong response to the threat. If not, then the pressure on our ecology of those hundred and fifty-four various and voracious new species will surely shatter what remains of life as we know it on this planet.

"It is this simple: *our ecology is under attack by a far more successful ecology.* The home planet may be half a billion—I said *billion*—years older than the Earth—with all the corresponding advantages of extended evolution that implies for the member species of that planet's ecology. The implied age of the ecology and its host planet may also be a clue to *why* this infestation is occurring at all. The host planet may be wearing out. Or its sun may be going cold. What we are seeing may very well be an attempt by an intelligent species to outlive the death of its home system.

"And—if we are correct about the age of the Chtorran ecology, that is also why we will not be able to use terrestrial microorganisms against the Chtorran life forms. If the Chtorran life forms that we have seen are the products of an extra umpteen million years of evolution, then that implies that they would also have the cumulative immunities against every mutation of every germ that has evolved on their home planet. And that suggests that they would therefore have a greater spectrum of resistance to unknown microorganisms. Our germs are going to be no threat to them, because to them, our ecology is simpler—much simpler. We are the great reptiles looking at the appearance of grass and blossoming flowers and therapsids in our ecology and wondering what the hell is happening to our world. We have no *natural* defenses here."

She leaned out across the podium as if to look into the face of every one of us in that auditorium. "If we accept this hypothesis—and I do not see how we can avoid it—then the motive of the initiating agency is no longer in question. There is only one possible interpretation of the situation: *we are at war!* A war unlike anything ever experienced or even conceived in the history of this planet!" She stopped herself, as if she were embarrassed at her own intensity. She covered it with a drink of water, just a sip, then continued. "The problem is that we have no evidence of the agency behind this invasion. It has to be there, but where is it? Again we come back to the question: where are the *real* Chtorrans?" Dr. Zymph let the question hang there in the air for a moment. She looked over her notes and rubbed the bridge of her thick nose between thumb and forefinger.

She looked up again, and when she spoke, it was like a burst of gunfire. "Actually, we might be asking the *wrong* question. We have to look at the situation from an invader's point of view. I refer you now to the Skotak-Alderson studies on how to colonize a planet. In those papers, of course, the authors were talking about Venus and Mars, but the general principles they laid down are extensible to any world.

"Briefly, Skotak and Alderson broke the colonization process down into sections. Part I is Terraforming and Phase I involves producing an atmosphere that Terran organisms can survive in. Phase II begins with the introduction of selected life forms to create a favorable protoecology on the world to be colonized.

"Now, applying that to our own situation, obviously some intelligence somewhere is working its own Phase II here on Earth. They are *Chtorraforming* the planet, if you will.

"Just as we would need to establish grasslands to feed our cattle, cornfields to feed our chickens, forests to provide our paper and lumber and plastics, bees to pollinate the blossoms of our plants so we can have fruits and vegetables, so must our unknown Chtorran planners need to establish the equivalent support species necessary to the survival of their civilization. That is precisely what is happening now. And will continue to happen.

"Based on a weighted Skotak-Alderson simulation, the infestation of the Earth will occur in three, perhaps four, distinct stages. Each stage will see a specific level of species support established before the next level appears. In other words, they won't bring in the Chtorran equivalent of coyotes until the Chtorran rabbits are fat, and they won't bring in the Chtorran rabbits until the Chtorran pastures are green—or in this case, purple—and they won't plant the pastures until the Chtorran earthworms have softened the ground. That puts us at a disadvantage, because we'll be seeing each species out of context, not knowing where each one fits in the larger pattern. It'll be as difficult as trying to extrapolate the rest of the symphony, when all you have is the sheet music for the tympanist and the third trombone.

"That's why we can't give you the hard answers yet. What facts we do have are still unconnected. We can only give you the larger pattern that all the facts point to. This infestation of the Earth is their way of clearing the land. It's the easiest way to deal with the local residents—clear them out before you move in. We're supposed to be long gone before the new tenants arrive. If you'll pardon an unpleasant metaphor, what we are experiencing is the Chtorran version of a slum clearance. A neighborhood improvement project—"

She pointed to the screen behind her. It lit up with slides of the nightwalker, the millipedes, the sea sludge, the red kudzu, the stingfly, the puffball creature, the pipe cleaner bug and a whole bunch of other things I didn't recognize. Dr. Zymph said, "—and these are the *shock troops*—the advance men for a highly competitive ecology; these are the bugs and beasties that are intended to soften up this planet for the rest of the ecology to follow. Let me say it again: the present infestation is only the first wave of a much larger and *meaner* infestation still to come. What comes next are *the creatures that eat these!*"

She bent to her notes for a moment, frowning, then looked up at us again. Her expression was grim. "Don't be misled by those who would minimize the situation. We are not going to find any *easy* controls for this or later infestations. We do not have the necessary competition on this planet. We human beings may not even be competitive enough, *ruthless and vicious enough,* to muster the necessary effort. I hope I'm wrong. But I don't think I am." She paused a moment to let that sink in.

"We must recognize from the very beginning that our natural defenses are not going to work. Our only possible countermeasures will be developed by finding the weaknesses within the Chtorran ecology. We must discover the interrelationships of these creatures and sabotage them in any way we can. We must use this invading ecology *against itself!* We must start today! It will not be an easy task! It will require a massive mobilization—the complete and total mobilization of every human being on this planet! And we must begin it *immediately!*"

She stopped to wipe her forehead. She was beginning to show the strain of what must have been for her a very difficult task. I was beginning to suspect something from the audience reactions around me. These delegates hadn't come here to be frightened out of their wits, but that was exactly what she was trying to do. From their continual disturbed murmuring, I guessed that they had come with the idea that they were going to be reassured that everything was under control—we just need an increase in next year's appropriations, no problem, and then we can all go home, back to our newly claimed wealth. Only it wasn't working out that way.

Dr. Zymph was talking about the end of the world. And I could see the hostility on some of the faces of her listeners.

She was saying, "—I will not try to soften this for you, because I do not think the dangers can be understated. We are facing *extinction.*

"We are *not* being invaded," she said. *"Not yet.*

"But—we are *going to be invaded.*

"How soon it will happen, we don't know. How long this phase will last, we don't know. What kind of creatures have initiated it, we don't know. What kind of creatures will appear next, we don't know. But I promise you—we *will* find out. If we live.

"It is inevitable. *We are going to be invaded.* By something.

By the next level of this ecology. By the life forms that feed on these. And whatever comes, whatever form it takes, will be umpteen times more competitive—meaner, nastier and more vicious—than the things we're seeing now. What you see up there"—and she pointed toward the screen again, her arm stretched up and back, her finger stabbing like a pistol at the last of her slides, the gaping maw of a full-sized crimson Chtorran—"is just a candle before the firestorm!"

And with that she was through. She did not say, "Thank you," but it was clear that she was finished. She switched off her clipboard and strode from the stage.

There was no applause.

Twenty-One

DR. ZYMPH'S remarks had not gone over well. You could feel the resentment. The audience boiled out of the auditorium like a nest of hornets. Their voices rising shrilly, they clustered into angry knots. Small arguments were breaking out all over, some erupting into shouting matches.

"—outrageous!" fumed one little man, shoving rudely past me. He was dark-skinned, he wore an expensive suit and he had a thick Middle-East accent. "Lies and propaganda! Next we're going to be told that the only answer is a military one! But my government isn't going to buy their horror stories! They're using this as an excuse for their own rearmament—" The rest was lost in the hubbub.

"I'm telling you she did not!" A tall, bald man with glasses was surrounded by a score of other scientists. "If anything, this was the toned-down version! If there's been *any* misstatement in the facts, it's been on the side of caution!"

The roar and buzz of a thousand separate voices swirled in the air above the lobby. A large crowd surrounded a huge fat man and a small loud one who were alternately booming and sniping at one another—a duel between a foghorn and a magpie. I couldn't get close enough to hear what they were saying, and the spirited reactions of their listeners were drowning out the meaning, leaving only the shredded sounds of their voices.

Behind me, someone else was preaching; I turned to see a bulldozer-shaped woman backing a nervous-looking man up against a corner. "—and we have the papers to prove it! Have you read them yet? No? I'll send you copies. Marsha got a letter from the man himself, saying how impressed he was by her volume—"

I faded sideways, almost into the center of another conversation, a very quiet one. The speaker was a well-mannered black man, very soft-spoken. His listeners were a group of reporter types, each one holding his or her recorder out like a shield. ". . . The people have had enough bad news. They want to hear something good for a change. Of course, Dr. Zymph's remarks are not going to be popular—I expect to see a lot of resistance. But now let me add this. If the threat *is* real, you can be sure that the American people will shoulder their fair share of the responsibility. We'll handle it."

I'd heard enough. I headed out toward the lounge area. I was confused at the reaction of the delegates—didn't they realize?—and angry at them as well. I stood in the middle of them and fumed. I would have liked to have stuffed a few of them into the nearest Chtorran in full view of their colleagues. That would change some minds, all right!

I was still hesitating, standing in the middle of the crowd and wondering what to do next, when I heard my name called. A hand was waving at me from halfway across the lobby. Ted's. I began working my way over to him. He was standing with a short, barrel-shaped man who was wearing a dark suit and a frown; he looked constipated, perpetually glaring out at the world through thick-lensed horn-rimmed glasses. "This is Martin Miller," Ted said, "managing director of the Erewhon Project."

"Oh," I said. I looked around. "Um, what happened to Dinnie?"

Ted shrugged. "I dunno. We got separated. No problem."

"I thought you two were, ah . . ."

"Huh? You've gotta be kidding!"

"Then what was that business about eleven orgasms?"

Ted put his hands on my shoulders and looked me straight in the eye. "Jim, trust me. Someday, you'll know this for yourself—when you finally manage to lose that legendary virginity of yours—but until then, take my word for it: *it is impossible even for a normal healthy male in the peak of physical condition to come eleven times in one night.*" And then he added, "I know—I've tried. But the most I've ever managed was seven. And it wasn't with Dinnie."

"She seemed to think so."

"Jim, I am telling you the truth. I only came once. And I had to think of raw liver to do even that. Let her believe what she wants."

"Then why the hell did you—"

"Shh! Keep your voice down! I'm gonna teach you one of the secrets of success. If you need to get to know a great number of people in a hurry—especially important people—find yourself the most ambitious social climber you can, and flatter her. Or him. You can get into a lot of otherwise closed doors that way. Look, you don't mind, do you?" He had slipped one arm around my shoulder and turned me sideways away from Miller. "This could be very big. For *both* of us. He's not even twenty-five yet and he's making multimillion-casey decisions. I'll talk to you later, all right?"

"Huh—? But you called me!" But Ted had already turned back to his conversation. Something about flash-doming urban tracts for future redevelopment. Miller was explaining how preservation grants would allow them to claim large areas of already developed but abandoned property, and Ted was babbling about getting the Reclamation Office to foot most of the bill. I didn't think either one was hearing a word the other was saying.

"Listen, you've got to stop seeing it as a set of political moves," the woman behind me was saying. She was speaking to a small cluster of Fourth-World delegates. She looked deceptively friendly. Her face was framed with dark curls and her mouth looked like a kiss looking for a place to happen. Her nametag said S. DORR. "I understand your concerns, I really do. Your governments are justifiably afraid that the United States is using this ecological infestation as an excuse for rebuilding its military strength. And certainly, that would be a legitimate concern under any ordinary circumstances. But these are *not* ordinary circumstances. You heard Dr. Zymph's presentation." Her badge identified her as a deputy ambassador to the United Nations. She spoke calmly and with authority. "Perhaps you've seen the reports, perhaps not, but the United States is the only nation left on this planet that can still muster the human resources necessary to meet this challenge. If you don't allow the passage of the Allowance Act, you're hurting yourself as much as us. These are the hard, cold facts—Europe is in ruins, barely surviving; Africa is at war with itself; most of South America is out of communication—all we know about are a few major cities; Russia's in turmoil; and we have no idea how bad the situation is in China. At least the United States still has a workable military organization. That's because this country did *not* mobilize its military for civilian population control during the plagues. We were forbidden to mobilize, so we kept our units isolated and as a result most of them survived. We now represent a reservoir of ability that the international community of nations desperately needs to draw upon—*must* draw upon—*despite the fact* that it would require the one thing that a majority of nations in the U.N. are most opposed to: an extraordinary American military reconstruction! But that's what's needed if we are to mount realistic opposition to this invasion." She held up a hand to forestall an interruption. "Please—I need to make the point understood. What we intend is *not* a military campaign in the traditional sense of armament and mobilization—there simply isn't the manpower for that—but rather a worldwide call to purpose with the same sense of discipline and urgency that are the hallmarks of a successful military operation. We would use the existing structure of the United States Civilian Operations Corps as a foundation on which to build our proposed worldwide ecological defense—because it's there and it's ready to go to work, and we don't have the time to spare making everything politically satisfactory for all concerned parties.

"We know that several members of your delegation were upset by Dr. Zymph's remarks, but my government is prepared to stand behind them. We are also prepared to share our knowledge freely. Your scientists are welcome to verify our facts; we're sure that they'll come to the same conclusions."

Her audience listened politely and patiently, but when she finished, the leader of the group spoke up. His English was thickly accented, but his words were blunt. "And if we don't do as you wish—what then? You go ahead and do it anyway, right? Who is to stop you now? Who has the power to stop anybody anymore? So what you're asking is not permission, not even cooperation—but approval. I cannot see my government granting that, Ms. Ambassador. I cannot see *any* government going out on that limb."

The woman flushed. Was it anger or embarrassment? Her tone of voice was too deliberately calm. "Dr. T!Kai, you disappoint me. If the United States were able to do this alone, we would already be in the process of doing it—that is how serious we consider this situation. But we are not able to do this alone; that is the purpose of this special conference, to demonstrate the scale of the problem and to call for worldwide cooperation—"

He interrupted her. "I find a flaw in that reasoning, Comrade Deputy Ambassador. First you tell us that we are not capable, that only the United States is capable. Now you tell us that you cannot do this without us. Which is it, please? You cannot have it both ways?"

This time, it *was* obvious. She was angry. "Dr. T!Kai, you are supposed to be a man of science, a visionary among your own people. You have even been called the mastermind of the African social revolution. We have been putting facts before you for three days now. We have many more facts to put before you. Please listen to them. *Realize what they mean.* If you have any questions at all, the entire staff of the National Science Center is at your disposal. You've seen the live specimens—if you need to see them again, it can be arranged. But *please* hear what we are trying to tell you!"

He looked at her calmly and said, "I am hearing. I am hearing all too well." He shook his head. "What I hear are excuses and justifications. I do not want to hear any more. Excuse me, please." He gestured to his retinue, and the group of them turned away and moved off down the hall.

Deputy Ambassador Dorr looked after them, tears welling up

in her eyes. She mouthed a phrase that looked like *Damn fools!* Then she caught me looking at her and she smiled with embarrassment. She said, "You weren't supposed to hear that."

I said, "I've seen the Chtorrans. You're right."

"Yes," she said. She didn't look happy about it. "But this isn't about being right."

Twenty-Two

WHEN THE conference resumed, there were some conspicuously empty places in the auditorium. I wasn't the only one who noticed; behind me, I heard someone say, "Good. Now maybe we can get something accomplished."

I found a seat closer to the front this time. Almost immediately, two MP-types dropped into the empty places on my left and a narrow-looking scientist type with curly black hair, glasses and a big nose plopped himself down on my right. He was carrying a clipboard. Funny—there were a lot of people carrying clipboards today; most of them looked like they were part of the cadre that was running this operation. Professional, determined and grim. The foreign delegates had a more casual air, and they had secretaries and aides with them instead of clipboards—an almost ostentatious display of wasted labor.

Dr. Olmstead called the conference back to order then and introduced the next speaker, Dr. Indri Kwong from the Asian Control Center. Dr. Kwong was very thin and very old. He wore one of those quasi-military suits that all those Asian officials like to wear. And he was tiny; they had to lower the podium for him.

There was something wrong with his right arm—he kept his hand tucked into his pocket and used only his left.

He fumbled around with his notes for a moment, then began. "Is that screen working? Ah, yes—good. Thank you." His English was almost too good—he spoke in precisely clipped phrases. "Thank you. Thank you for inviting me to address this conference. But if you will forgive the presumption of an old man, it is entirely appropriate that this section be the responsibility of the Asian Control Center. We were not only the first to isolate and identify specimens of the Chtorran gastropedes, but we have also compiled the greatest record of experience with these creatures. I wish to point out, however, that the term 'gastropede' is a misnomer. The creatures are only superficially sluglike under their fur. They actually have many small pairs of legs—so, if anything, they are giant, pink, fur-covered caterpillars."

He stopped then and paged slowly through his notes. I thought it was strange that he was using hard copies instead of a clipboard or a terminal, particularly because of the extra burden of having only one hand to manipulate the pages with.

"May I have the first slide, please? Ah, thank you. This is the first public presentation of these photographs, and we believe them to be the best set of photos yet obtained. Perhaps I should take a moment to present the background here. It has been only recently discovered that the mountainous regions of Manchuria are the site of a rather heavy infestation of gastropedes and associated ecology. On somewhat short notice we organized a small caravan of armored vehicles and airlifted them into the area. They were able to send out the following pictures before contact was lost. I wish to point out that the loss of the caravan does not necessarily imply that the gastropedes reacted with hostility to the human presence. The area is also known to be a staging site for several well-organized bandit gangs—"

"Hmp," muttered one of the MPs on my left. "They won't let him admit they've got a rebellion on their hands. Those are probably guerrillas."

"—and it's equally possible the caravan may have been attacked by one or more of these gangs."

I looked at the MP, and whispered, "How come everybody is so reluctant to admit that the worms are dangerous?"

"Eh?" He looked annoyed at me, but before he could answer, the curly-haired fellow on my right shushed us both.

Dr. Kwong was saying, "The evidence of these pictures should effectively dispel several of the more pernicious rumors that the creatures feed on human flesh. As you can see here—ah, yes, here's the shot—this particular individual is stripping the bark off a tree. During this entire sequence of photos—until the creature realized it was being observed—it felled several small saplings and ate most of the smaller branches and leaves. Later on, other individuals were seen to duplicate this behavior."

Huh? But what about—

I shut my mouth and listened.

Dr. Kwong adjusted his glasses on his nose and looked out over the audience. "We do not dispute that there have been attacks on humans, but we do believe now that such incidents are atypical. Not all tigers are maneaters either. A tiger has to learn that a man is easy to kill. Um . . . let me digress here. A tiger perceives that a human being is larger than he actually is because a man stands erect and seems to tower over the tiger. The tiger's perception of the man's height overrules his perception of the size of the man's body. So there is probably the element of, say, surprise for the tiger that a human being is easier to kill than he might have thought. But even that is not enough to turn a tiger into a man-eater. Human flesh does not taste good to the average predator—particularly the big cats. No, the tiger has to have a susceptibility, a *need,* before it can turn into a man-eater. Salt is one of its primary needs. A lack of it is usually enough to turn the tiger into an enemy. We suspect that the gastropedes that have attacked human beings may be suffering from a similar kind of dietary deficiency and human flesh may inadvertently be one of the sources for whatever the element is that they need."

Another picture came up on the screen. Obviously a telephoto shot. A small Chtorran carrying a sapling across the ground.

"We suspect that the natural behavior of the creatures is closer to that of the North American beaver. This colony was observed for quite some time performing a very pastoral set of behaviors. As you can see here, they are in the process of damming a small stream.

"This is one of the larger Chtorran settlements that the team discovered. Notice that there are three domes here, and an equal number of domes still under construction—"

"Those are corrals," I said. I folded my arms across my chest. Dr. Kwong didn't see that the Chtorrans were predatory, so he obviously couldn't recognize their corrals for what they were.

The curly-haired man on my right gave me a look. "You know something?"

"Damn right I do."

"Better keep it to yourself. This isn't the place." He didn't intend it angrily, but I didn't want to hear it.

Dr. Kwong was saying, "—we do find it interesting that the Chtorran gastropedes come three to a nest. Never more than that—"

"Excuse me, sir," somebody said, standing up. It was me.

Heads swiveled to look at me. Dr. Kwong stopped in mid-phrase, unable to ignore me. He blinked twice and said, "I beg your pardon?"

"Have you ever found *four* Chtorrans in a nest?"

Dr. Kwong looked mildly annoyed. "Young man, I just finished saying that there were *never* more than three."

"Are you *sure* about that?"

"Young man, what is the purpose?"

"I'm sorry, sir. But they do come four to a nest. I've seen it."

Beside me, the curly-haired man was tugging at my sleeve. "*Sit down!*" he hissed. I ignored him.

Dr. Kwong wasn't angry—just surprised that someone would display the incredibly bad manners to interrupt him. "Are you arguing with me, young man?"

"No, sir. I'm correcting you. I've seen it. Four worms—Chtorrans—in a nest. I was there."

"I see. Young man, I am the Director of the Asian Control Center. We have a network of observers that spans the largest continent on this planet. This is the first time I have ever heard of a fourth Chtorran in a nest. So perhaps you can understand my reluctance to accept this information. Particularly in *these* circumstances. I'm sure your story merits investigation. Perhaps some anomaly has occurred, but this is neither the time nor the place, so if you would resume your seat, I might continue—"

Something brittle snapped. "If *this* isn't the place, then *where the hell is?* I have information! I saw this myself." I said it loudly, and there was anger in my voice. "There was a hut and a corral and the corral was full of millipedes and the hut was full of eggs. And when the Chtorrans came out of the hut, *there were four of them.*"

By now, the people around me were calling for me to sit down, but I ignored them. Curly-hair was slumped in his seat, one hand over his eyes.

Dr. Kwong motioned away a concerned aide. "No, no, let him be—I can handle him." Everything he said was amplified by the PA system, whether he faced the microphone or not. He said to me, "Young man, may I ask, on what do you base your knowledge? What is your credential?"

"United States Army. Sir. My name is James Edward McCarthy, and I hold the rank of corporal."

Somebody behind me snorted. Somebody else called, "That's as low as they have left. They can't find anyone willing to be a private anymore."

My mouth opened again and said, "United States Army, Special Forces Operation. I was assigned as an exobiologist and an observer."

"Special Forces?" There was something odd about the way he repeated it.

"Yes, sir."

"And your duties involved . . . ?"

"I was on a reconnaissance mission and on a Chtorran-hunting mission."

"A *what—?*"

"Uh—to say it in plain English—which is something nobody else around here has done yet—we went out to burn some worms. And we killed three of them. And then the fourth one came out and killed my friend. And I had to burn them both."

"I beg your pardon? Did you say *burn?*"

"Yes, I did."

He was leaning forward intently. "What do you mean, 'burn'?"

"Burn! Flamethrowers, sir. Napalm. Jellied gasoline. It's the only thing that'll stop a worm fast." There was a startled reaction from the audience, loud gasps and cries.

Dr. Kwong was holding up his hand. "Please, please—may we have some order? Napalm? Are you sure?"

"Yes, sir. I had to kill one of the best men I've ever known. It was the only way. I wouldn't lie about a thing like that."

"You used *napalm?* Napalm is an illegal weapon!"

"Yes, sir. I know that. I raised the same objection myself. But you missed the point, sir. There were *four* worms in that hut!"

"Young man, there are some very good reasons why napalm was outlawed as a weapon of war. If you'll wait a moment, I'll show you one of them—" He was fumbling with his jacket. One of his aides stepped up to help him, but Dr. Kwong brushed him peevishly aside. He unzipped the tunic and dropped it to the floor, then he opened his shirt to reveal a withered right arm and a mass of white scar tissue that stretched from his neck to his waist, and probably a good way down his leg as well. He walked with a slight limp as he stepped around the podium. "Take a good look—this is what napalm can do to a human being. I was seven years old. United States soldiers came to my village, looking for the enemy. The enemy was long gone, but they burned the village anyway. And most of the villagers too. I have lived all of my life carrying the scars of your country's crime against mine.

"Many other nations had to suffer the same ravages to discover sanity in the ashes—and it took a long time for it to happen—but the peace-loving nations of this world finally enforced a lasting peace against the imperialistic savageries of the United States. Napalm was the most pernicious of the American weapons to be restricted. There are too many thousands of crippled men and women who can tell you why. Look and see what it does to the human body, young man. There is no easy healing here—there is no healing at all, only scars. And now—you stand there in your ignorance, your bare-faced naïveté, and dare to tell me that the United States is using such weaponry again? In disregard of all the treaties and United Nations mandates?"

"That's not the issue!" I was screaming now. "You grandstanding son of a bitch! You think the worms are so goddamned friendly, why don't you go in and see for yourself? They have one here at the center! He's in a glass-walled room—why don't you go in and try hand-feeding him! Then you'll find out if they're man-eaters!"

"Sit down!" That was Dr. Olmstead, pointing at me and shouting through a bullhorn—where the hell had he gotten that?

Dr. Kwong was shouting back at me, "I've seen the specimen—and that's a feral animal. It has no inhibitions and only animal intelligence. It may be that the other creatures we've observed *do* have some intelligence. Had you let me finish, I would have discussed that point. We have been making attempts to establish contact with them, but since you and your cohorts have been burning every one of them you come in contact with, you've made it impossible for us. You're the ones who've made them into an enemy—you and your execrable military mind-set!"

Off to my right, one of the African delegates was standing and shouting now. "Don't be sidetracked! Let's deal with this napalm issue! The United States is in violation of—"

"What about the fourth Chtorran?"

"You can't bomb your way to peace," called someone else, and still another voice responded, "It's a helluva start!"

"Come on," the curly-haired man said, grabbing my arm. "You're getting out of here!" He gestured to the MPs. "That way—"

"Huh? What is this? You can't—"

"Shut up, stupid! You want to get out of here in one piece?" He pushed me roughly forward.

"Wait a minute! What about the fourth Chtorran—? Wait a minute!"

Twenty-Three

THE TWO MPs moved through the crowd like destroyers. One of them had my arm in a steel grip and was pulling me after him—I caught quick glimpses of roaring faces turning toward me, but I couldn't even shout. Curly-hair, holding my other arm in an equally painful vise, brought up the rear. We were out the side door of the auditorium so fast we could have been on rails.

"This way—" the MP said, jerking me sideways into a hallway. Behind us, I could hear the angry outcry rising. "Damn!" said curly-hair bitterly. "You just started a riot."

"Uh, sorry about that."

"Be smart for a moment. Shut up." To the MPs he said, "Tailor shop."

"Right." They grabbed me between them, one on each side—one hand under the armpit, the other under the elbow—and we *moved.* They held me like I was furniture; it didn't matter if I moved my feet or not to keep up—we *moved.* Curly took the lead, angling right into a dark service corridor, then left into a broom closet, opening up a door where no door should be.

We stepped through and there was silence. We were in darkness.

"Wait a minute." Curly was punching something into a wall terminal. Dim red ceiling lights came up and I could see we were in another corridor, only this one was featureless. To the MPs he said, "You can let go of him now. You, come with me."

I followed him into a small room. There were a desk and two chairs. He slapped his clipboard down onto the desk and sat down behind it. He pointed at the other chair and I sat down too. He opened a drawer and pulled out a pack of cigarettes, shook one out and lit it. He did not offer one to me.

So—this was to be an interrogation.

I remembered something I had seen in a movie. I leaned forward and shook a cigarette out of the pack for myself.

"I didn't say you could smoke."

"You didn't say I couldn't." I glared back at him.

He grinned abruptly. "It won't work. I saw the same movie."

I shrugged and stubbed the cigarette out. "I don't smoke anyway."

He didn't laugh. He let the grin fade and studied me for a moment, thoughtfully. At last he said, "You have something for me?"

"Huh?"

"You were trying to find me this morning, weren't you?" He tapped his chest.

"Huh?" And then I saw it. His name badge. WALLACHSTEIN. *"Oh!"* I said, realizing. "But the directory said you don't exist."

"You better believe it." His chair creaked alarmingly when he leaned back. "I'm not even here now. This is all a hallucination you're having. Now, I believe you have something for me?" He held out his hand.

I was still smarting. I folded my arms. "I want some answers first."

His hand was still outstretched. "Listen, stupid, you're in big trouble, so be a good boy for a while and maybe I can get you out of here quietly. Maybe." The air had gotten noticeably chillier.

"I didn't ask to be rescued from anything. You dragged me in here against my will—"

"You want to go back? That can be arranged too. Just give

me the package that Obie gave you, and Sergeants Kong and Godzilla will put you right back in the center of what you started. Although I think you'd be a lot better off with us. We did you a favor and you might want to say thank you."

"Yeah—and I might want to say 'fuck you' too! I'm getting really tired of all the 'oughts' and 'shoulds' and 'musts' that are being dropped on me. And all without explanations. Nobody ever explains anything. And then you get pissed off because I'm not following the rules! So fuck you! I was told that if I couldn't find you I should destroy the package. Well, I couldn't find you. You don't exist. Now, which way is out—?"

"Sit down, Jim," he said. "You made your point. Besides, the door's locked until I'm ready to unlock it."

It was his use of my name that stopped me.

He'd been expecting me. And something else—he'd purposely sat down next to me in the auditorium! And the MPs too! They'd had me bracketed since . . .

"How long?" I asked.

"How long till I unlock the door?"

"No. How long have you—whoever you are—been watching me?"

"Oh, that. Since about three minutes after you checked my name in the directory. You've been under surveillance ever since."

"The woman on my right—the one during Dr. Zymph's presentation?"

"Uh huh, and the two lieutenants on your left as well. I don't know what you're carrying, but Obie says it's important." He added, "I don't mind telling you that I'm curious to see what Obie thinks is too dangerous to send over a wire—even a secure and coded one." He leaned forward to drop his cigarette into an ashtray. "May I have it, please?"

I took a breath. I exhaled. "Yeah, I guess so."

He raised an eyebrow at me. "No more argument?"

"You called her Obie."

Wallachstein grinned. "You know something? You're not so stupid."

I pulled out the lockbox and passed it over to him. He turned it over and laid it face down on the desk. I didn't see exactly what he did with his fingers, but the back of it slid off, revealing a thin false bottom. There was a single memory clip inside. Wallachstein picked it out and dropped it into his jacket pocket as casually as if it were something he did every day; then he looked up and noticed my expression. "Something the matter?"

"Uh, I've never seen one like that."

"And you'll probably never see another one either."

"Can I ask why? The false bottom, I mean."

"Sure. These things aren't too difficult to break into, not for a skilled laboratory." He turned it over and slid it across. "Here. What's your birthday? Punch it in."

"My birthday?"

He nodded. I tapped it out on the keyboard and the box popped open. Inside was a package of fifty thousand-casey notes.

"Happy birthday," he said.

"Huh?"

"Courier fee. You got your message through without being killed. The money's unimportant. It's just a decoy, in case you lose the box. The wrong person opens it; he thinks that's what's being transported. Burn the paper wrapper—just in case they're not fooled by the money, there's a microdot on the wrapper. It's nothing but a very long random-number sequence. You could go crazy trying to decode it, because it won't. It's just hash. Another decoy. A practical joke, even—but the idea is to distract the enemy, draw him away from the real trick. We're all so marvelously subtle these days—on both sides—that no one stops to think there might be an easier way."

"Uh . . . sir . . . *the enemy?*"

"You're already met them. Out there." He pointed at the door. He dropped the money out of the box onto the table before me and slid the box into a desk drawer. "Go ahead, take it. Better spend it before it goes *completely* worthless."

"Uh, shouldn't I be discreet? I mean, won't people wonder where it came from?"

"Don't bother. Nobody else does. We're all stealing from the dead one way or another anyway. Nobody's going to question you." He picked up his clipboard and stood up, all in one motion. "I'm going to ask you to wait here while I go and see what's on this." He tapped his jacket pocket meaningfully. "You want coffee?"

"Yeah, thanks."

"Right." He was already out the door.

He'd given me a lot to think about. Just what was going on here? What had I stumbled into? And how was I going to get *out?*

I tried the door. He'd locked it behind him. I sat down again.

Then I got up and tried the drawers on the desk. They were locked too. I shrugged and went back to my chair. Then I wondered if I'd done something stupid. Did the walls of this room have eyes as well as ears? I hoped I hadn't picked my nose in front of one of their cameras.

The door to the room slid open and one of the two MPs came in carrying a tray. He closed the door behind him, crossed to the desk and set the tray down. He pushed it toward me: a pot of coffee, one cup, a cream pitcher, a sugar bowl and a spoon. He sat down in the chair behind the desk, folded his arms casually and leaned back in the chair. It complained loudly. He stared at me.

I poured myself a cup of coffee and tasted it carefully. *Ugh!* Had they sent all the way back to Sergeant Kelly's kitchen for this?

"Well. Here we are," I said. "Uh, are you Sergeant Kong or Sergeant Godzilla?"

He opened his mouth and said, "Shut up."

I shut.

It was a very uncomfortable half-hour. At least, it felt like a half-hour. We sat and glowered at each other the whole time.

At last Colonel Wallachstein came back. He motioned Sergeant Kong—or maybe it was Godzilla—out of the room with a jerk of his head and sat down at the desk again. He pushed the coffee tray to one side without even looking at it. He waited until the door was closed before he said. "I believe you. About the fourth Chtorran. You've had a rough time of it, haven't you?"

I shrugged. "Who hasn't?"

"You'd be surprised. The world's full of opportunists. Never mind. Obie says you're okay. She also asked me to honor the obligation. If I thought it appropriate."

"Obligation?"

"I think she may have mentioned it already. Every member

of the Special Forces not only has the right, but the obligation, to understand the responsibilities of his orders—"

"You mean I have the right to ask questions after all?"

He nodded. "And I have the responsibility to answer them."

"Well, it's about time. Yeah, I have a lot of questions. First of all, just what the hell is going on? Not just here, but out there? Why won't any of those bozos take the Chtorrans seriously? And—"

He held up a hand to slow me down. He waited until my questions petered out on their own. He looked unhappy. "I said, 'if I thought it appropriate.' I'm sorry, but I don't. Not yet. Maybe not at all. You're a real pain in the ass, you know that? Unfortunately . . ."

"Unfortunately *what?*"

He glanced at me wryly. "Unfortunately, you're a *smart* pain in the ass." He looked unhappy. He looked at his watch and looked even unhappier. "I don't know what to do with you. And I have to get back. I have to monitor something this afternoon. I hate to leave you hanging, but I don't have any choice—and I'm sorry, but it wouldn't be a good idea for you to go back to the conference. Not today, at least. There're a few people looking for you, and not too many of them are friendly. We still have to figure out how to handle this—what you started. Um, listen, I'll arrange for you to monitor the rest of the conference by remote, and we'll cover your disappearance for a couple of days too. At least until Tuesday when most of the foreign delegates are on their way out. I owe you that much at least. And maybe by then I'll have figured out what to do with you."

"Uh, don't I get any say in the matter?"

"Haven't you said enough today?"

"All I did was stand up and ask a question. I still haven't gotten any answers."

"Did it ever occur to you that there may not be any to give?" He stood up. "You wait here." And he exited again.

This time I didn't have to wait as long. The door slid open and Major Lizard Tirelli stuck her head in. "McCarthy?"

"Huh? Yeah—hi!"

She looked annoyed. "Come on," she said. I followed her out into the darkened hall and to the right. Now where were we going? The door was back the other way.

We stopped in front of an elevator alcove. The door slid open at our approach. I followed her in. There was only a single button on the control panel. She pressed it and the door closed. The elevator slid upward.

"Where are we going?"

"Thirteenth floor," she said.

"Huh? Hotels don't have thirteenth floors."

"This one does," she said. Her voice was brittle. Obviously, she didn't want to talk. At least, not to me.

I shut up and we rode the rest of the way in silence.

Twenty-Four

THE THIRTEENTH floor looked like any other floor of the hotel—except it only had *one* elevator door.

My dad had told me about controlled-access architecture a long time ago. I'd just never seen any firsthand. Apparently, the builders of this hotel had intended the architectural camouflage for business purposes, probably to provide a floor of private suites and offices for visiting dignitaries and other celebrities who needed tight security.

If someone were to notice that there was a physical gap between twelve and fourteen, and were to ask about it—and he'd probably have to walk the fire stairs to figure it out—he'd probably be told it was a "service area." Which it was, sort of. He just wouldn't be told what service. The purloined letter again. Like a lockbox with a false bottom.

I would bet, however, that the present occupants of the thirteenth floor were not the ones for which it had been originally intended. Or were they?

We stopped before a featureless gray metal door. Room 1313.

"Am I going to be locked in?" I asked.

Lizard ignored me as she slid the room card into the slot. She punched a number and the door slid open. She handed me the card. "You can change the combination if you want. You can leave if you want."

"But I thought—"

"What?"

"—that Colonel Wallachstein wanted me to wait."

"Who?"

"Colonel Wallachstein—the man who pulled me out of the auditorium and interrogated me and—"

She stepped close to me. "Listen, stupid. The man you're talking about doesn't exist. There's nobody in Denver by that name. Do you understand?"

No, I didn't. "Uh, I guess so. Can I ask something?"

She looked annoyed and impatient. "What is it?"

"What the hell is going on?"

"I can't answer that."

"Am I under arrest?"

"You're free to go any time you want. It just wouldn't be a good idea. There are people looking for you—some of them you wouldn't like very much."

"Oh. Then I'm being held in protective custody?"

"You're not being held at all."

"Then why am I here?"

"I don't know. It's not my job to answer your questions."

"Is *anyone* going to answer my questions? Or am I just going to be shoved from place to place until I'm out of everyone's way?"

"That sounds like a good idea. Oh, you can't phone out from here without clearance, but you can get room service."

"Which is the way out?"

"For you? Take the fire stairs up to fourteen or down to twelve and catch an elevator from there. But you won't be able to get back. My advice is for you to do exactly what you're told and wait here." She turned to go.

"Um—Major?"

She stopped and looked at me.

"Am I in trouble? I mean, should I be worried?"

I guess I was scared. I guess it showed in my voice, because she caught herself. A flicker of annoyance had started to cross her face, a reflex reaction to another stupid question, but then she realized the concern behind the question and softened. She said, "You didn't do anything that at least half a dozen other people didn't want to do. You just didn't know why you shouldn't have."

I felt the pain of embarrassment flooding into my face—of being identified as the guy who'd screwed things up. "Is anyone ever going to tell me?" I asked.

She wanted to go, I could see that, but instead she took my arm and dragged me into the room, closing the door behind us. "Sit down." She looked at her watch. "All right, I have time. You want coffee? No? Well, I do." She stepped over to the apartment's kitchenette and opened a cupboard. "You'd better enjoy your coffee today, Jim—there won't be much of it tomorrow."

"Huh?"

"Never mind. Listen—what did you major in?"

"Biology. Software. Humanity Skills. Problemantics. The usual."

"Right. Did you take any history?"

"Only the basic requirements."

"Damn." She was silent a moment. I didn't know if her outburst was because I hadn't taken any history or because she'd spilled some water. She turned back to me.

"Did you have a Global Ethics course?"

"Yeah. Everybody did. It was required study."

"Uh huh. Do you know why?"

"To prevent another Apocalypse."

"Right. What do you know about the Apocalypse?"

"Um, not a lot, I guess. Just what we were taught in class."

"Go on," she encouraged.

"Well—you sure you want to hear this?"

"I said, go on."

"Well—um, there was a war. In the Middle East. There are always wars in the Middle East, but this one got out of control. It was between Israel and I forget who, but there were a lot of other countries lined up against Israel. And there were African and Chinese mercenaries involved. And finally it got so bad that Israel had no choice but to threaten to use nuclear weapons. And finally they did."

"And then what happened?"

"The United States withdrew its support for Israel and Israel had to surrender."

"And?"

"Everybody was so scared at what had almost happened that they all went to Russia and signed the Moscow Treaties."

"Yeah." She looked skeptical and turned back to the coffee. "You want milk or sugar?" she asked as she poured. I shook my head. As she handed me the cup, she said, "That version is the one they teach in the schools—but it's so simplified, it's almost a fairy tale. Israel didn't drop those bombs. We did."

"Huh? But that's not—"

"Of course that's not. But the truth is a little less palatable. That was *our* war and we told Israel to drop those bombs, because we thought it would bring an end to the war. Well, it did—but not the way we thought it would. What they didn't tell you is that the President lost his nerve."

"Huh?"

"What did they teach you in class?"

I shrugged. "The way we heard it, there was a midnight Cabinet session and all of his advisors were arguing loudly back and forth about how many people would die in each exchange and whether or not our third-strike capability would survive, and the President was just sitting quietly at the end through all of this, puffing on his pipe like he always did. And finally, after several long hours, one of the Joint Chiefs of Staff summed it up by saying, 'The moral arguments are irrelevant here. The war is *inevitable.*' And that's when the President said, *'Like hell it is!'* "

"Yeah, that's the story. But it's not true. That is, it's only half true. The part you don't hear is about the ultimatum that the Soviet ambassador had handed him just that afternoon. If Israel launched any more nuclear weapons against Soviet allies, the Soviet Union would view those attacks as originating in the United States, and would respond accordingly. It was the same ultimatum that John F. Kennedy handed Nikita Khrushchev in October of 1962, when Russian missiles were discovered in Cuba—and the Russians were aware of the irony of the situation. They used the exact same phrasing in their note."

"I never heard about this," I said.

"You weren't meant to—but that's what was on his mind during that meeting. That the other side had decided that all-out nuclear war was inevitable too."

"But, I always thought he was a hero."

Major Tirelli looked wistful. "So did I—I still do. And maybe he was—maybe it takes more guts to stay *out* of a war. But either way, we inherited the consequences of that decision."

I sipped at the coffee. It was hot. And bitter. I said, "What we were taught was that he made a speech, an extraordinary speech, in which he said that the responsibility had been handed to him whether or not the world should be plunged into Armageddon. And regardless of the morality of any other issue, this one fact remained uppermost in his mind: if it could be stopped, it had to be stopped, and he would do whatever was required of him to prevent the deaths of millions and millions of human beings. He said that by the act of using nuclear weapons, a nation disqualifies itself from the community of rational thought."

"I heard the speech," she said. "My parents made me stay up to hear it. But I didn't understand what it meant until later. That man went to Moscow, hoping that it would be seen as a gesture of sanity. Instead, they saw it as capitulation and forced him to accept a crippling peace, a debilitating compromise. The tragedy is he knew exactly what they had done to him. Oh, he looked like a hero—he was being hailed as a courageous man all over the world—but he knew what he had given away: America's right to protect her foreign interests. What do you think Pakistan was about? It was an attempt to reestablish the old prerogative. And it failed. This time it was the Chinese who handed us the ultimatum. And this time, the treaties were even more crippling. Do you know what the allies did to Germany after the First World War? They took away that nation's right to an army. That was what was done to us. The United States was told that our existence as a nation would continue only so long as we maintained no direct threat to any other nation on this planet. And the cooperation with that agreement would be monitored by an international committee."

"We never heard this," I said.

"I told you, you weren't meant to. It's a part of our history that we aren't very proud of, so officially, it doesn't exist—like all the other pieces of history we don't acknowledge."

I hid my reaction behind the coffee cup again. When I lowered it, I said, "Is that why the foreign delegates are so paranoid about the way we want to fight the Chtorrans?"

"Right. Very few foreign governments see the Chtorrans as the threat we do. The reasons are varied. Some of them don't see science as anything more than a way to make the crops grow bigger. Others don't think the Chtorrans will be a threat next year because they aren't a threat this year. Most of the people we're dealing with don't even comprehend the scale of death produced by the plagues—so how can they comprehend that the plagues are only a small part of a much larger infestation?"

"Then Dr. Zymph was right?"

"If anything, she was understating the case. You've had enough direct experience with the Chtorr to know what they're like. But try to tell that to someone who's never seen one in action. They won't comprehend it. They don't want to."

"Doesn't that get frustrating?"

Lizard nodded wearily, and grinned. "Incredibly so!" She sipped at her coffee, then said, "Dr. Zymph knew that was how the delegates would react. She was willing to have it. We have to keep putting the facts out, but it happens every time the subject is raised in the international community. The delegates go crazy. They see the Chtorrans only as America's latest rationalization for rearmament. Listen, we're already rearming ourselves. We don't *need* a rationalization." She shook her head sadly. "But they're frightened; that's what it really is. Just about every nation on this planet is in trouble of one sort or another—there isn't one of them that isn't vulnerable to the first serious military threat that occurs. They're not concerned about the Chtorrans because they've never been bitten by one—but they're sure as hell scared of American military power, because they're still carrying scars. At least we're a threat they can comprehend, so they're displacing their fear and their anger onto us." Lizard looked at me. "Now do you see what kind of cow pasture you stepped into?"

"Ugh," I said.

She glanced at her watch. "I gotta go—but look, you can use the terminal here to tap into the History section of the Library of Congress. You might find it interesting. You probably don't know it, but as a member of the Special Forces, your security clearance is high enough to get you access to most of what you need to know."

"I didn't know that."

"Then you've got an interesting afternoon ahead of you. It'll be a while before anyone can get back to you. Be patient, okay? There are some decisions that have to be made first—"

Twenty-Five

I HADN'T thought about Whitlaw in a while.

I wondered if he was still alive. I'd never given it any thought before; I couldn't imagine him dead. I'd always just assumed he would be one of the survivors.

But then again, I couldn't imagine Shorty being dead either. Or my dad. And they were—so what did it matter whether I could imagine it or not? The universe was going to do what it damn well wanted regardless how I or anyone else felt about it.

Whitlaw ran his class the same way. He didn't care how we felt either. "You don't get to vote," he used to say. "You already did when you put yourself in this class. You belong to me, body and mind, until I'm ready to turn you loose upon the world."

The class was a two-semester unit. Toward the end of the first semester, Whitlaw abruptly asked, "Does anyone here know *why* this is a required course?"

"If we don't take it, we don't graduate." That was one of the mindless lurches who usually roosted in the last row of seats. A couple of his buddies laughed.

Whitlaw eagle-eyed the hulk over the heads of the rest of us. He gave him a thorough half-second of examination and then said, "That isn't the answer I was looking for, but considering the source, I guess it's the best I could have expected. Anyone else?"

No. No one else.

"It'll be the first question on your final exam," he prompted. Someone groaned.

Whitlaw stumped back to his desk. I wondered if his limp were bothering him. He didn't look happy. He opened the loose-leaf binder he used as his source book and paged through it silently, until he found the page he was looking for. He studied it with a thoughtful frown. After a moment, he looked up again. "No takers?"

No. We'd gotten too smart for that.

"Too bad. All right—we'll try it this way then: How many of you think it's appropriate for a population to rebel against tyranny?"

A few hands went up immediately. Then a few more, tentatively, as if terrified that they were volunteering to be on the front lines. Then a few more. I raised my hand. Pretty soon almost everyone had. Whitlaw didn't wait to see if it would be unanimous. He pointed at one of the abstainers. "How about you? Don't you think so?"

"I think you have to define your terms. You're being too general. What tyranny? Which one?"

Whitlaw straightened and eyed the fellow with narrowed eyes. "Are you on the debate team? No? Well, you ought to consider it. You're doing everything but confronting the issue. So all right, I'll make it easy on you—" He closed his book.

"—Let's say this room is the nation of Myopia. I'm the government. You're the citizens. Now, you know governments are not free. So the first thing I'm going to do is collect taxes. I want one casey from each of you." He started striding down the aisles. "Give me a casey. No, I'm not joking. These are your taxes. Give me a casey. You too. Sorry, I don't accept checks or paper money. What? That's your lunch money? Gee, that's tough, but your government's needs come first."

"But that's not fair!"

Whitlaw stopped, his hand full of coins. "Who said that? Take him out and execute him for sedition!"

"Wait a minute! Don't I get a fair trial?"

"You just had one. Now shut up. You've been executed." Whitlaw kept collecting. "Sorry, I want exact change. You don't have it? Don't worry about it. In your case, I'll levy a four-casey surcharge. Consider it a penalty for paying your taxes with paper money. Thank you. Thank you—fifty, seventy-five, a casey, thank you. All right, I've got forty-eight caseys here. This'll buy me a good lunch. Everybody be sure to bring another casey tomorrow. I'll be collecting taxes every day from now on."

We looked at each other nervously. Who was going to be first to complain? Wasn't this illegal—a teacher taking money from his class?

A tentative hand. "Uh, sir . . . your majesty?"

"Yes?"

"Uh, can I ask a question?"

"Mm, depends on the question."

"Can we ask what you're going to do with our money?"

"It's not your money anymore. It's mine."

"But it was ours to start with—"

"—and now it's mine. I'm the government." He slid open his desk drawer and dropped the coins loudly into it. "Eh? Your hand is still up?"

"Well, it just seems to me—to all of us—"

"To *all* of you?" Whitlaw looked at us with raised eyebrows. "Is this an insurrection that I see before me? I guess I'd better hire an army." He stumped to the back of the room, pointing at the huskiest boys in the class. "You, you and, ah, yes, you too. And you. Come up front. You're now in the army." He opened the drawer and scooped up coins. "Here are two caseys for each of you. Now, don't let any of this rabble near the royal palace."

The four boys looked uncertain. Whitlaw shoved them into position between himself and the class. "Now then—you were saying?"

"Mr. Whitlaw!" Janice MacNeil, a tall black girl, stood up. "All right! You've made your point. Now give everybody back their money—" Janice was in student government.

Whitlaw peered between the shoulders of two of his tallest "soldiers." He grinned. "Uh uh," he said. "This game is being played for keeps. Now, what are you going to do about it?"

Janice didn't fluster. She said, "I'll go to a higher authority."

Whitlaw was still grinning. "There aren't any. This class is autonomous. See that plaque on the wall? That's the charter of the Federal Education System. You've been in this classroom nearly every day for eighteen weeks, and I'll bet you still haven't read it, have you? Too bad—because that's the contract you agreed to when you entered this classroom. I have total authority over you."

"Well, of course, I *understand* that!" she snapped. "But I'm talking about the *real world* now. You have to give us back our money!"

"You *don't* understand." Whitlaw grinned at her. "This *is* the real world. Right here. And I *don't* have to. I am empowered by the federal government to do whatever is necessary to fulfill the course requirements. And that *includes* taxes—if I so deem it necessary."

She folded her arms. "Well, we don't have to cooperate."

Whitlaw shrugged. "Fine. I'll have you arrested."

"What? You'll send me to the principal's office?"

"No, I mean arrested, as in read you your rights and throw you in the slammer, the lockup, the hoosegow, durance vile, the Bastille, the Tombs, the Tower of London, Devil's Island and Alcatraz—do I make myself clear?"

"You're kidding."

"No, I'm not. Look it up."

"But that's not fair!"

"So what? You already agreed to it, so what are you complaining about?" He tapped two of his troops. "Throw her out of here—and that other fellow too, the one we executed earlier. They're automatically flunked." Whitlaw's army didn't look happy about it, but they started down the aisle.

Janice looked genuinely scared, but she scooped up her books and clipboard and went.

"You'll wait next door until the period is over," Whitlaw said.

"Anyone else want to question the authority of this government?"

No. Nobody else did.

"Good." Whitlaw sat down and put his feet up on his desk. "I'm flunking everyone who opens his mouth out of turn." He picked up a book and an apple, opened the book and started reading. Periodically, he would take a loud bite from his apple, audibly reminding us of his presence.

The army looked uncertain. "Should we sit down, sir?"

"Of course not. You're on duty."

The rest of us exchanged glances. What was the point of this? The fellow to whom Whitlaw had recommended joining the debate team leaned over and whispered to a friend, "He's daring us to try something."

"Well, you try. I don't want to get thrown out."

"But don't you see, if we all organize—"

Whitlaw stood up suddenly, glowering. "What's that? Sounds like subversion to me!" He stepped forward and grabbed the debater by his shirt, pulling him out of his seat. "I won't have that!" He dragged the boy out of the room.

In the brief moment that he was gone, there was bedlam.

"The man's a loonie—"

"—This is crazy—"

"—Can't we do something?"

I stood up. "Listen! We outnumber him! We don't have to let him get away with this."

"Shut up, Jim! You're just gonna get us all in worse trouble!"

"Let him talk—"

"You got an idea, Jim?"

"Well, no . . . but . . ."

Whitlaw came back in then, and I slid back into my seat fast enough to feel the heat.

Whitlaw turned to his troops. "What kind of army are you? I leave the room for less than a minute, and I come back to find rabble-rousers preaching sedition in the aisles! I want you to arrest and expel every one who complained—or you'll get thrown out too!"

There were five of us.

"Is that all?" Whitlaw bellowed. "If you missed anyone, I'll have your heads!"

The army looked scared. After a moment's whispered conference, they picked three more people and all eight of us trooped out. "But I didn't even say anything!" Joey Hubre looked close to tears. "Tell him!" he appealed to his twin.

"You do," shouted Whitlaw, "and you go too. In fact, you'd better go anyway—you're probably both trouble!"

There were twelve of us in the next-door classroom. We sat glumly looking at each other. Confused, puzzled and very hurt. We could hear Whitlaw bellowing. And then, abruptly, there was silence. A moment after that, three more exiles joined us.

"What'd he do? Execute the class?"

"Naw—he declared a national silence," said Paul Jastrow. "That's why he threw us out. I passed a note. He said I was publishing treason."

"What's he trying to prove?" complained Janice.

"Tyranny, I guess. That's what started this, remember?"

"Well, what are *we* supposed to do about it?"

"Isn't it obvious? We're supposed to rebel!"

"Oh, sure! We can't even open our mouths to complain! How are we going to organize?"

"*We* can organize," I said. "In here. We'll form an army of liberation. The other class members will support us."

"You sure of that? He's got them so terrified they're pissing in their pants."

"Well, we've got to try," said Hank Chelsea, standing up. "I'm for it."

"Count me out," said Jastrow.

I stood up. "I think it's the only way."

Janice stood up. "I—I don't like this, but I'll go along with it because we've got to show him he can't do this to us."

Two of the other boys stood up, and one of the girls. "Come on, John. Joey?"

"Uh uh. I don't want to get yelled at anymore."

"Aren't you angry?"

"I just want my money back."

"Paul?"

"He'll just throw us out again."

"Wait a minute, Jim." That was Mariette. "Just what is it you want us to do anyway? What's your plan?"

"We go in there and declare the dictatorship over."

"Oh, sure, and then he yells at us some more and his army throws us out again. He's hired two more thugs."

"They're not thugs, they just look like it."

"All football players are thugs to me. Anyway, there's six of 'em now. So what are you gonna do about that?"

Six people started to answer her at once, but Hank Chelsea

held up his hand and said, "No, wait—she's right! We need a plan! Look, try this. We open all three doors of the room at once—that startles everybody. Then, before he can say anything, the girls have got to go for the army—no, listen to me. I'm betting that they won't hit the girls. What you do is put one girl on each soldier. She gives him a big hug and a kiss and tells him to join us—"

"Yeah, and then what?"

"—and that we'll pay them *double* what he's paying them!"

"He's paying them three caseys each now."

"No, they'll join us. But only if each girl takes one boy. Grab his arm and start talking to him. Say whatever you have to, and don't let go until he agrees to join us."

"Yeah, right, Mr. Big Shot. So you get the women to do the dirty work. What are the men going to do?"

"We're going after the honcho and reclaiming the national treasury."

We debated the plan for a few more minutes, during which time two more exiles joined us. They agreed to join the revolution almost immediately and suggested some refinements to the attack. We were almost ready when Joey Hubre sniffled and said, "What if someone gets hurt? What about that?"

That stopped us for a moment, and we had to rethink our plan again. But Paul Jastrow said, "Well, what of it? This is war, isn't it?"

"No, he's right," said Hank. "Maybe Whitlaw wouldn't care if he hurt anyone, but we're supposed to be an army of liberation. We're not going to hurt anyone."

"Unless they ask for it," muttered Jastrow.

"No, not even then," snapped Hank.

"Who appointed you general? I didn't!"

"All right—" Hank put up his hands. "We'll take a vote—"

"No!" I said. "We have a plan. We're ready to go! Armies don't vote!"

"They do now!" said Jastrow.

"But not in times of war! Is there anyone who needs to vote?"

"Yeah, I want to go over this war plan again—"

"Oh, terrific! There goes the revolution! Let's have a parliamentary battle instead. Wait a minute, I've got a copy of *Robert's Rules of Order* here—"

"McCarthy, shut up! You're an asshole!"

"Yeah? Then why are you the one who's giving us shit?"

"Hey, wait a minute—we're being distracted from our goal by this! We're forgetting who the real enemy is." Hank Chelsea stepped between us. "Now, look, we've got a plan. Let's do it! All right?"

Jastrow looked at Chelsea's proffered hand skeptically. "I don't like this—"

"Aw, come on, Paul," said Mariette and Janice, and then everybody else said it too, and Paul looked embarrassed and shrugged and said, "All right," and we went and invaded Mr. Whitlaw's Global Ethics course.

He was ready for us.

All the desks had been piled up to form a barricade across half the room. The kingdom of Myopia had built a Maginot Line.

We stopped and looked at each other.

"I've heard of paranoia, but this is crazy!" said Janice.

"Yeah. Well, I told you it wouldn't work," growled Paul.

"Now what do we do?" said Mariette.

We stood there exchanging glances. "Can we pull it down?"

"We could try," I said. "But I don't think that's the way we're supposed to solve this problem."

"Okay, Mr. Megabyte," said Paul Jastrow. "What's your solution?"

"I don't have one. I just said, I didn't think the physical way is the answer. I think we're supposed to use our brains here." I shut up then. I realized I was looking straight through the barrier at Whitlaw. He was making notes on a clipboard, but he had paused and was looking at me with a slight smile. "Um . . ." I tried to continue, but my train of thought had disappeared. "Let's have a conference. In the hallway. I think I have an idea."

We trooped out to the hall. I said, "I think we should go in and try to negotiate a peace treaty."

"He's not going to negotiate with us."

"Yes, he is," I said.

"What makes you so sure?"

"Because they can't get out of there unless they do. We have the side of the room with the doors. I don't think they're going to want to climb out of a third-story window."

There was a moment of appreciative silence. You could almost hear the smiles spreading.

"Yeah, let's go. Who's got a handkerchief? We need a white flag—"

We trooped back in and announced, "We come in peace. We want to negotiate a settlement."

"Why should I? You're a bunch of radicals and subversives who were thrown out of the system because you wouldn't cooperate with it."

"The system doesn't work," said Janice. "We want a better one."

"Yeah," said Mariette. "One we can be a part of."

"You're already part of the system. You're the rebels. We have to have rebels to punish as examples."

"Well, we don't want to be rebels anymore!"

"Too bad," said Whitlaw from behind his barrier. "You're troublemakers. The only role for you is rebels. That's what you're good at." We could see him grinning.

"You gotta take us back, Whitlaw—" That was Paul Jastrow.

"Eh? I don't *gotta* anything!"

"Yes, you do," I said. "You can't get out of the room until we let you."

"Ahh," he said. "You found something to bargain with. All right, what is it you want?"

"We want our money back!" screamed Joey Hubre. Joey?

"We want to come back to class," said Janice.

"—amnesty!" said Paul.

"—a fair deal!" I said.

"—respect!" said Mariette.

"—the rights of Englishmen," said Hank quietly, and we all turned to look at him. "Huh?"

But Whitlaw was grinning. "You—your name? Chelsea? Right." He made a note on his clipboard. "A for the day. Now let's see if you can keep it. What are those rights?"

Hank was standing before the barrier of desks, his arms folded. "No more taxes, Mr. Whitlaw, unless we get some say in how the money is to be spent. No more expulsions from the class unless there's a fair hearing. No more unfair use of force. We want the right to disagree with you, and the right to express our disagreements freely without you throwing us out."

"It's my classroom and the law says I can run it any way I want."

"Well, then we want that law changed."

"Sorry, that's one law I didn't make. I can't change that."

"It doesn't matter. You can change the way you run your class. You said you have autonomy. Let's negotiate some changes that'll make this class acceptable to all of us."

"Since when do students have the right to tell teachers how to teach?"

"Since we have all the doors!" cried Paul.

"Shh!" said Hank.

"Who appointed you president?"

"Will you shut up? One person is supposed to talk for all of us!"

"I didn't agree to that!"

"It doesn't matter what you agreed to—it's the way things are!"

"You're just as bad as he is! Well, the hell with you, then!" Paul marched to the end of the room and sat down, glowering.

Hank looked around at the rest of us, a little panicky. "Listen, people—if we don't cooperate with each other, this isn't going to work. We can't show any weakness."

"Yeah," said Janice. "Hank's right. We can't bog down in arguments among ourselves."

"Yeah, but that's no license for you to take over," said Mariette. "Paul's right. We didn't have an election."

"Wait a minute," I said. "I don't want to argue—and I agree with you that we've all gotta pull together or we'll certainly be pulled apart—but I think we have to recognize that each of us is in this rebellion for a different reason and each of us wants to have a say in the negotiations. I want the same thing Paul wants—to be heard."

"May I say something?" John Hubre stepped forward, the silent twin. "Let's draft a list of our demands, and vote on the ones that we want to make Whitlaw adhere to."

Hank looked defeated. "All right. Who's got some paper? I'll write 'em down."

"No," said John. "We'll put them on the screen, where everyone can see them. And I think the entire class should discuss them and vote on them. Is that okay by you, Mr. Whitlaw?"

"Do I have any choice?"

John looked startled. "Uh . . . no. Of course not."

"May I offer a suggestion?" asked Whitlaw.

"Uh . . . all right."

"Let's dismantle this mountain of furniture so we can operate in a more civilized situation. The rest of this war is cancelled until further notice."

In short order, we looked like a classroom again, except that instead of tyrannizing us, Whitlaw was standing quietly to one side, observing—and only occasionally offering suggestions.

The list of demands grew to thirty in less than five minutes.

Whitlaw looked them over, snorted and said, "Don't be silly."

The class reactions ranged from, "Huh? What's wrong with these demands?" to "You don't have any choice!"

He held up a hand. "Please—I want you all to take another look at this list. Most of your grievances appear to be legitimate, but take another look and see if you notice something about your demands."

"Well, some of these are kind of petty," said Paul Jastrow. "I mean, like number six. No more ripping shirts. Maybe that one's important to Doug—but how important is it to the rest of us?"

Janice said, "And some of them are redundant—like the right to express ourselves freely encompasses the right to assemble and the right to speak and the right to publish—so we don't have to list all three, do we?"

And then other voices chimed in with their opinions. Whitlaw had to hold up a hand for silence. He said, "You're all right, of course. It's important to have protection for every situation, whether we specify it or not. I suggest that what you're looking for is an umbrella under which you can operate—an all-purpose rule."

He let us argue for only a few moments, then brought us back to the issue again. "Your demands are valid. Look at your rules again, and see if you can boil them down to one or two sentences."

We did as he suggested. With a little help, eventually we came up with "The government shall be accountable to the people for its actions. The people shall have the right to express their differences freely."

"Congratulations," smiled Whitlaw. "Now what happens if I refuse to accept it?"

"You don't have any choice," said Mariette.

"Why not?"

"Because if you don't, we'll just rebel again."

"Uh huh. What if I hire some more football players?"

"You can't afford to hire as many as you'll need."

"I'll raise taxes."

That prompted some groans and an immediate response from one of the boys who had not been expelled. "Where do I sign up to join the rebellion?"

"That's why you don't have any choice," Hank said. "You don't have the tax base."

"You're right," Whitlaw said. He went back to the front of the room. "All right, then—are we in agreement on this point? That if a government is not accountable to its citizenry, that citizenry is justified in removing that government from power—by whatever means necessary?"

There was general assent.

"I see. The kicker in there is the last line. 'By whatever means necessary.' Obviously it includes open rebellion. How about terrorism? How about assassination? And at what point do you decide that those actions are necessary?"

Paul Jastrow was still sullen. He said, "When there's no other course of action left to us."

"All right, let's consider that. Was your rebellion justified?"

General assent.

"Because I didn't want to listen to what you wanted to say, right?"

Again agreement.

Whitlaw said, "Suppose I had set up a complaint box. Would the rebellion still have been justified?"

There was a thoughtful pause while each of us considered it. I raised my hand. "What would you do with the complaints put into the box?"

Whitlaw grinned. "I'd throw them away at the end of each day without reading them."

"Then, yes," I said. "The rebellion would have been justified."

"What if I read the complaints?"

"What would you do about them?"

"Nothing."

"It's still justified."

"What if I acted on those I agreed with? All the ones that didn't inconvenience me personally."

I thought about it. "No, that's still not good enough."

Whitlaw looked exasperated. "What is it you people want?"

"A fair system of handling our grievances."

"Ahh, now we're getting somewhere. Do you begin to understand now? Your credo up there is very pretty, but it's worthless without the legal guarantees to back it up. What kind of system are you asking for—uh, McCarthy, is it?"

"Yes, sir. How about an arbitration panel of three students? You pick one, we pick one and they pick the third. My father's union uses that system to handle disagreements."

"All right, suppose I decreed that's the kind of system we'll have?"

"No, sir, it has to be voted on. We all have to agree to it. Otherwise, it's still a case of you dictating to us."

Whitlaw nodded and looked at his watch. "Congratulations. In just a little more than an hour, you've recreated more than a thousand years of human history. You've overthrown a government, established a charter for a new system and created a court system with which to enforce it. That's a fair day's work."

The bell rang then. We'd used an entire ninety-minute class period. As we started to gather our books, Whitlaw held up a hand. "Hold it. Stay in your seats. You're not going to your next class today. Don't worry, your other instructors have been informed. They know not to expect you. Does anyone need to pee? Okay, take ten minutes. Be back here and ready to go at eleven-forty."

When we resumed, Joey Hubre was the first to raise his hand. "When do we get our money back?"

Whitlaw looked at him severely. "Don't you understand? You *don't.* The government always plays for keeps."

"But . . . but . . . but we thought this was—"

"What? A game?" Whitlaw looked a little angry. "Weren't you paying attention? This was tyranny! Would you have overthrown the government if you thought I wasn't playing for keeps? Of course not!"

"All I want is my money back—"

"It's part of the national treasury now. And even if I wanted to give it back, I couldn't. I've been overthrown. It's up to the new government to decide what to do with the money."

The classroom was getting tense again. Janice stood up and said, "Mr. Whitlaw! You were wrong to take our money!"

"No, I wasn't—as soon as I declared myself a government, I was within my rights. You were wrong for letting me get away with it. Ever single one of you. You!" He pointed at the first student who had handed over a casey. "—you were wrong for handing me that first coin. Why did you do it?"

"You told me to."

"Did I tell you I was going to give you anything in return for it?"

"No."

"Did I tell you I was going to give it back to you when we were through?"

"No."

"Then why did you give it to me?"

"Uh . . ."

"Right. You gave it to me. I didn't take it. So why are you telling me I'm the one who did wrong?"

"You had an army!"

"Not until after you gave me the money to pay for it." He said to the whole class, "Your only mistake was your timing. You should have rebelled when I declared myself your government. I had no right to do so, but you let me get away with it. You should have demanded accountability then—before I had enough money to hire an army."

He was right. He had us there. We all looked a little embarrassed.

"Well, what do we do now?" wailed Mariette.

"I don't know. I'm not the government anymore. You overthrew me. You took away my power. All I'm doing now is following orders. Your orders. I'll do anything with this money that a majority of you can agree on."

It took less than thirty seconds to pass a resolution requiring the disbursement of all funds collected in the recent taxation.

Whitlaw nodded and opened his desk drawer. He started counting coins. "Uh, we have a problem—there are forty-four of you in this class. But there are only thirty caseys here. If you'll remember, the former government spent eighteen caseys on an army."

Four people stood up to author the next resolution, requiring the return of funds paid to former members of the Imperial Guard. Whitlaw vetoed that. "Sorry. Doesn't that fall into the realm of confiscation? Remember the five-casey note I took unfairly? You just had a rebellion because you didn't want a government able to do that. Now you're setting up a new government to do exactly the same thing."

"But this is different—"

"No it isn't! Confiscation is confiscation! It doesn't matter who does the confiscating—the person still loses something!"

"But . . . then how do we redress previous wrongs?"

"I don't know either. You're the government now. You tell me."

"So why can't we just take the money back?"

"Because the army was fairly paid. They did their job and they were paid a fair wage for what they did. You can't take that money away from them now because it's theirs."

"But you had no right to give it to them!"

"Yes, I did! I was the government!"

Hank Chelsea was standing then. "Wait a minute, sir! I think we all understand what you're trying to teach us. We have to find a fair way to do this, don't we?"

"If you can, you'll be a better man than I am. In the eleven years that I've been teaching this class, not one session has ever found a way that was both *fair* and *legal* to take money out of one person's pocket and put it into another's." He motioned for Hank to sit down. "Let me give you this to think about: a government—*any* government—is nothing more than a system for reapportioning wealth. It takes money from one group of people and gives it to another group of people. And when it happens that enough people decide that they don't like the way the wealth is being reapportioned, that's when that government will be replaced by another one more to the people's liking. As has happened here! But you cannot use the new government to redress all of the wrongs of the previous government—not without creating far more problems than you'll ever clean up. You'll end up with a government entirely concerned with past events and not present ones. That's a sure way to set yourself up to fail. If you're going to win at this game, you have to deal with circumstances the way they are, not the way they used to be or the way you'd like them to be. In other words, only operate on those events you *have* control over. That's the only way to produce results. The real question, then, is, what *do* you have control over? We'll probably spend the rest of the semester tackling that one. Right now, let's handle the immediate problem." He opened his desk drawer. "There are forty-four of you and only thirty caseys here. If you don't reimburse the six members of the Imperial Guard, you're still going to be eight caseys short. And one of you is going to be at least four caseys short because I took a fiver off him."

It was moved, seconded and approved to return four caseys to Geoff Miller to bring his loss into line with the rest of ours. This left the national treasury at twenty-six caseys. We were now short twelve caseys if we wanted to return the money equally.

One of the former members of the Imperial Guard stood up. "Here, I'll give you back the extra two caseys that Whitlaw paid me. I don't think it's fair for me to keep it." He poked his buddy, who also stood up. "Yeah, me too." Two more former soldiers also chipped in then, but the last two just sat in the back of the room with their arms folded.

"We earned it fairly. We're entitled to it."

"Well," said Whitlaw, "that brings the national debt down to two caseys. Not bad. Now all you have to do is decide who gets the short straws."

"This isn't fair!" said Mariette again.

Whitlaw agreed with her. "You're beginning to see it. No matter how hard we try, the government *cannot* be fair to everybody. *Cannot.* The very best that it can do is treat everybody equally *un*fairly."

The immediate classroom problem was finally resolved when John Hubre realized that the casey isn't indivisible. Thirty-eight students, each of whom had paid one casey in taxation, were repaid ninety-four cents each. There was twenty-eight cents left over. Whitlaw started to pocket it, but Hank Chelsea said quickly, "Sorry—that's the national treasury. We'll have one of our own hold it, if you don't mind."

Whitlaw passed it over with a grin. "You're learning," he said.

Twenty-Six

"ALL RIGHT," said Whitlaw. "Obviously, there was a point to that little exercise. No, put your hands down. I'm just going to give you this straight out. There's no such thing as a government."

He looked around the room. "Point to it. Show me the government. Show me *any* government." He waved our hands down again. "Forget it. You can't. You can show me some buildings, and some people and some rules written down on paper, but you can't show me a government. Because there's no such thing in the physical universe. It's just something we made up. It exists only by our agreement that it does. You just proved that here. We agreed that we wanted some stuff managed and we agreed on some rules for how it should be managed. The agreements are the government. Nothing else.

"How big the government gets depends on how many agreements you make. If enough people agree, we'll build some buildings and hire some people to work in them and manage the agreements for us. Now, here's the question—how do you know if something is the business of the government or not?—that is, the business of the people we've hired to work in our buildings and manage our agreements for us. How do they know what to manage? What's the test?

"No—put your hand down. It's too simple. A person, place, or thing is in the jurisdiction of a government if it *tests* that government's agreements. If it doesn't, it isn't.

"The government doesn't have to manage the people who *keep* the agreements. They don't need managing. They're being responsible. It *is* the business of the government to manage those people who *test* the agreements. This is it. The *whole* of government consists of the art of managing people to keep the agreements—*especially* those who do the managing."

Whitlaw moved thoughtfully to the back of the room. He sounded as if he were speculating idly aloud. "Now . . . management is decision-making, right? Anyone not see that? So, the question is—what are the guidelines by which the managers make their decisions? What is the meter-stick?" He looked around at us.

Marcie something-or-other: "The agreements, of course. The rules."

Whitlaw snorted. "Not bloody likely. The rules are just the context—the *authorization* for the decisions. In fact, the history of this nation is about men and women *not* following the rules. History is a list of who tested what agreements.

"Every time an agreement is tested, the person whose responsibility that agreement is, is also being tested. So, what does that person use for guidelines?—particularly when there are no guidelines! What is the *source* of that person's choice?" Whitlaw shoved his hands into his jacket pockets and turned slowly around, making sure we were all paying attention. When he spoke, his voice was low and quiet. "The truth is that ultimately every single choice . . . is a reflection of the integrity of the individual making it."

"You might want to notice that—that everything we've done in this country, *everything* that we've accomplished—good or bad—in nearly two and a half centuries, has been done out of the integrity—or lack of integrity—of people *like ourselves* who are willing to make decisions and be responsible for them, especially when they know those decisions will be unpopular."

I wondered what he was working toward. He wandered back

to the front of the room and sat down on his desk, facing us with an anticipatory expression on his face.

"Do you think the Moscow Treaties were fair?" he asked abruptly.

The class was divided. Some thought yes, some thought no. Most weren't sure.

Whitlaw said, "Well, let's look at it from the rest of the world's point of view. How do you think we looked to them?"

"We're the home of the free, the land of the brave—all the refugees come here." That was Richard Kham Tuong. He had almond eyes, brown skin and curly blond hair. He said it proudly. "People come here looking for freedom. We're a source of hope."

"Uh huh," said Whitlaw, unconvinced. He stood up and strode casually back to stand directly in front of Richard Kham Tuong. "Let me run some statistics by you. One half of the world's population goes to bed hungry every night. There are nearly six billion people on this planet—but the three hundred million who are lucky enough to live in the United States consume one-third of the planet's resources every year. For most of the last century, it was closer to one-half, by the way. Do you think that's fair?"

"Uh . . ." Richard recognized that as a loaded question and did the only thing he could. He stalled.

"Or let me try it another way," Whitlaw went on. He was sandbagging Richard now; we all knew it. "Suppose we order a couple of pizzas for this class. There are twenty-two very thin slices in a pizza, so there should be just enough for everybody to have a little bit. But when they arrive, I take fifteen of the slices for myself and leave the rest of you to fight over what's left. Is that fair?"

"You're loading the question, sir. Obviously, the way you say it, it's *not* fair."

"Well, what do you think we should do about it?"

"Everything we can, I guess."

"All right. Let's see. Are you willing to give up all of your clothes except what you're wearing now? Are you willing to survive on one meal of rice and beans per day? Are you willing to give up your automobile? And all use of electricity? Because that's the kind of sacrifice it would take—every single American would have to give up that much before we would be able to start paying back our debt to other nations. Are you ready to agree to that?"

There was silence in the classroom. Nobody wanted to be the first to admit it.

"It's all right," encouraged Whitlaw. "You'll notice I'm not ready to go hungry either."

"Okay, so we're selfish—what's the point?"

"That is the point. That's how we look to the rest of the world. Like pigs. Rich and fat and selfish. Let's go back to the pizza analogy. Here I am sitting with my fifteen slices. Are you going to let me get away with it?"

"Of course not."

"Then you think you're justified in restricting me?"

"Of course."

"All right, now you understand part of what the Moscow Treaties were about. Yes, there was a war—and the Moscow Treaties were aimed at the causes of it. A very large part of it was the perception that the United States had been selfish with the world's resources."

"Wait a minute!" Paul Jastrow said. "That's only in the eyes of the other nations. There's another side to that argument, isn't there?"

"I don't know," Whitlaw said innocently, his blue eyes twinkling. "Is there? You tell me."

Paul Jastrow sat down, frowning. He had to think about this.

Joey Hubre raised his hand. "Sir, I read somewhere that the problems that the United States has been experiencing for most of our history have been the problems of success, not failure."

"So?"

"Well . . . I mean, um, I hope I get this right. The article said that the size of a success is proportional to the amount of energy invested, and that all of the technological advances that have occurred in this country could have only occurred because of the huge amount of resources available to apply to the problems."

"And—?"

"Well, the point was that this justified our prodigious energy appetite. You have to put fuel in the jet if you want it to go. The other nations in the world have benefited from our advances. They can buy the fruits of the technology without having to invest in all the research. Um, the article used energy satellites as the example. A poor nation—a landbound one—doesn't have to develop a whole space program to have an energy station in space. They can buy one from us for only two million caseys. It was the United States that spent billions of caseys developing the industrial use of space, but everybody benefits."

"I see—and that justifies it?"

"Would it have been better for us to have spent that money on food for the poor? We'd still have lots of poor people today, but we wouldn't have energy stations in space. And those energy stations may eventually make it possible for poor nations to feed all their people."

Whitlaw kept his face blank. "If you were one of those poor people, Joey, how would you feel about that? No, let me be even more graphic. If you were a poor farmer, and your wife and three children were so malnourished that together the five of you weighed less than a hundred kilos, how would you feel about that?"

"Uh . . ." Joey sat down too.

Where was Whitlaw going with this? A lot of people were starting to get angry. Were we wrong for enjoying what we had?

Paul Jastrow spoke up for all of us. He was slouched low in his chair and had his arms folded angrily across his chest. "It's our money," he said. "Don't we have the right to say how we want to spend it?"

"Sounds good to me—except what if it isn't all your money? Remember, we've been consuming nearly one-half the world's resources for most of a century. What if it's *their* money too?"

"But it wasn't their money—it was their resources. And they *sold* them to us on a free market."

"A free market which they claim we manipulated to our advantage."

"And they haven't manipulated back?"

"Ah, I didn't say that." Whitlaw was trying to keep a careful neutrality. He held up a hand. "I don't want to repeat the whole argument—that's not what we're going for today—but are you beginning to understand the *nature* of the disagreement? Do you see the validity of *both* points of view?"

A general murmur of assent swept the room.

"Now," said Whitlaw, "we've seen how a group of people can

make a decision that affects all of them, and that decision can still be unfair. Most of the nations on this planet think the Moscow Treaties were fair. Do you?"

We thought about it. Some of us shook our heads.

"Why not?" Whitlaw pointed.

"Our economy was almost destroyed. It took us over a decade to recover."

"Then why did we agree to those treaties?"

"Because the alternative was war—"

"They had us outnumbered—"

"We didn't have a choice—"

"All right, all right—" He held up his hand again. "All of that is all very well and good—but I want you all to consider something else now. Isn't it possible that your perception of the treaties' unfairness is a *biased* perception, a product of your own subjective points of view?"

"Uh . . ."

"Well . . ."

"Sure, but . . ."

"No." That was Paul Jastrow. Everybody turned to look at him. He said, "It doesn't matter how many people say it's right if it isn't. We just spent a whole session learning that everything a government does is going to be unfair to somebody, but a good government tries to minimize the unfairness."

"Uh huh. . . ." Whitlaw nodded. He was wearing his devil's-advocate expression and using a pleasant, noncommittal tone of voice. "But isn't that what the Moscow Treaties were supposed to do? Establish a more equitable distribution of the world's resources?"

"Yes, but they did it wrong—they were confiscatory. And you just demonstrated to us that you can't redress old wrongs that way without creating new wrongs."

Whitlaw picked up his clipboard and made a note. "You're right." He sat down on the edge of his desk and did something very unusual—for Whitlaw. He *lowered* his voice. He said, "A large part of this course is supposed to be about the Moscow Treaties, so you'll understand why they were necessary. And I think now you understand why many Americans resented them. It felt like we were being unfairly punished for being successful. And it didn't matter to the other nations that all of our studies and data models and simulations showed that most of their starving populations were beyond saving—they still felt that they had to make that commitment to try—"

"But not with *our* resources—"

"Hush a moment, Paul," said Whitlaw, uncharacteristically polite. "Let me finish this. It didn't matter what we felt. We were outvoted. The other nations of this world were going to see that we coöperated whether we wanted to or not—because data simulations or no, they still *had to try* to save their starving populations. And yes, it was unfair the way it was done—and that's a large part of what I wanted you to realize—but that was the best solution they could come up with. And yes, it was a punitive one—"

He stopped to catch his breath. He looked a little gray. Janice MacNeil said, "How come it was never explained this way before? I mean, all the news ever said was that it was our own noble sacrifice to help the rest of the world. I never heard before that they were holding a gun to our heads."

"Well, which would you rather believe? That you're doing something because you're being charitable or because you're being forced to? If you were President, which would be easier to sell to the electorate?"

"Oh," she said. "But didn't anybody notice?"

"Sure, lots of people did. And they said so, very loudly—but nobody wanted to believe them. Remember, most people were so relieved at having avoided a nuclear war they were willing to believe that its nonoccurrence was proof of the nobility of both sides. They were *eager* to believe it, rather than that someone had blackmailed someone else under the table. People who complained were called extremists; after all, you don't have to listen to extremists. It's easier than you think to devalue a truth that you don't want to hear. And remember this: *any* unpopular idea is going to look extreme, so you want to be responsible in how you present it. It is almost always dangerous to be right—and it is *certainly* dangerous to be right too soon."

"Well—um, does the government know now? I mean, what did we do about it? Or what *are* we going to do about it?"

Whitlaw said, "The process of making that decision has been going on for almost twenty years now. We are doing it every day. We are surviving. We are continuing—and we're *contributing.*

"You see, this is the hard part to accept. In retrospect—now that we have had the benefit of twenty years of hindsight—we can see that what was done was perhaps the very *best* thing to do under the circumstances. If you want to look at it from a nationalistic point of view, those treaties were only temporary setbacks, because they did not cripple us permanently. And furthermore, they made it possible for us to deal with the rest of the world in an atmosphere of reduced hostility because they finally felt they had evened the score.

"Now, you need to know just *how* we paid our reparations. We only shipped food and farm machinery; instead of cash, we gave them energy satellites and receiving stations. That way, they all had a vested interest in keeping our space program going. We shipped teachers and technicians. We exported ourselves—"

And suddenly, three years later and a thousand miles away, the coin dropped. Whitlaw had never come out and said so, but he had made it pretty clear that we had lost that war. And that we knew we had lost the war—and it seemed as if we had actively cooperated in the process of our own punishment. Or had we?

There were a lot of government programs that only made sense in retrospect—like the Teamwork Army, for instance. That was only supposed to be a peacetime solution for massive unemployment—the regimen was exactly like that of the regular army, except they didn't drill with guns; but then, how long does it take to learn how to use a gun? Six weeks?

And the space program—as long as we had mass-drivers on the moon, there wasn't a city on Earth that was safe. We didn't need atom bombs—we could drop asteroids.

And all those shipments of food and farm machinery—that helped our economy more than theirs, because we got to retool our assembly lines to build a new generation of technology.

And all those energy satellites—every nation that accepted one would be dependent on us for its maintenance.

And our export of more than half a million teachers to the underprivileged nations—the next generation of world leaders would be taught with American values.

It made a crazy kind of sense. I could almost imagine the President saying, "What if we only *pretended* to lose?"

I thought of a lockbox with a false bottom and a suite of rooms on the thirteenth floor. You can't hide anything forever—you can only misdirect the attention of the searcher.

The rest of the world would be looking for evidence of military buildup—and we were hiding it as economic recovery and reparations and civilian solutions to unemployment! And the best part of it was that those things were always exactly what they *seemed* to be, even when they weren't.

And something else—

Even Whitlaw's class had been a sham.

I'd always wondered why there was a Federal Education Authority. Now it made sense. Under the guise of teaching us history—how we lost a war—Whitlaw was teaching us how to win the next one without ever fighting it. He'd taught us to outthink our enemies, because it was easier than outfighting them.

I felt like a grenade had gone off in my belly. A grenade that Whitlaw had shoved down my throat three years before and had taken this long to explode.

I'd never thought about the Special Forces before—they were just another military unit, one specifically trained for crisis deployment. I guess I'd thought that meant natural disasters and riots—I hadn't realized there was a second Special Forces hidden in the one place nobody would think to look: inside the regular Special Forces.

I realized that and my heart popped. What was the Special Forces *really* for? What had I been a part of?

Twenty-Seven

THERE WERE four of them. Colonel Wallachstein, Lizard, a tiny, friendly-looking Japanese lady with graying hair, and a dark fellow in a black suit. They seated themselves around the small table facing me.

Wallachstein said, "No introductions, McCarthy. Understand something. This meeting didn't happen. And these people don't exist. Neither do I. Got that?"

"Uh, yes, sir."

"Good. I hope so. Because this comes under the jurisdiction of the National Security Act. If you commit any further violations you're likely to disappear. Permanently."

"Yes, sir."

"Now, before we begin, there are some things I have to say. I'm required by law to do this." He looked at a sheet of notes before him, and read, " 'A fair trial presupposes that the defendant is a responsible human being, capable of understanding the difference between right and wrong and able to gauge his actions and their consequences on that basis. Therefore, the outcome of this hearing is dependent on your ability to deal with the information available to you.' " He looked up at me. "Do you understand this?"

I nodded. My throat had gone dry again. Was I on trial? For what?

Wallachstein was frowning. "Is something the matter?"

"Sir," I managed to croak, "what kind of hearing is this? I mean, under what authority—?"

He held up a hand. "Let me finish first." He resumed reading. " 'Under such operating conditions, we cannot judge "guilt" or "innocence" as absolute moral value—nor should we attempt to. Instead, we are determining an organism's ability to deal rationally with its environment. Instead of seeking punishment, revenge or even rehabilitation, it is the purpose of this tribunal to determine the *value* of the individual's contribution to the social environment versus the cost of his continued existence in that environment.' " He pushed the sheet of paper aside and looked directly at me. "Do you understand that?"

I nodded.

"Right. Now, one other thing. What I just read you is in compliance with the Revised Legal Code of 2001. In this hearing, in any area where there is conflict between the Revised Legal Code and the standards of the National Security Act, the standards of the National Security Act shall have precedence. Do you understand that?"

"Uh, I think so. But . . . ?"

"Yes?"

"May I ask questions?"

He said, "You have the right to establish for yourself the authority of this tribunal and its jurisdiction over you. Your question?"

"I have several," I began.

"Let's hear them."

"What's going on here? Who are you? What is your authority? And what am I charged with?"

Wallachstein exchanged glances with the Japanese lady. She smiled sweetly and spoke in a lightly accented voice, but she slurred some of her consonants and I had to concentrate to be sure I understood all of her words. "As a member of the Special Forces Warrant Agency, you are under the direct command of the National Security Office, Military Branch, and therefore you are under the multilevel jurisdiction of the National Security Code, the United States Military Code and the United States Civilian Code, in that order. The purpose of this hearing is to determine the circumstances that resulted in a breach of security that occurred this morning in front of some two thousand witnesses, among whom were individuals known to be agents of hostile foreign governments. The members of this tribunal are authorized to act on behalf of the National Security Office. For reasons of national security, no other identification of the officers of this court will be made. Do you understand?"

"Yes, ma'am."

She smiled sweetly back at me.

"Um," I said, "I have some other questions."

They waited expectantly.

"First, I'd like to know how long the Special Forces has been the cover for a secret military operation. I want to know what the nature of that operation is and whatever else you can tell me about it. I understand that as a member of the Special Forces, I'm entitled to be fully briefed."

Wallachstein exchanged a glance with the dark fellow. He looked at me and said, "Who told you that?"

"Nobody. I put the pieces together myself. It wasn't hard."

Wallachstein said, "There is no secret military operation within the Special Forces. At least, not on paper. However, the internal nucleus of the organization has stood ready to handle necessary but nasty security operations for over a hundred years. The current operation is almost exclusively targeted at controlling the Chtorran infestation. It is a secret operation because we are using weaponry that has been proscribed by international agreement—as you are well aware. What else do you want to know?"

"I want to know what the Chtorrans are. Are they really from another world or are they a biological weapon developed here?"

The Japanese lady said, "Dr. Zymph's report on the infestation, which you heard, is our best assessment of the situation to date."

"How do I know you're telling the truth?"

"You don't." She added, "I will tell you that Dr. Zymph is too proud a lady to lie for anyone, if that helps."

"That may be, but the Chtorrans are too well adapted to this ecology. And the United States is taking too much advantage of the situation."

"Yes," she said. "I see." She didn't say anything else. She just blinked at me.

"Well, aren't you going to answer those points?"

She shook her head. "Unfortunately, there are no satisfactory answers—at least none that will satisfy you right now."

"Well, give me the unsatisfactory answers then."

She said, "I can't tell you anything about the Chtorrans that you don't already know. Yes, they are terribly well adapted to our ecology. We've noticed it too. Someday we hope to find out why. I will tell you that if any nation on this planet had the ability to create—in absolute secrecy—several hundred new species of virulent life forms, totally unrecognizable to state-of-the-art genetic tailoring, it would have to be the United States. We know that we didn't do it. What we're seeing is beyond our ability to construct. And we know that no one else has the capability to do it either.

"Now, as to the second part of your concern: yes, the United States *is* exploiting the situation—but we did not create the situation, nor would we have if we did have the ability. But it does exist and we will use it. We would use any situation that occurred. We have a responsibility to the remaining member population of this nation to manage the affairs of state in a way that best serves their interests. If we didn't, they would have the right to replace us with individuals who would."

"I can't say I like that very much," I said.

She nodded. "I told you that the answers were unsatisfactory. I'm afraid that you will have to resolve your conflict with them for yourself."

She looked to Wallachstein. He looked at me. "Is that it? Or is there something else?"

"Just one thing more, sir. How did *I* end up in the Special Forces?"

For the first time, he smiled—it was a grim smile, but it still qualified: the corners of his mouth twitched. He said, "By mistake. The . . . ah . . . plagues destroyed several key lines of communication. We lost some of our most valuably placed people. The individuals who replaced them were not aware of the unique status of the Special Forces. We've been very successful in establishing ourselves as our own cover organization, but even we were not untouched by the plagues, and it took a while to re-establish all of our necessary controls. Unfortunately, during that time, a number of individuals—like yourself—were assigned to Special Forces units that they should not have been. For the most part, we've been able to locate and isolate those individuals who were unable to meet our special . . . criteria. You, unfortunately, have proven to be something of a difficult case. Had you made the attempt to contact me immediately upon arrival, I might have been able to prevent the scene in the conference hall this morning." He cleared his throat, then allowed himself another grim smile. "On the other hand, in all fairness, there are a number of people who feel exactly as you do and who would have liked to have done the same thing you did—except that they knew the reasons why they shouldn't."

"Oh."

Wallachstein and the Japanese lady whispered together for a moment, Lizard and the dark fellow listening in. Dark fellow shook his head about something, but Lizard shook her head harder, disagreeing with him. I caught the phrase "—can't afford to waste personnel—" and then they shut up when they realized they were getting too loud.

Wallachstein said, "I think I have to agree with Major Tirelli's assessment." He turned to me. "McCarthy, let me be honest with you. I don't give a damn what happened this morning. I'm not so sure that you did any serious damage to us, and you may even have done some good by drawing off some of the heat from Dr. Zymph's presentation. We expected there to be fireworks over that, because there were individuals in attendance whose sole purpose in attending was to create fireworks and embarrass the United States. We knew about them in advance. You seem to have stolen their thunder and embarrassed one of their most respected spokesmen."

"*I* embarrassed *him?*"

"You dealt with the issues. He didn't. More importantly, you kept him from making his presentation. He was going to minimize the Chtorran problem in favor of a global reconstruction plan—it would have been a very attractive plan too, because the United States would have ended up paying for most of it. Essentially, we would be shipping out every unclaimed machine in the country, every vehicle, computer, airplane, TV set and toaster. And if we couldn't do it fast enough, they'd send in volunteer troops to help us. To be honest, McCarthy, I couldn't have staged a better diversion if I'd wanted to. And believe me, I wanted to. I didn't because I thought it would be too obvious. And that's the problem here. You called attention to yourself as a member of the Special Forces Warrant Agency, and even though you didn't know what you were doing, you have given the United Nations Inspection Authority additional reason to suspect the Special Forces as an undercover operation. Our enemies are already claiming that this morning's events were carefully planned to discredit their position. They're right and wrong at the same time. If we had thought we could have gotten away with something like what you did, we would have done it—but we didn't think we could have. And you proved that our estimation of the situation was correct. In your ignorance, you did the right thing—that's why it was wrong, because it was so right. Do you understand?"

"Uh, sort of, but not really."

Wallachstein was grim. "I'm not sure what I should do with you, McCarthy. I can't give you a medal and I don't have time to hang you. Do you have any suggestions?"

I thought about it for a moment. They waited patiently. When I finally spoke, it was with carefully chosen words. "I'm interested in Chtorrans, sir. I'm not interested in playing spy games. Up in the mountains, we knew who the enemy was. He was big and red and always screamed before he leaped, and there wasn't anybody to say how we should or shouldn't fight back. We just did what we had to."

Wallachstein said, "In that, I envy you. There have been occasions when I wished for the application of a flamethrower to solve some of my problems down here." He opened a notebook in front of him and scribbled something on a page. He ripped the page out and shoved it toward me. "Here. I want you to go someplace this afternoon."

I took the paper and looked at it. "A doctor?"

"A psychiatrist."

"I don't understand."

"Have you ever heard of survivor's syndrome?"

I shook my head.

He said quietly, "When you wipe out three-quarters of the human race, all you have left are orphans. There isn't a human being on this planet who hasn't been affected in some deep way. The dying has touched us all. I'm sure you've seen some of the reactions, the herds of walking wounded, the manics, the zombies, the suicides, the sexual obsessives, the ones who are so desperate for stability that they've become drones, and so on. I don't know if you've seen much of the opposite side of that coin though. Like any ordeal, the plagues destroyed the weak and tempered the strong. There are a lot of people who are just coming alive now because they have something *worthwhile* to do. Before you can become a *real* member of this Special Forces, we have to know which kind of survivor you are."

I blurted, "I don't know. I never thought about it. I mean, I just picked myself up and kept on going. It seemed the only logical thing to do—"

Wallachstein held up a hand. "Don't tell me. Tell the doctor. We'll recess this hearing until . . ." He glanced at his watch, scowled. ". . . until further notice. Take a scooter from the car pool, McCarthy. Major Tirelli will show you where to go. Don't talk to anyone else. Go directly back to base and plug into Dr. Davidson. Get something to eat at the base commissary. Better get a change of clothes too, and then come back here immediately."

"Uh, sir?"

He looked up. "Eh?"

"I thought I was . . . under arrest. I mean, what's to keep me from getting on the scooter and heading west?"

"Nothing," he said. "In fact, it'd probably solve a lot of problems if you did. It's not something many people know, but not a lot of traffic is getting over the Rockies these days. Something keeps stopping the cars and peeling them open like sardine cans. Besides"—he looked me straight in the eye and his expression was taut—"you're not the kind who bolts. You'll come back. By then we'll have Dr. Davidson's report and we'll know what to do with you. Major Tirelli, will you escort McCarthy to the car pool? We have some talking to do here."

Twenty-Eight

THE ROOM was empty.

A rug. A chair. A table with a pitcher of water and a glass on it. Nothing else. No other doors except the one behind me.

"Please sit down," said a disembodied female voice. I looked, but I couldn't see a speaker system. I sat down. The chair creaked, but it was comfortable. It was a swivel-rocker, upholstered in dark brown leather. It felt reassuring.

"Your name, please?"

"McCarthy, James Edward."

"Ah, yes. We've been expecting you. Dr. Davidson will be with you shortly. While you wait, I'll play a short film for you."

"Um—" But the room was already darkening. The wall in front of me began to glow and images began to solidify in the air. I shut up, decided to relax and enjoy it.

The film was . . . a montage. What they call a tone poem. Music and images wrapping around each other, some sexual, some violent, some funny, some happy—two naked children splashing in a rocky stream dissolved into a tiny jeweled spider weaving a diamond tapestry against a blue and velvet background—that shimmered into an eagle soaring high above a desolate landscape as if looking for a haven—the eagle became a silver sailship hanging effortlessly in space below an emerald-shiny Earth, and then a pair of male dancers, clad only in briefs, whirled around each other, their bodies glistening with sweat—resolving now into a cheetah racing hard across the veldt and bringing down a zebra, terrified, in a cloud of stinging dust—

It went on like that for ten or fifteen minutes, a tumble of pictures, one after the other, faster than I could assimilate. A couple of times I felt frightened; I didn't know why. Once I felt angry. I didn't like the film. I wondered why they were showing it to me. This was boring. And then, just when I started to get interested again, it ended.

When the lights came back up, a quiet voice said, "Good afternoon." The voice was male. Quiet. Very mature. Grandfatherly.

I cleared my throat again, and I found my voice. "Where are you?" I asked.

"Atlanta."

"Who are you?"

"You may call me Dr. Davidson, if you wish. That's not my real name, but that's the name I use for these sessions."

"Why is that?"

He ignored the question. "If you'd like to smoke, please feel free," said Dr. Davidson. "I won't mind."

"I don't smoke," I said.

"I meant dope."

I shrugged. "I don't do much of that either."

"Why not?" he asked. "Do you have strong feelings about it?"

"No. I just don't like it much." Something was making me uncomfortable. I said, "Can you see me?"

"Yes, I can."

"Is there any way I can see you?"

"If you mean, is there a screen for two-way video, I'm sorry, there isn't. If you mean you'd like to see me face to face, you'll have to come to Atlanta. I'm something of an invalid. That's one of the reasons why we don't have two-way hookups. Sometimes my . . . ah, condition can be disconcerting."

"Oh." I felt embarrassed. I didn't know what to say.

Dr. Davidson said, "Please tell me about yourself."

"What do you want to know?"

"Why do you think you're here?"

"I was told to come here."

"Why?"

"They want to know if I'm too crazy to be trusted."

"What do you think?"

"I don't know. The way I always heard it, the crazy person is the worst one to judge."

"Just the same, what do you think?" Dr. Davidson's voice was mild—and incredibly patient. I began to like him. A little.

I said, "I think I'm doing okay. I'm surviving."

"Is that your gauge of success? That you're surviving?"

I thought about it. "I guess not."

"Are you happy?"

"I don't know. I don't know what happiness feels like anymore. I used to. I don't think anyone's happy since the plagues."

"Are you unhappy? Do you feel depressed?"

"Sometimes. Not a lot."

"Hurt? Confused?"

"Yeah. A little."

"Angry?"

I hesitated. "No."

There was silence for a moment. Then Dr. Davidson asked, "Do you *ever* feel angry?"

"Yeah. Doesn't everybody?"

"It's a normal response to frustrating situations," Dr. Davidson admitted. "So what makes *you* angry?"

"Stupidity," I said. Even talking about it, I could feel my muscles tightening.

Dr. Davidson sounded puzzled. "I'm not sure I understand that, Jim. Could you give me some examples?"

"I don't know. People lying to each other. Not being honest. . . ."

"Specifically?" he urged.

"Um—well, like the people I met at the reception last night. And the scientists this morning. And even Colonel Wa—the people who sent me here. Everybody's talking to me. But so far, nobody wants to listen."

"I'm listening, Jim."

"You're a shrink. You have to listen. That's your job."

"Did you ever wonder what kind of person becomes a psychiatrist, Jim?"

"No."

"I'll tell you. Somebody who is interested in other people enough to *want* to listen to them."

"Well . . . but it's not the same. I want to talk to the people who can answer my questions about the Chtorrans. I want to tell them what I saw. I want to ask them what it meant—but it doesn't seem like *anyone* wants to listen. Or, if they listen, they don't want to believe. And I *know* I saw a fourth Chtorran come out of that nest!"

"It's difficult to prove, isn't it?"

"Yeah," I grumbled. "It is."

"Why don't you sit down again."

"Huh?" I realized I was standing. I hadn't remembered getting out of the chair. "Sorry. When I get angry, I pace."

"No need to apologize. How else do you deal with your anger, Jim?"

"Okay, I guess."

"I didn't ask you how well you thought you dealt with it. I asked you specifically what you *do* to deal with it."

I shrugged. "I get mad."

"Do you tell people when you're angry?"

"Yeah. Sometimes."

Dr. Davidson waited. Patiently.

"Well, most of the time."

"Really?"

"No. Hardly ever. I mean, I blow up sometimes, but most of the time, I don't. I mean . . ."

"What?"

"Well—um, I don't really like to tell people that I'm pissed at them."

"Why not?"

"Because, people don't want to hear it. They only get mad back at you for getting mad at them in the first place. So when I get mad at someone, I—try not to let it get in the way, so I can deal rationally with the other person."

"I see. Would it be fair to say that you suppress your anger, then?"

"Yeah, I guess so."

There was a longer pause this time. "So you're still carrying a lot of it with you, aren't you?"

"I don't know." And then I looked up. "What do you think?"

"I don't think yet," said Dr. Davidson. "I'm looking for patterns."

"Oh," I said.

"Let me ask you something, Jim. Who are you angry at?"

"I don't know. People talk to me, tell me what to do—no, they tell me who I am and I know that's not who I am. They talk to me, but they don't want to listen. My dad—whenever he would say, 'I want to talk to you,' he really meant, 'I'm going to talk and you're going to listen.' Nobody wants to hear what I have to say."

"Tell me more about your dad," said Dr. Davidson.

I rocked back and forth in the chair for a moment. Finally I said, "Well, see, it wasn't that my dad and I couldn't communicate. We could—but we *didn't*. Not very often, that is. Oh, once in a while he tried—and once in a while I tried—but most of the time both of us were too involved with our own concerns to be involved with each other."

I said, "You know, my dad was famous. He was one of the best fantasists in the country. Not the most popular—he didn't go in for a lot of flash and dazzle—but still he was one of the most respected, because his simulations were intelligent. When I was a kid, a lot of people used to tell me how lucky I was—even my own friends—because I got to play all his programs before anybody else. They couldn't understand my matter-of-fact attitude about his work, and I couldn't understand their awe."

"How *did* you feel about his work?"

I didn't answer that immediately. I wanted to interrupt and give Dr. Davidson a compliment—he was asking the right questions. He was very astute. But I realized I was sidetracking myself. And I realized why. I didn't want to answer that last question.

Dr. Davidson was very patient. The chair arms were warm. I let go of them and rubbed my hands together. Finally, I admitted it. I said, "Um . . . I guess I didn't realize it at the time, but I think—no, I *know*—I resented my dad's work. Not the games themselves, but his total involvement with them. I was jealous, I guess. My dad would get an idea—say, like *Inferno* or *Starship* or *Brainstorm*—and he'd turn into a zombie. He would disappear into his office for weeks at a time. That closed door was a threat. Do not disturb under penalty of immediate and painful death. Or possibly something worse. (Beware of Yang the Nauseating.) When he was writing, it was like living with a ghost. You heard sounds, you knew there was someone in the house with you, but you never saw him in person. And if by chance you did, it was like meeting a stranger in your living room. He'd mumble an acknowledgment, but he'd never lose his million-light-year stare.

"I don't know how Mom learned to live with it, but she did. Somehow. Dad would be up before seven, fix his own breakfast and then disappear for the day—only coming out of his office to help himself to something from the refrigerator. Mom made a point of leaving plates of food for him, so all he had to do was grab the plate and a fork and he could vanish back into his study. Usually we wouldn't see him again until after midnight. This could go on for weeks at a time.

"But we always knew when he had reached a halfway point—he took three days off to recharge his battery. It wasn't for us that he took the break; it was for himself. He'd take us out to dinner and a show, or we'd take a couple of days and go to an amusement park, but it was always strained. Maggie and I didn't know how to react around him because we'd been tiptoeing past his office for so many days in a row. Now, suddenly, he wasn't a monster anymore; he wanted to be our friend—but we didn't know how to be friends with him. He'd never taken the time to give us a chance to learn.

"For a long time I was jealous of his computer, but then I learned how to survive without a real dad and then it didn't matter anymore. Pretty soon, the hard parts were only when he was trying to make up for lost time. We all felt so uncomfortable, it was always a relief when he 'd finally stretch his arms out and say, 'Well, I guess I'd better get back to work. Somebody's got to pay the bills around here.'

"Mom had her own work, of course—but she was able to switch off the terminal and walk away from it without looking back. Dad never was—when he had a problem to solve, he gnawed at it like a puppy with the legbone of a steer. Later, when I was old enough, I was able to appreciate the elegance of Dad's work. His programs not only played well, but they were so beautifully structured they were a joy to read. But no matter how much I respected the products of his labors, I still resented the fact that so much of his emotional energy went into his creations that there was only a little left for me. For the family.

"When Dad was finally finished with a program, he would be *completely* done. He wouldn't go near the machine for . . . I don't know—it seemed like months. He wouldn't even play other authors' games. Those were almost okay times, because he'd try to make the effort to learn how to be a real human being again—a real father. But by then, we'd learned to recognize the signs—that he couldn't really do it. Whenever he got too close, he'd get just so close and then he'd retreat again. He'd suddenly —*conveniently*—get another idea and he'd be gone again.

"So Maggie and I—well, I don't know about Maggie, but it *seemed* that she felt the same way—had that gap in our lives, and we either had to look somewhere else for something to fill it or learn to live with the lack. Which is mostly what I did—lived with the lack—because I didn't know that a family *wasn't* supposed to be that way. Maggie—well, she found her own answer. We weren't that close.

"Anyway, that was before the plagues. When we went up to the cabin, something in Dad changed—not better, just different. At first I didn't notice, because I didn't have enough experience with him to know, and then when I did, I didn't know what to make of it. I guess it scared me. As if I didn't know who he was after all.

"Several times a week, he and I would make the rounds of our security sensors—no one could have approached within a mile of the cabin without our knowing about it, not even a deer. We never had any people come near, but the system kept us in fresh meat and I learned how to skin a carcass and hang it. At first, Dad and I each kept mostly to ourselves, but after a while, he began talking to me. As if I were a real person. As if he'd just been waiting for me to grow up first.

"It confused me. I mean—hell, how can you expect someone to suddenly be a *real* son when you've spent twenty years ignoring him?

"And yet, even as I resented the goddamned presumption of the man, I still wanted him to finally be my father. So I stopped hating him for a while and began to discover what an interesting person he really was. I'd never known some of the things he'd done when he was my age—you know, he once met Neil Armstrong!

"I guess that was when Dad and I finally got to know each other. And I know this sounds strange, but those days up at the cabin were probably the happiest time of my life. It was a vacation from reality, and for a little while, we were a real family. It was nice. For a while. . . ."

After a while, Dr. Davidson prompted, "Go on, Jim."

"Huh?"

"What happened?"

I shrugged. "We came down from the mountains too soon. And we got caught in the last wave of the plagues. And the boys died. And—um, Dad never forgave himself. My sister never forgave him. And my mother—well, she never stopped pitying him because she knew what private hell he was living with. I guess he couldn't take that."

"Jim—"

"Huh?"

"You didn't say how you felt."

"Yes, I did. I said I loved him."

"How did you feel about coming down from the mountain too soon?"

"Uh . . . it was a mistake, but it was an honest one. I mean, anyone could have . . . I mean, it wasn't his fault—"

"Jim," Dr. Davidson said very quietly, "you're not being honest with me."

I jerked my hands back from the arms of the chair—

"Yes," he admitted. "There are sensors in the chair—but that isn't how I know you're lying. I can hear the stress in your voice."

I felt suddenly flustered—and angry. I jumped up out of the chair—

"How *did* you feel, Jim?"

"None of your damn business! I'm tired of people telling me who I am, who I have to be. I'm tired of people lying to me! Everybody lies. Obama lied. Duke lied. You're lying now, I'll bet. I'm tired of it—tired of being used and manipulated. It isn't fair! It wasn't fair when my father did it!" The words were tumbling out now. I knew what I was saying, but I couldn't stop myself—I didn't even know if I meant any of it. "He didn't listen to me either! I wanted to stay up in the mountains longer! We were happy there!" The words caught in my throat and I choked. I started coughing.

After a polite pause, Dr. Davidson said, "There's water on the table."

I stepped over to it and poured myself a glass. I drank it, then poured another and downed half of it too. My throat still felt dry. I carried it back to the chair with me. I sat down again. I tried to perch on the edge of the seat, but the chair wasn't designed for it; I had to lean back.

"You said you were happy there, in the mountains," Dr. Davidson prompted.

"Yes," I admitted, glad to finally have it out. "I was. I wasn't competing with the computer anymore. We were involved with living. Surviving. I mean, it wasn't easy; we had to chop our own wood and do a lot of maintenance on the solar panels, but we were *involved* with what we were doing—and with each other. We talked to each other about what we had to do. We shared our experiences. We *cooperated.* Oh, there were fights, a lot of arguments—especially at first—but we were a family finally. And it wasn't fair to end it. We could have stayed up there longer. We should have waited. I didn't want to come back. I wanted us to stay up there—"

"So it wasn't the boys at all?" asked Dr. Davidson.

"No," I admitted. "Not for me. It was . . . I was afraid I was going to lose him again."

"So you were angry at your father?"

"Yeah, I guess so. Yeah, I was."

"Did you tell him how you felt?"

"No, I never did. I mean, there wasn't any point. Once he'd made up his mind, that was it. Oh, I tried—I did tell him. I said we shouldn't go down yet, but he said we had to. I didn't want to, but you couldn't argue with him, so I didn't. I just figured he was going to have his way, so I started putting up the walls again. You know, I'd let them down for a while, but now that he was making plans to come back, I had to protect myself again and—" I stopped to take a sip of water.

"Did he notice it? Did he see a change in your behavior?"

"I don't see how he could have missed it. I was a real asshole there for a while."

"I see."

There was silence. While I realized. It wasn't just Maggie's anger. Or Mom's pity. It was me too. My resentment. Was that what he'd been trying to tell me that last day at the depot? Did I drive him away too?

"What are you thinking about now?"

"Nothing," I said. "I'm just wondering who I should be angry at. My dad? Or me? He was there when I needed him. But I wasn't there when he needed me. I abandoned him because . . . because . . ." My face was getting hot. This was the hard part to admit. I could feel my throat tightening up. ". . . I thought he was going to shut me out again and I wanted to shut him out first—to show him what it felt like, to show him he couldn't jerk me around like that! I mean, everybody else does it, but not my dad! It wasn't fair!" I started coughing then, and my eyes were blurry. I rubbed my palms against them, realized I was starting to cry—and then broke down and bawled like a baby.

Dr. Davidson waited patiently. Finally he said, "Are you all right?"

"No," I said, but I was. I was *relieved* to have finally spoken it aloud. It was as if I had released a great pressure that I hadn't even known was there until the words had given it form. "Yes," I said. "I'm all right. Well—a little better, anyway. I hadn't realized I was living with such . . . guilt."

"Not just guilt, Jim. Anger too. You've been carrying your anger for such a long time, Jim, it's become a habit. It's part of you. My job is to assist you in giving it up. If that's what you want."

I thought about that. "I don't know. Sometimes I think my anger is all that keeps me going."

"Maybe that's because you haven't experienced anything else as intense. Have you ever been in love?"

I shook my head.

"Perhaps you ought to think about that—consider what it is you expect a lover to be. We could talk about that next time."

"Next time?"

"If you wish. You can call on me any time you want. That's what I'm here for."

"Oh. I thought this was only a one-time interview."

"It doesn't have to be."

"Oh," I said. Then, "Thank you."

Twenty-Nine

DINNER WAS a thick steak (medium rare), real mashed potatoes, green peas (with melted butter on them), fresh salad (bleu cheese dressing) and a chocolate soda. All of my favorite foods. Even an army commissary couldn't do too much damage to a T-bone steak. Although they tried.

I wondered about Ted. I wondered where he was and what he was up to now. Or who.

I'd never been able to keep up with him. And I knew why.

Paul Jastrow said it to me once—I didn't remember the argument, but I did remember the insult: "Hey, McCarthy—there are human beings and there are ducks. You're a duck. Stop pretending to be a human being. You're not fooling anyone." Some of the people around him laughed, so after that, whenever Paul wanted to get a laugh, he'd turn to me and start quacking, then he'd turn to his friends and explain, "You have to talk to them in their own language if you want them to understand anything."

I never understood why he'd picked me out for the honor of that particular humiliation—not until much later when I saw some comedian on TV do the exact same routine to an unsuspecting member of the audience. It wasn't personal; he was just using the fellow—he was someone to hit with the rubber chicken. That's when the nickle dropped. Paul had been imitating this comic. Maybe he hadn't even meant it personally—it was just a cheap way to get a laugh. But nobody had let me in on the joke. So I didn't get to laugh too. And even though I understood it now, in retrospect, it still didn't lessen the hurt. I could still feel it, could still hear the laughter.

I think it hurt the most because I was afraid it might be true.

I was looking at my half-finished steak. I was wishing I had someone to share the meal with. It's no fun eating alone.

I pushed myself away from the table. I wasn't hungry anymore. I hated to waste food, but—

—and then I had to stop myself, or I would have laughed out loud. There weren't any children starving in Africa anymore—or India, or Pakistan, or anywhere else! Nobody was starving anymore. If there was one good thing the plagues had accomplished, they had ended world hunger. It didn't matter if I wasted this steak or not. There was steak enough for everybody now. There was steak to waste! It was an eerie realization.

But I still felt guilty about not finishing. Old habits die hard. If you train yourself to think a certain way, will you keep on thinking that way, even after it's no longer a valid way to think?

Hm.

Did I think like a duck? Was that it? Did I keep on doing ducklike things because I didn't know how to do anything else? Was it that obvious to the people around me?

Maybe I should stop being me for a while and start being someone else—someone who didn't have so much trouble being me.

I wasn't hungry anymore. I got up, took my tray to the bus window and left the commissary.

I wondered if I walked funny. I mean, I was short and a little pudgy around the bottom. Did I look like a duck? Maybe I could learn to walk differently—if I stood a little taller and carried my weight in my chest instead of in my gut—"*Oof!* I'm sorry." I had been so busy walking, I hadn't been looking, and had plowed straight into a young woman. Quack. Old synapses never die, they just fire away. "I'm really sorry—oh!"

It was Marcie. The thin girl with the large dark eyes. From the bus. Colonel Buffoon.

"Hi—" I flustered for words. "Uh, what are you doing here?"

"Feeding my dog—they give me the scraps." She showed me the package she was carrying.

I held the door for her. She stepped through, but didn't say thanks. I followed after.

She stopped on the sidewalk. "Are you following me?"

I shook my head. "No."

"Well, then, go away."

"You're very rude, you know."

She stared at me blankly.

"You don't even give people a chance."

She blinked. "I'm sorry. Am I supposed to know you?"

"Uh—we were on the bus together, remember? Last night?"

She shook her head. "I don't remember anything from last night. Were you one of the boys I screwed?"

"Huh? No . . . I mean . . . *what?*"

"He doesn't use me at all. I know that's what people think, but he's never touched me. But he likes to watch me do it with the young men he picks out. And then he likes to—well, you know."

"Why do you stay with him?"

She shrugged. "I don't know. I don't have anywhere else to go." And then she added, "I really am sorry. I don't remember you at all. I was stoned last night. He had some Atlanta Blue. I don't think I did it with anyone, but I'm not always sure. Were you there?"

"I told you. We were on the bus together. Remember? The bus into town?"

"Oh, yeah. I'm sorry. Sometimes I don't remember things at all. If you say so." She turned away from me then, bent to the ground and unwrapped her package to reveal a large pile of meat scraps and bones. "He's going to love this. Rangle!" she called. "C'mon, boy. Here, Rangle, come and get it or I'll give it to the dog!" She turned back to me. "I don't like to do dust, but—well, it helps sometimes. You know. Sometimes I get . . . lonely. You know?"

"Yeah. I know."

"That's funny, isn't it? There are still lots of people, if you know where to go, but it's all crowds of strangers. I don't know anybody anymore."

"I know what you mean. And everybody always seems so *agitated.* It's like—you know, the social Brownian movement has been speeded up—"

Her expression was blank. She didn't know.

I said, "It's because there are less people now—we all have to move faster to make up for the difference."

She was staring at me. Had I just said something stupid? Or had she not gotten it? She said, "I used to be smart. Like you. Only it stopped being useful to be smart. So I stopped being smart." She looked sad. "The dust helps a lot. You can get real stupid real fast with dust." She caught herself then, as if she'd said something she shouldn't have. She lifted her voice again. "Hey, Rangle! Come on! Where are you, boy?" There was an edge of impatience in her tone. She turned back to me. "You'll like him. He's really a very friendly dog—I just don't know where he is now."

"Oh, well . . . maybe he got caught up in traffic, or something."

She didn't react to the joke. She turned her wide-eyed stare on me again. "Do you think so?"

"Are you still dusted?" I asked.

"Oh, no. I haven't sniffed since yesterday. I don't like it. Why do you ask?" Before I could answer, she clutched my arm. "Am I being weird? I'm sorry. Sometimes I get weird. It happens. But nobody ever tells me if I'm weird or not. That scares me sometimes—that I might be so weird that no one will tell if I am or not. One time, everybody else got dusted and I had to stay squeaky—because it was my period and I didn't want to risk hemorrhaging—and I was really bored. They didn't understand why I wasn't giggly like them—"

"Yes," I said. "You're being weird."

She looked into my face. Her eyes were very large and very dark. She looked almost like a little girl right then. She said, "Thank you. Thank you for telling me that." She blinked and I saw the tears welling up in her eyes. "I don't know anything anymore, except what other people tell me. So thank you for telling me the truth.

"Do you hate me?"

I shook my head.

"Do you feel sorry for me?"

"No, I don't." I thought about my father for an instant. "No, I don't feel sorry for anyone anymore. It only kills them."

She kept on looking at me, but she didn't say anything for a long moment. We stood there in the Colorado dusk, while overhead the stars began to come out. To the west, the mountains were outlined in a faint glow of orange. The breeze was warm and smelled of honey and pine.

The silence stretched until it was uncomfortable. I began to wonder if I should apologize for being honest with her. Finally she said, "I wish I knew where that damn dog went to. It's not like him to miss his dinner! Rangle!" She looked annoyed, then as if embarrassed to have been angry, she said, "I don't know why I'm getting so upset—he's not my *real* dog. I mean, he's just a stray. I sort of adopted him—" And then she admitted, "—but he's the only person I know who . . . well, he doesn't care if I'm weird. Rangle doesn't care. You know?"

"Yeah, I do. We all need someone these days." I smiled at her. "Because we're all we've got."

She didn't answer immediately. She was staring at the paper with the meat scraps on it. Overhead, the street lights came on, filling the twilight with a warm glow. When Marcie finally spoke, her voice was very soft. "You know, I used to know what was important in life and what wasn't. Being beautiful was important. I had my nose fixed—my whole face—because I wanted to be beautiful. Like, you could have that bump on your nose fixed—"

"It was a motorcycle accident," I said.

"—only you'd still be you inside, wouldn't you? Well, that's what happened to me. I had my face remodeled—only afterwards, I was still me. I think that's what's happened to the world. We're all still who we were last year—only our outsides have changed and we don't know it yet. We don't know who we're supposed to be anymore. I'm nervous and I'm scared—all the time," she said. "I mean, what if I do find out who I am, and then someone comes up and tells me no, that's not who I am after all? Do you know what I mean?"

I said, "Ducks. We want to feel like swans, and they keep telling us we're ducks—and not even very good ducks at that."

"Yeah," she said. "That's good. You do understand. Sometimes I wonder if there's anyone else in the world who feels what

I do—and sometimes I find someone who does; but it's always a surprise to find out that I'm not completely alone."

She shivered and I put my arm around her. "I know."

Petulantly, she said, "I just wish I knew where Rangle was. He'll probably show up tomorrow, grinning and wagging. He's a real practical joker, but I don't like worrying. You've seen him around, haven't you? Sort of halfway between brown and white, almost pink—real shaggy, with big floppy paws like bunny-feet slippers. Big brown eyes and a black gumdrop nose."

Yes, I had seen him.

From a glass booth above a circular room.

Last night. With Jillanna.

He had been—dessert.

I could feel my stomach tightening. Oh, shit. How should I handle this one?

Marcie looked at me. "Did you say something?"

"Uh—Marcie, I—uh, don't know how to tell you this, but—" *Just tell the truth,* the voice in my head said. "—uh, Rangle is dead. He was—uh, hit by a car. It happened late last night. I saw it happen. He was killed instantly. I didn't realize that was Rangle until you described him."

She was shaking her head. "Oh, no—he couldn't be! Are you sure, Jim?" She searched my face for some sign that I was mistaken.

I swallowed hard. My throat hurt. I remembered something I'd heard in the booth, about how this dog had been scrounging around the commissary for a while. "Marcie," I said. "I'm sure. He was about so high, right?"

She nodded slowly. She gulped for a moment, as if she couldn't get air. And then she put her hands to her face and held them there. It was as if she were shattering into a thousand screaming pieces all at once, and only the sheer pressure of her hands was keeping all those pieces from flying off into space.

And then, abruptly, she straightened up and her face was like a mask. When she spoke, her voice was flat and dead. "I'll be all right." She shrugged. "He was only a dog." She was a zombie again.

I stared at her as she bent and picked up the package of meat scraps that Rangle would never eat. She folded the paper up neatly and walked over to a nearby garbage can and dumped it in. "Now I can stop caring."

"Marcie, it's all right to care. We all have to have someone to care about."

"I don't," she said. She pulled her coat around her, as if to shield herself against the cold—but it was a warm night and it wasn't the cold she was shutting out. She brushed past me and started walking away.

"Marcie!" She kept on walking and I felt powerless to stop her. It made me angry—the feeling of helplessness; it was the same feeling as when my father walked away from me for the last time. "No, goddammit! I'm tired of people walking out on me!" Something flickered like a frame in a movie and then I was moving across the space between us and grabbing her arm. I pulled her around to face me. "Knock it off!" I snapped at her. "This is really stupid. I've seen other people do it. You start retreating from life because it hurts. You do it one step at a time, but pretty soon it becomes such a habit that you do it automatically—you run from everything. Of course it hurts! How much it hurts shows how much you care! And that proves just how much alive you are!"

"Let go of me! I don't need a sermon!"

"You're right! You don't! You need a year in a rubber room!"

She broke free of my grip, her eyes wild. "Don't say that!" she shrieked. Her hands were like claws.

"Why? Because it might be true? You said you were terrified of being weird, that you might be one of those ladies with the fried eggs on their foreheads, but nobody would tell you. Well, I'm telling you. If you run away from me now, that's the first step toward the fried egg."

She looked as if I'd slapped her, blinking at me in the glow of the street lights. Her expression seemed to dissolve as the meaning of the words sank in. I could almost see them penetrating, layer after layer. "I've been there," she said. "I don't want to go back."

"So *don't.* You don't have to. It's all this running from stuff that keeps you crazy. You think you're the only one who's crazy? The rest of us are just as wacko! All you have to do is look. The only difference is we don't let it stop us." I added, "Too much."

"But it hurts!"

"So what? Let it hurt! At least that way you get it over with! What you're doing now sure isn't producing results, is it?"

She nodded and gulped, and then her eyes welled up and she clutched my shirt and she grabbed me and started bawling. I pulled her close and held onto her, as if I could shield her from the pain—only it wasn't pain from the outside anymore, it was pain that bubbled up from the inside and burst out through her eyes and nose and mouth. "It isn't fair! It isn't fair! Why does there have to be so much dying?!! I want my dog!! Oh, Rangle, Rangle! I want my Rangle back!" She sobbed and screamed into my jacket. She gulped for air and sobbed again. The tears were streaming down her cheeks now. "It isn't fair! Everything I've ever loved—I don't want to love anything anymore! I'm tired of losing! It hurts too much to care! I want an end to it! I want my dog!"

I thought about the men who'd captured Rangle and thought about what I'd like to do to them. Marcie was right—it wasn't fair. They killed the dog, but I had to deal with the guilt and the grief! Why did I have to clean up their mess?! All of their messes?!! I could feel my fists tightening against Marcie's back. Her shoulders heaved. She began coughing and I unclenched my fists and started thumping her gently. "It's all right, baby," I said. "It's all right. Let it out, that's the way, it's good to cry. It shows how much you cared. Just scream it out, that's the girl—" I just kept babbling, trying to comfort her and slowly ease her back. It was amazing how much she cared about that dog. She just kept on crying—or was she crying for more than just the dog right now? I held her and let her weep. Two soldiers walked past us without stopping. They took us for granted. Such scenes were common nowadays.

Marcie sniffed and looked up at me. "Jim?"

"Huh?"

"I'm all right now. You can let go."

"Oh. I'm sorry."

"No. Don't. Thank you."

"Come on. I'll walk you back to your room."

"Okay."

We walked in silence. She had a small apartment in the second building past the commissary, one of the co-ops we'd seen on the way in. It was austere, but homey.

Once inside, she put her arms around me again and held me close. "Thank you," she said. I put my arms around her and we stood that way for a while.

"Jim," she said softly, "will you make love to me?"

I could smell the perfume in her hair; it made me dizzy. I didn't speak; I just nodded, then brought my face around to hers. Her eyes were wide—she looked like a frightened little girl, afraid I'd say yes.

I said, "Yes," and her eyes closed gently. She laid her head against my chest and I could feel her body beginning to relax. She was all right. At last she knew she was all right. Because I was all right, and I said so.

I stroked her hair with my hand. She was . . . so tiny, so pale, so thin. So fragile. So warm.

There were a thousand things to say.

I didn't say any of them.

After a while, we moved to the bed.

"Turn off the light?" I said.

"I'd rather leave it on."

"Oh. Well . . . okay."

Thirty

I FLOATED in the land of Afterward, drifting toward the land of Nod—until suddenly, I jerked awake and sat up in a cold sweat. "Holy buffalo shit!"

Next to me, Marcie rolled over, alarmed. "Huh? What is it?"

"I have to go—I have to be back at the hotel! What time is it? Oh, sweet Jesus—it's almost midnight! They're gonna hang me for sure!"

"Jim, are you all right?"

"No—I'm not!" I was already pulling on my pants. "Where are my shoes?"

"Don't go—"

"I have to!" And then I saw the look on her face—that hurt, used expression—and I sat down next to her and pulled her into my arms. "Marcie, I'm sorry. I wish I could stay here with you, but I can't. I—I'm under orders. I know this looks like I'm running out on you, but I'm not. Please believe me."

"I believe you," she said, but I could feel her stiffening in my arms. She rubbed at her eyes. "I'm not angry. I'm used to it."

I tilted her face toward mine and kissed her. "I'm not like that, Marcie."

"Yeah, I know. Nobody's like anybody else anymore—only everybody's still running from everybody else."

I started searching for my shirt. "I'm not running *from,* I'm running *to.* If you knew—"

"Uh huh. You've even got a secret mission. Like everybody else." She threw herself back in the bed, rolling up in the blankets, pulling a pillow over her head. "Just go away, Jim—quietly! Okay?"

I sat down on the bed next to her while I pulled on my shoes. "Listen, I'll come back, all right? If it's not too late. I want to."

"Don't bother," she mmfled from under the pillow.

"Marcie, please don't be angry with me. I wish I could tell you, but I can't." I bent to kiss her, but she wouldn't let me pull the pillow away from her head. "All right, have it your own way."

I drove back to the hotel, feeling like something that had crawled out from under a rock and not knowing why. Dammit—the harder I tried to be honorable the worse I felt. Why couldn't I just be a shit like Ted and have everybody falling all over me?

The only answer I could think of to that was that I didn't know how to be a shit. I was doomed to go through life always trying to be nice. Always trying to rationalize. Always trying to understand.

I switched on the auto-terminal angrily, and punched for channel fifteen. It was a replay of one of the Free Forum sessions at the conference, but listening to it only made me angrier. Why were they broadcasting this bullshit anyway? If these people wanted to be stupid, that was their business—but how many innocent people were going to be endangered because they believed what they heard on the network? I was almost trembling with anger when I finally pulled into the hotel's underground parking.

I circled down into the concrete bowels of the building. There was a ramp marked SERVICE and I pulled into that. The robot guard scanned my card, looked at my face and cleared me without question. The elevator also checked my identity before delivering me to the thirteenth floor.

There were no armed guards waiting for me when the elevator doors slid open. I let out the breath I had been holding all the way up.

I went back to the room they had assigned me and checked in at the terminal. "Request instructions."

The screen cleared, then flashed: "Please wait at this location until further notice."

What did that mean?

I sat in front of the terminal and waited, staring at the screen. How long?

Had Wallachstein and the others already met and decided my fate? While I hadn't been there to speak for myself?

I went into the kitchen and got myself some tomato juice, then I came back to the keyboard and sat down again. Still nothing. I thought of Marcie. I could still smell the honey-warmth of her hair. It made me feel warm and toasty inside—until I remembered the bitterness of my abrupt exit. I wondered if she'd forgive me.

Well, maybe I could do something while I waited. I cleared the screen and punched for Library Service. The screen flashed: "Sorry. This terminal is locked."

Huh?

I tried again. Same answer.

I pulled my card out of the reader-slot and went to the door.

It wouldn't open. "Invalid code."

I came back into the room, stood in the center of it and looked around for another way out. The balcony?

I opened the sliding door and stepped out, leaning out over the railing to see how high I was. Too high. Thirteen stories. It wasn't the fall that was dangerous, it was the abrupt stop at the end.

What about climbing over the railing to an adjacent balcony? Not possible. The balconies were isolated for privacy. Another service of your security-conscious Marriott.

I looked down again, then went back into the room and took inventory. Two sheets, king size. Two blankets, king size. Not enough. Even with the drapes, I'd probably be four stories short.

I sat down in front of the terminal again and began to drink my tomato juice. It was tart. It made the salivary glands at the back of my mouth hurt. Did I have any other options?

I couldn't think of any.

Why did I want to escape anyway?

Because they had locked me in.

And why had they locked me in?

Because they were afraid I might try to escape.

And what did that imply? That they had made a decision? That they had something planned for me that I might not like?

And I had rushed from Marcie's bed to come here? No wonder so many people thought me a fool.

I downed the rest of the juice in a few quick swallows, then sank back in the chair and glowered at the implacable screen of the terminal.

It was totally disconnected. Before it would respond again, it would have to be cleared by someone with a priority code.

I thought about Marcie and my promise to call her. I wouldn't even be able to do that.

I thought about Wallachstein and his barely veiled threats. Had I failed the psychiatric examination?

What if they did decide to make me disappear? Wasn't I entitled to a fair trial—or had I already had it? How would they do it? Would I get any warning? How did they make people disappear anyway?

I realized I was sweating. I couldn't sit still. I got up and searched the room again, the balcony, the door—

The door beeped.

I started to call, "Who is it?" and then stopped. What if it were a firing squad? Would they do it here in the room? Or would they take me somewhere else to do it?

I stood there, debating whether to holler for help or try to hide.

Before I could make up my mind, the door slid open. "May I come in?"

"Huh? Who—?" And then I placed him. Fromkin. The man who ate strawberries and lox while talking about global starvation. The pompous asshole.

"I said, 'May I come in?' I'm not interrupting anything, am I?"

"Uh, no—I—uh, how did you open the door?"

He held up a card with a gold stripe on it for me to see.

"Oh," I said.

I made room, he stepped inside and the door slid closed. I looked at it, wanting to see if it would open for me now, but I resisted. I followed him into the room and we sat down. He sank into his chair with easy grace. How old *was* he, I wondered?

He studied me for a moment with sharp dark eyes, then he said, "I'm here because a *mutual friend* of ours suggested that I talk to you. Do you understand?"

"No names, huh?"

"That's right." He repeated, "Do you understand?"

Wallachstein had asked the same question several times. A phrase floated into my mind: *the comprehension of the defendant.* It was an important legal consideration. There had been a Supreme Court decision about it once. I wondered, was this part of my trial too?

"Is this official?" I asked.

He looked annoyed. "Unless you answer my question, I have to leave. Do you understand?"

"Yes," I said quickly. "I do. I understand. Now answer my question. Is this an official visit, or what?"

"If you want to look at it that way, yes. Our *mutual friend* thought we ought to have a little chat. It's to your benefit."

"Is it? Really?"

Fromkin looked annoyed, but otherwise he ignored the question. He said, "In case you're wondering, yes, I did see your performance this morning—and yes, I also remember you from last night. For someone who only got in town yesterday, you've certainly let people know you're here." I must have looked embarrassed, for he added, "To be fair, it's not *all* your doing. This city is just another small town these days. The number-two indoor sport is gossiping about the number-one indoor sport—and who's playing which position. You and your boyfriend just got caught in the middle, that's all."

"We're not boyfriends. The middle of what?"

Fromkin scratched his head. "Uh, let me explain it this way. There's a certain group of people; rumor has it that they're very important. Although nobody knows who's in the group, or even who does what, or even what the group is supposed to be doing, everybody suspects that anybody who knows anything must be in that group. It just so happens that some of those suspicions are very accurate. So when one of those supposed-to-be-important individuals is suddenly called away from her—ah, personal affairs—to bring in a Very Important Delivery, well, then, naturally there's going to be a great deal of interest in that delivery."

It took me a moment to translate that, and then it took another moment for it to sink in. Right. It was worse than I thought. I said, "Ted and I are not boyfriends. Or any other kind of friends. And I don't know how important our delivery was or wasn't—we were told it wasn't."

"I don't know about that." Fromkin spread his hands wide in a gesture of innocence. "That's not what I want to talk about anyway. Do you mind if I record this?" He held up his unit. I shook my head and he switched it on. "Did you see any of the playbacks of the conference sessions?"

"Only a little. I heard some of it while I was driving back here this evening."

"What did you hear?"

"A lot of uproar. About how to deal with the worms. Apparently there's a faction that wants to try to establish peaceful contact."

"Do you believe that's possible?"

"No."

"Why not?"

I blinked. "Uh, you don't know much about the Chtorrans, do you?"

"That's not germane. I'm asking *your* opinion."

"I never saw a Chtorran who wanted to stop and chat first. We never had any choice but to kill them."

"How many Chtorrans have you seen?"

"Live or pictures?"

"Total."

"Um, well—I've seen the Show Low photographs—"

Fromkin nodded knowingly. "Go on."

"—and I've seen the nest I mentioned this morning. The one with the fourth Chtorran. The one I burned."

He waited expectantly. "Is that all?"

"Um—no, there was one more. The one here at the Science Center."

His eyes narrowed. "Tell me about that," he said slowly.

I shook my head. "It was just . . . there."

He looked into my eyes and said, "I know about those sessions, son. Is that what you saw, one of them?"

I nodded. "There were some dogs. They fed them to the Chtorran. Live. Do you know about that?"

Fromkin said, "They say that Chtorrans won't eat dead meat—they have to eat their prey live."

"That's true. At least, as far as I know it is."

"Mm hm. And those are all the Chtorrans you've seen?"

"Yes."

"Are you an expert on Chtorrans?"

"No, of course not. But I've had more experience than most other people have had—at least those who've lived to tell about it. Some of those assholes this afternoon were talking about making friends with Chtorrans. And that's no more possible than a steak making friends with a dog—except from the inside."

"Couldn't it be that your experience with Chtorrans is limited, and that's colored your perceptions of them . . . ?"

"You mean, maybe there are peaceful ones, but I don't know about it?"

He nodded.

I weighed the possibility. "Well, yeah—maybe there *are* peaceful ones. I've never heard of any. And I don't think anybody else has either—or else we'd have heard about it by now. Somebody would have said something this afternoon. Somebody would know about it, wouldn't they?"

Fromkin didn't answer.

"What's this all about, anyway?" I asked.

He shook his head. "Just for information. Raw material. You know. The truth can only be seen when looked at from many points of view at once."

I shook my head. "You're not asking for information. You're digging for something specific."

"You're too suspicious. I'm a civilian, son. Can we go on?"

"There's more?"

"Just a little. This afternoon, you stood up in front of a crowd of people and said you had to burn a man because he was being attacked by a worm."

"Yes, I did." Part of me was insisting that I put up a defensive barrier against this man's probing, but another part was insisting on telling the truth, no matter who heard it. The only way we would defeat the Chtorrans would be by telling the truth. I added, "It was the kindest thing I could do."

"Kindest—?" He raised an eyebrow at me. "How do you know that?"

"I beg your pardon?"

His expression had turned hard. "Have you ever been on the receiving end of a flamethrower?"

"No, I haven't."

"Then where do you get your information?"

"That's what I was told by Shorty."

"Who's Shorty?"

"The man I had to burn. *Sir.*" I said that last deliberately.

Fromkin was silent for a moment at that, turning the information over to see if it was mined. Finally he said, "I'm told—by someone who *knows*—that death by fire has to be the most horrible thing imaginable. When you're hit by napalm, you can feel your flesh turning into flame."

"Sir," I said stiffly, "with all due respect, when a wave of fire from a flamethrower hits you, there isn't time to feel either the heat or the pain. It's a sudden descent into unconsciousness."

Fromkin looked skeptical.

"I was there, sir. I saw how quickly it happened. There wasn't any time for pain."

He studied that thought for a long moment. "How about guilt?" he asked finally. "Was there time for that?"

"Huh?"

"Do you feel guilty about what you did?"

"Guilt? I did what I had to do! What I was told to do! I never questioned it! *Hell, yes,* I feel guilty! And ashamed and shitty and a thousand other things that don't have names!" Something popped for me. "What's this all about anyway? Are you judging me too? Listen, I have enough trouble living up to my own standards—don't ask me to live up to yours! I'm sure your answers are better than mine—after all, your integrity is still unsullied by the brutal facts of practicality! You've been sitting around eating strawberries and lox! I'm the guy who had to pull the trigger! If there is a better answer, don't you think I want to know? Don't you think I have the first right to know? Come up to the hills and show me! I'd be glad to find you're right. But if you don't mind, I'll keep my torch all charged and ready—just in case you're wrong!"

He waited patiently until I ran down. And even then, he didn't answer immediately. He got up, went to the kitchen and got a bottle of water from the refrigerator. He took a glass, filled it with ice and came back into the living room, slowly pouring the water over the cubes. He eased himself back down into his chair, took a drink and studied me over the glass. When he spoke, his voice was quiet and calm. "Are you through?"

"Yeah. For now."

"Good. I want to ask you some questions now. I want you to consider a couple of things. All right?"

I nodded. I folded my arms across my chest.

"Thank you. Now, tell me this. What difference does it make? Maybe it's a kindness to burn a man, maybe it isn't. Maybe he doesn't feel a thing—and maybe it's the purest form of pain, a moment of exquisite hell. What difference does it make, Jim, if a man dies crushed in the mouth of a Chtorran or burned by napalm? He's still dead. *Where* does it make a difference?"

"You want me to answer?"

Fromkin said, "Go ahead. Take a crack at it."

I said, "It doesn't make a difference—not the way you ask it."

"Wrong," he said. "It does. It makes a lot of difference to the person who has to pull the trigger."

I looked at that. "I'm sorry. I don't see how."

"Good. So look at it this way. What's more important? Killing Chtorrans or saving lives?"

"I don't know."

"So? Who do I have to ask to find out?"

Huh? Whitlaw used to ask the same question. If I didn't know what I thought, who did? I said, "Saving lives."

"Good So what do we have to do to save lives?"

I grinned. "Kill Chtorrans."

"Good. So what happens if a human being gets in the way? No, let me rephrase that. What would have happened if you had tried to save—what was his name, Shorty?"

"We'd have both bought the farm."

Fromkin nodded. "Good. So what's more important? Killing Chtorrans or saving lives?"

"In this case, killing Chtorrans."

"Uh huh. So does it matter what justification you use?"

"Huh?"

"Does it matter whether you believe that a man dies painlessly under the flame or not?"

"Well, no, I guess not."

He nodded. "So how do you feel about it now?"

I shook my head. "I don't know." I felt torn up inside. I opened my mouth to speak, then closed it again.

He gave me another raised eyebrow.

"I don't know," I repeated.

"All right," he said. "Let me ask it this way. Would you do it again?"

"Yes." I said it without hesitation.

"You're sure of that?"

"Yes."

"Thank you. And how would you feel about it?"

I met his gaze unashamedly. "Shitty. About like I feel now. But I'd still do it. It doesn't matter what the policy is." I added, "The important thing is killing Chtorrans."

"You're really adamant about that, aren't you?"

"Yeah, I guess so."

He took a long breath, then switched off his recorder. "Okay, I'm through."

"Did I pass?"

"Say again?"

"Your test—this was no interview. This was an attitude check. Did I pass?"

He looked up from his recorder, straight into my eyes. "If it were an attitude check, what you just asked would probably have flunked you."

"Yeah, well." My arms were still folded across my chest. "If my attitude leaves something to be desired, so does the way I've been treated. So we're even."

He stood up and I stood with him. "Answer me something. Are there peaceful Chtorrans?"

He looked at me blankly. "I don't know. What do you think?"

I didn't answer, just followed him to the door. He slid his card into the lock-slot and the door slid open for him. I started to follow him out, but there were two armed guards waiting in the hall.

"Sorry," said Fromkin. For the first time, he looked embarrassed.

"Yeah," I said, and stepped back. The door slid shut in front of me.

Thirty-One

I STOOD there staring at that goddamned door for thirty seconds without saying a word.

I put my hands on it and pressed. The metal was cold.

I rested my head against the solid wallness of it. My hands clenched into fists.

"Shit!"

And then I said a whole bunch of other words too.

I swore as long as I could without repeating myself, then switched to Spanish and kept on going.

And when I finally wound down, I felt no better than when I had started.

I felt used. Betrayed. And stupid.

I began to pace around the apartment again. I kicked the terminal every time I passed it. Useless hunk of junk. I couldn't even use it to call room service.

I wandered into the kitchen and opened the fridge—it was surprisingly well stocked. But I wasn't hungry. I was angry. I started opening drawers. Someone had thoughtfully removed all of the carving and steak knives.

And swearing didn't do any good anymore. It only left my

throat dry. And me feeling foolish. The minute you stop, you start to realize how silly it looks.

What I really wanted to do was get even.

I walked back into the living room of the suite and gave the terminal another kick. A good one—it nearly toppled off the stand, but I caught it in time. And then I found myself wondering *why.* The damn thing wouldn't communicate with me—I didn't owe it any favors.

I shoved it off the stand and onto the floor.

It hit with a dull thud.

I picked it up and shook it. It didn't even sound broken.

"I know—" I carried it out to the balcony and threw it over the side.

It bounced and scraped down the sloping side of the building and shattered on the concrete below with a terrifically satisfying smash.

I threw the stand after it.

And then a chair.

And a lamp.

And a small table.

The TV screen was bolted to the wall. I hit it with the second chair—it took three tries to smash it—and then threw the chair after its companion.

Bounce, bounce, scrape, slide, crash, smash. Great.

What else?

The microwave oven.

The nightstand from the bedroom.

Three more chairs.

Two more lamps.

The dining-nook table.

A hassock.

All the hangers from the closet.

Most of the towels and sheets.

A king-size mattress and box spring. Those last were particularly difficult.

It was while I was struggling with the box spring that I realized a crowd had gathered below—at a safe distance, of course. They were applauding each new act of destruction. The more outrageous it was, the louder the cheers.

The bedframe and headboard drew a standing ovation.

I wondered what I could do to top it. I began to clean out the kitchen.

All the dishes—they sounded great as they clattered and crashed on the street below—and all the pots and pans.

All the flatware.

The contents of the refrigerator—and the shelves as well.

Almost all the bottled water. I opened one for myself and took a long drink. I stood there on the balcony, catching my breath and wondering why nobody had come up to stop this rain of terror. I finished the bottle and it too sailed out into the night to shatter somewhere in the darkness below.

I looked back into the apartment. What else? What had I missed?

The bar!

I decided to start with the beer. There was a nearly full keg in a half-fridge under the counter. It clanged and bonged all the way down, exploding in a sudsy fountain when it hit. There were screams from the ones who got drenched.

The half-fridge followed the keg. Shit! Wasn't anything built in anymore? What kind of lousy workmanship was this anyway?

I stopped, arm cocked in the act of defenestrating a bottle of scotch.

No. Some things are sacred.

What was it Uncle Moe used to say? Never kill a bottle without saluting it first? Right.

I took a swig and sent it to its death.

There were three bottles of the scotch. I toasted every one. Then I murdered the bourbon. I began to realize that I was going to have to take smaller swigs. This was a very well-stocked bar.

I assaulted the rums, both light and dark.

Exterminated the vodka.

Executed the gin.

Raped the *vin rosé*.

There were fewer shouts coming from below now. Apparently, once I had stopped dropping the big exciting stuff I had lost most of my audience. Well, just as well. Spectacle may be impressive to the unsophisticated, but the real artist works for elegance.

I staggered back and finished off the liqueurs and the brandies. I saved the sherry for last—after all, it was an after-dinner drink.

There was a selection of different glasses on a crystal shelf. They followed the bottles. And so did the shelf.

I prowled around the room, looking for things I'd missed. There wasn't much. I wondered if I could roll up the rug.

No—I couldn't. I was having too much trouble standing.

Besides, I had to pee first. I stumbled into the bathroom and threw up. Then I peed.

"How about a shower?" I hiccuped. "Okay," I agreed with myself, and turned the water on. I found a towel that I'd forgotten to throw and some soap. I also found a box of Sober-Ups in the medicine cabinet. No—I wasn't ready to sober up yet. I put them aside.

The shower had terrific acoustics. The resonance was perfect for singing. It was all the encouragement I needed. "*When I was a lad in Venusport, I took up the local indoor sport—*" I went through the complete librettos of *A Double Dose of Love* and *A Bisexual Built for Two* before I ran out of soap.

The nice thing about hotels, though—you never run out of hot water.

But you can't sing without soap. It just doesn't feel right.

I turned off the water, found the forgotten towel and began to dry my hair. Still singing, still toweling. I walked back into the living room—

Wallachstein, Lizard and the other two were standing there, waiting for me.

"Uh—" I said. "Hi." And lowered the towel to my waist. "Can I, uh, offer you a . . . seat?" Only Lizard smiled; she turned her head to hide it. The others just looked grim.

"Thank you," said Colonel Wallachstein. "I think we prefer to stand."

"Well—" I said. "It's nice of you to drop in like this. I wish you would have phoned ahead, though, so I could have tidied up a little—"

If Wallachstein was angry, he hid it well. He kept his voice flat and emotionless. His dark eyes were unreadable. He indicated the empty room. I'd pretty well stripped it bare. "Is there some explanation for all this—?"

I shifted my weight to what I hoped was an assured stance. "Yes. I was bored."

"I beg your pardon?"

"Someone locked me in. Disconnected the terminal. I didn't have anything else to do. I began to experiment with the psycho-acoustic properties of falling objects, trying to determine which common household items made the most satisfying crashes."

"I see . . . and what did you determine?"

"Ceramic lamps are very nice. So are beer kegs. And almost any liquid-filled bottle. Chairs and mattresses are impressive, but dull."

Wallachstein nodded thoughtfully. "I'll remember that for future reference. In case I'm ever in a situation where I need to use those facts." He looked at me curiously. "Is there anything else you want to add?"

"Yes, I think there is," I said. I started off slowly. "I'd like to know why I was locked in here, for one thing! You asked me to cooperate with you. Is this how you guarantee it? Or is there something else going on that I don't know about? Have you and your disappearing committee that doesn't exist already decided my fate? Do I still exist? I suppose you don't want my opinion in the matter, do you? And while I'm at it, I want to know what ever happened to fair trials. I still don't even know what I'm charged with! I think I want an attorney present before we go any further." I folded my arms across my chest—then had to grab my towel to keep it from falling. I resumed the pose, but the effect had been spoiled.

Wallachstein took a moment before answering. He glanced around the room as if looking again for a place to sit, then looked back at me. "Well, yes—I suppose we do owe you an apology for that. It was a mistake."

"Was it?" I demanded. "How come everything is always a mistake? Doesn't anybody around here do anything on purpose anymore?"

"Like the furniture?" he prompted.

"Yeah, like the furniture! That was on purpose." I shoved my chin out in what I hoped was a pugnacious expression. "You want me to pay for it? I have fifty thousand caseys."

He shook his head, held up a hand. "Don't bother. This room doesn't exist. Neither does the furniture. Neither do I. And, perhaps—neither do you. If you'll shut up and listen for a moment. . . ."

That brought me down. I shut up.

"The fact that you were detained against your will is unfortunate. I assume full responsibility. I gave an order and it was misinterpreted. I apologize. I can understand—and sympathize—with your reaction. In fact, it's something of a healthy sign. It indicates you have a side that is not only independent, but occasionally downright antisocial. For our purposes, those are valuable traits." He rubbed his chin thoughtfully and went on. "Now, as to your other questions: there was no hearing. You were never on trial. You were never charged. Do you understand?"

"Uh . . ." There was that question again. "Yes, sir. I do."

"Good. The paperwork has been destroyed. There's nothing on record to indicate that you committed a breach of security. Furthermore, I've placed on record a copy of your orders, which you received yesterday morning *in writing,* instructing you to report the information about the fourth Chtorran to the members of this conference, in whatever forum available. Do you understand?"

"Uh, yes, sir."

"Good. Now go get dressed. There's something else we have to talk about, and I'd prefer to do it a little more formally."

"Yes, sir." I retreated to the bathroom, downed a handful of Sober-Ups and pulled on my clothes. It was while I was running a brush through my hair that I overheard raised voices. One of them was Lizard's.

She was saying, "—still disagree. It isn't fair."

"It's a fact of life, Major! We're all expendable." I didn't recognize the voice. Mr. Darkfellow?

"That's not the point! It's this particular operation! It's slimy!"

"It's *necessary!* We've been forced by circumstance. The decision has already been made—"

And then, suddenly, there was silence—as if someone had realized how loud they were all getting and had hushed them. I frowned at myself in the mirror. What the hell was going on now? What kind of rabbit hole was I falling into this time?

I clipped my hair in the back, splashed some more water on my face, toweled carefully, counted to ten and came back into the room.

Only Wallachstein was left. The others were gone. Lizard. The Japanese lady. Mr. Darkfellow.

Wallachstein said, "I asked them to leave. It was getting a little loud."

"Something you didn't want me to hear?"

"Perhaps. I have a job to offer you. It's rather dangerous. But I think you're qualified for it."

"Why?" I asked.

"Because you're one of the few personnel around who has both a scientific background and first-hand experience with Chtorrans in the field."

"What's the job?"

"I want to put you into the Chtorran Control Section of the Agency."

"I thought that's where I was already."

He shook his head. "That's not a permanent operation. It's only a temporary holding of the line while we try to figure out what we're really up against. We're putting together something a little more *responsible.* You'll do pretty much what you were doing up at Alpha Bravo—searching out and destroying pockets of infestation. The only difference is that we'll be using the team to develop methods of capturing Chtorrans alive—if we can. The only live specimen we have to date may be an atypical example. You've seen it, I've heard."

I nodded.

"So how does that sound to you, McCarthy?"

I shrugged. "It's not exactly what I had in mind. I want to be attached to the Science Center here. I want to finish what I started with those specimens."

Wallachstein shrugged it away. "Don't bother. Let one of Molly's button-pushers play with that stuff. We find those things every time we find a hut. The only reason we still collect them is to keep Dr. Partridge's section so busy they can't get into trouble anywhere else. So far, it works. We keep a man in her section to keep us posted if anything interesting comes in. I believe you met him. By the way, that was a nice piece of work, figuring out that the Chtorrans live under a red sun."

"Thank you. But the job isn't finished."

He shook his head. "It's unimportant. Those specimens are unimportant."

"Huh? Then why were we flown in on a priority flight?"

"You figure it out. What did you deliver?"

"Millipedes. Plants. Scrapings—"

"Worthless. We've got specimens."

"—Chtorran eggs!"

"Mm hm. Maybe. We'll know when they hatch." Wallachstein was unimpressed. "What else? What did you bring in worth fifty thousand caseys?"

"Oh!" The lockbox. "The memory clip."

Wallachstein nodded. "All that other stuff was just a cover. To tell the truth, I wish you'd left it behind."

"Huh? Why?"

"Look around—you see this city? It looks like it survived, right? Wrong. It's too big. It's not supportable. We don't have the people. It's just a matter of time until it breaks down."

"I thought the government wanted to bring the people back into the cities."

"It does. But militarily, it's not a good idea. What if we have another plague? We lose everything all over again. We can't risk it. No, we're more convinced than ever of our need to decentralize, especially our labs. I want every unit in the country to be studying the Chtorrans independently. We'll have the network fully reestablished by the end of next month, so you'll be in full communication with everyone else's work at the same time. I can offer you that. You'll be in communication with some of our best brains."

"I don't understand this," I said. "This afternoon I was nothing but a pain in the ass to you. An embarrassment. What changed?"

"We figured out how to make an asset of a liability, that's all."

"Oh?"

He smiled gently. "You're not stupid, McCarthy. Not when you sit down with a terminal. But sometimes you don't see what's in front of your own face. I'd have thought you'd have figured it out by now."

"Well, I haven't."

"It's like this. You are uniquely valuable. You know something that nobody else does. You know that there are sometimes four Chtorrans in a nest."

"But nobody believes me."

"I do," he said. "And so do a lot of other people. Some very important people."

"Huh?"

"That memory clip. You were wearing a helmet, remember?"

It took a second for me to realize what he was talking about. "But—Obama said the clip glitched."

"She was protecting you. She didn't know if it was important or not. She couldn't assess the impact by herself. So she passed it by a nonstandard channel. You carried it yourself."

"You've seen it—?"

He nodded. "All of us. And the inquest. It's pretty scary stuff."

For a moment, I couldn't catch my breath.

"Are you all right?"

"No," I said. I looked at him. I could feel my heart pounding. "I need to know. What did the clip show? Did I . . . screw up? I mean—could I have saved Shorty?"

He said it quietly. "Yes."

I felt as if I'd been slammed by a wall of guilt. I sank to the floor, to my knees. I was hurting too hard to cry. I put my hands on the rug to hold myself up. I felt like I was falling. My head was burning and I was trapped inside it. I wanted to puke. My stomach jerked and heaved. I wanted to die—

I came to with my head in Wallachstein's lap, crying. He was patting my face gently with a cool, damp towel. When he saw my eyes were open, he put the towel down. He stroked my hair gently. "How are you feeling, son?"

"Shitty." The tears were still rolling down my cheeks.

"Good. That's what you should be feeling." He kept stroking my hair. I was willing to lie there and let him. It didn't seem odd at all.

"I want to go home," I said. "I want this thing over! I don't want it this way!" I was crying again. "I want my mommy to tell me everything is going to be all right again!"

"Yeah," said Wallachstein. "Me too."

And then I started laughing. It hurt too much to cry anymore. All I could do was laugh.

And cry.

And then laugh some more.

Wallachstein mopped my face with the wet towel again. "How are you feeling now?"

"Better. Thank you." I realized how odd this scene must look and I felt uncomfortable. I tried to get up. He pushed me back down into his lap. "Stay. I want to talk to you."

"Yes, sir." I let myself stay.

"We've known that there's been something happening with the Chtorrans for seven or eight weeks now. We started losing teams and we had no idea why—just that they'd go out to handle a nest and they wouldn't come back.

"We had some guesses but no proof, so we sent out teams with cameras and radios. We lost two of them and still didn't know any more. Your team is the first one that returned. Your clip is the answer we needed. We've already found two more huts with four Chtorrans in them. Both have been neutralized. We're already changing your procedures. You saved a lot of lives."

"I wish somebody had told me some of this before."

Wallachstein patted my forehead with the towel again. "I think you'd better review your actions since you arrived and answer that one yourself. We weren't sure what kind of bozos you and your friend were. We're still not sure about your friend, but he's keeping himself busy and out of the way, and I suppose I should be thankful for that much at least. Eventually I'll find something for him, something where he can't get into too much trouble."

I let it all sink in. It didn't change anything. "I still didn't save Shorty."

"That's right. He's still dead." Wallachstein added, "And likely to remain that way."

I sat up and looked at him. "That's pretty callous."

"I suppose it looks like that. Jim, whether you could have saved him or not, does it make a difference anymore?"

"No, I suppose not."

"Good. Real good," he said. "Fromkin was right about you."

"Fromkin?"

"What do you think that interview was about? I wanted to know what your feelings were about killing Chtorrans, and how candid I could be with you."

"What did he say?"

"He said I should tell you the whole truth and nothing but. He said you'd be difficult about it too."

"Am I?"

"Yep." He grinned. "Now, do you want the job?"

"I don't know. I'll still be on the front lines, won't I?"

"There's a commission involved."

"How high?"

"Second lieutenant."

"You're kidding."

"I wish I were. But only officers can be cleared for Chtorran security. So if we want to add a member to the team, we have to make him an officer."

"Can't I stay 'Civilian Personnel, Attached'?"

He shook his head. "No nonmilitary personnel are going to be allowed access to the Control Arm's operations. So what's your choice?"

"Can I have some time to think it over?"

"I need your answer tonight. That's why we were late getting back to you. We had some decisions to make. Some of them were triggered by the events this afternoon. And you're a part of those decisions too. I had to twist some arms to bring you aboard. Now, either take it or leave it."

"What if I leave it? Then what?"

"I don't know. We'll find something to do with you. I promise, you won't like it."

"So I don't really have a choice, do I?"

He looked annoyed and apologetic, both at once. "Son, I don't have time to play games. There's a war on. Do you want to be a part of it or not?"

I looked into his face. "Yes, I do—it's just that I'm not used to straight answers, so you'll understand if I'm a little skeptical."

He didn't answer that. He said, "You'll take the job?"

"Will you make me a first lieutenant?"

He blinked. Then he laughed. "Don't push too hard. I'll go for first. I won't go as high as captain." He looked around. "Did you throw the Bible out too? No—there it is. Stand up. Raise your right hand. Repeat after me—"

Thirty-Two

I ENDED up with a rifle in my hands and a feeling of *déjà vu.*

The rifle was an AM-280 with tunable laser sight. The output was set high in the UV and I had to wear an EV-helmet with retinal-focused eyepieces to see the beam. It spat high-velocity bursts of eighteen-grain needles, as many as three thousand per second. You pointed the beam at your target and pulled the trigger. The needle bursts would tear holes in a steel door. They said you could slice a man in half with a 280. I didn't want to try.

I hefted the rifle and looked at it. I had a sour feeling in my stomach. I'd trusted Duke and Obama and ended up with a torch in my hands and Shorty on the receiving end. It'd left me with a bad feeling about weapons. I could admire the technology here. It was the use which bothered me.

The lieutenant slid two boxes across the counter toward me. "Sign here that you've received the rifle and ammo."

I held up a finger. "Wait a minute. Who's supposed to check me out on this?"

"I don't know anything about that."

"Then I'm not signing for it."

"Have it your own way." He shrugged and started to turn away.

"Hold it. Is that phone secure?"

"You can't use it."

"Slide it over here. This is company business."

He started to say something else, then thought better of it. He pushed the phone at me. I slid my card into it and punched the number Wallachstein had given me.

The line beeped as it switched to code mode and Wallachstein came on the line, "Joe's Deli, Joe ain't here."

"Uncle Ira?"

"Speaking."

"I've got a problem."

"Tell me about it."

"I'm not taking this weapon."

"Why not?"

"Nobody seems to know who's responsible for checking me out on it."

"Don't worry about it—"

"I am worried about it."

"—you're not going to have to use it. It's for show."

"I'm sorry, sir, but that's not good enough."

"Look son, I don't have anyone free to check you out on that piece before this afternoon. All I want you to do is stand there and look like a soldier. I'll see that you have a thorough course of instruction in it before the week is out."

I started to protest. Instead, I said, "May I have that in writing, sir?"

There was silence from the other end of the line. Then he said slowly, "What's the matter, son?"

"Nothing, sir. But it's like I told you last night. I'm not taking anybody's word for anything anymore."

He sighed. I could almost see the expression on his face. I wondered if I'd overstepped myself. He said, "I'll put it in your file. You can check it yourself this afternoon."

"Thank you."

"Right." He signed off.

I hung up the phone and turned back to the lieutenant. "Have you got a manual for this thing?"

He looked sour. "Yeah. Somewhere. Wait a minute." He

disappeared into the back and came back with a thin booklet which he tossed onto the counter. "Anything else?"

"No, thanks." I put the book in the rifle case along with the two boxes of clips, and closed it. I signed the receipt and picked up the helmet.

As I turned to leave, the lieutenant said, "You know something? I don't believe you're a lieutenant any more than I believe any of the other stories I've heard about you."

I met his gaze. "I really don't care. What you believe is none of my business."

I went outside and tossed the rifle and helmet into the trunk of the car and locked it. Instead of going back to my barracks, I pulled the base map out of the glove compartment and looked for the practice range. There it was, on the far north end of the camp. It took ten minutes to get there—I had to take the long way around.

There was no one there when I arrived. Good. I wanted privacy. I unpacked the rifle and sat down in the car with it across my lap while I read the manual. I locked both safeties, and practiced loading and unloading it. An empty magazine would be automatically ejected. A full one could be snapped into place as easily as inserting a memory clip into a recorder. Good.

Now, how did the laser sight work?

According to the manual, the laser randomly retuned itself every ten-thousandth of a second to a different point in the spectrum, but always beyond the range of visible light. The laser would fire its microsecond bursts at randomly computed intervals. There was no regularity either in the frequency of the beam output or in its frame rate. Only an EV-helmet, when it was plugged into the rifle, could track the myriad infinitesimal packets of coherent light. The wearer would see the laser as a steady beam. No one else—goggled or otherwise—would see anything at all, except perhaps an occasional subliminal flash. The idea was to prevent enemy snipers from homing in on the human end of the beam. Without sophisticated equipment, tracking it was impossible.

Next I tried on the helmet.

It was like looking into hell. I was staring into a *glowy,* ethereal-looking world, colored all in shades of red and gray. The helmet sensors scanned the spectrum from beyond ultraviolet to below infra-red, then the image was digitized and new color values were assigned; the resynthesized image was projected directly onto the retina. Clever. But it hurt my eyes. It would take some getting used to.

I retuned the color spectrum and lowered the brightness of the image. Now the scene was multichromed, but individual objects were not. Every building, tree, car, or whatever, was painted only in shades of one dominant color—pink or green or blue. The horizon and distant landscape appeared as layers of purple and gray while closer objects stood out in translucent, almost glowing pastels. They seemed to float against the dingy background. There were no shadows.

It was an eerie and compelling kind of imagery. The world was both familiar and surreal. I could identify objects, I could see them in better detail than I could with the unaided eye, but at the same time, everything had a shimmering aura in this ghostly twilight landscape.

I looked at my hands; they were pale, shading almost to green. In fact, my whole body looked green. Would all human beings look this color?

I got out of the car and turned around slowly, examining the world around me as if I'd never seen it before. And in this sense, I never had. Finally, and with a definite sense of regret, I went back to the car for the rifle.

I connected the helmet-control wire to the stock of the weapon and switched the laser on.

Nothing.

No beam.

I switched it off. I took off the helmet. I reset the laser for standard operation. I switched it on. A bright red beam stabbed across the practice field.

Great. The laser worked.

I reset it for coded operation and put the helmet back on.

Nothing.

I took off the helmet and double-checked its batteries and all connections. They appeared to be in order. I double-checked the connection to the rifle. Again correct. Hm. I put the helmet back on, waited for the image to solidify and turned on the beam again. If it was working, you couldn't prove it by this helmet.

I switched everything off and went back to the manual. It took only a few minutes to find the appropriate section. In large block letters, it said: "IMPORTANT: BE SURE THAT THE SETTING OF THE CODE KEYS IN YOUR HELMET IS IDENTICAL TO THE SETTING OF THE CODE KEYS IN YOUR WEAPON."

It took a few minutes to find the section on the code keys—there were matching panels on both the helmet and the rifle. The laser sent a control pulse to the helmet every time it fired. Both the rifle and the helmet had identical random-number generators, but if they weren't starting from the same seed—the setting of the code keys—the helmet wouldn't track with the laser as it continually retuned itself every ten-thousandth of a second.

You could use the weapon without its laser sight, but with nowhere near the same kind of accuracy.

I reset the code keys on both helmet and rifle and put the helmet on again. Once again, I stood at the center of a surreal world: a landscape of gray, populated with glowing pastel trees and buildings. But this time, when I switched on the laser, the beam appeared as a luminescent bar that seemed to be all colors at once: pink, green, white, blue, yellow, red—it flickered through the spectrum faster than the eye could identify individual hues. I saw only the afterimages as they blurred into each other, and the effect was the perception of colors that I'd never seen before. They were intense and glorious. The beam sliced across the nacreous landscape like a razor. I wrote my name across the sky with it, and I could see the afterimage as a shimmering blur. Was that my eyes or the sensors or something in the digitizing process? No matter, it was eerily beautiful.

You could easily become addicted to this other-worldly sense of perception. It was very distracting.

Finally, I stopped. I couldn't stall any longer. I loaded a clip into the rifle and switched off both the safeties. I touched the beam to one of the haystacks on the other side of the field. I pulled the trigger.

Someone kicked my arm and the haystack exploded.

I locked both the safeties on and flipped the goggles of the helmet up.

Yes, the haystack had exploded.

The AM-280 was supposed to be recoilless, but it wasn't. No

gun is ever completely recoilless. You have to be careful with repeating weapons because they'll "walk up" on you. That's what had happened to me here. Instead of punching a hole in the haystack, I had sliced it vertically upwards.

I flipped the goggles back down, switched off the safeties and blew up another haystack. It took three more tries before I could control the weapon well enough to just punch holes in them. The trick was to focus on the end of the beam and lean into the action of the rifle to steer it. I sliced up the last two haystacks, just to see if the rifle could be used as an axe. It could. Good.

Maybe I could even cut a Chtorran in half with it.

Except I didn't know if I was looking forward to that opportunity or not.

I went back to the car and put the gun back into the case and locked it in the trunk, the helmet too. I drove back to the barracks feeling curiously happy. As if I'd proven something to myself, although I wasn't sure what.

Thirty-Three

THERE WAS a box on the bed when I came in. Inside was a uniform, with appropriate insignia. Only one. There were supposed to be two. Typical army efficiency—half the job is always done on time. I took it out and looked at it. Something was giving me a vaguely uneasy feeling—and it wasn't just the after effects of last night's booze. I'd thrown up most of that before it had gotten into my bloodstream, and the Sober-Ups had neutralized the rest before it could do any real damage. No, this was something else, but I couldn't put my finger on it. I just knew that I wouldn't feel quite right wearing this uniform. It had come . . . too easily.

Still pondering, I hung it up in the closet.

I was in the shower when Ted staggered in. He didn't even take off his clothes; he just stepped into the shower with me and held his head under the spray.

"Good morning," I said.

"Oh," he said. "Is it morning?"

"For a little while longer anyway." I pulled him away from the shower head so I could rinse off. He sagged against the wall.

"What day is it?" he asked.

"Sunday."

"Of what year?"

"Same one." I got out of the shower and grabbed a towel. I didn't particularly want to talk to Ted right now.

I was half-dressed when he sloshed out of the bathroom after me. "Hey, Jim—" he began.

"Eh?"

"I'm sorry I wasn't here yesterday. Or last night. Or this morning. Things just got away from me, that's all."

"Oh?"

He must have sensed my coolness. "Look, you've got to understand—I was doing it for us, trying to make some connections! And I did! I didn't even see any of the sessions yesterday."

"Oh?" Then he must have missed the scene in the conference hall. I didn't ask.

"No. I was scouting."

"I'm sure."

"Listen, it paid off! I've been offered a commission in the Telepathy Corps. I go in for my operation on Wednesday. I'll be getting one of the new multiband implants."

"Oh, terrific."

"It is, Jim!" He grabbed my shoulders. "Before the plagues, it would have taken an Act of God—or at least an Act of Congress—to get into the corps. Now they're so desperate, they're even willing to waive the psychological requirements."

"I can see that."

"No, you know what I mean."

Yes, I did. "What else did you do for *us?*"

"I'm sorry, Jim. I did speak up for you, but you weren't qualified. I've got the electronic-language background. And I can travel."

I pulled away from him and went to the closet.

"But listen to me—that's not all. Remember that Chtorran that we heard about, the live one that they captured?"

"Yeah . . . ?"

"Well, I got to see him last night. He's amazing!"

"Oh . . . ?"

"Yeah—I met that girl you were talking about, Jillanna! You were right. She's really something! That's why I wasn't here last night. I spent the night with her. She's with the project, and she got me in to see him. Really extraordinary. It was feeding time, and—"

"Ted! *Stop!*"

"Huh?"

"I don't want to hear about it, okay?"

He looked at me confusedly. "You're sure?"

"I'm sure."

He peered at me. "Are you all right?"

"I'm fine."

"Are you upset because I didn't come looking for you so you could see it too?"

"No, I'm not."

"—because if that's what it is, Jimbo, I'm sorry, but this was an invitation only for one. If you know what I mean."

I pulled away from him and started getting dressed.

He said, "Hey—you'll get your chance. They're going to show it to the conference this afternoon! They're trucking it over to the hotel right now."

I ignored him. I opened the closet door.

"Hey!" said Ted. "Terrific! They've already delivered my uniform! Great!" I stepped back and he pulled it off its hanger. "How do I look? Lieutenant Theodore Andrew Nathaniel Jackson?"

"Uh—" I didn't say it. I closed my mouth and went back into the bathroom to get a hairbrush instead.

"Oh, come on, Jim—don't be a spoilsport! Say congratulations!"

"Congratulations."

"Like you *mean* it!" he wailed.

"Sorry, I can't do that. I am not going to sleep better tonight, knowing that you are helping to defend America."

"Well, then that's your problem."

"Don't slam the door on your way out," I said.

He didn't.

"Shit," I said.

Thirty-Four

"IS THAT thing armed?"

I looked up. The speaker was another one of those cranky-looking officers I had been running into every since getting off the chopper.

"Yes, sir. It is."

"By whose authority?"

"Special Forces."

He shook his head. "Sorry, soldier, Not here. This operation is regular army." Somehow, the way he said it, he meant the *real* army.

I looked at his bars. "Major," I said, "I was given orders to stand right here and wear this helmet and carry this rifle. I was told to do this because there is a large, purple and red, man-eating caterpillar in the cage under that curtain. The theory is that if that creature should somehow break loose, I'm supposed to stop it."

The major put his arm around my shoulder and led me off to a corner of the stage. The curtain was still closed. "Son—" he started to say warmly.

"Don't call me 'son.' I'm an officer."

"Lieutenant," he said stiffly, "don't be an asshole. I want you off this stage—and the other jerk-off too." He pointed to the rifleman on the other side of the stage. I hadn't exchanged more than two words with him. All I knew about him was that his name was Scott and he stuttered.

"I'm sorry, sir. I can't do that."

"Listen to me, stupid. Under the terms of the conference charter, this is supposed to be an entirely civilian operation. The military is only to provide supplementary aid and keep a very low profile. I am *ordering* you off this stage."

"Yes, sir. Would you put that in writing, sir?"

He hesitated. Then he said, "Listen to me—the glass walls of that cage are laced with doped silicon monofibers. Do you honestly think that creature is likely to break through those panels?"

"It doesn't matter whether I think it's likely or not, sir. Would you put those orders in writing?"

"Who's your commanding officer?" he scowled.

I could have kissed him for asking. "Uncle Ira," I said.

"I see. . . ." He said it slowly. I could almost see the wheels turning in his head. "Those are his orders, then?"

"Yes, sir."

"Well"—he had to say something—"lock those safeties on. I don't want any accidents."

"Yes, sir."

"All right. Thank you. Resume your post."

I went back to the side of the cage. As soon as the major left the stage, I flicked the safeties off again.

A few minutes later, Dr. Zymph walked through. She took one look at me and another at the other lieutenant on the other side and frowned. She disappeared into the wings of the stage for a moment, and when she came back, she came straight toward me.

"Lieutenant?"

I flipped the goggles up. "Ma'am?"

Apparently she didn't recognize me from yesterday, not with the helmet on. Just as well. She said, "Would you mind standing in the wings where the audience can't see you?"

"I thought you said these things were dangerous."

"I did and they are. But I want you out of sight. Please?"

I thought about it. "Sure. No problem." I moved off. She went and spoke to Scott on the other side and he did likewise.

Dr. Zymph waved to an aide—it was Jerry Larson from Molly Partridge's office. I wondered what he was doing here. He gestured to someone else offstage and the stage lights shifted to a dimmer, redder color, and after a few tests with some sophisticated light sensors, Dr. Zymph was satisfied. She nodded to Larson and he and another aide began undraping the glass case with the Chtorran in it.

Without thinking, I flipped my goggles down over my eyes and switched the laser beam on. The red light of the stage turned gray. The beam appeared as an eerie bar of flickering luminescent color.

They were undraping the other side first, so I didn't see the Chtorran—only the reactions of those who were looking toward it. Their faces were pearly green. Their expressions were stiff. They looked like zombies. I wondered how the rest of the conference would react when the main curtain went up. And then the last of the drape came off the glass case on my side and I could see the Chtorran too. It was a bright silvery worm. Its color was *beautiful* in the adjusted image of the goggles. It *glowed.*

Almost instinctively, I brought the rifle barrel up. The flickery beam played across the Chtorran's soft fur. Immediately—as if it could *sense* the beam, somehow—it turned to look at me. Its great lidless eyes focused on me with dispassionate interest. The same look it had given the dogs.

Was this the last thing Shorty had seen?

I lowered the beam. I didn't know if the creature could sense it or not, but I didn't want to irritate it. The Chtorran continued to study me. It unfolded its arms and pressed them against the glass. Then it moved forward and pressed its face—if you could call it a face—against the cold surface. Was it tasting?

It slid even further forward then, lifting a third of its bulk up the side of the cage. It leaned on the glass. The frame creaked ominously.

"Don't worry, it'll hold," someone behind me said. I didn't turn to look. I just brought the beam back up and held it on the Chtorran's belly until it slid back down again.

"Trrlll . . ." it said.

Dr. Zymph walked up to the cage then, ignoring the Chtorran, and bent to inspect the front of the platform supporting it. She looked worried. She lifted the edge of the dust ruffle and peered at the supports. She called Larson over and the two of them bent together to look. "I thought I heard it creak," she said. "Does that look correct to you?"

He nodded. "We're okay." He looked at his watch. "You'd better get started."

"Right." She stood up then. "Everybody please clear the stage." She raised her voice and repeated the command. "If you're not wearing a red badge, you're not authorized to be here." She came over to my side of the stage and peeked out through the edge of the curtain. She nodded, satisfied.

"Counting the house?" I asked.

"Eh?" She looked at me, as if surprised I could speak. "Just checking the seating arrangements." She picked up her clipboard from the stand where she'd left it, gave a thumbs-up signal to Larson on the opposite side of the stage and stepped out in front of the curtain.

They must have hit her with a spotlight then, because I could see it from this side as a bright spot shimmering in the folds of cloth. Her shadow was a silhouette in the center. She switched on her microphone and began to speak. We could hear her clearly backstage. "I don't suppose I have to make much of an introduction this afternoon, even though this is something of an unscheduled event. But after the, ah, heated discussions of yesterday as to just how *dangerous* the gastropedes may be, we thought it best to bring our one live specimen out for display and let you judge for yourselves."

The Chtorran was looking at me again. I wished it would turn around and look at the fellow on the other side. He was meatier than I.

"Now, before we open the curtain, I want to caution all of you against taking any flash pictures—and we also request that you please try to be as quiet as possible. We're going to bring the lights all the way down and put a spotlight on the gastropede. We're not sure how it will react to a large audience, so we're going to keep it dazzled by the light. For this reason, it's imperative that you not make any unnecessary sounds."

The Chtorran was fascinated by Dr. Zymph's voice. It kept cocking its eyes back and forth, trying to locate the source of the sound. If it had any external ears, I couldn't see them. I wondered if that suggested a higher-density atmosphere. That would certainly go with a heavier gravity. Sound waves would be more intense—experientially louder. The creature's ears could be a lot smaller. But would its hearing be better or worse on Earth? Or maybe it didn't need ears. Maybe it could hear with its whole body. Maybe it could even *see* with its whole body.

"All right, now—" Dr. Zymph was saying, "—remember to keep very very quiet. Can I have the curtain opened, please?"

It slid open like the doorway to a hanger. A single pink shaft of light streamed directly in, widening as the curtain opened. The Chtorran turned to look at it. I could hear gasps from the darkness beyond.

Dr. Zymph didn't say anything. The Chtorran's presence was statement enough. It unfolded its arms and began exploring the front surface of the cage, as if trying to reach the light.

I touched the contrast knob on my helmet and the shaft of the spotlight faded. The audience appeared beyond it in a dim green gloom. I turned the knob another klick and the bright parts of the image faded further; the darker areas brightened again. I could see the whole auditorium now. The audience was very upset and restless. I could see them whispering excitedly to one another. I could hear them rustling in their seats.

The Chtorran slid forward, lifting the forward third of its body up against the glass. I heard sudden gasps. The creature must have heard them too—it hesitated and stared, trying to focus on the space beyond the light. It remained poised in that position. This was the third time I had seen a Chtorran reared up like that; what did the position mean in Chtorran body language? Was it a challenge? Or a prelude to attack?

I looked at the audience again. I could pick out faces in the first few rows. There was Lizard, sitting at the far end of the front row. I didn't recognize the fellow with her; he looked like the same colonel I had seen her with the day before. Next to him was Fromkin, wearing another of those silly-looking, old-fashioned frilly shirts. All of them looked odd, painted in shades of pale green. While I watched, an aide came up to Lizard and bent to whisper something to her. She nodded and got up. The colonel got up with her. Fromkin waited a moment longer, then followed them off to the side of the auditorium. I knew that exit. That was the door Wallachstein had hustled me through.

The Chtorran slid down from the glass then. It turned around in its cage, exploring the length and breadth with its oddly delicate hands. It looked at me, and then it turned and looked at the guard on the other side. Did it understand why we were here? It must have. It brought its gaze back to me again. I was afraid to look it in the eye. It turned to study the audience. It peered out through the spotlight, blinking. It blinked and blinked again. I couldn't hear the *sput-phwut* through the glass. It kept blinking and I wondered what it was doing. It looked as if its eyes were shrinking. It peered out at the audience again and this time it acted as if it could see them through the spotlight.

There were other empty seats in the auditorium now, most of them near the ends of rows. I didn't see anyone else I knew, only a couple that I recognized. There was that constipated fellow Ted had been talking to. And Jillanna. Was it my imagination, or was her face shining a little brighter than those of the people around her?

The Chtorran slid forward again, this time with a more deliberate motion. It slid forward and forward, lifting more than half its length up against the front of the glass. I held my beam directed against its side.

In the audience, a couple of people were standing nervously, pointing. A few were even backing up the aisles. I wondered how close we were to panic. Dr. Zymph's silent presentation was more effectively terrifying the members of the conference than anything else she could have done. A movement caught my eye. Dr. Zymph was picking up her clipboard and stepped back away from her podium. Was she pointing to someone on the opposite side of the stage—?

I heard the *cra-a-ack* of the glass before I knew what it was.

I turned in time to see the Chtorran falling forward through a shower of glass fragments. They glittered around it like tiny sparkling stars. In one smooth movement, it poured through the glass and flowed down off the stage and into the shrieking audience. It hit the front rows like an avalanche.

I sliced my beam across to follow—hesitated half a second as I realized I'd be shooting into a crowded auditorium—then pulled the trigger anyway.

The Chtorran reared up, a struggling woman in its mouth. It dropped her and whirled around—I could see that there were several other people pinned beneath it. I fired again. Where the beam touched its side, I was digging out great gouts of flesh—but I wasn't even slowing it down! I couldn't tell if the other rifleman's beam was working or not—I didn't think so. I could see that he was firing too—there was a line of bloody black divots across the Chtorran's silver back, but it was ragged and uneven. He was having no more effect than I was. The Chtorran whirled and swung and pounced. It rose and fell and rose again, its eyes swiveling this way and that, its maw working like a machine. Even from this distance, I could see the blood spurting. The creature raised up high again, another victim in its mouth. The other rifleman dropped his gun and ran.

The auditorium was a screaming madhouse now. The green-lit mannequins streamed toward the exits. The crowds were piling up at the doors in great knots of struggling bodies, jamming and trampling. The Chtorran noticed them; its eyes angled first one way and then the other. It dropped the body it was holding in its maw and *moved.* The Chtorran leaped across the rows to land among the screaming people, flattening them to the floor or pinning them against their seats. It *flowed* up the aisle. It picked the people up and threw them, or pounced upon them as it had the dogs—but it wasn't eating! It was in a killing frenzy!

I didn't know what I was doing. I ran forward, dropping off the edge of the stage—almost losing my balance—catching myself and racing toward that silver horror. I angled the blue-white-crimson beam at it and pulled the trigger, pulled the trigger—trying to slash a line across the Chtorran's flesh, trying to carve the beast in half. There were people lying all around it. Most were motionless. A few were trying to crawl. I stopped worrying if they were in my line of fire. It didn't matter. Their only hope was if I could stop this creature quickly.

I skidded on something wet and sprawled sideways. I could see my beam slicing sideways across the wall—*Oh, God! This is it!* But the Chtorran wasn't even turned toward me. Yet.

I scrambled back to my feet. The Chtorran was terrifyingly close. It had swung around and was working its way back down the aisle again. I saw now, in dreadful clarity, exactly how it killed. It raised the forward part of its body high and brought it directly down upon its victim—this time, a member of the Chinese delegation, a slender young man—no, a girl! She couldn't have been more than sixteen. The creature pinned the screaming girl to the floor with its gnashing maw; then, holding her down with its black, peculiarly double-jointed arms, it tried to pull away—but its mouth was like a millipede's, with rows and rows of inward curving teeth. It couldn't stop eating! It couldn't stop chewing something once it started—not unless the object was deliberately pulled out of its mouth! That's why the creature held the bodies down when it backed away—so it could pull free.

The effect was to rend the body as thoroughly as if it had been pulled apart by a threshing machine. The Chinese girl screamed and jerked and twitched and then was still. The Chtorran lifted up then and began to turn—and I could see that there were human entrails hanging from its mouth. There were bodies on the floor around it—they were badly ripped and mauled. They had died horribly.

I touched my beam to the creature's shoulder. The arms were anchored against a hump on its back. If I could keep it from holding the people down, it wouldn't have the leverage to pull back and free. It would be struck with the one victim! I squeezed the trigger hard and dug gobbets out of the Chtorran's silver body. But the hideous arms kept moving! And the creature started swiveling toward me—

I kept firing! The Chtorran's side was an exploding mass of flesh. Suddenly the arm collapsed—the limb fell useless, hanging and waving. It jerked and twitched erratically and black blood spurted from the wound. In the hellish view of the helmet, I could see the steam as pinkish vapor rising from its silver body. The rest of the world was a gray and green and orange backdrop to this horror.

I couldn't see the other arm to shoot at it; the Chtorran's body blocked my shot, I touched the beam to its eyes and squeezed the trigger! Again and again! The rifle dug against my shoulder as it shrieked, as it roared. One of the Chtorran's eyes disappeared, replaced by a bloody hole. The whole mound of flesh burst like jelly.

The Chtorran raised up then, up and up and up, revealing its darker mottled belly—was it going to throw itself at me?—and then it screamed! An agonizing, high-pitched howl of rage! "*Chtorrrr! Chtorrrrr!*" Without thinking, I skittered back, my feet slipping on the bloody carpeting of the auditorium. A row of seats had been broken from their anchors by the weight of the creature and there were people from the row behind pinned under them. The monster didn't notice. It broke its scream and focused. It looked at me and *knew.* For one single terrifying instant the two of us—human and Chtorran—shared a communication that transcended words! I knew it like a shout of rage and pain: *Kill!*

The moment broke.

And then it came toward me. It arched its body forward and poured itself across the seats, flowing toward me like a river of teeth.

I stabbed the beam into its other eye and fired—tried to fire. Nothing happened—out of ammo—the empty clip popped up and out and clattered on the floor. I fumbled with a second magazine, sliding it into place even as I kept moving backward. When I squeezed again, the creature's other eye exploded in a vaporous cloud.

It didn't slow the creature down! Even blind, the Chtorran could still sense its prey! Did it smell my terror? I was screaming now, a wordless rage of profanity, a wall of obscene fury that I flung against the horror! I had moved beyond my terror, was in a state where every action happened in slow motion, so slowly I could see the spurt of every droplet, the flex of every muscle, but even so could not move fast enough to escape the charging death.

The Chtorran reared again, and this time it was close enough to strike. I stabbed the beam into its mouth and carved it into bloody jelly. I squeezed the trigger hard and dug a screaming gory line straight down the monster's front and up again. The silver fur was streaked with red and black.

The Chtorran towered over me, shuddering with each punch of needles from the rifle, one arm hanging useless, the other grabbing, clutching frantically—its eyes were scarlet pudding, its mouth was twitching teeth—

Somewhere in that jerking mass of flesh, there was a brain,

a control center—something! I squeezed again and the second empty clip popped up. I grabbed my belt for another magazine——and then the Chtorran toppled forward onto me and I went out.

Thirty-Five

SOMEBODY WAS calling me.

Uh uh. Go away.

"Come on, Jim. Time to wake up."

No, leave me alone.

She was shaking my shoulder. "Come on, Jim."

"Leemea lone—"

"Come on, Jim."

"What're you want—?"

She kept shaking me. "Come on, Jim."

I went to brush her hand away. I couldn't move my hand. "What do you want, goddammit?"

"Come on, Jim."

I couldn't move my arm! "I can't move my arm!"

"You're connected to an IV. If you promise not to pull it loose, I'll untie your arm."

"I can't move my arm—!"

"Do you promise not to pull the IV out?"

"Untie me!"

"I can't do that, Jim. Not until you promise."

"Yes, yes, I promise!" I knew that voice. Who was she? "Just untie me!"

Somebody was doing something to my arm. And then it was free. I could move it around. "Why did you wake me up?"

"Because you have to wake up."

"No, I don't. Leave me alone."

"Uh uh. I have to stay with you."

"No, I want be dead again. The Chtorran killed me—"

"No, he didn't. You killed him."

"No. I want to be dead. Like everybody else."

"No, you don't, Jim. Ted wouldn't like it."

"Ted's an asshole. He isn't even here." I wondered where here was. I wondered who I was talking to. She was holding my hand. "I want to be dead too. Everybody else gets to be dead—why can't I?"

"Because once you're dead, you can't change your mind about it."

"I don't want to change my mind. Being dead can't be all that bad. Nobody who was dead ever complained about it, did they? Like Shorty. Shorty's dead. He was my best friend—and I didn't even know him. And my dad. And Marcie's dog. And the little girl. Oh, God"—I started to cry then—"we shot a little girl! I was there, I saw it! And Dr. Obama—she told me it was all right! But it wasn't! That's all bullshit! She's still dead! We didn't even try to save her! And I didn't see any Chtorrans! Everybody else said there were Chtorrans, but I didn't see any Chtorrans!" I wiped at my face, wiped the snot away from my nose. "I didn't believe in the Chtorrans. I never even saw the pictures. How was I to know?" The words bubbled up in my throat, tumbling out one after another. "I saw the Chtorran kill Shorty. I burned it. And I saw them feeding dogs to the Chtorran. Marcie's dog. I saw them bring the Chtorran onto the stage. Dr. Zymph checked the glass—oh, God—I saw it break. The Chtorran just boiled out into the auditorium. I saw the people running—I saw it—" I was choking on my own sobs now. She was holding my hand tight—

I wiped at my face again, but she was there with a tissue. I took it and mopped at my nose and eyes. Why was I crying, I wondered. And why was I saying all of this? "Don't go away!!" I said suddenly.

"I'm right here."

"Stay with me."

"It's all right, I'm right here."

"Who are you?"

"It's Dinnie."

"Dinnie? I don't know any Dinnie." Or did I? Why did the name sound familiar? "What's wrong with me?"

She patted my hand. "Nothing's wrong with you that won't get better. Are you through crying?"

I thought about it. "Yeah, I guess so."

"You going to open your eyes?"

"No."

"Okay. Don't."

I opened my eyes. Green. The ceiling was green. The room was small and dimly lit. A hopital? I blinked in confusion. "Where am I?"

"Reagan Memorial."

I turned my head to look at her. She wasn't as weird-looking as I remembered. She was still holding my hand. "Hi," I said.

"Hi," she said. "Feeling better?"

I nodded. "Why did you wake me up?"

"House rules. Anyone on pentothal has to be awakened when they come out of surgery, so we're sure they can handle their own breathing."

"Oh," I said. I was covered with blankets. I couldn't feel anything. "What happened?"

She looked unhappy. "The Chtorran killed twenty-three people. Fourteen more died in the panic. Thirty-four were injured, five of them critically. Two of those are not expected to live." She eyed me critically. "In case you're wondering, you will."

I started to ask, "Who—" But my voice cracked and I didn't finish the sentence.

" 'Who' what?"

"Who was killed?"

"They haven't released any names yet."

"Oh. So you don't know."

I couldn't fathom her expression. She looked oddly satisfied. "Well, I can tell you this—some of the Fourth World delegations are going to have to be restaffed. We've filled up two wings and the morgue with them. They were all sitting in the first five rows. And the worm threw himself across that whole section."

Something occurred to me then, but I didn't say it. Instead, I asked, "How did it get out?"

"They had the wrong kind of glass in the cage. They thought they had hundred-strength. It was only ten. There's going to be an investigation, but it looks like there was some kind of foul-up in supply. Nobody knew."

I tried to sit up and couldn't. I was strapped to the bed.

"Uh, don't," Dinnie said, putting her hand on my chest gently. "You've got five broken ribs and a punctured lung. You're lucky you didn't hit a major blood vessel. You were under that Chtorran for fifteen minutes before we got you out. You were on CPR maintenance for at least thirteen of those minutes."

"Who—?"

"Me. And you're lucky, buster, because I'm damned good at it. It's a good thing you took a step back before he fell on you, else I wouldn't have been able to reach your face with the mask—or your chest with the thumper. It took seven men to roll that Chtorran off. They wanted to flame it, but I wouldn't get out of the way. You can thank me later. They *weren't* too happy about it. Who have you got mad at you anyway? I never saw so many angry men with torches. But I don't abandon my patients. By the way, I think one of those broken ribs is mine. Don't ask. I couldn't be gentle. Oh, and you've also got a fractured kneecap. You were on the table five hours." She hesitated and then mouthed the words, "On purpose."

"Huh?"

She leaned over me to fluff my pillow, and as she did her mouth came very close to my ear. "Somebody didn't want me to save you," she whispered.

"Huh?"

"Sorry," she said out loud. "Here, let me fluff that better." Again, she whispered, "And they wanted to let you die on the table. But you're under medical protection here, and nobody's going to be allowed to see you without a nurse present. Me."

"Uh . . ." I shut my mouth.

Sitting back again, she said, "By the way, you may be a hero. Some of the doors in that room were jammed. No telling how many people that thing might have killed if you hadn't stopped it before the rest of the cavalry arrived."

"Oh." I remembered the Chtorran swinging around and starting toward me, and suddenly, I was nauseous—

Dinnie saw the look of alarm on my face, and was there with a basin almost immediately. My stomach lurched and my throat convulsed—and there were cold iron claws digging into my chest—

"Here!" She shoved a pillow into my arms, wrapped me around it so it splinted my abdomen and chest. "Hang onto that."

—nothing came up. I retched again, and then once more. Each time the pain dug into me again.

"Don't worry about your incision—you're well-glued. I did it myself. You won't splatter."

But the feeling has passed. The pain had blotted out the need to vomit.

I looked at Dinnie. She grinned back. And in that moment, I resented her all over again. For her presumption of such familiarity. And then I felt guilty for resenting her when I owed her so much. And then I resented her for making me feel guilty.

"How are you feeling now?"

I took inventory. "I feel like shit."

"Right. You look like it too." She got up then and went to the door and whistled. "Hey, Fido—!"

A ROVER unit trundled in then and wheeled up to the bed. She plucked a handful of sensors out of the basket on top—they looked like poker chips—and started sticking them to various points on my chest and forehead, neck and arms. "Three for EKG, three for EEG, two for pressure and pulse, two for the pathologist, one for accounting and an extra one for luck," she said, reciting the nurse's mnemonic.

"Accounting?" I asked.

"Sure. It automatically checks your credit rating while you're lying there, so we know how much to charge."

"Uh, yeah."

She turned to the ROVER unit and studied its screen. "Well, bad news for your enemies. You'll live. But a word of advice: next time you try to make love to a Chtorran, you be the boy. You're a lot safer on top."

She peeled off the sensors then and dropped them back into the basket. "I'll leave you now. Can you fall asleep by yourself, or do you want a buzz-box?"

I shook my head.

"Terrif. I'll be back with your breakfast."

And then I was alone again. With my thoughts. I had a lot to think about. But I fell asleep before I could sort things out.

Thirty-Six

I WAS back in Whitlaw's classroom.

I felt panicky. I hadn't studied for the test—I didn't even know there was to be one. And this was the final exam!

I looked around. There were people here I didn't know, but as I looked at them, their faces solidified into familiarity. Shorty, Duke, Ted, Lizard, Marcie, Colonel Wallachstein, the Japanese lady, the dark fellow, Dinnie, Dr. Fromkin, Paul Jastrow, Maggie, Tim, Mark—and Dad. And then a lot of other people I didn't recognize. A little too many.

Whitlaw was in front of the room, making sounds. They didn't make sense. I stood up and said so. He looked at me. They all looked at me. I was in the front of the classroom and Whitlaw was in my seat.

A little girl in a brown dress was sitting in the front row. Next to her, just sliding up, a gigantic orange and red Chtorran. He turned his blackeyed gaze to me and seemed to settle down to listen.

"C'mon Jim!" Whitlaw hollered. "We're waiting!"

I was angry. I didn't know why. "All right," I said. "Listen, I know I'm a screwup and an asshole. That part is obvious. But, see, what I've been doing is assuming that the rest of you *aren't.* I mean, here I am listening to you people making noises like you know what you're doing, and I've been believing you! What an asshole I am! The truth is, you people don't know what you're doing either—not any more than I do—so what I'm telling you is that my experience is just as valid, or just as *in*valid, as yours. But whatever it is, it's my experience, and I'm the one who's going to be responsible for it."

They applauded. Whitlaw raised his hand. I pointed at him. He stood up. "It's about time," he said. He sat down.

"You're the worst, Whitlaw!" I said. "You're so good at pouring your bullshit into other people's heads that it keeps floating to the top for years afterward. I mean, you gave us all these great belief systems about how to live our lives and then when we tried to plug into them, they didn't work. All they did was create inappropriate behavior."

Whitlaw said, "You know better than that. I never gave you a belief system. What I gave you was the ability to be independent of a belief system, so you could deal with the facts as they happened to you."

"Yeah? So how come every time I try to do that, you come in and give me another lecture?"

Whitlaw said, "If you've been inviting me into your head and letting me run my lectures on you, that's *your* fault. It isn't me who's doing that. It's you. You're the one running those lectures. I'm dead, Jim. I've been dead for two years. You know that. So quit asking me for advice. You're living in a world I know nothing about. Quit asking me for advice and you'll be a helluva lot better off. Or ask me for advice, if it's advice you want—and if it isn't appropriate, then ignore it. Get this, asshole: advice isn't the same as orders; it's only another option for a person to consider. All it's supposed to do is widen your perspective on the thing you're looking at. Use it that way. But don't blame me if you don't know how to listen."

"Must you *always* be right?" I asked. "Sometimes it gets *awfully* annoying."

Whitlaw shrugged. "Sorry, son. But that's the way you keep creating me."

He was right. Again. He always would be. Because that was how I would always create him.

There were no other hands. "Then we're clear? I'm running this life from now on? Right."

I looked at the little girl in the brown dress. She didn't have a face. And then she did. It was Marcie's face . . . and Jillanna's face . . . and Lizard's face. . . .

I turned to the Chtorran. "I have some questions for you," I said.

It nodded its eyes, and then looked into my face again.

"Who are you?" I asked.

The Chtorran spoke in a voice like a whisper. "I don't know," it said. "Yet."

"What are you? Are you intelligent? Or what? Are you the invaders? Or the shock troops?"

Again the Chtorran said, "I don't know."

"What about the dome? Why was there a fourth Chtorran inside?"

The Chtorran waved its eyes from side to side, the Chtorran equivalent of a headshake. "I don't know," it said, and its voice was louder. Like the wind.

"How did you get here? Where are your spaceships?"

"I don't know!" it said. And it was roaring now.

"How can we talk to you—?"

"I DON'T KNOW!" And it was raising up in front of me as if to attack—

"I AM IN CHARGE HERE!" I bellowed right back at him. "AND I WANT SOME ANSWERS!"

"I DON'T KNOW!!" the Chtorran shrieked—and exploded into a thousand flaming pieces, destroying himself, destroying me, destroying the little girl sitting next to him, the classroom, Whitlaw, Shorty, all the people, everything—dropping it all into darkness. . . .

Thirty-Seven

TED WAS sitting in the chair, looking at me. His head was bandaged.

"Did it get you too?" I asked.

"Did what get me?"

"The Chtorran. Your head is bandaged—did the Chtorran get you too?"

He grinned. "Jim, it's Wednesday. I just had my surgery this morning. They wouldn't let me in to see you before this."

"What surgery?" And then I remembered—"Oh!"—and came awake. "Wednesday?" I started to sit up, found I couldn't, and fell back into the bed. "Wednesday? Really?"

"Yup."

"Have I been unconscious for three days?"

"No more than usual," Ted said. "You know, with you it's hard to tell sometimes." Then, seeing my expression, he added, "You've been floating in and out. You've also been heavily drugged. So's most everybody else. They've had so many casualties to treat that they just plugged everybody into their beds and kept them on maintenance. You're one of the first to wake up.

I had to pull a few strings to do that. I wanted to have a chance to see you—to say goodbye."

"Goodbye?"

He touched the bandage around his head. "See? I had my surgery. They did the implant. I'm in the Telepathy Corps now. My transfer became official when the implant went in."

"Is it working? Are you receiving?"

Ted shook his head. "Not yet. Not for a while. First I have to go through a two-week training to learn how to experience myself more intensely. But I'm already sending. They're continually recording me, calibrating my connections and storing my sense of self so I won't lose touch with who I really am, all that kind of stuff. It gets very complex. The training is designed to rehabilitate your ability to experience. Do you know we spend most of our lives being unconscious, Jim? Before you can be a telepath. you have to wake up—it's like having a bucket of ice water thrown in your face. But it's incredible!"

"I can see," I said guardedly. His eyes were bright. His face was shining. He looked like a man possessed with a vision.

He laughed then—at himself. "I know—it sounds *weird.* To be a telepath is a daring adventure, Jim—you have to surrender yourself to the network. But it opens up a whole new world!"

"Have you done any receiving yet?"

"Just a little. Just enough so they would know that the connections were in. Jim, I know this sounds stupid, but I've been doing the most *wonderful* things! I tasted vanilla ice cream! That is, somebody else tasted it, but I tasted it with her! And I kissed a redhead. And I smelled a flower. And I touched a kitten. And an ice cube! Have you ever really felt what *cold* is?"

I shook my head. I was startled by the change in Ted. What had they done to him? "Uh, why? What was the purpose?"

"To see if I could *experience* things," he explained. He said it quietly. "You know—like pressure, heat, cold, taste, smell, vision—all that stuff. Once it's certain that the incoming linkage is working properly, then we test the broadcasting connections. Only first I have to train my natural ability to experience living. So I don't send spurious messages—like if I'm feeling cranky one day, it would color my perceptions. So I have to give that up. God, it's terrific! I love it!" He stopped and looked at me. "So, Jim. What's new with you?"

I couldn't help it. I started giggling.

"Well, I killed a Chtorran. Another one."

"Yeah. I heard about that. I saw the tapes. It's been on all the news channels. You can't believe what's going on! It's the greatest game of uproar I've ever seen."

"Really?"

"It's the best! It's the funniest political circus since the vice-president was found in bed with the attorney general. Everybody's running around and screaming that the sky is falling, and why isn't somebody doing something about it? The Africans are the most upset. They lost some of their loudest mouthpieces."

"Wow," I said. "Who?"

"Well, Drs. T!Kung and T!kai—and Dr. Kwong, the one you had the argument with."

I snorted, remembering. "It's poetic justice. Who else? I saw Lizard in the audience. Was she hurt?"

"Who?"

"Major Tirelli. The chopper pilot."

"Oh, her. No, I saw her at the funeral. They had a mass service for the victims. Cremated the remains in case the Chtorran bite had bugs in it."

"Oh. Good."

Neither of us said anything for a moment. We just looked at each other. His face was glowing. He looked like a very shy schoolboy, eager and excited. He did not look like the same person.

In that moment, I found myself actually *liking* him.

"So," he said. "How do you feel?"

"Fine, I guess. Numb." I smiled. "How about yourself?"

"Pretty good. A little scared."

I studied his face. He looked back at me unashamedly. I said, "You know, we haven't had much time to talk since we got here."

He nodded.

"This may be the last time I get to talk to you."

"Yeah, it may be."

"Yeah," I said. "I wanted to tell you how pissed I was at you. That I thought you were acting like a real asshole."

"S'funny. I was thinking the same about you."

"Yeah. But I guess—I just want you to know that I—uh, I appreciate you. A lot."

He looked embarrassed. "Yeah. Me too." And then he did something uncharacteristic for him. He came over to the bed, sat down on it, leaned over me and hugged me gently. He looked into my eyes, leaned down and kissed me once, very lightly on the lips. He brushed my cheek with his hand.

"If I never see you again—" he said, "—and there is that possibility—if I never see you again, I want you to know this. I do love you. You're an asshole most of the time, and I love you in spite of yourself." He kissed me again, and this time I didn't resist it. There were tears in my eyes and I didn't know why.

Thirty-Eight

THIS TIME, when I awoke, it was daylight.

And the Very Reverend Honorable Dr. Daniel Joseph Fromkin was sitting quietly in a chair studying me.

I raised my head and looked at him. He nodded. I looked around the room. The blinds were drawn, and afternoon sunlight filtered through the narrow vertical slats. Dust motes danced in the beams.

"What day is it?"

"Thursday," he said. He was wearing a muted coppery-gold suit—almost, but not quite, a uniform. Where had I seen—oh, I got it. Mode. He was a Modie.

"I didn't know that," I said.

He saw that my glance was on his tunic. He nodded an acknowledgement and asked, "How are you feeling?"

I looked. I wasn't feeling anything. "Empty," I said. I wondered if I was still under the influence of the drug. Or its after effects.

"Anything else?" asked Fromkin.

"Naked. As if I've been stripped and held up for display. I

have memories that I'm not sure actually happened or if I just dreamed them."

"Uh huh," he said. "Anything else?"

"Angry. I think."

"Good. Anything else?"

"No, I don't think so."

"Great." He said, "I'm here to debrief you. Are you up to it?" He looked at me expectantly.

"No."

"Fine." He rose to leave.

"Wait a minute."

"Yes?"

"I'll talk. I have some questions of my own."

He raised an eyebrow at me. "Oh?"

"Will you answer them?"

He said, "Yes. As a matter of fact, I am authorized to answer your questions."

"Honestly?"

He nodded his head slowly. "If I can."

"What does that mean?"

"It means I'll tell you the truth as I know it. Is that all right?"

"It'll have to do."

He looked impatient. "What's the question?"

"All right. Why was I set up to be killed?"

Fromkin sat down again. He looked at me. "Were you?"

"You know I was! That Chtorran was supposed to get me too. That's why I was assigned there—so when the glass broke, I'd be the first. I wasn't supposed to have a working weapon, was I? Except I took the manual and went out to the range and familiarized myself with the gun. So it didn't work, did it?"

Fromkin looked unhappy—not pained, just sad. He said, "Yes. That was the expectation."

"You didn't answer the question."

"I will. Let's hear the rest."

"All right. Why was the Chtorran supposed to break out? I saw Dr. Zymph check the case with an aide. They weren't checking to see if it was safe. They were checking to make sure it would break at the right moment. When the Chtorran put its weight on it. Right?"

Fromkin said, "That's what you saw?"

I nodded. "All those people were *supposed* to die, weren't they?"

Fromkin looked at the ceiling for a moment. Composing his answer? He looked back at me. "Yes, I'm afraid so."

"Why?"

"You already know the answer, Jim."

"No, I don't."

"Go over it again. Why do you think the attack was set up?"

"After the fact, it's pretty obvious. Most of those people disagreed with the United States position on the Chtorran threat, so you invited them to a first-hand look at how one *feeds.* That's the guaranteed shock treatment. It always works. It worked on me, and all I had seen were the Show Low pictures. These people got the special live performance. It was set up so that none of our people were killed or injured, only those who opposed us." I studied his face. His eyes were shaded. "That's it, isn't it?"

"Pretty much," Fromkin said. "You're only missing the context."

"The *context?* Or the *justification?*"

Fromkin ignored my jibe. "You saw how the convention was progressing. Can you give me a *better* alternative?"

"Have you tried education?"

"Yes! Do you know how long it takes to teach a politician something? *Three elections!* We don't have the time! We have to make our point *today.*"

I must have been frowning, for he said, "You heard those delegates. They were running everything they saw and heard through the filter that the United States was using the Chtorran menace as an excuse to exploit the rest of the world again."

"Well? Isn't that true?"

Fromkin shrugged. "Frankly, it's irrelevant. The war against the Chtorr is going to last anywhere from fifty to three hundred years—if we win. That's our window for a *best-case* approximation."

"And? What's the worst case?"

"We could all be dead within ten years." He said it dispassionately, but the words came out like bullets. "The situation calls for extraordinary crisis-management skills. It demands the kind of unified effort that this planet has *never* seen. We need a controlling body that can function free of the usual inertia common to an accountable government."

"You're advocating a dictatorship?"

"Not hardly. I'm advocating universal military service for every man, woman, child, robot, dog and computer on the planet. That's all." He allowed himself a wry smile. "That's hardly a dictatorship, now, is it?"

I didn't answer. He stood up and went to the window and looked out. "The irony of the situation," he said, "is that the only surviving institutions who have the resources to handle the situation are the very ones least able to apply those resources—the world's great technological nations. The conference is dominated by Fourth Worlders who are still in a pre-Chtorran consciousness—you know the one: 'They've got theirs, now I'm going to get mine.' And they're not going to let us play any other game while they still see themselves as not being equal partners. And the fact of the matter is, they're already equal partners. The Chtorrans find them just as tasty—they don't care!"

Fromkin turned to face me. He came back to the chair, but didn't sit down. "Jim, every day that passes without a program of unified resistance to the Chtorran invasion pushes the window of possible victory two weeks farther away. We're rapidly approaching the point where the window becomes totally unattainable. We don't have any time. They've taken the position that the United States is their enemy, one who will use any devious means to exploit them. They don't dare give up that position, because giving it up looks exactly like admitting they've been wrong. And that's the hardest thing in the world for a human being to do—be wrong. Do you know that people would rather die than be wrong?"

I saw the Chtorran pouring itself off the stage again. I heard the screams of terror. I smelled the blood. Those people died because they were wrong? I looked into Fromkin's face. His expression was intense. His eyes were hurting.

I knew it wasn't true even as I said it, but I had to say it. "So they're wrong—and you're right?"

Fromkin shook his head. "We did what we had to do, Jim, and the only way to explain it is so unsatisfactory that I don't even want to try."

I thought about it. "Try me anyway," I said.

He looked unhappy about it. "All right, but you won't like it. This is a different game—with different rules, one of the most important of them being 'All previous games are no longer valid.' And anyone who keeps trying to play the old game in the middle of the new is in the way. Got that? So we put all of our biggest problems in the front rows. We didn't like it, but it was *necessary.*"

"You're right. I don't like it."

He nodded. "I told you that you wouldn't." He continued, "But, Jim—every single one of those survivors has now *experienced* the war at close range. It is no longer just another political position. It's a bloody scar on the soul. The people who came out of that auditorium know who their enemy is now. What you saw—what you participated in—was a very necessary piece of shock treatment to the community of world governments."

He sat down again, leaned forward and put his hand on my arm. "We didn't want to do this, Jim. In fact, as of last week, we had decided not to. We were hoping then that the facts alone would be enough to convince the delegates. We were wrong. The facts aren't enough. You demonstrated that when you stood up in front of the entire conference. You demonstrated to us just how completely crystalized the Fourth World position was."

"Oh, sure—that's right," I said. "Blame it on me now!"

Fromkin leaned forward and said intensely, "Jim, shut up and listen. Stop showing off your stupidity. Do you know what you've given us? The lever with which to engineer a massive realignment of political intention. The tapes of the conference have been released to the public channels. The whole world has seen that Chtorran attacking a roomful of their highest leaders. The whole world has seen you bring that Chtorran down. Do you know you're a hero?"

"Oh, shit."

Fromkin nodded, "I agree. You're not the one we would have chosen at all, but you're the one we got, so we just have to make the best of you. Listen, the public is alarmed now—we *need* that. We didn't have it before. It makes a difference. We're seeing some very powerful people suddenly declaring their intentions to martial every resource necessary to resist the Chtorran invasion."

I leaned back in the bed and folded my arms across my chest. "So the United States wins after all, right?"

Fromkin shook his head. "That's the joke, son. There may not even be a United States when this war is over—even if we win. Whatever is necessary for the human species to defeat the Chtorrans is of such overriding importance that the survival of any nation, as a nation, becomes a minor matter. Every single one of us committed to this war knows that the survival of *anything* is of secondary importance when weighed against the survival of the species. Period."

He leaned back in his chair again. I didn't say anything. There wasn't anything to say. And then I thought of something. "I can see that's *your* position. Now, what was the justification for including me? Remember, I was supposed to get killed there too—not be a hero."

Fromkin did not look embarrassed. He said, "That's right. And you weren't supposed to be rescued either. That nurse, Dinnie—she can be a perfect pain in the ass sometimes—she saved your life. She disabled two of our marines when they tried to pull her away."

"They were going to kill me?"

"Uh, not exactly. It just seemed, ah, politic not to rush to your aid. But nobody told her that. When they tried to pull her away, she crippled them. Broke one fellow's kneecap, the other one's collarbone, arm and sternum. She stayed with you the whole time, wouldn't let anybody near you unless she knew them personally."

"And what happened in the operating room?"

Fromkin looked started. "You know about that too?"

I nodded.

"A senior officer suggested that your treatment be . . . postponed. She invited him to leave the operating theater. He refused. She gave him a choice. Under his own power or otherwise. If otherwise, she guaranteed he wouldn't like it. She was right. He didn't like it. She's under arrest now—"

"Huh?"

"Protective custody. Until some things get sorted out. I promise you, she'll be all right. But you and I need to have this little chat first."

Something occurred to me then. "Why you and I? Where's Uncle Ira? Shouldn't he and I be having this conversation?"

Fromkin hesitated. "I'm sorry. Colonel Wallachstein is dead. He didn't get out of the auditorium in time." There was pain in his face.

"No—!" I cried. "I can't believe that!" I felt like I'd been slammed in the chest with a brick—

"He pushed three people out ahead of him," said Fromkin. "I was one of them. He went back for someone else. I waited for him at the door. He never came out."

"I—I don't know what to say. I hardly knew him. I don't know if I liked him—but I respected him."

Fromkin waved it away. "He respected you for killing that fourth Chtorran. He told me so. In fact, he authorized your bounty check Sunday morning, just before the session."

"Bounty check?"

"Don't you know? There's a one-million-casey bounty for every Chtorran you kill. Ten million if you capture one alive. You're a millionaire now. Twice over. I'll authorize your second check. I'm taking over certain responsibilities for the Agency. That's why you and I are having this chat."

"Oh. Are you my superior officer now?"

"Let's just say I'm your, ah, liaison."

"With who?"

"You don't need to know their names. They're the people who worked with Uncle Ira."

"The same people who decided I should be killed?"

Fromkin exhaled in quiet annoyance. He folded his hands into his lap and collected himself. He looked me in the eye and said, "You need to understand something about that. Yes, you were supposed to die. The people you work for made that decision."

"Nice people," I said.

"You'd be surprised."

"I'm sorry, they don't sound like the kind of people I *want* to work for. I may be an asshole, but I'm not a stupid one."

"That remains to be seen." Fromkin went on quietly, "Until Sunday afternoon, as far as anyone could tell, you were a liability. Nobody figured on you bringing that Chtorran down. I admit it, I'm *still* surprised—but when you did that, you stopped being a liability and started being a hero. You're an asset now, son.

Sunday's pictures demonstrate that a human being *can* stop a Chtorran. The world needs to know that. You've become a very useful tool. We want to use you—if you're willing to be used. The earlier decision is inoperative now. You can thank Dinnie for that. She bought you enough time so we could come to that realization. Hm," he added. "We may have to recruit her."

I didn't know whether to feel relieved or angry. I said, "That's all I am? A tool? You can tell them I'm grateful. I hope I can do the same for them sometime."

Fromkin caught my sarcasm. He nodded in annoyance. "Right. You'd rather be right. You'd rather exercise your righteousness."

"*I'm angry!*" I shouted. "It's my *life* we're talking about! That may not mean much to you, but being eaten by a Chtorran could ruin my whole day!"

"You have every right to be angry," Fromkin said calmly. "In fact, I'd worry about you if you weren't, but the thing you need to get is that it's irrelevant. Your anger is *your* business. It means nothing to me. So handle it so you can get on with your job."

"I'm not sure I want the job."

"You want to kill Chtorrans?"

"Yes! I want to kill Chtorrans!"

"Good! We want you to kill Chtorrans too!"

"But I want to trust the people behind me!"

"Jim, *stop taking it personally!* Any of us—*all* of us—are expendable, if it will bring the rest of us closer to the goal of stopping the infestation. Right now, our problem is the resistance of every person who doesn't see that the Chtorran problem is the overriding one—especially those who are *entrusted* with the responsibility for *handling* this circumstance. They're in the way. If they're in the way, they have to be moved *out* of the way. So don't get in the way. And if you do, don't take it personally."

"I think that makes it even *more* horrifying," I said. "The sheer callousness of it."

Fromkin was unimpressed. "Oh, I see—your ideals are more important than winning the war. That's too bad. Do you know what a Chtorran calls an idealist? Lunch."

I glanced at his uniform. "Is that an *enlightened* position?"

"Yes," he said. "*It is.*" He didn't expand on it.

I said, "You still haven't answered my question."

"Sorry. Which one?"

"What was the justification for wanting me dead too?"

Fromkin shrugged. "It seemed like a good idea at the time."

"I beg your pardon?"

"You looked like a liability, that's all. I told you, don't take it personally."

"Is that it?"

"Uh huh." He nodded.

"You mean it was just calmly decided—just like *that?*"

"Yep."

I couldn't believe it. I began to splutter at him. "You mean to tell me that you—and Colonel Wallachstein—and Major Tirelli—just calmly sat around and decided my death?"

He waited till I ran down. It was a long wait. Then he said, "Yes—that's *exactly* how it happened. Calmly and unemotionally." He met my furious stare with an unashamed expression. "In the same way that we calmly and unemotionally decided to turn the Chtorran loose on a roomful of our colleagues. In the same way that Duke calmly and unemotionally decided to handle that little girl in the brown dress. Yes, I know about that too." He added, "And in the same way that you calmly and unemotionally decided to handle Shorty and that fourth Chtorran. There's no difference, Jim. We just left out some of the hysteria and drama. But otherwise, there's no difference, Jim, in what we did and what you did.

"You accepted the responsibility when you accepted that flamethrower in the first place. The truth is, the things we did that you don't like are really the things *you* did that you don't like. Right?"

I had to admit it.

I nodded. Reluctantly.

"Right. So give the people around you a break. It isn't any easier over here. We just don't have to be drama queens about it. So you can spare me your goddamned self-righteousness! If I want to be beaten up, I can do it far better than you can! In fact, I already have. I know the arguments—better than you, probably! You think I haven't gone around this bush myself a few times?"

"I hear you," I said. "It's just—I hate the way I've been treated."

"I got it," Fromkin said. "And that's understandable. The fact of the matter is, the agency owes you several dozen apologies—we owe you more than we can ever repay. But would it make a bit of difference? Or would it use up time we need for more immediate problems?"

I stopped the anger I was building up long enough to look at his question. No, it wouldn't make a bit of difference. I looked at him again. "No, it wouldn't."

"Right. What we did was wrong. You know it. We know it. We thought it was necessary—and the fact of the matter is that we never expected to have this conversation. But now we've got it and it's my responsibility to clean up the mess—so consider it an acknowledgment of the contribution that you've made that I'm taking the time. So pay attention. I have a job for you."

"Huh?" I sat up straighter in bed. "That's it? That's how you say thank you?"

"That's right. That's how we say thank you. We give you another job."

"Most people at least say, 'Attaboy. You done good.' "

"Oh," said Fromkin. "You want me to pat your fanny and blow in your ear first, is that it?"

"Well, no, but—"

"—But, *yes.* Listen, I don't have time to waste telling you how wonderful you are—because you won't believe it anyway. If you need to be reminded, then you've got a question about it, don't you? So I'm going to give you the short cut to wonderfulness, so you'll never have to worry about that one again. Ready? What are you doing that makes a difference on the planet? That's your meter stick by which to measure your worth. Got that?"

I nodded.

"Good. Now we have a job for you. The Agency wants to put you to work. Does that tell you anything?"

"Uh, yes. It does," I said. I held up a hand for time. I needed a moment to think this through. I wanted to say it clearly. "Look, I think one of us has got to be a fool—and I know *you're* not. And I'm not sure *I* want the nomination."

"I beg your pardon?" Fromkin looked puzzled.

"How do I know you won't find me . . . ah, what's the word, *expendable* again some time in the future?"

"You don't."

"So there's no guarantee, is there?"

"Right. There's no guarantee. You want the job?"

"No." I didn't even have to think about it.

"Right." He stood up to go—

"Wait a minute!"

"You've changed your mind?"

"No! But—"

"Then we have nothing further to talk about." He started for the door.

"Aren't you going to try to . . ."

"What? Convince you?" He looked genuinely puzzled. "Why should I? You're a big boy now. At least that's what you've been telling us for the past three days. You can choose it or not. You don't need the sales pitch. And I don't have anything to sell."

"Aren't you at least going to tell me what it is?"

"No. Not until I know what your agreement is."

"Agreement?"

He looked annoyed. "Your commitment. What is it we can count on you for?"

"To kill Chtorrans. You can count on me for that."

"Good," he said. He returned to his chair. "Now, quit being an asshole about it. We're on the same side. I want the same thing you do. Dead Chtorrans. I want to put you to work. Do you want to work? Or do you want to screw around with politics—like our Fourth World friends?"

I glared at him. I didn't like this at all. But I said, "I want to work."

"Good. So get this—the time is *over* for games. And that *includes* self-righteousness. I'm telling you the truth now and you can count on me to keep on telling you the truth." His eyes were fierce. His expression was intense, but unashamed. I felt naked before him. Again.

I said, "This is very hard."

He nodded.

"I don't know if I can believe you or not."

"So don't believe me," Fromkin said. "Your belief is irrelevant. The truth is what's so, whether you believe it or not. The question is, what do you want to do about it?"

"Well—" I began. I felt myself smiling. "Revenge would be silly—"

"It's also out of the question." He smiled back.

"—so I might as well be useful."

"Good idea," Fromkin agreed. He leaned back in his chair. "You know, you may have forgotten, but you're an officer now. You fooled us. Nobody expected you to live long enough to use your commission. But you have, so now we've had to create an appropriate job for you."

"I've got one."

"Eh?"

"I've already got a job," I repeated. "I'm working on the Chtorran ecology. There are too many people making guesses without enough information. There aren't very many people out there actually gathering it. I had an instructor once who said that if you offered him the choice between a dozen geniuses for his lab or a couple of idiots who could handle field work, he'd take the idiots. He said it was more important to observe the facts accurately than to be able to interpret them, because if you observed enough of them accurately, you wouldn't have to interpret them—they'd explain themselves."

"Makes sense. Go on."

"Right. Well, you've got almost nobody out in the field. This war against the Chtorr doesn't exist yet because you—*we* don't have any intelligence on them!" I thumped my chest meaningfully. "*That's* my job! I'm an intelligence agent! That's where you need me the most. Because we don't even know yet who or what we're fighting—"

He was holding up one hand to stop me. "Hold it! You're preaching to the choir, son. I got it." He grinned broadly. It was the cheeriest expression I'd ever seen on him. "You know, it's a funny thing. That's *exactly* the same job we had picked out for you."

"Really?"

"Really." He nodded as he said it. "I'm making the assumption that we *are* on the same side, then?"

I looked at him. "I guess we are."

He said, "I know. It doesn't feel like it, does it?"

"No, not really. Not yet."

"So I'll tell you this. You don't get to choose your friends or your enemies. They're always thrust on you. All you get to choose is which category you're going to put them in." He grinned. "Wanna be my friend?" He held out a hand.

"Yeah." I took it.

"Thank you," he said, looking into my eyes. His gaze was intense. "We need you." He held onto my hand for a long moment, and I could feel his gratitude, almost like energy, flowing into me. I realized I didn't want to let go.

He smiled at me then, a warm expression like sunrise coming up over a cold gray beach. "You'll do fine. Major Tirelli will be by later to get you started. Do you have any other questions for me now?"

I shook my head. And then I said, "Just one—but it's irrelevant. Does the Mode training really work?"

He grinned. "Yes, it does. It did; I'm sorry it's such a low priority these days." His expression went wistful. "Someday, when there's more time, I'd like to tell you about it."

I said, "I'd like that."

That made him smile proudly. "I think you would." He stood up to go. "Oh, one more thing." He glanced at my meal tray. "Don't drink the orange juice."

"Huh?"

"I said, don't drink the orange juice."

I looked at his face. "I passed another test?"

"Right." He grinned again. "Don't worry, it's the last one."

"Is it?" I asked.

"I sure hope so, don't you?" He was laughing as he left.

I looked at the meal tray. There was a glass of orange juice on it. I poured it into the potted palm.

Thirty-Nine

THE MORNING sun was very bright, and I felt terrific. My knee hardly hurt at all. The doctors had replaced my kneecap with one grown in a tank and shaved to fit my bones; they told me to minimize my walking for a week—and to guarantee that I did, they put my leg in a case so tight I couldn't bend it. But I could limp—with crutches or a cane—and as soon as I could I was out of the hospital.

I found Ted at the bus station.

He was sitting quietly and waiting. He looked *subdued,* which surprised me. I guess I didn't know what I was expecting. Silver antennae sticking out of his head? But, no—he was just sitting patiently in a corner, a detached look on his face.

I hobbled over to him, but he didn't see me—not even when I stood in front of him. "Ted?" I asked.

He blinked twice.

"Ted?" I waved a hand in front of his face. He didn't see me. His expression remained unchanged. Not just detached—absent. Blank. Nobody home.

"Ted? It's Jim."

He was a zombie.

I sat down next to him and shook his leg. He brushed my hand away. I shook his shoulder and shouted in his ear. "Ted?"

Abruptly, he blinked—and then a confused expression came over his features. He looked like a sleeper awakening suddenly in a strange place. He turned his head slowly and looked at me. Recognition finally came to him. "Jim . . . ?"

"Ted, are you all right? I had to knock three times."

"Yeah," he said quietly. "I'm fine. I was just . . . plugged in."

"Oh. Well, uh, I'm sorry if I interrupted you. But I just got out of the hospital, and this was my only chance to say goodbye before you shipped out."

"Oh," he said. His voice was flat. Distracted. "Well, thank you."

He started to go emotionless again, but I caught his arm. "Ted, are you all right?"

He looked at me, a flicker of annoyance in his eyes. "Yes, Jim, I'm *fine.* But there's a transmission coming in from Capetown that I want to return to."

"I got it," I said. "But I want you to take a moment to be with me. Okay?"

He blinked at me. I knew the question. Bored patience. "What is it, Jim?"

"Well, I thought . . . just that . . . we might have some things to say to each other. . . ."

His voice went distant. "I saw your Chtorran again. We had a transmitter in the front row. He died. I experienced his death."

"Oh," I said. "Uh—that must have been very hard for you."

"It wasn't the first death I've experienced. I've been playing a lot of tapes." Suddenly, he looked very old.

I put my hand on his arm. "Ted, is it hard?"

He looked at me, but didn't answer. Was he listening to another voice again?

"Ted," I said, "what's it like?"

He blinked, and for just a moment he was the old Ted looking out at me from inside his body, and for just that moment I thought I saw stark terror. "Jim," he said intensely, "it's wonderful! And it's . . . terrible! It's the most intense and exhilarating experience a human being can have. I've been a thousand different people—I can't explain it. It's all still so confusing. I'm being bombarded with experiences, Jim! Constantly. And I don't know which of them are mine—if any! I don't even know if it's me sitting here talking to you. You could be talking to *any* telesend on the circuit. I can remote-access anybody else's experience and, if necessary, even take over control. And they can use my body too!".

I opened my mouth to say something, but he stopped me with a desperate hand on my arm.

"No—listen to me. I'm out of the circuit now, but only for a moment. The trainees have to take the dirtiest jobs—it's that way in all the services. I'm on call sixteen hours a day. Yesterday, I was . . ." He stopped, as if he were trying to form the words and finding it difficult. His eyes looked red. "Yesterday, I was . . . ridden. By a Russian government official. I don't know if it was a woman or a homosexual or—I don't know, but whoever it was used my body to make love to another man. And all I could do was do it. I had no control of my own."

"Did you file a grievance?"

"Jim, you don't understand! It was *wonderful!* It was complete and absolute *service!* Whoever it was gave me the opportunity to confront a different experience! That's what this is about—the expansion that comes from confronting the totality of human experience!"

"Ted, can't you get out?"

"Get out?" Ted looked incredulous. "Get out? Jim, don't you understand? I don't want out. Even while I was hating it, I was loving it—good *and* bad. The Telepathy Corps is a chance to share the experiences of a million other human beings. How else could a person ever get to live a million other lives?" His eyes were feverish now, intense. "Jim, I've played the tapes! I know what it feels like to die—in a hundred different ways. I've gone down in plane crashes, I've drowned, I've fallen off buildings, I've burned to death and I've even been eaten by a Chtorran! I've been afraid in more different ways than I ever dreamed possible—and I've been exhilarated in as many different ways too! I've climbed mountains and gone into space. I've lived in free fall and at the bottom of the ocean as a gillman. I've done so much, Jim—it's like making love to the universe! And I've made love a thousand different ways as well! It's all on the tapes. I've been a naked child in Micronesia and a fifteen-year-old courtesan somewhere in Osaka. I've been an old man dying of cancer in

Morocco, and—Jim, I know what it is to be a woman, a girl! Can you comprehend what it is to leave your own sex behind, like a fish discovering air—discovering how to fly? I've made love as a girl! And I've carried the child that resulted and given birth to it!! I've nursed it and raised it! And I died with it when the plagues came! Jim, I've experienced more life in just the past few days than I'd ever known in all the years before. And I'm terrified and excited because it's all coming down so fast I can't assimilate it. Jim"—he clenched my arm so tight it hurt—"Jim, *I'm disappearing!* Me—Ted! My identity is dissolving under the assault of a thousand other lives! I can feel it happening! And I know what it will feel like to stop existing as me, because that experience is recorded too! And, Jim, I want it even as I'm afraid of it. It's a kind of death. And it's a kind of *orgasm* too! This is incredible stuff! Jim, my life is over! Now, I'm a part of something else, something larger and—Jim, I want to say this to you while there's time—"

Abruptly, his grip on my arm loosened. His face relaxed, the tension disappeared and he became detached again.

"Ted?"

"I'm sorry, I'm on call now, Jim. I have to go."

He started to rise, but I pulled him back down. "Wait—you started to say something?"

"*Perdóneme?*" A strange voice came from his mouth.

"Uh, nothing." I let go in horror.

Ted's body nodded. "*Bueno.*" It got up and walked away. The last I saw of Ted, his body was just getting on a helibus. The chopper clattered up into the air and disappeared into the east.

I wondered where Ted was in the circuit now. I knew it didn't matter. The half-life of even a strong identity was less than nine months. I'd probably never see Ted again. His body, maybe, but the thing that animated it—where would that be? Experiencing what? Or whom? Within a few months, it wouldn't even be a personality anymore. Ted had known what he was getting into when he'd made the decision to receive the implant. He'd known what it meant. At least, that was what I wanted to believe.

I turned and hobbled back to the Jeep I'd requisitioned. I didn't feel so terrific anymore. I had a lot to think about. I levered myself in and said, "Science Section, please."

The Jeep replied "Acknowledged," and whined itself to life.

It waited till its whirring stabilized, then backed smoothly out of the parking slot. As it eased forward, it announced, "Incoming message."

I said, "I'll take it."

Marcie's voice: "Jim, I want you to stop calling me. And stop leaving messages for me to call you. I have nothing to say to you. And you have nothing to say that I want to hear. I don't want to see you and I don't want to talk to you. I hope I'm making myself clear. I want you to leave me alone, because if you don't, I promise you, I'll file a postal grievance."

The message ended abruptly, and the Jeep trundled across the tarmac. I thought about Marcie, tried to figure out what was going on. I remembered something Dinnie had said. "We're all crazy these days. *All of us.* We were crazy before the plagues too, but now we're *really* crazy." Or was that just a convenient justification? I didn't know.

Dinnie had said, "The thing is, none of us can see our own craziness, because it's the filter we look through. All we can see is what we project on the people around us. And then we blame it on them." She'd smiled and said, "Do you know how to tell if you're crazy? See if the people around you are."

I looked—and *everybody* around me was crazy.

That was the joke. You know you need help when the people around you are crazy.

The hell with her. I didn't have time to be crazy anymore.

The Jeep said, "Will there be a reply?"

I said, "No. And post this. Refuse all future messages from the same source."

"Acknowledged."

I still felt lousy.

Forty

THE JEEP lurched to a stop in front of the Science Section, and I climbed out carefully. There were no guards here. None were necessary anymore. Since the reorganization, no doors would open for you unless you had a red card or higher. I had a gold card.

Once past the fourth set of security doors, I pointed at two lounging aides and said, "You're temporarily requisitioned. I have some things I want loaded."

They grumbled and fell into line behind me. "I don't want to hear it," I said.

We went directly to the extraterrestrial specimen section. A woman in a lab coat looked up as I came in.

"Where's Dr. Partridge?" I asked.

"She doesn't work here anymore. She's been transferred to Administration."

"What about Larson?"

"Who?"

"Jerry Larson?"

"Never heard of him." She put her clipboard down and looked at me. "What can I do for you?"

"I'm McCarthy," I said.

"So?"

"I requisitioned some specimens." I pointed to the wall of cages. "Three millipedes and a incubator of eggs. They were supposed to be ready for me."

She shook her head. "The orders didn't come through here."

"Fine," I said. "I'll give them to you now—" I pulled my copy of the flimsies out of my pocket.

She blinked at me. Her face hardened. "Whose authority are you operating under, *Lieutenant?*"

"Special Forces Warrant Agency," I snapped. My leg hurt. I was tired of standing. I tapped the card pinned to my chest. "*This* is my authority. I can requisition any goddamned thing I want. If I want to, I can requisition you to Nome, Alaska. Now, I want those three bugs and that box of eggs." I gestured to the aides. "There's a Jeep out front. Load 'em in the back."

"Just a minute," she said, reaching for a phone. "I want confirmation—"

I hobbled over to her, leaning heavily on my cane. "One," I said, "I gathered those specimens. Two, I killed a Chtorran to get them here. Three, I haven't seen one piece of research out of this lab, so as far as I'm concerned, the effort in bringing them here was wasted. Four"—I was unfolding the orders that had been handed me that morning by Major Tirelli—"I have all the confirmation you need right here. And five, if you don't get out of my way, I'm going to place this cane in a most uncomfortable place. And if you don't believe I can do it, I'm the fellow who killed the Denver Chtorran."

She read the orders, then handed them back without comment. She sniffed. "No, you're not."

"I beg your pardon?"

"You didn't kill it."

"Say again?"

She raised an eyebrow at me. "Do all lieutenants have lousy hearing? I said, 'You didn't kill it.' "

I turned to the aides. "Load that stuff on the Jeep. I'll be right out."

"Hold it!" She barked. "You touch those cages, I'll have you shot." The aides stopped where they were. She poked my chest. "Let's you and me settle some things first."

I looked at the woman in the lab coat. She wasn't wearing a name badge. She had green eyes. "What's your name?" I demanded.

"Lucrezia Borgia."

"Is there a rank in front of that?"

"Just Doctor."

"Right. Well, Dr. Borgia, do you want to start making some explanations?"

She pointed at a set of double doors at the end of the room. "Two rooms down," she said.

I hobbled through the double doors. She followed after me. I was in a wide hallway with another set of double doors at the end. I pushed through those and—

—there was the Chtorran, almost motionless in the center of a large room. The room was brightly lit. The Chtorran's flanks heaved regularly as if its breathing were labored. There were men attaching probes to its sides. There were ladders and scaffolds all around the creature.

"I . . . uh . . ."

"Didn't kill it." She finished for me.

"But I—never mind. What're they doing to it?"

"Studying it. This is the first time we've ever been able to get close enough to a live one to poke it and prod it and see what makes it tick. You crippled it. It can't see, it can't hear, it can't move. At least we don't think it can see or hear. We're sure it can't move. It certainly can't eat. Your gun pretty well destroyed its mouth. We're pumping liquids into it."

I didn't ask what kind of liquids. "Is it safe to approach?"

"You're the expert." She said it acidly.

There were men and women all over the animal. I hobbled forward myself. Only one or two of them looked up at me. Dr. Borgia paced me quietly. She took my cane and poked at the creature's mouth. "Look here," she said. "See that?"

I looked. I saw a clotted mass of flesh. "What am I looking for?"

"See that row of bumps? New teeth. And if you could climb the ladder, I'd show you the creature's arm stumps. And its eyes. If we could get underneath, I'd show you its feet. The thing is regenerating."

I looked at her. "How long?" I asked.

She shrugged. "Three months. Six. We're not sure. Some of the gobbets we've carved off it show signs of trying to grow into a complete creature too. Like starfish. Or holograms. Each piece has all the information necessary to reconstruct the original. You know what this means, don't you?"

"Yeah. They're almost unkillable. We *have* to burn them."

She nodded. "As far as the rest of the world is concerned, you killed this thing. They even paid you for it. But the truth is, you only stopped it. So don't you ever come into my lab again, throwing your weight around and acting like an expert! You got that?"

I didn't answer. I was looking at the Chtorran. I took a step toward it and reached out and touched its skin. The creature was warm. Its fur was silky. Oddly alive. It felt electric! My hand tingled as I stroked it.

"Static electricity?" I asked.

"No," she said.

I took another step forward, almost leaning on the warm side of the Chtorran, almost pressing my face into it. Some of the strands of fur brushed softly against my cheek. They felt like feathers. I sniffed deeply. The creature smelled warm and minty. It was oddly inviting. Like a big friendly fur rug you wanted to curl up in. I continued stroking it.

"That isn't fur," she said.

I kept petting. "It isn't? What is it?"

"Those are nerve endings," she said. "Each individual strand is a living nerve—appropriately sheathed and protected, of course—and each one has its own particular sensory function. Some can sense heat and cold, others light and darkness, or pressure. Some can smell. Most—well, while you're busy petting it, it's quietly tasting you."

I stopped petting it.

I pulled my hand back. I looked at her. She nodded yes. I looked at the Chtorran fur again. Every strand was a different color. Some were thick and black, Others were fine and silvery. Most were various shades of red—a whole spectrum of red, shading all the way from deep purple to bright gold, and touching all the bases in between: magenta, pink, violet, crimson, orange, scarlet, salmon and even a few flashes of bright yellow. The effect was dazzling.

I brushed my hand against the fur again, parting it gently. Beneath, the Chtorran skin was dark and purple, almost black. It was hot. I thought of the skin on a dog's soft underbelly.

I realized the Chtorran was trembling. Every time I touched it, the intensity of the shivers increased. Huh—?

"You're making it nervous," Lucrezia said.

Nervous—? A Chtorran? Without thinking, I slapped the creature's flank. It twitched as if stung.

"Don't," she said. "Look—"

A shudder of reaction was rippling up and down the Chtorran's body. There were two technicians on a platform hanging just above the Chtorran's back. They were trying to secure a set of monitor probes. They had to pull back and wait until the Chtorran stopped shuddering. One of the technicians glared at me. When the creature's flesh stopped rippling, she bent back to her work.

"Sorry," I said.

"The creature is incredibly sensitive. It can hear everything that goes on in here. It reacts to the tone of your voice. See? It's trembling. It knows you're hostile. And it's afraid of you. It's probably more afraid of you than you are of it."

I looked at the Chtorran with new eyes. It was afraid of me—!

"Remember, it's just a baby."

It took a moment for me to grasp the implications of that—not just for here in the lab, but for outside as well, out there, where the wild ones were.

If this was a baby—if all of those *out there* were babies—then *where were the adults?* The fourth Chtorran—?

"Wait a minute—this can't be a baby!"

"Oh?"

"It's too big—I brought in eggs! A baby Chtorran should only be . . ." I spread my hands as if to hold a puppy. ". . . oh, about yay big. . . ."

"Have you ever seen one?"

"Uh—"

"What's the smallest Chtorran you've *ever* seen?"

"Uh—" I pointed. "This one."

"Right. Have you ever heard of heavy metal accumulation?"

"What about it?"

"It's a way of measuring the age of an animal. The body doesn't pass heavy metals, like lead or mercury; they accumulate in the cells. No matter how clean a life you live, it's inevitable that you'll pick up traces just from the atmosphere. We've tested this creature extensively. Its cells are remarkably earthlike. Did you know that? It could almost have evolved on this planet. Maybe someday it will. But there's the thing: it doesn't have enough trace metals in its system to be more than three years old. And my guess is that it's actually a lot less. Maybe eighteen months." She held up a hand to forestall my objection. "Trust me—we've tested it. We've deliberately introduced trace metals into its system to see if perhaps it doesn't have some way of passing them. And yes, it does—our estimate of its age is based on *that* equation. And that's no anomaly, buster. All of our supplementary evidence supports the hypothesis. Eighteen months. Maybe two years at the most. It's got an incredible growth rate."

I was shaking my head. "But what about my eggs—?"

"Oh, that's right. Your eggs. Your *Chtorran* eggs. Come with me." I followed her back to the room we had just left. She brought me up to the row of cages. "Here are your eggs," she pointed. "See all the baby Chtorrans?"

I stepped close to the cage and peered.

Inside were two small millipedes. They were sleek and wet-looking. They were busily chewing on some pieces of shredded wood. A third baby millipede was just now chewing a hole in the shell of its egg. It paused abruptly and looked straight out at me. I felt a cold chill.

"The only thing interesting about these babies," she said, "is the color of their bellies. See? Bright red."

"What does that mean?"

She shrugged. "Means they're from Rhode Island. I don't know. Probably it doesn't mean anything. We've found all kinds of color bandings on these creatures' bellies."

"When did they hatch?" I asked.

"Early this morning. Cute, don't you think?"

"I don't get it," I said. "Why would the Chtorrans keep millipede eggs in their dome?"

"Why do you keep chicken eggs in your refrigerator?" Dr. Borgia asked. "What you've found is the ubiquitous Chtorran version of the chicken, that's all. These things eat the stuff that's too low on the food chain for the worms to bother with. They're convenient little mechanisms to gather up food and store it till the worms are hungry."

"I'm confused. Those eggs looked too big to have been laid by a millipede."

"Do you know how big millipedes get?"

I shook my head.

"Look down here."

"*Jesus!*" I yelped. The thing in the cage was a big around as a large python. It was over a meter long. "Wow!" I said, "I didn't know that."

"Now you do." She looked at me, and her green eyes flashed smugly. "Any *more* questions?"

I stepped back and turned to her. I said, "I apologize. I've been a jerk. Please forgive me."

"We're used to dealing with unpleasant creatures." She smiled innocently. "You were no problem at all."

"Ouch. I deserved that. Listen, it's obvious that you know what you're doing here. And that just hasn't been my experience elsewhere in the Center. I didn't even know this section existed until this morning."

"Neither did anybody else until we took custody of Junior in there—" She jerked a thumb over her shoulder at the other room.

"I'm really sorry," I said.

She swung to face me. "I got that. Now listen up and listen good. I don't give a damn how sorry you are. I really don't. It's over. Now, let it be something you can learn from."

"Uh, yeah."

"You're an officer now. So I'll give you the bad news. Every damn schmuck who sees those bars on your arm wants you to succeed, you know that? He wants to know that he can trust you *totally* when his life is on the line. That's how you want to feel about your superiors, don't you? Well, that's how your men want to feel about you. You act like a jerk and you blow it—not just for yourself, but for every other person who wears the same bars. So get yourself tuned in to what this is about. Those stripes are not a privilege! They're a responsibility."

I was feeling a little sick.

I guess it showed. She took me by the elbow and turned me to the wall. She lowered her voice. "Listen, I know this hurts.

And here's what you need to know about that: criticism is an acknowledgment of your ability to produce results. I wouldn't be giving you correction if I didn't think you could take it. I know who you are. I know how you got those stripes. That's fine; you deserve 'em. I've heard a lot of good things about you. Believe it or not, I don't want to see you screwing up. You got that?"

"Uh, yeah. I got it."

"Is there anything you want to say to me?"

"Uh . . . thanks—I think." I added, "I'll know when the bleeding stops. Uh, I'm awfully embarrassed."

"Listen, all new officers make the same mistake. You're lucky you made it here instead of someplace serious. You think the bars change you somehow. They don't. So don't let them get in the way. You're not your rank—you're just a person being trusted with that amount of responsibility. So I'll let you in on the secret. Your job isn't to order people—it's to *inspire* them. Remember that and you'll be very successful."

"Thank you," I said again. There was something about the way she spoke. "Are you related to Fromkin?"

She grinned. "I trained with him. Nine years ago." She stuck out her hand. "My name's Fletcher. Call me Fletch."

I shook hands gently. My wrist was still sore.

She said, "If you still want the bugs, take them."

I glanced back at the cage. The third baby millipede had finally gotten out of its shell. It was trying to crawl up the surface of the glass. Its belly was bright red. It stopped and stared at me. Its eyes were large and black and unnerving.

I shrugged. "I don't know now. I only wanted them back because I thought nobody around here *cared.* Now, I see that's not so. If you can do a better job . . ."

Fletcher grinned again. "Yes, we can."

I made a decision. "Well, then—keep 'em here. I just want to know what there is to know about them."

"I'll put your name in the computer," she said. "You can plug into the files any time you want. Our job here is to disseminate information, not hide it." Then her eyes twinkled and she added, "Visiting hours are every day from noon to five. Next time, bring flowers."

"I will," I said. I dropped my gaze away from her eyes. For

some reason, they were suddenly too beautiful to look at. I made a show of looking at my watch. I was embarrassed again, but this time for a totally different reason. "Well—" I said "—I guess I'd better get going. I have a plane to catch. Thanks again. For *everything.*"

I turned awkwardly toward the door. She stepped in front of me. "Just one thing. That *was* a pretty fair piece of shooting. I was there. My compliments." And she stretched upward and kissed me warmly on the lips.

I could feel myself blushing all the way to the Jeep.

Forty-One

WE WERE on a high hill overlooking a shadowed valley, almost a canyon. At the bottom, a glittering stream sluiced down between the two sheer slopes, zig-zagging from north to south and forming a wide, shallow pond where the canyon opened up. The surface of the water reflected back the sky; it looked like blue glass. At the far end of the pond, the water poured gently over the edge of a low earth-and-wood dam.

A long shelf of land bordered the little lake. Near the dam was a rounded dome, almost unnoticeable against the black earth of the hill behind it. I studied it through the binoculars for a long time. The dome seemed darker than usual. It looked as if mud had been smeared all over its surface. Not a bad camouflage, but still not good enough to fool the computers. Satellite reconnaissance was monitored, processed and analyzed on a twenty-four-hour basis for telltale changes in local terrain. The particular rounded bump of the worm hut, the dam, the local harvesting of trees—any of these things alone could have triggered an investigation; all of them together had put this valley on the Immediate-Attention list. It had taken us three weeks to get to it.

I passed the binoculars over to Duke. He peered through and grunted.

"They're getting smarter," I said.

He nodded. "Yeah. This one is just plain inaccessible. There's no way we can get down there unnoticed."

Larry was studying the canyon upstream. "Can't raft in," he said.

Duke nodded in agreement. "Didn't think we could." He turned to Larry. "Call the blimp. We're dropping the team in." Larry nodded and thumbed his radio to life. Duke looked toward me. "What are you thinking?"

I said, "It puts it all on the shoulders of the first man. He's got to hold the position until the others are safely down." I closed my eyes for a second and visualized what it might be like. "I'll do it," I said.

"You don't have to," Duke said.

"Yes, I do."

"All right," said Duke. "Fine. Do you have any problems with the plan?"

"No," I said. And then I shrugged and grinned. "I hate it—but I have no problems with it."

Duke eyes me steadily. "What's that about?"

"I hate blimps. I have this thought the worms will hear us coming. Or see the shadow."

"Anything else?"

"Yeah. I hate heights."

"Is that it?"

"Yeah."

Duke looked at Larry. "You?"

"I'm fine."

"I don't get that from you—what's going on?"

Larry shook his head.

"You still obsessing about Louis' death?"

Larry shook his head. Louis had died two weeks after his finger had been bitten. He'd started shivering one afternoon, then collapsed. He sank into a coma that evening and was dead the following morning. The autopsy showed that almost every red blood cell in his body had been exploded—from the inside. The killer was a virus that behaved like malaria. There were now thirty-four viral or bacteriological agents that had been identified as active agents in the Chtorran infestation. Louis had been lucky. His death had been quick, and relatively painless.

Duke said, "Larry, are you going for revenge?"

Larry didn't answer.

"—Because if you are, you'll stay behind. It'll get in the way."

"I'll be fine!"

Duke looked at Larry. "You fuck up, I'll put a stake through your heart. I promise you."

Larry grinned, "I got it, boss."

"All right." Duke included me again. "Let's get moving. Be sure your teams are clear. We'll have a final briefing just before we go." Duke looked at me. "Jim, you and I will go over the attack plan with the pilot. You're right about the shadow—we have to keep it off the dome—and the engine noise, so let's see what the wind is doing. If it's light enough, we'll *float* across the valley."

We slid back down the hill. We'd left our Jeep a quarter-mile away, on a fire road. It took us another half-hour to get to the landing site where the blimp was waiting. Our three attack teams were going through a last check of their equipment as we pulled up. Larry hopped out even before the Jeep had finished rolling to a stop. "Only three torches—" he called. "There's too much fire danger. We'll use the bazookas—"

Duke poked me. "Let's talk to Ginny."

I followed him to the command tent, where a 3-D map of the valley was displayed across the situation table. He nodded perfunctory greeting to the watch officers and tossed his pack to one side. "All right, let's get to work." He stepped up to the table and picked up a light pen. He drew a red target circle in the large clearing next to the dome. "That's where I want to put the team."

Captain MacDonald stepped up to the table opposite Duke and frowned. Her white hair was pulled back into a crisp military bun. She wore a tight jacket, trousers, a sidearm and a stern expression. She pointed. "I've got fifteen knots of wind coming from the southeast. It's going to be tight."

Duke dialed down the magnification. The image shrank as if it were dropping away. The tabletop now included several square miles of surrounding mountains. "I got that. And we need thirty seconds over the landing site." He pointed at the now reduced red target circle. "Can we do it with the engines off?"

Ginny closed her eyes and thought a moment. She said, "Tricky . . ." She typed something into the keyboard and studied the monitor. "Looks like a split-second drop. Your men are going to have to take their cues from the box—"

She stopped and looked at us. "I can't promise to do it with the engines off. I *can* promise to give you forty-five seconds over the target site—and I'll keep the engines off as long as possible."

Duke didn't look happy. "There's a real potential for disaster here." He turned to me. "Jim, I don't want anyone dropping in the water. And I don't want anyone dropping too near the dome. Can we trust your team?"

"We'll hit our marks."

"Can I count on it?"

"I'm the one taking the biggest risk." I met his eyes. "You can count on me."

"All right." Duke turned back to the display. He dialed the image up to maximum and centered it on the dome. "What does that look like to you?"

I checked the scale indicator at the edge of the table. "It's too big. How old is this picture?"

Ginny looked at the monitor on her side of the table. "Eighteen hours. This is yesterday afternoon."

"Thank you." I picked up the light pen. "Here—this is where to look. Around the perimeter of the dome. Look for purple coleus or wormberry plants. Every time we find evidence of cultivation, we also find a fourth Chtorran. There's none of that here yet. Nor is there a totem pole in front—that would also be evidence. But"—I shook my head—"this dome is too big. I want an extra watch at the back of it."

Duke looked at me sharply. "Reason?"

"I don't have one. Just a feeling something's weird here. Maybe it's the location of the dome, maybe it's the mud camouflage. But I get a sense there's some intelligence here."

Duke nodded. He studied the terrain again. "I'll buy it. Ginny?"

Captain MacDonald nodded too. She touched the keyboard in front of her and wind lines appeared across the map. She studied the monitor screen for a second, then said, "There's your course, the red line. If the wind holds, you'll have fifty seconds over the target area. I'll come across the valley from the southeast." She pointed with the light pen. "Now, look, we're coming down a very narrow track. I've got mountains on one side and water on the other. The shadow will be north and west of us. And so will the dome. I can't promise I'll miss it, not without the risk of dropping men in the water, unless you want to wait till later in the day."

Duke shook his head.

"All right. I'll do my best, but your first man will have to start down the rope even before we clear the dome. And he'll be hitting the ground awfully close—"

Duke looked at me. I shook my head. "No problem."

"—otherwise, the last of the team will be falling in the water."

"They had their baths this month," I said. "Don't worry about it."

"Anybody have anything else to add?" asked Duke. "No? Good. Let's go. Load 'em up." As we stepped out of the tent, he clapped my shoulder. "How are you feeling?"

I said, "Who's good idea was this anyway?"

He grinned back. "Right."

My team was to jump first, so that meant we boarded last. While we waited beneath the curve of the huge sky-blue blimp, I briefed them quickly. The job is routine, the jump's a little tight. Any questions? None. Good. Any problems or considerations? Larry had handled them already. Fine.

I moved among them quietly, double-checking the charges on their weapons and the expressions on their faces.

"How's it look, Cap'n?" That was Gottlieb. He had apple cheeks, a frizz of curly hair, and a perpetually eager smile. Right now he looked worried. I could tell because his smile was uncertain.

"Piece of cake."

"I heard the valley's awful narrow—"

"Yep. It is. That's just to make it interesting. These things are turning into turkey shoots. We don't want you falling asleep." I looked into his face. There was still too much tension there. I wondered if I should pull him. I put my hands on his shoulders and leaned over and whispered in his ear. "Listen, asshole—I promise you, you're going to do fine. You know how I know? Because if you don't, I'm going to rip your arms off."

He knew I meant it. He grinned. "Yes, sir!"

He'd be okay now. He was more afraid of me than he was of the worms. The worms didn't stand a chance.

"Two minutes!" called Larry.

I turned and found myself looking at Amy Burrell. Eighteen years old, tiny frame, large eyes, dark hair. Trembling in her boots. She was wearing the helmet camera and carrying an AM-280. "Sir—?"

I knew what she was about to say. I didn't give her a chance to say it. "Ah, Burrell—good. Once you hit the ground, I want you to stay close. I'll be moving around to the back side of the dome. Keep fifty feet behind me and you'll do just fine. Keep your camera running, and if anything comes out of the dome, just keep looking at it. We need the pictures. Oop—the line's moving. Get going!" I turned her and pushed. I slapped her on the backside. From here on, she wasn't going to have time to be scared.

The blimp took us up quickly. Captain MacDonald was sharp. She turned into the wind immediately and headed south. She was going to give herself lots of maneuvering room before heading for the target.

The engines thrummed with quiet power. We could feel their high-pitched whine in our butts and our backbones. Beneath us, the ground tumbled away like a rumpled brown sheet. The wind whistled coldly past us. I licked my lips and wondered if they were going to get chapped.

We were on two platforms mounted on the sides of the gondola. Each one of us had his or her own rope. On the signal, all the ropes would be dropped simultaneously. On the count, we would drop as our numbers were called. I tugged experimentally at my pulley. It was fine. I realized I was fingering the double-breakaway punch on my chest and stopped.

Captain MacDonald swung the blimp around then, heading us back toward the target. I watched our shadow as it moved across the treetops below. When she cut the engines, we were plunged into an eerie silence. Burrell looked at me nervously. The absence of sound was deafening.

I was about to thumb my microphone to life, to say something to fill the moment—when abruptly, music filled my earphones. Williamson's *Angry Red Symphony.* A perfect choice! Ginny was more than a pilot—she was an artist. I shut up and listened.

Too quickly, the approach to the target appeared before us. I recognized the escarpment at the top that looked like a dragon's backbone. And there was the fire road, and the place we had parked the Jeep. And now, as we came closer, there was the canyon and the valley beneath it. The blimp shadow was sliding down the slope—*and suddenly turned sideways.* Were we heading in at an angle? Had the wind changed? Abruptly the engines came whining back to life—*damn!*

The computer interrupted the music then. "Team One: stand by to drop."

There was the dome. And the blimp shadow was moving uncomfortably toward it—

"Five seconds!" said the computer. Something clicked, and all the ropes began dropping away, snaking to the ground like yellow spaghetti. "Three seconds!" I stood up. The blimp shadow moved across the dome. *Goddammit!* "Two!" I released the safety on my pulley. And—"Drop Alpha!" I lifted my knees and fell forward into nothingness. The pulley shrieked and screamed as it careened down the rope. "Drop Beta!" Above me, I could hear an echoing shriek, and then another and another.

The ground rushed up toward me. The ropes below were crackling and undulating like live wires. And two of the largest Chtorrans I'd ever seen came streaming purple out of the hut—"*Chtorrrrr! Chtorrrrrrr!*"

"Shit!"

I yanked a grenade off my belt, pulled the pin, and sighted below. There wasn't time, I was falling too fast. I dropped the grenade—

It fell short. The blossom of fire went off in front of the first charging worm, deflecting it but not slowing it down. The roar of the blast kicked upward like a hammer-blow. I grabbed for another grenade, knowing it was already too late—and then the worm was hit by two more sudden explosions, one right after the other. The shock of them kicked me momentarily upward. Somebody above me must have dropped grenades—I hoped they hadn't dropped any more.

The Chtorran was writhing on the ground. It had been cut

in half by one of the blasts. The second Chtorran was almost directly beneath me now, and the third and largest one was just coming out of the dome. I released the safety on my torch and pointed it straight down. I hoped Shorty had been right about this. The second Chtorran was reared up and reaching for me and I was dropping right into his churning maw—I could see straight down his throat. I pulled the trigger. The air beneath me exploded into flame. I couldn't see the Chtorran through it. The burning ground rushed up to meet me. I didn't even know if there was still rope for my pulley anymore. I pointed the torch sideways and fired again and the jet kicked me away from the burning worm. I released the trigger and hit the ground hard. I fell on my ass—*"Oof!"*—and had the breath knocked out of me—

The third worm was charging straight toward me. *"Chtorrrr! Chtorrrrrrr!"* I didn't even have time to stand. I just pointed the torch and fired—

When I finally let go of the trigger, there was nothing left of the worm but a snaky dark mass of writhing, burning, rubbery flesh. It smelled terrible.

And then Duke was there, standing over me, offering me a hand. I thanked him as I pulled myself to my feet. He glanced around at the three burning worms. "You want to remember you're a guest here and leave something for the rest of us?" And then he was away, pointing and directing the rest of his team to fan out.

I looked at the three worms myself. "Babies, huh?" And shook my head. I didn't know if I wanted to meet Mama or not.

Larry's team was already moving to the far side of the dome. My team was moving into position, but uncertainly; several of them were staring at me and the still-burning carcasses. They looked stunned. I clicked on my microphone. "Goddammit! Move out! Haven't you ever seen a man burn a worm before?" I started striding toward the back of the hut. "Burrell! Get your ass in gear!" I wondered how badly mine would hurt tomorrow from that hard landing. I wasn't going to worry about it now. I hit the breakaways on my chest, kicked out of the drop harness and kept going.

I planted myself directly in front of the back wall of the dome.

I gave it a lot of room. I checked the charges on my tanks. Still half full. Good. More than enough.

I glanced around behind me. Amy Burrell, white as a sheet, was fifty feet away. She held her rifle in a death grip. But she was ready. I looked at the wall again. Nothing. I checked the rest of my team. They were ready too.

My mike was still on. I switched channels and said quietly, "Apple."

"Baker," said Larry.

"Charlie," said Duke. "Hold your positions."

I looked at the rear wall of the dome. It was blank and featureless.

"All right," I barked. "Bring me a freeze machine. *On the double.*"

The freeze machine was a large plastic crate filled with styrofoam doodles. Inside the doodles were two tanks of liquid nitrogen and a spray nozzle. They'd been dropped after everyone else was down safely. We had two of them.

If we hadn't wakened the Chtorrans with our arrival, we would have used the liquid nitrogen instead of the torches. Gottlieb and Galindo wheeled up one of the kits. Riley and Jein were just unloading the other. They touched the release and the crate popped open with a *thump.*

"I'll take the kit. Michael, you cover me with the torch." Gottlieb grinned as I passed it over to him. He loved the excitement.

The nozzle for the freeze machine was lighter than the torch, and I didn't wear the tanks on my back. It was Galindo's job to move them—if we had to move. I wore a pair of insulated gloves so thick they could have been used in a boxing match. I closed the faceplate on my helmet again and I was ready.

The back wall of the dome remained unchanged.

Duke's voice whispered in my earphones. "You okay, McCarthy?"

"I'm fine. But when this is over, my ass is going to hurt."

"You did good."

"I know," I said. And then I added. "Thanks."

There was silence for a bit, so I asked, "What happened with the blimp?"

"I don't know. I didn't have time to ask. We came over the

edge and the wind shifted. But Ginny did her job. Nobody hit the water."

"When we get back, I'm going to buy her flowers."

"Do that. Better yet, buy her a bottle. It looked like a quick save." He was silent a moment, then asked, "Jim, how long do you want to wait?"

"At least a half-hour. Remember what happened to that team in Idaho."

"Right." Duke said, "There was a lot in that report to worry about."

"You mean the tunnel they found?"

"Yeah. If the worms are changing their nesting behavior . . ." He didn't finish the sentence; he didn't need to. The job was already difficult enough.

I studied the wall some more. There was no evidence of a hidden exit.

"Do you want to send in the Robe?" asked Larry. The blimp had also dropped a meter-high mechanical walker—a more sophisticated version of Shlep, the Mobe, only it didn't have Shlep's good looks or personality.

"No," said Duke.

Larry argued for it half-heartedly for a few moments, then trailed off. Duke didn't reply. I couldn't see either of them. There was just me and the wall.

"Jim?"

"Yeah, Duke?"

"You want to switch positions?"

"Naw, I'm fine."

"You sure?"

"I'm sure."

"All right."

The wall was unchanged. Something very small and loud buzzed around me. A stingfly? It was too fast to see. I waved it away with one gloved hand.

"Burrell? Time check."

"Twelve minutes, thirty seconds."

"Thank you."

I could feel myself sweating. I was starting to feel clammy inside the insulated battle-suit. I wished the fourth goddamn worm would quit waiting and come on out already. "Come on, worm!

I've got a nice cold bath for you! Just the thing for a hot summer afternoon!"

There was silence.

Something hooted.

I found myself growing drowsy. I shook myself back awake; I stamped my feet, jumping back and forth from leg to leg for a moment.

I squeezed the trigger, just a touch, and let loose a cold cloud of freezing steam. It put a chill into the summer air and a cold pain into the eyes. Water droplets crystalized and pattered on the ground. That would keep me awake for a bit.

We'd been freezing worms for a month now. It was still a new technique. I didn't like it. It was more dangerous. And you still needed a backup man standing by with a torch, just in case.

But Denver had this idea that if you could freeze a Chtorran, then you could map it internally, so we'd been freezing them and sending them to the photo-isotomography lab in San Jose. I'd seen the process once. It was impressive.

You take a frozen Chtorran, you put it up on a big frame and you point a camera at one end. Then you start taking thin slices off of it, taking a picture of the cross section after each slice. You do this with the entire worm. Then you give the pictures to the computer.

The computer gives you back a three-dimensional map of the internal structures of the Chtorran body. Using a joystick and a screen you can move around inside the map and examine specific organs and their relationships to each other. We still didn't know half of what we were looking at, but at least we had something to look at now.

The process had been successfully completed with four gastropedes of varying sizes. We didn't know why, but they seemed to be from four different species. Denver was going to keep freezing and mapping worms until the discrepancies were resolved.

"Duke," I said.

"Yeah?"

"Why do you think the fourth worm always waits so long to attack?"

"Beats the hell out of me."

"Yeah. Well, thanks anyway."

"No trouble at all, son. If you don't ask questions, how will you ever learn anything?"

The wall in front of me began to bulge.

I studied it offhandedly. Odd. I'd never seen a wall do that.

It bulged a little more. Yes, the dome was definitely being pushed out of shape. I raised the nozzle and pointed it directly at the center of the bulge.

"Duke, I think we got something. Burrell, pay careful attention now. I'll show you how this is done."

The dome began to crack ominously. The crack suddenly stitched up from the ground and across and then down again, and then the outlined piece began to topple outward—

"*CHTORRRRRRRR!! CHTORRRRRRRRRR!!*" This worm was the largest of them all! Was there no limit to their growth? Or was *this* the adult form?

It came sliding toward me like a freight train. I pulled the trigger and screamed and released a cloud of icy steam and a deadly spray of freezing liquid nitrogen. It spread out in sheets, enveloping the Chtorran. For a moment, it was hidden by the clouds and spray, and then it came plunging through, its fur streaked with white and icicles.

"Hold your torches!" I shouted, but it kept coming! And then, in a single startling instant of terror, the Chtorran raised itself up and up and up! The worm was three tons huge! It towered above me, crackling, wreathed in shining ice and silvery burning steam! And in that moment of deadly cold confrontation, I thought for sure that this was finally it—this brilliant beast of hell was about to topple down across me! This final frozen fury would be its last revenge! And then, instead, the momentum of its upward thrust continued and it began to slowly teeter sideways, farther and farther, until at last it toppled and came crackling and crashing down across the ground like a mountain of collapsing, shattering ice.

I could smell the cold like a knife within my brain, across my eyes. The pain of it was exquisite! The Chtorran was a fallen chimney. It lay shattered on the ground. Its fur was crystalizing in the sun, the ice was streaked along its sides in sheets and sprays and icicles. Something inside the creature exploded softly with a muffled *thump*—and as if in answer, one of its arms broke quietly off and slid and clattered to the ground.

How many more?

I turned away from the shining carcass and looked to the mountains climbing away to the north and west. How many more were out there? This was the twentieth I'd killed. But I didn't feel joyous—I felt only frustration. The job was taking too long!

The noise of the choppers pulled me back to the present. The first of the landing craft were already dropping down over the hill. They'd be bringing the rest of my science team and our equipment.

The security squad was just following the Robe unit into the hut. Not until they'd searched every room and tunnel would anybody else be allowed to enter. It was fine by me. I'd seen my share of worm huts. They were starting to look all alike to me.

For just a moment I felt tired. I didn't feel my usual exhilaration. I didn't even feel satisfied.

"Jim?" That was Duke, an ever-present voice in my ears, in the middle of my head.

"I'm fine," I responded.

"Good. Check out the corral, will you?"

"Right." I secured the freeze machine and headed around the dome. It didn't matter how I felt. That was irrelevant—I still had a job to do. I looked up at the corral and I remembered a little girl in a torn brown dress—

—and suddenly the feeling passed. And I knew why I was here. Because there was no place else that I would rather be. There was nothing else for me to do but *this!* It was perfect. The job was going to be done, and suddenly it was a beautiful day! I started toward the landing site to pick up the rest of my team.

Just one thought remained—

There has to be a better way!